Stolen Passions
by Crystal Jordan

Lyra Marcus tries to avoid her werewolf family's political entanglements. Instead, she heals the wounds of the never-ending border skirmishes between lycans and wereleopards. It's a bitter irony that she's about to die in that war.

When she awakens after an attack, the horror of her situation dawns. She's a wounded werewolf in the middle of wereleopard territory. And standing over her is a son of its most powerful family, Zander Leonidas. Her fate may be a swift and bloody end, but she intends to go down fighting.

Zander has no plan to fight the little she-wolf who's landed at his Refuge Resort, a place where shifter species are free to be what they are—except wolves, of course. Yet Lyra fits him in a way she shouldn't, and the urge to mark her as his mate is irresistible. A match like theirs, though, would rock the foundations of their world.

He intends to find out who left Lyra for dead on Leonidas land. And keep her safe from whoever wants to finish the job—not to mention the werewolf alpha who wants his niece back - at any cost...

Passions Recalled
by Loribelle Hunt

When both his mate and his father died in a freak accident, Jason, the oldest Leonidas brother left home and became a park ranger in the Florida Panhandle. The distance and solitude suit him. After all, the less he cares, the less he hurts.

With a hurricane bearing down on the coast, his job is to secure and evacuate the park. As the storm worsens to a point where evacuation is no longer possible, he discovers Celeste Lykaios injured and unconscious. The problem is…his mate died over a year ago.

Celeste's world has turned upside down. After being gravely injured in a plane crash, Jason abandoned her. In a mere twenty-four hours she finds out her werewolf step-father lost her birth father's land, her family hid her survival from Jason, and her new fiancé is a killer. She goes to the only person she is certain can keep her safe, driving straight into a hurricane only to be attacked before she finds him. She wakes up in Jason's home with no idea how she got there or why.

They take shelter from the storm to unravel the betrayal that split them apart, but first have to face the danger stalking Celeste.

When the storm passes, one question remains. If his mate–a human–survived the airplane crash that was supposed to have taken her life and the life of his father…what happened to the stronger wereleopard leader?

Fleeting Passions
by Crystal Jordan

Ecstatic that she's found a place to hide—and a job—at Refuge Resort, Cleo Nemean toasts her escape a few too many times and ends up having a one-night stand with a seriously hot leopard shifter. The catch? It's Adrian Leonidas, her new boss…and they accidentally mark each other as mates.

Nothing could be worse than losing her hard-won freedom. Until her werebear ex, Trevor, tracks her down. His obsession has already cost one life. Determined to never again be the cause of another death—especially Adrian's—she flees the safety of the refuge. And her new mate's protection.

Only Cleo has ever caused Adrian to lose his formidable control. Accidental or not, the lovely lion shifter is now his woman. He's not about to let anything harm her before they've explored the undeniable heat between them. There's only one way to eliminate the threat to her life: use her as bait to lure Trevor into a trap.

When the trap is sprung too soon, however, there's no time to wonder if whoever tipped Trevor off is tied to his father's disappearance. Not when there's a gun pointed at Cleo's head…

Renegade Passions
by Loribelle Hunt

Wereeagle Alexandra "Ajax" Petros is destined to lead her people...and running from that fate. She's spent several years in the Messenger Corps, the elite werebirds who carry communications between the different were species.

As a bird, she's neutral and her people have enjoyed and prospered under that neutrality. When she uncovers a plot by one of her own to not only steal her throne, but destroy the leopards and wolves in the process, what will she decide? Face the threat on her own and take her rightful place, or stick to her neutrality in the coming war?

Only one man has the power to make her choose, the power to make her forsake her oath to her people's ways. But what does Nicodemus Leonidas want from her? Her help...or her soul?

Nico is the family's coldly methodical security expert. The last thing he wants while trying to discover what happened to his father is the werebird who literally drops into his lap. She's driving him crazy, but their chemistry is incredible–and if she insists on sticking her messenger nose into the middle of wereleopard business, who is he to stop her?

Except everyone in this game has secrets and Ajax's are the biggest of all. When the dust has settled and Nico's family is reunited what will become of the mate he was so reluctant to claim? He must either convince her to stay with him or follow her as she pursues her own destiny. For the first time in his life, Nico lets his heart–not his mind–decide his fate.

Forbidden Passions

Crystal Jordan
&
Loribelle Hunt

Forbidden Passions
Print ISBN: 978-0-9860944-4-6

Stolen Passions Copyright © 2017 Crystal Jordan
Passions Recalled Copyright © 2017 Loribelle Hunt
Fleeting Passions Copyright © 2018 Crystal Jordan
Renegade Passions Copyright © 2018 Loribelle Hunt

All rights reserved. Without limiting the rights under copyright reserved above, no part of this publication may be reproduced, stored in or introduced into a retrieval system, or transmitted, in any form, or by any means (electronic, mechanical, photocopying, recording, or otherwise) without the prior written permission of both the copyright owner and the above publisher of this book.

This is a work of fiction. Names, characters, places, brands, media, and incidents are either the product of the author's imagination or are used fictitiously. The author acknowledges the trademarked status and trademark owners of various products referenced in this work of fiction, which have been used without permission. The publication/use of these trademarks is not authorized, associated with, or sponsored by the trademark owners.

CONTENTS

Stolen Passions
Crystal Jordan
~1~

Passions Recalled
Loribelle Hunt
~61~

Stolen Passions
Crystal Jordan
~135~

Renegade Passions
Loribelle Hunt
~191~

Stolen Passions

Crystal Jordan

CHAPTER ONE

It was the heat that woke her.

Something rough rasped against her cheek, and sweat slid in slow beads down her face. It stung her eyes when she opened them to see the blazing sun overhead. Sand. It was sand scraping the skin on her face. From the smell of it, she was in the desert, no longer in the humid air of New Orleans. She was so hot, she felt as if her blood was boiling. Exhaustion sapped at her strength, willing her to return to oblivious slumber, but questions nagged at her, buzzing around like insistent gnats.

Where was she, and how had she gotten here? Why was she outside?

When she tried to lift her head to get a better look at her surroundings, every muscle in her body screamed in protest. Oh, God. She remembered now. She'd been attacked after she'd finished a late shift at the clinic in New Orleans—a clinic just for people like her. Shape-shifters. Wereanimals.

The last thing she remembered seeing was a gloved fist slamming into her jaw—and it packed the kind of strength behind it that a human couldn't manage. It had to be another shifter. The physician in her began cataloguing injuries even as the wolf wanted to rip someone's throat out for doing this to her. Multiple lacerations and contusions, possible fibular fracture and a serious case of dehydration. If she didn't get to water soon, she was so screwed.

The anger whipping through her made it easier to ignore the shrieking agony that threatened to make her collapse back to the sand. It didn't matter if it hurt—she was going to die if she stayed here. She wiped sweat and dried blood from her face, pushing her long black hair back over her shoulder.

Lifting her nose to the wind, she inhaled and tried to catch the scent of civilization…or water, whichever was closer. West. The faintest aroma of people came to her, so she turned in that direction. Her gait was a broken stagger, but she was moving. She stumbled again and again, crashing hard to the ground and scraping skin from her palms and elbows.

A hopeless sob was wrenched from her chest, but she forced herself to get up, to keep going. She didn't want to die. She didn't want to give the son of a bitch who'd done this to her the satisfaction. The wide expanse of rocky desert terrain stretched before her endlessly, broken only by stark mountains rising to the north. Sweat burned the cuts on her face. Gritting her teeth, she pushed on. If she gave in to the pain, she'd never get to see them punished. A grim smile pulled at her cracked lips. Revenge was a great motivator.

When her ankle twisted and gave out from under her, she tumbled down a short ravine, landing on her back. Squinting against the glare of the sun, she saw a large bird pass in front of it. Probably a buzzard coming to pick her bones when she died. Groaning, she braced her hands on the ground and tried to force herself up again, but her arms collapsed, and her head slammed down to the ground. Her ears rang with the force of the impact.

It was almost funny that she, Doctor Lyra Marcus, fastidious to a fault and niece of the most powerful werewolf Alpha in America, was filthy, bloodstained, lying in the dirt and couldn't do a damn thing about it. A giggle that bordered on hysteria bubbled from her throat. Well, at least she remembered her own name. That was something. She clamped a hand over her mouth to stifle the laughter.

Get a grip, Lyra.

Digging down deeper inside herself than she ever had before, she used the side of the ravine to pull herself upright, to stand, to lean against as she shuffled along again. The farther she walked, the more her thoughts grew fuzzy around the edges, and that wasn't good. No, not good at all. Eventually the ravine ended, and she staggered out into an arid wasteland. It wouldn't be much longer before she couldn't get up if she fell, couldn't go any further. And then the scavengers would have their turn at her. The thought didn't scare her as much as she knew it should, and time slid away as she put one foot in front of the other.

She lifted her head as she smelled something worse than death on the wind, and the horror of her predicament finally hit home.

Wereleopard.

The sworn enemy of her kind. She was in the desert, which meant that if she was still in the United States, she was deep into the western territory the cats claimed for their own. A place where no sane wolf would ever go.

She couldn't see it among the scraggly brush and broken rock, but she knew it was there. The way her wolf senses screeched danger was no lie. She picked up her pace, tried to run, tried to escape. To where, she didn't know, but she wasn't being taken in enemy territory without a fight.

And there it was, all tawny fur and dark spots—huge, sleek, and undeniably male. His gaze locked on her as he pursued her at a ground-eating pace, hunting her. She snarled, more the wolf now than woman. Her fangs erupted from her gums, but she didn't have the energy left to shift into full wolf form. Too weak to defend herself.

Weak, and probably dead before the vultures ever got a piece of her. It was her last thought before she tripped over a sunken boulder, and the ground came rushing up to meet her.

The world went dark, and she knew her life was over.

Zander slowed to a lope to circle the unconscious woman. Confusion and anger had flooded him the moment the scent of werewolf had reached his nose. Someone was trespassing on his family's land, and he'd needed to investigate. This wasn't what he'd expected to find. His claws dug into the loose sand as he paced around her, looking for a trap. The desert was eerily silent. He hadn't seen anyone else out here, couldn't smell anything but her on the wind. It was distracting, that smell. Titillating in a way that he shouldn't allow it to be. Still, it didn't answer the most important questions. What the fuck was going on here? Who was she, and how had she gotten here?

He nudged her shoulder with his muzzle, pushing her limp body over on to her back. Whoever she was, she was in bad shape. Blood caked her nostrils and the corners of her mouth. Ugly bruises mottled her creamy skin. Horror and rage fisted his belly as he saw distinct handprints on her flesh. Someone had done this to her deliberately—beaten this woman until she collapsed. He fought the urge to track down the bastard and return the favor. Every muscle in his body locked as he got a stranglehold on his temper. It was unlike him to react so violently, and he shook his head hard.

She sucked in a quick breath, her eyes flaring open for a moment. The unusual liquid silver color snared him, fascinating the cat within him. Her lips moved, but no sound emerged. She growled a warning at him, her fangs baring. But he read the fear and desperate helplessness under the fierceness in that gaze. He wanted to reassure her, let her know that she was safe, that he would never allow anyone to hurt her again. But then she was gone, her eyes closing and her body relaxing against the ground as she passed out.

Some emotion he couldn't name gripped his chest as he stared down at her. Whoever she was, she was his responsibility now. She was his now. A shudder of foreboding ran through him, but he pushed that aside the way he had his unexpected anger. He had more vital matters to deal with, like saving this woman from dehydration under the blazing sun.

He stretched, his body shifting from leopard to human form. The spotted fur retracted until he was left crouching naked beside her. He gingerly scooped her up and cradled her slim form to his chest. Protectiveness flooded him as he felt how delicate she was compared to him. He could get all his questions answered about her after he got her out of the desert heat. Sweat already slid in rivulets down his back and stuck his skin to hers.

After only a few steps, the hot sand managed to scorch and blister his very human feet. He bit back a curse as he started the long trek home.

Over twenty-four hours later, he sat by her bedside while she slept fitfully. Her silver eyes rolled back for a moment before she opened them fully to meet his.

"Welcome back." Zander dropped the financial report he was reading to the bedside table and leaned forward in his chair. It looked like his uninvited guest was finally awake.

Neither he nor his brothers had been able to figure out who she was or how she'd ended up on their land. He did know that if he hadn't had a meeting and needed to cut short his daily run around his family's extensive property, he never would have found her. If he hadn't taken that shortcut, she'd be dead.

And that would be a damn shame. A woman this lovely shouldn't have to die that way. Once he'd cleaned her up and the natural healing ability all shifters possessed kicked in, he could see the fine bone structure, the full lips, the lovely face framed by a pool of inky black hair against the white pillowcase. Those locks had trailed to her waist when she'd run from him. As beat up as she'd been, he had no idea how she'd managed to run at all. The way she'd bared her fangs showed a predator's nature. Her strength impressed the hell out of him, and his reaction to her on every level made her unlike any woman he'd ever known before, regardless of species. She'd been in and out of consciousness, and he'd forced liquids down her throat every time she came to.

His brothers had offered to take turns sitting with her, but he'd refused. The first moment Zander had seen those gray eyes focus on him, he'd been caught by something more powerful than he'd ever experienced before. It hadn't relaxed its grip on him since. The leopard in him wanted her, the animal as intrigued as the man. He couldn't walk away. So here he sat, alert to every breath she took as her body rapidly restored itself. She appeared to be completely healed, so he watched and waited for her to awaken and not just resurface briefly as she had before.

Her gaze was blank and glassy as she returned to awareness by degrees. "W-where am I?"

That low voice reminded him of chicory and hot, humid nights on the bayou.

"The infirmary at Refuge Resort." Leaning farther forward, he caught a lock of her silky hair between his fingers and slid it away from her face. Her scent came to him the way it had that first moment in the desert, sweet, rich and all woman. He sat back with a jerk, pushing away the errant thought.

"Refuge? That's in Arizona." She blinked hard, raising herself onto her elbows. Her movements made the narrow cot squeak. The thin sheet slipped down to bare a dusky nipple. His gaze dropped to it, to the slight, firm curves of her body, and his body reacted, cock going rock hard. She lifted a hand and covered herself without haste. Not a scrap of embarrassment shone on her face when he met her gaze. He arched a brow, and her mouth quirked at the corners. "Sorry, kitty cat. I'm not shy. I'm a doctor, so nudity doesn't bother me."

"Good to know." He let a lascivious smile curl his lips as his gaze swept over her body. The sexual response he had to her was outside of his control, but what he did with it wasn't. And he always kept the upper hand.

But…kitty cat? As if a leopard could be compared to a domestic house cat. He snorted. The woman was more than bold. It was too bad he liked that in his women. He shifted in his seat to adjust the fit of his khaki slacks—his hard-on hadn't let up and fire balled in his gut. Damn, he had to be desperate if he was getting this hot over a wolf. Even if she was well enough now to play, she was a werewolf. He'd smelled the wolf on her before he'd even seen her, and the way she'd bared her fangs when she'd seen him told him she was no stranger to the conflict between their species.

His older brothers would want to know she was awake, especially Nico, the resident security expert at the resort. Hell, the security expert for the vast empire of companies the family owned. The whole operation was based in a collection of offices here at the resort. If she'd been a man, Nico would have suggested putting her back out in the desert to rot, but harming a woman was one of the few lines even the half-feral Nico wasn't willing to cross. He had wanted to cuff her to the bed though, and Zander had flatly refused, which meant Nico was now in a thoroughly pissed off frame of mind.

The air conditioning kicked in, and the vent over her bed spewed cool air. She shivered, goose bumps rising on her skin. The sunset made her ebony hair shimmer as she jerked her chin at the fading daylight coming through the windows. "Why was it so hot outside? It's not even June yet."

He grinned, tried not to stare at the way her nipples hardened under the sheet, and stretched a leg out straight to give his straining erection some room. Jesus, what was it about this slip of a woman that had him so horny? He swallowed and reined in his thoughts—and hormones. "Never been to the desert, huh? We're getting near record highs, but Tucson can get over a hundred even in March and April. For about a week we've been hovering just under one-ten. It'll cool off a little when the monsoon season hits."

Where was the smooth tongue he was so famous for? There were a million things he needed to speak to this woman about, and the weather wasn't one of them.

That silver gaze swept over him, pinned him in place. "Which one are you?"

"Excuse me?" He arched a brow. Where had that question come from? Maybe she wasn't quite as awake as he'd assumed.

She sighed and sat all the way up, wrapping the sheet around her toga-style as she swung her long, shapely legs over the side of the small cot. "You're one of them. The Leonidases. You're not just a leopard."

He chuckled. No, she was definitely awake. And sharp. There was nothing sexier than a smart woman. He forced himself to derail his totally inappropriate lustful admiration and respond to her question. "Got it in one."

"There are four of you, aren't there?"

"Yes, but only three of us still live in Arizona." Since the airplane accident that had taken his father's and sister-in-law Celeste's lives. He didn't let himself finish the sentence. His eldest brother, Jason, had been gone for months, unable to remain and live with the daily reminders of his dead mate. That left Adrian, Nico and Zander to lead the leopard clan of this country. He swallowed and forced an easy smile to his face. "What gave me away?"

"Like every werekind, I've seen pictures of your father in the papers. The resemblance is there." One creamy shoulder lifted in a shrug, and a single ebony curl slipped down to curve around her breast. Lucky curl.

"Huh." He rubbed a hand over the back of his neck, working out a kink from sitting beside her bed for so long. "Adrian was always the one who looked like our father."

And Jason had been the odd one out. If it wasn't their father singling Jason out and shoving him up on the dutiful pedestal reserved just for the Leonidas heir, it was the fact that he looked nothing like anyone else in the family.

As a melanistic leopard, Jason might have the same green eyes as his younger brothers, but his blue-black hair was a sharp contrast to their lighter brown. The difference was only accentuated in animal form when his dark coat and cream colored spots were the exact opposite of a traditional leopard's. Melanism was a genetic anomaly known to big cats in the wild as well as shifters, where regular cubs were born in the same litter as a black cub.

Now the distance was physical as well as psychological. Zander sighed, suddenly weary. Their family had never been a peaceful one—especially since Jason's one act of rebellion against their father had been to mate with the werewolf Alpha's human stepdaughter. Hector had always regretted letting Celeste come to Refuge to do a story for one of the werekind newspapers. Even then, the Leonidas brothers had always had one another's backs against all outsiders.

And Zander damn well missed his family.

The she-wolf tilted her head and answered his unvoiced thought. Her gaze softened with quiet sympathy. "You must miss him. I'm sorry your father died."

"You know, I actually believe you." And he did. The sincerity in her eyes and on her pretty face couldn't be faked. His face felt as though it might crack as he forced another small smile to his lips. It had been harder and harder in the last few months to maintain the optimism that used to come so naturally to him.

He shook the moroseness away. It wouldn't help, and his family was none of this woman's business. For all intents and purposes, she was a trespasser on Leonidas land...and a member of an enemy shifter species. Just because she was beautiful didn't mean she needed to know anything. He scooted forward in his chair, preparing to rise. It was time to let Nico and Adrian have a go at her.

She cleared her throat and seemed to grope for a more neutral topic. She waved a hand to encompass their surroundings. "If you have a clinic, where's your medic?"

"Died in the same crash that killed my sister-in-law and father." The smile was more a baring of teeth this time.

"Ah." She swallowed audibly and glanced away.

There was one piece of information he'd get before he left. He braced his hands on his thighs and leaned into her space. "And who are you, Doctor Wolf?"

"Marcus." Her gaze flashed to him again as their knees brushed. "Doctor Lyra Marcus."

"Lyra." He rolled the name on his tongue, savoring the sound. Lovely. It suited her. Then realization snapped through him as her last name connected to what he knew about the wolf clan. "Marcus…the werewolf Alpha's—"

"Niece." She finished the sentence for him.

"You're Celeste's cousin."

"Yes. Though we were never close, and I haven't been on wolf clan land since long before she died." She crossed her arms over her chest and lifted her chin. "Is any of that a problem for you?"

Shit. How the hell hadn't he made that connection already? Now that he viewed her objectively, he could see the resemblance in the high cheekbones and gray eyes. A knot of dread fisted in his belly. Michael Lykaios was the werewolf Alpha, the wolf equivalent of Adrian, who led the leopard clan in the States. One of Lykaios's sisters had mated to a wolf named Marcus. Zander didn't remember the man's first name, but it didn't matter. That the Alpha's niece had been left for dead on leopard land made this situation a lot more complicated than it had been a few minutes before.

"No, it's not a problem for me. Wolves only come to the resort with special permission, and they aren't generally allowed west of the Mississippi." He leaned back in his chair, folding his arms. "But a woman in your family would know all that. So, what are you doing on leopard land?"

"I don't know. I'm a doctor at a werekind clinic in New Orleans." She shook her head, confusion and anger flashing in her gaze. Staring at the floor, she seemed to concentrate on something only she could see. "All clinics are neutral territory, so I'm not sure what happened. I was the last one out and locked up the clinic that night, and I was attacked. I woke up in Arizona. Trust me, this little trip wasn't my choice, but since I know you have a small charter airport here, if you'll point me to a phone, I'll make arrangements to get on the first plane out of here."

"No." The thought of her leaving was unacceptable. He arched a brow and shook his head when she looked startled. "Absolutely not."

Her eyes narrowed to dangerous slits. "You can't keep me here."

"We don't know who left you here, but we sure as hell know they want it to look like leopards had a part in what happened to get you here. You're not leaving until I know this isn't going to land back on my doorstep." Not until he knew it was safe for her to be out of his sight. Protectiveness fiercer than he'd ever known for anyone outside of family members swamped him, but he didn't fight it. For as long as she was on his resort, the woman was his responsibility. Hell, she was just his. It didn't matter that the thought sounded insane even to him. It simply was. Some fundamental instinct inside him claimed it was so.

"Well…when you put it that way. Shit." She sighed and rubbed a hand over her forehead. "You never told me which Leonidas brother you are. From what you've said, I can only guess you're not Adrian."

"I'm Zander."

"The youngest." Her breath caught when their legs slid against each other again, the same awareness he'd been fighting since she woke up flashing in her pale gray eyes.

"Yes."

She licked her lips, staring at his until he wanted to grab her and shake her for tempting him. But if he touched her he wasn't going to shake her. No, he had much more carnal things in mind for her. She inched forward until she sat on the very edge of the cot, until he could feel the heat from her slim body. "You run Refuge Resort."

"Right again." It was hardly a secret what his job was. Or that Nico took care of security, or Adrian was the Leonidas CEO. When your family ruled a species, everyone knew everything about you. Or thought they did.

She rose, and he stood with her, wrapping his fingers around her biceps to steady her in case she might fall. The feel of her satiny skin under his fingertips made his cock ache and turned the supportive action into something far more sexual than he intended.

He couldn't help but wonder what it would be like to have her long limbs and soft hair wrapped around his body as he drove himself inside her until this insane hunger was spent. He barely bit back a groan, his fangs sliding forward a bit as the leopard within him fought for feral supremacy.

She jerked back, tripping over the edge of the sheet in her haste to escape him. He snorted and caught her close to keep her upright. Her body pressed to his, and an audible gasp erupted from her. How the hell had he gotten himself into this? The instincts that kept him by her side when she was unconscious had only intensified since she'd awoken. The fierce intelligence and strength of character shone from her face, drew him in. Fire fisted tight in his belly as her curves molded to his harder body. She was tall for a woman, tall enough to fit him just right. Unusual. Intriguing. Far too tempting.

Her jaw jutted pugnaciously, a challenge filling her narrowed eyes. "I'm fine. You don't have to coddle me. I've completely healed."

"What's the matter, little she-wolf? Are you scared?" He lowered his head until his breath ruffled the short hairs at her temple, and he felt how she shivered in response. His grip shifted on her arms to draw her closer when she tried to pull away. He'd never been able to resist a challenge. "If I wanted to hurt you or take advantage of you, I had all the opportunity in the world. I've touched all that pretty naked skin. We don't have a doctor, so who do you think washed the dirt off you?"

"Oh, God."

"What?" Grinning down at her, he rubbed his thumbs in slows circles on her arms. "I thought you weren't shy, Doc. So it won't shock you to hear I've been hard since the moment you opened those lovely gray eyes and looked at me. You won't be surprised when I tell you the feel of you makes me wild, that I want to suck your pretty nipples into my mouth until you scream and claw my back."

Her gaze burned incandescent with a desire that punched hard through him. His muscles shook with the need to rip the sheet away and stroke over her supple flesh again. Sucking in a breath, he caught the scent of her dampness. Nothing was ever as sweet as that lush fragrance, heady and provocative.

"I can smell how wet you are for me. All for me. Would you be hot and tight around me if I slid my cock into you right now?" He wanted to know. Desperately. Lust wound tight inside him, squeezing off his ability to breathe. She whimpered, lifting her hands to stroke across his chest. He damn near purred at the feel of her petting him.

"Zander." His name was a breathless whisper on her lips, and he wanted nothing more than to plunge his tongue into her mouth, his cock into her hot, slick body.

He swallowed. "Are you seeing anyone, Lyra?"

The very idea was repugnant, made him want to hunt someone down and hammer his fists into them, but he had to ask. He'd be a fool not to know that this was going somewhere, and he didn't share.

"No." Her head fell back to expose her neck, her mouth opening on a low moan that exposed her elongated canines. He sensed the wolf within her clawing for freedom.

With the thought came a harsh slap of reality. What was he doing? Forcing some small distance between them, he pried his fingers off her arms one by one. It was madness. He shouldn't touch her. She was a wolf. An enemy.

And he wanted her.

CHAPTER TWO

Lyra reached for him. A tiny part of her mind wondered what the hell she was doing, but her hormones bitch-slapped those sensible thoughts into submission. His nearness, his scent, his naughty words were driving her mad with want, making her burn in a way she never had before. Every instinct within her sang, the wolf wanting to taste him. The leopard was a breed apart from the men she'd been with in the past. The predator was there, enticing the animal within her, but the man lured her in just as surely with his light, wicked smile. So different from the men in her clan. He was exotic, intoxicating. Hers, for the moment. If she took what she desired.

It was complete madness, and she didn't care. Her sex clenched as her nipples brushed against the hard muscled planes of his chest. His breath hissed out, and she smiled, loving the way he reacted to her touch. Good. At least she wasn't alone in this. Her breath raced out. Her heart pounded. No man had ever gotten to her this fast, made her so wet she ached, made her skin feel hot, flushed, and tingly—the way her body shrieked for more shocked her, but she couldn't stop it. And she didn't want to.

He backed away, toppling his chair in the process. She followed him, fisted her fingers in his navy T-shirt and pushed him against the wall next to the bedside table. The sheet fell away, slithering down her body and making her shiver. He cupped her hips as his back hit the wall. The pads of his fingers were rough with calluses, the friction making goose bumps ripple over her arms and legs. His grip bit into her flesh, stilling her movements when she rubbed herself against his hard length, the heavy muscles of his chest, the impressive erection between his thighs.

A harsh groan ripped from his throat. "This is a bad idea."

"Wouldn't be the first one I've acted on." Or the last, she was sure. She couldn't argue with him though, and her body wanted no part in logic. Cupping her fingers around his cock, she stroked him through his khaki pants.

He went rigid, his hips thrusting into her touch. A strained laugh rumbled in his chest. "You're my kind of woman."

"Prove it." Narrowing her gaze on his handsome face, she made it a challenge—to please her, to make her scream. She caught a flash of white teeth before he whipped her around and shoved her back against the wall. She gasped when his hands closed over her breasts. Shutting her eyes, she let the excitement twist within her when his hot mouth closed over her nipple.

Heat flowed through her veins like lava, making her back bow as she tried to get closer to that talented tongue. He flicked it against her nipple, teasing her. Then he switched to the other breast, and the damp skin cooled in the air-conditioned room. She shuddered at the contrast of heat and chill as he sucked her nipple deep into his mouth. When she felt the sharp points of his fangs and the rough texture of a cat's tongue on her sensitive flesh, she sobbed out a breath. She'd never experienced anything like it before. It was too much. Her breath exploded out in frantic gasps. His claws raked lightly against her hips as he held her still.

"Zander. Oh, my God."

Her nipple popped out of his mouth as he sank to his knees before her, stroking his fingertips down her body as his claws retracted. A flush of need ran under his tanned skin, and his chest heaved for breath. His voice was rough when he spoke, but a roguish grin curved the corners of his full lips. "You wanted me to prove it, didn't you? I never back down from a challenge."

"I—I'll keep that in mind." She smiled down at him, lifting her leg to hook it over his shoulder and open herself to him. "Since you're down there… Don't stop now."

"I won't." The teasing left his tone, and his green gaze burned into her flesh as he looked at her. He curled his hands over the top of her thigh, holding her in place. She shivered, her anticipation building the longer he waited. Tension ran through her muscles until she shook with it. Sliding her fingers into his thick, golden brown hair, she let her head fall back against the wall. A single finger trailed up the inside of her thigh until he stroked the slick lips of her pussy lightly.

She moaned, her hips arching to offer herself up for more. Perhaps it was how forbidden it was to let him touch her, but no one had ever excited her this way. Anticipation boiled in her veins, made her heart pound and her breathing speed until she panted. She tightened her fingers in his hair. "Now, Zander. No more playing."

Two fingers speared her, thrusting deep into her pussy. She screamed, her pelvis jerking forward. He spread her lips wide, leaning in to swipe his tongue in a long, slow lick. "So fierce, but eating your pussy tastes sweeter than sugar."

She rolled her head against the wall, and she clenched her jaw to keep from howling. Her fangs punched through her gums, and she wrestled to keep the wolf at bay as his lips settled over her clit, sucking and biting at the hard nub. Her sex clenched around his fingers as he built a slow, hard rhythm inside her. The feel of his tongue against her, the occasional rasp of a cat with the soft heat of a human man made her choke.

The muscles in her legs shook as she fought to stay upright. Beads of sweat broke out across her forehead and gathered between her breasts to slip down her skin. The combination of sensations was beyond erotic. His hands and mouth worked her faster and faster until she tugged on his hair insistently, demanding more. It was already more than she could handle, more than she'd ever had before, but still she craved him. Every thought was wiped from her mind. All that was left was the drive toward orgasm. She could feel it rising like a tidal wave inside her, and she arched her hips away from the wall. His fingers slipped away from her as he pulled back.

She sobbed a denial, fisting her fingers in his hair with a wolf's superhuman strength—so tight it had to hurt. But he was bigger than she was, stronger.

Jerking to his feet, he towered over her. "Here. Taste how good it is."

His lips slammed down over hers, his tongue shoving into her mouth. And she did taste. Herself and him, mingling on his hot tongue. The flavor shocked her, but it also turned her on even more. Her pussy flexed on nothingness, craving the feel of his hard cock pounding inside her. She moaned when he pulled away for a moment. "You can't stop!"

"Are you fucking kidding me? I'm just getting undressed." And he suited action to words, stripping so fast she was surprised he didn't rip his clothes. Though with the fire burning inside her, she wished he would just hurry this up. She was dying here.

"Thank God." Wrapping her arms around his neck and her legs around his lean hips when he stepped forward again, she tried to get as close to him as humanly possible. They both groaned at the full skin-to-skin contact. The light furring on his chest rasped against her hardened nipples. His big hands gripped her ass, lifting her to rub the head of his cock against her pussy. He shoved himself deep, going to the hilt in one hard push. She bared her claws, digging into his shoulders as pleasure and pain rocketed through her system. He was so damn thick, the stretch of it hurt. And she liked it. Her body twisted to get closer, seeking a fuller penetration.

His breath rushed against the side of her neck, cooling the sweat there and making her shiver. "You're so hot, so tight. And the way you smell…wetness and woman. Do you know how good your pussy feels around my cock, Lyra?"

"Jesus," she breathed. Amazingly, she grew slicker at his words. She'd never been with a man who said the kinds of things he did to her. It was dirty and raw and so naughty it made her hotter for him.

He withdrew until just the head of his cock remained inside her, then he shoved back in. She pressed her hips forward to meet him, and the sound of their naked skin slapping together echoed in the wide room. The rhythm they set was desperate and almost punishing in its speed. She didn't want to think of anything outside of this moment with a man who made her burn.

Rolling his pelvis against hers, he changed the angle of his thrusts. "Do you like this, sugar?"

"Yes." The position was so fucking perfect, his cock hitting her just right as her walls clamped around him. He groaned, his fingers biting deeper into her ass as he pulled the cheeks apart. Flames danced inside her, heating her skin until they threatened to explode. She threw her head back. "Yes."

His chuckle vibrated against her chest, and he brushed his lips over the base of her throat. "Me, too."

"Make me come, Zander." She closed her eyes and smiled, remembering his warning. "If you can."

Drawing a hand back, he slapped the fleshy part of her thigh. She jolted at the shock of sensation, one more piling on top of those that already threatened to overwhelm her. Her pussy flexed around his thrusting cock, and she cried out as he smacked her again. Her eyes snapped open to meet his, and the green of them burned into her. She couldn't look away, caught by the intensity of what transpired between them.

She dug her fingers into his shoulders as they moved faster and faster, racing each other to orgasm. Heat swamped her system, and her sex began to pulse around his cock each time he filled her. She was close. So very close. He rotated his hips, changing his intense angle. Then it broke within her so hard and fast it left her sobbing. He hammered inside her, and aftershocks rocked through her, made her shudder as it went on and on in endless waves.

Then he froze, his big body ramming his cock inside her one last time as his heat flooded her. She growled low in her throat, the sound ripping out of her. He hissed, his fangs glistening in the last glimmer of sunlight streaming through the windows. "Lyra."

Her palms pressed to his sweaty back, slipping down his skin. His face buried in her throat as his muscles shook under her stroking fingertips. Reality returned slowly as her body stopped shaking, her heart stopped galloping, and her chest stopped heaving for breath. It was an ugly reality.

Her uncle would kill her—if her father didn't get to her first. Niece or not, the Alpha would not take this kind of behavior well, and she would be in a shitload of trouble. That would be quite a homecoming for her considering she hadn't seen or heard from either one of them for almost three years. Not since she left the clan in Tennessee and took the clinic job in New Orleans. Uncle Michael was beyond pissed and her father…well, the words they'd parted with were the kind that meant it was years before they would speak again. If ever.

It might have been safer if Zander had left her out in the desert. How the hell had he done this to her? She'd never even slept with a man on the first date, let alone the first twenty minutes. She never let anyone get this close this fast. Or at all. Her family had taught her very clearly that if she stepped out of line, or became a problem, they wouldn't stick by her. No one would ever want her, need her or love her enough for that. And she was one enormous problem for Zander Leonidas at this point.

Whoever had dumped her here in the first place hadn't finished what they started. She wasn't dead. Neither the desert nor the leopards had done it. But, why her? And why now? She wasn't close to her family, no matter how high ranking it was. What was the end game? Who benefited from her going missing? She didn't have any enemies—at least, she didn't think so. If her family wanted her dead, they'd had years to get it done.

It made no sense, and that's what scared her the most.

The wolf bitch was a loose end. Ramon Guerra didn't like loose ends. If he was hired to do a job, he did it. End of story. He was the best for a reason.

His client wasn't happy about this delay—about the fact that Lyra Marcus was still alive. And was fucking Zander Leonidas. Ramon eased away from the rear of the infirmary, fading into the desert landscape that surrounded the resort.

She had to die on leopard land. Why, Ramon didn't know, and he didn't want to know. He had a target, and that was all he needed. If it weren't for the werebird hunting in the desert who had interrupted Ramon while he was dumping the Marcus woman off, he'd have made certain she was dead before he'd left her. She'd gotten lucky once. It wouldn't happen again. Her life would be over in a matter of days. The wild cat inside of him purred in agreement—nothing assuaged the ocelot's feral nature like a fresh kill.

Though most species of shifter cats pledged loyalty to the Leonidas family, Ramon didn't give a damn about all that. He suspected his client had hired him specifically because he was a cat-shifter, but he didn't let himself dwell on the thought. Instead, he methodically went over the last forty-eight hours, cataloguing what had gone wrong and planning his next steps. He didn't like how complicated this operation had become.

He was bringing in reinforcements. That hadn't been his original plan, but plans changed. Every situation was fluid. Usually he liked to work alone, but the fact that the she-wolf was shacking up with a leopard was worrisome. He didn't like surprises, and the Leonidas family was one he didn't want to tangle with. His business depended on him keeping a low profile. Attracting the attention of the ruling leopards wouldn't do that for him.

Yeah, the bitch was a loose end he needed to tie up. Now.

CHAPTER THREE

The next morning, Zander strode out of the building that housed the corporate offices for Leonidas Industries. It had taken him the better part of two hours and a whole lot of fast talking to get Adrian and Nico to agree to keep Lyra here until they figured out what was going on. All of them were going to start digging discreetly to see what new shifts in wolf politics were in the works. That Lyra had ended up on leopard land wasn't a coincidence. Someone had gone to a lot of trouble to get her here, wanted to start something, to make a statement, and they needed to know who and why.

Not knowing made frustration crawl through him. Whatever had happened spelled trouble for his family, and they'd had more than their share lately. He wanted it done. But there was nothing more he could do at this point. It was a waiting game. In the meantime, he had work to do for the resort. His assistant manager had handled everything while Zander played nursemaid, but the younger man couldn't do everything himself. Zander had a lot of catching up to do.

His gaze swept the resort grounds as he walked toward the main hotel that housed his office. Palm trees littered the premises, shading a sparkling blue pool and the creamy stucco and wood Spanish-style buildings. Mountains rose in the distance to one side of the resort while the desert opened in the other. His place. Under his leadership, it was more successful than it ever had been. At his insistence, Refuge was a neutral-territory resort exclusively for shifters, where they were free to be whom and what they were. Since wolves vacationed here as well, Nico was anal about maintaining tight security.

An hour later, Zander's intercom buzzed and his secretary's voice came through. "Sir, I found a guest who's the same size as your…new friend." There was a slight pause while the line crackled. "And you have a one o'clock appointment in Tucson today. You're going to need to leave soon."

"Right." Zander pulled in a deep breath, the scent of sand and a hundred different shifters reaching his nostrils. Including Lyra's. His pants grew uncomfortably tight as his cock stirred. He'd taken her to his house on the edge of the resort's main compound last night. He'd reached for her again and again before dawn broke, burying his cock in her tight, silky sheath. Shaking his head, he snorted. The most intense orgasms of his life and he should be half-dead, not horny again.

Something he didn't understand had happened between Lyra and him. It confused the hell out of him, and he didn't like it, but he wanted her. Now. Again. He'd never had a problem getting women, but there was something about her that made him react. Never in his life had he had to fight to keep from biting a woman. But with her, his fangs had come out, and every instinct inside him had screeched for him to mark her, to make her his forever.

She wasn't staying, so he had no business going there. It didn't matter how pretty she was or how good a lay. He held back a wince at the crude thought—wolf or not, she didn't deserve it, but it was a good reminder to himself. She wasn't for him. Biology and destiny weren't things he could argue with or charm into his way of thinking. He could talk his brothers into keeping her until they knew what was going on, but it wasn't permanent.

He couldn't forget that even for a second.

He clenched his fists as frustration rocketed through him. What a fucking mess. Why did she have to be a wolf? Their world wouldn't survive a mating between their species. It was bad enough that Jason had mated with the Alpha wolf's human stepdaughter, but a leopard and a true wolf? It wouldn't happen. It couldn't happen.

Every shifter species could trace its existence to the blessing of a benevolent deity. For leopards, it went back to King Leonidas of Sparta. He'd become legend for his bravery in the face of an onslaught of Persian forces under the command of Xerxes. So impressed with Leonidas's courageous death, the hunter goddess Artemis had made his sons more than men. The god Zeus, jealous of his daughter's powerful creations, had made a wereanimal of his own. Wolves. King Lycaon of Arcadia had been the first, and his fifty sons had followed in his footsteps.

Wolves and leopards had scattered to the four corners of the globe, but their war for dominance had never abated, even centuries later. The peace between their two species was tenuous at the best of times. A kidnapped and battered wolf on leopard land wouldn't help with that, but every instinct demanded Zander keep Lyra safe…and near.

There were no other options.

"Thanks. I will." Setting the receiver in the cradle, Lyra hung up the phone and sighed. Her head throbbed, her body screaming with tension.

She hadn't told the hospital where she was—just that there'd been an emergency and she'd had to leave suddenly. Zander's suggestion. He said it wasn't safe. She knew he was right, but why had she trusted him? Why didn't she call her family? Her uncle and father would help her. She knew it. But…what if Zander was right? What if someone inside her family had done this to her? Clan politics could get nasty, and she wasn't involved in that world enough to know if someone was making a play for power. Had her family made any new enemies? She didn't know. That was the problem with all of this.

She didn't know.

She didn't know who would do this to her or why. Didn't know who she could turn to, who she could trust, who she could count on so that she didn't end up dead. What had happened to her wasn't an accident, but she didn't know why.

And whoever had done this…she wanted them to pay. She wanted them to hurt the way she had when she was crawling through the desert, knowing she wouldn't survive. She wanted them to feel that moment of absolute terror, of absolute certainty, that they were going to die, just like she had when Zander found her. Was that wrong of her? She didn't know. As a doctor, she'd taken an oath to do no harm, but the wolf within her didn't give a damn about oaths. It wanted revenge, painful and bloody. It wanted to hunt her attacker down and end this once and for all. If she ever found out who they were.

Rubbing at her temples, she tried to ease the ache there. Nothing helped. Tears of frustration welled in her eyes, and she swiped them away. Crying wouldn't help her out of this mess she'd fallen into, wouldn't make it all better. Someone wanted her dead; that much was clear.

Whether it was wise or not, she was going to trust Zander to help her figure this out.

Some fundamental part of her knew he wouldn't hurt her. Ever. And he wouldn't allow anyone else to harm her either. She felt...safe. Protected. Was this how Celeste had felt when she'd gone against the clan Alpha and mated with Jason? When she'd heard about her cousin's mating, Lyra had thought Celeste insane. It could only cause more strife between the clans. Then again, Lyra was *persona non grata* in the wolf clan herself. So much so that her mother had made it clear she shouldn't come home for Celeste's funeral. Lyra wasn't welcome to share the family's grief. That still chafed. But Lyra now understood the pull of Leonidas men. While she wasn't a woman to cower behind a man, it was nice to have someone to watch her back. She hadn't known that kind of security since...ever. Not even when she lived on clan land.

It never occurred to her how much she might need it. Until Zander. But she also knew it couldn't last. For many, many reasons, including the fact that a relationship with her would cause him problems with his family. And hers. No, when this was all over, she'd never see him again. The thought made her heart ache and her throat close, but she shoved the feelings aside. Reality was what it was.

She pulled in a slow, deep breath and let herself look around. He'd brought her to his house last night. She hadn't wanted to stay by herself at the infirmary. A dart of terror went through her, made her heart seize. She clenched her jaw and rode out the fear that threatened to overwhelm her. It was easier to ignore now, in the daytime, but she'd have to get used to being on her own again. But, not yet. Not yet. For the moment, she'd let herself lean on someone else. Just until they got to the bottom of her kidnapping.

His home had obviously been professionally decorated in the same Southwestern style as the rest of the resort, but it was the personal touches that interested her. Unframed family photographs propped against a wooden mantle showed four tall green-eyed boys in various poses, some surrounding an unsmiling man. Hector Leonidas. It was odd to think of the leopard rulers as a family. The realization was unsettling. They'd always been others. Enemies. Until she'd moved to New Orleans, she'd had very little exposure to leopards.

She stood to wander around, touching the heavy wooden furniture, the curved walls that never actually formed a corner as they led from one room to the next. Anything to distract herself from the danger that weighed so heavily on her chest. It was an oppressive cloud that refused to dissipate. She pulled a soda out of the fridge and leaned against the counter to drink it.

Zander drove up in a Jeep, parking in front of the bay window over the kitchen sink. If she lived here, she'd grow herbs in that window. She shook the thought away. Stupid. She was only here for a few days. No settling in. She had an apartment of her own to get back to in Louisiana.

He loped around the side of the Jeep toward the house. God, he was big. He had to be about six and a half feet tall. It was amazing. At five-eleven, she'd never been with a man who made her feel petite, but he did. He fit her in every way. And it was wrong. She knew it was. Wrong, stupid…and totally forbidden. Even thinking about marking him as hers was unbalanced, but she'd been more than ready when they'd had sex. Her instincts tore at her insides demanding she satisfy the bone-deep need to claim. If her father and uncle knew, they'd check her into the psych ward of the nearest werekind hospital.

Any way she looked at it, her time with Zander was limited.

No more Zander to whisper in her ear, to stroke his fingers down her skin, to make her scream with pleasure. It wasn't logical. It wasn't like anything she had ever known before. Everything with Zander was carnal. He drowned her in the sheer visceral reaction of a woman to a man.

She wanted more. And she couldn't have it. Why did it have to be him who did this to her? Why did it have to be now when she could least afford to be distracted by sex? She should be focused on finding out who kidnapped her, not worrying about having to leave Zander when she did. Knowing all that didn't seem to be stopping her. She sighed, too many emotions ricocheting through her. Rage, frustration, hopelessness, fear and something heart-stoppingly sweet when she focused on the leopard walking toward her.

A petite young woman got out of the other side of the vehicle and followed Zander to the front door. She had a bag in one hand and a cigarette poised in the other. Her hair was so pale a blonde it reminded Lyra of a moonbeam.

Lyra met them at the door, opening it to let them in. The way Zander's eyes lit and a wicked smile curled his lips when he saw her dissolved any jealousy that might have tried to rear its ugly head.

The blonde woman waved her cigarette around and indicated she'd stay outside. She handed Zander the bag, and he walked in with it. Lyra glanced from him to the girl. "What's going on?"

He handed the knapsack over. "Clothes for you. You looked to be about the same size."

"Except you're about a foot taller, so I put some skirts in there so it won't matter." The other woman's cheery, musical voice sailed in through the open door.

Lyra leaned around Zander to smile at her. "Thanks."

Walking into the bathroom, Lyra opened the sack to inspect the contents. She set it on the counter, slipped out of the cotton pajamas she'd stolen from Zander and tried on a few of the skirts until she found one that couldn't double as a belt on her. Considering she had no underwear, concealment was of the essence. She slid her feet into a pair of flip-flops that were also in the bag and pulled a dark polo shirt over her head, thanking God she didn't need to wear a bra.

When she stepped out, Zander was nowhere to be seen, so she went to give the extra clothes back to her guardian angel. After rounding the corner to the front door, she leaned against the jamb as the young woman took a deep drag on her cigarette.

"Thanks for the clothes."

"Oh, no problem. My parents got me a whole new wardrobe for my college graduation present, and they sent me to Refuge for a week to celebrate." She cocked her blonde head and gave a blinding smile. "Zander didn't tell me why you didn't have any clothes, but I hope it's kinky, because he's a hottie."

That startled a laugh out of Lyra. It was so incongruous to hear this Miss-America-contestant-looking girl say things like kinky while watching her suck on a cancer stick. "Those things will kill you, you know."

"I'm a shifter, so it's a lot harder to kill me than regular people." The blonde woman shrugged. "Besides, everyone deserves a vice, and chain-smoking is mine. I can't be too cute or I'd make even myself sick."

Arching her brows, Lyra chuckled. Well, she was pageant queen perky, but at least she was self-aware. "Okay, I give. What kind of shifter are you?"

A sheepish look crossed her face, but her lips curled into an adorable grin. "Swan."

Oh, that was just too perfect. It completed the uber-pretty and sweet package. Lyra struggled not to break into a fit of giggles. "What's your name?"

"Victoria Haida. Tori."

Offering her hand to shake, she said, "I'm Lyra."

Tori held the hand with the cigarette behind her and reached out with the other. "Nice to meetcha."

"Okay, it's about that time. Let's get going." Zander stepped out of the house and set his hand on Lyra's shoulder.

A shiver went down her spine at the light touch, and she gritted her teeth to keep a whimper of need in. "Where are you going?"

"We are going into Tucson for the day. As nice as Ms. Haida is to give up her wardrobe, you need clothes, and I need to meet with one of the local beverage distributors about deliveries to the resort's restaurant and lounge."

Since she obviously didn't have any money with her, he was going to have to foot the bill for her new clothes. Whether he liked it or not, as soon as she was out of this mess, she was paying him back. She didn't voice the thought out loud. She had a feeling he'd protest.

"And I'm going to hit the pool. I want to work on my tan." Tori lifted an already golden arm.

"Thanks again, Tori." Zander gave her a charming smile, cupped his big hand around Lyra's shoulder, and shut the front door behind them. It beeped as a security system engaged. Tori took off toward the rest of the resort while Lyra and Zander piled into the Jeep. The wind from the open top ruffled through her hair as they pulled away from the house and onto a two-lane road. She tilted her head back to let the bright sunshine bathe her face.

"Did you call the hospital?" Zander stroked his fingers down her arm.

"Yes. Before you ask, I didn't tell them where I was." She shoved her dark hair back, despising how helpless she was in all of this. She wasn't raised to be weak and hide from problems. It didn't sit well with her. But if her other option was ending up beaten and back in the desert—or dead—she was just going to have to deal with it. A sigh eased past her lips. "I'm going to lose my job over this."

He grunted, but made no other acknowledgment of her words.

"Gee, your concern is touching." Asshole. She didn't add that last word, but she was pretty sure he heard it by the way he chuckled.

Turning his head, he pierced her with an inscrutable glance. "We need a medic here."

She couldn't help the way her heart leapt, raced and then tripped at the very idea of staying with him. He wanted her to stay here. Stomping down on her momentary joy, she gave a derisive snort. "You're insane. If most of my family stopped speaking to me for leaving the clan to work in the borderlands, do you know what they would do to me if I worked for leopards?"

"Refuge is neutral territory."

"So are all werekind hospitals. That's not going to impress my uncle or my father. Or my cousins, my mother, my Great Aunt Hattie Jane."

"You have an aunt named Hattie Jane?" His white teeth flashed in a grin as he said it.

She rolled her eyes at him. "I'm from the south, of course I have an Aunt Hattie Jane."

"Do they call you by your middle name too?"

A growl slid from her throat. "Not if they want to live."

"What's your middle name?"

"Jane," she snarled. "It's a family name."

"That's pretty." He put a fake country twang in his voice. "Lyra Jane."

She fought a smile and lost, so she turned to look out the window and coughed into her fist to smother a laugh. "Only my mother calls me that. Just Lyra, thanks."

"Whatever you say, sugar."

Sugar. She winced. Not because she didn't like it, but because she did. She'd never been the pet-name type. Her world was sterile, clinical. Her patients relied on her to be calm, focused and impartial in her judgment of their injuries and ailments. None of that had ever led her to believe she was capable of the kind of caution-to-the-wind, wall-banging, screaming animalist orgasms Zander had dragged out of her all through the night.

And she wanted to do it again. The chemistry between them was beyond mind-blowing.

They'd gotten maybe five miles down the road when she caught Zander slanting her a glance. His eyes were a brilliant shade of green that danced when he gave her a wicked grin. "You're not wearing anything under that skirt, are you?"

"What do you think?" The muscles in her thighs tensed in anticipation. Wetness flooded her sex, and she wrapped her fingers tight around her seatbelt to keep from reaching for him. How had he done this to her? She'd gone years without sex before and never had a problem. It had only been a few hours since Zander had fucked her and she was dying for his touch.

His deep voice rumbled, almost a purr. "I think if I slid my hand up your leg I wouldn't just find you going commando. I'd find your pussy lips wet and hot, ready for me to finger-fuck."

Christ, he said dirty things. She swallowed hard, her body flashing hot with tingles. "Wh-why don't you find out, then?"

"I thought you'd never ask, sugar." He dropped one hand from the steering wheel and reached over to stroke her knee. He moved his hand slowly, making her squirm in mounting excitement. She wanted his fingers on her, in her, thrusting deep. The wind captured her soft whimper, blowing it away. She spread her thighs as wide as her skirt would allow. He pushed it up as he went. "Lift your ass."

She did, and he shoved her skirt up to her waist. The air caressed her damp flesh, and she shuddered. His fingertips brushed over her clit and skimmed her swollen lips before he dipped inside her soaking channel. His gaze flicked from the road to her and back again as he worked her flesh and controlled the vehicle with cool efficiency. The deep flush that raced under his skin gave him away—he wasn't as unaffected as he might appear.

"Zander, please." She raised her hips to meet him, and his movements were quick and forceful, catapulting her to the edge of orgasm. She arched her neck against the headrest, rolling her face toward him. "I don't want to come without you. I want you inside me."

He hissed, his fangs elongating as he looked over at her. Jerking the wheel, he pulled over to the side of the road, unclipped his seatbelt and reached between his legs to slide his seat back. That was all the encouragement she needed. She unsnapped her seatbelt, climbed over the center console and straddled his lap. He shoved her shirt up, yanking it over her head. And then his hands were on her bare breasts, her nipples in his mouth as he sucked her hard. Her back bowed, pressing her closer. His tongue flicked over her tight, flushed skin until she sobbed for breath. It wasn't enough. She craved the way his cock filled her. She needed it. Him.

Tugging up his shirt, she ran her hands over the muscled planes of his stomach and chest. Her nails flicked over the flat discs of his nipples. They hardened under her touch. His mouth left her breasts so he could jerk his shirt off and toss it aside. "Touch me, Lyra. I love your hands on me."

Her heart hammered so loud she could hear it in her ears. She unbuttoned his jeans and shoved the zipper down. Reaching in, she pulled his cock free of his boxers and stroked it. "Is this what you had in mind?"

"Oh, yeah." After a few moments, he moved her hand away, gripped her hips, and pulled her forward. "Ride me, sugar."

"You don't have to tell me twice." She braced her hands on his broad shoulders for leverage, rubbing the head of his dick against her lips. A whimper broke from her throat at the heat that thrummed through her.

He gave her a lopsided grin, fire flickering in his green eyes. "This is my favorite position, you know?"

"You have a favorite?" She chuckled, and it brushed her nipples against the springy hair on his chest. "I would have thought any position that got you laid would do the trick."

"Oh, it does. But there's something about watching a woman pump herself on my cock, the feel of her pussy all slick and tight, knowing she wants me so much she'll drive herself crazy going faster and faster to try to get more. The look on a woman's face when she fills herself with me—goddamn, there's nothing hotter than that."

She bit her lip and sank down on him, knowing she was giving him exactly the look he'd just mentioned. The way the corner of his mouth kicked up confirmed it. His big hands bracketed her hips, his thumbs digging into her flesh just below her pelvic bones as he guided her descent. Molten heat slid over her skin, made her back arch. His cock stretched her wide, and she rolled her hips for sweet friction. Her eyes dropped to half-mast as her concentration focused on his flesh in hers as she moved.

"You're so fucking beautiful, Lyra." Something tender flashed in his gaze as he lifted one hand to cup her cheek.

"Zander." She leaned forward, laid her hands along his jaw, and pressed her lips to his. He groaned, thrusting his tongue into her mouth to the same rhythm that his dick moved inside her. She curled her finger into claws on his shoulders, digging into his flesh as their pelvises ground together. Sweat rolled down their bodies, sealing them together with each downward movement. The muscles in her thighs flexed as she lifted and lowered herself on his thick cock. Faster and faster, harder and harder until she threw back her head and screamed, the sound half-woman and half-wolf. Orgasm crashed through her, and her pussy milked his dick, fisting around him.

Zander froze beneath her for a long, protracted moment before his hips hammered into hers. His hands held her down, seating her fully on his cock. Then he came, his jaw clenched tight, and his eyes flickering with green fire. She slumped against him, her fingers relaxing their grip on his shoulders.

Meeting his eyes, she grinned and tried to slow her breathing down, stop her muscles from shaking. "You know, I've never made it in a car—not even when I was a teenager."

An answering smile formed on his lips. "Everyone should try it at least once."

CHAPTER FOUR

Lyra watched Zander's gaze sharpen suddenly, focusing on something beyond her shoulder. Before she could glance back to see what it was, his arms snapped around her to roll her away from his door and smash her between him and the center console. It was such a protective gesture that she had to swallow and clear her throat so she didn't get choked up. When was the last time someone had put themselves between her and danger? Not since she'd left home to study medicine. She pulled in a deep breath and realized what he'd seen. A bird.

The loud flap of wings told her it was a bird of prey before she'd even managed to wriggle enough to see. Zander tightened his arms around her when she shoved her shoulder against him. "You're crushing me."

He didn't move, just kept his steely gaze pinned to the bald eagle that spun in a precise circle to land beside the Jeep. A rustle of feathers and the enormous bird shifted into a naked woman. She had short, spiky platinum hair and the most amazing breasts Lyra had ever seen. She heaved a disgruntled sigh at the mere teaspoonfuls of cleavage she had received. If she caught Zander staring, she'd kick his spotted leopard ass.

The faded scars on the eagle-shifter's body made Lyra arch her brows. It took an incredible amount of damage to scar a were. Battle scars. She knew about the warrior existence of those enlisted in the Messenger Corps—the werebirds who delivered messages from one group of werekind leaders to another—but she'd only met one or two of them in her life. None of them had ended up in her clinic.

"If you wouldn't mind stepping out of your vehicle for a moment. I'm here to deliver a message, and then I'll let you get back to your…business." Not a single expression crossed the wereeagle's face, but Lyra got the distinct impression the other woman was amused.

A warning growl vibrated through Zander's chest. "Who are you?"

"Alexandra Petros, Commander of the Messenger Corps. Call me Ajax."

Lyra swallowed. How important could the message be that they'd rated the Corps Commander to deliver it? Dread twisted through her, made the tips of her fingers tingle.

Zander tucked his cock back into his boxers, but didn't bother to zip his pants. He popped the door to the car, and Lyra stepped out after him. He shoved her back, so she was safely behind him and trapped by the open door. She sighed and wriggled to the side a bit so she could see, but wasn't dumb enough to try and go around him. He wouldn't let her and she knew it—no matter how capable a wolf was in defending itself from harm. Usually. Her track record in that area hadn't been so wonderful lately. Then again, if it had, she might never have met Zander. She tried to ignore the pang that hit her chest at that thought.

"What's the message?" he barked out.

The eagle woman raised a brow at his rudeness. "The wolves want the daughter you kidnapped back. Felix Marcus has approached the Alpha for assistance in this. If she's not returned, it's war."

He shook his head, his brown hair flying. "I had no part in her kidnapping."

"It's true." Lyra put her hand on his arm and leaned to the side to speak to the messenger. "The Leonidases saved me and took me in."

Cool indifference flashed over the eagle's face. "I'm sure you believe that."

"They can't take her from me," he hissed. "She doesn't have to go back if she doesn't want to."

She held up her hand. "Birds are neutrals. We don't involve ourselves in your disputes. This isn't my problem."

Lyra's voice held more entreaty than she would have liked, but the idea of leaving Zander sent panic exploding through her. And that scared her more than anything else. "But couldn't you—"

"I deliver messages. That's all. Personal feelings don't enter into the equation." Ajax's gaze was hard and unrelenting.

Zander sliced his hand downward, ending the conversation. "Then tell the wolves what we've said here and that the leopard leader will be in touch."

"Done." With a great leap, she shifted mid-air and swooped away.

They stood together until she was no more than a fading speck on the horizon. Lyra turned her face into Zander's shoulder, pulling in a deep breath to savor his scent. "I have to go."

"No." That warning growl she'd come to expect when he was pushed to dangerous limits sounded, but it couldn't be helped.

"War, Zander. My uncle and my father rarely agree on anything." Except that she shouldn't have gone to New Orleans. Her lips formed a bitter twist at how often their agreements hurt her. She pulled Zander around so he faced her, so he could see how serious she was. "My father doesn't issue idle threats." No, he didn't. And he'd probably use this as the excuse he'd been looking for to drag her back to Tennessee from New Orleans. Living as a shifter in a border city was dangerous because that was where violence between the species was most likely to break out. Which was exactly why she was needed there.

It wasn't that she craved the adrenaline of the emergency room, but no one needed her back home—there were other doctors for those clinics. And there was no way in hell she was going home with her tail tucked between her legs because her father was scared of what might happen to her. They'd had this battle before, and she'd go toe to toe with him again if she had to. Lyra sighed and focused on Zander. "If my father's gone to the Alpha—"

"No, sugar. You are not leaving." His tone was implacable, his face set in stone.

She cupped his jaw in her hands, trying to make him understand. "Imagine what open war would do to our people. It wouldn't just cost lives, but the secrecy that keeps all weres safe from humans. I have to go back. A phone call—even from your brother—isn't going to cut it."

"You don't know who did this to you. How do you know it wasn't someone your father and uncle trusts? How do you know this didn't have something to do with wolf clan politics? How do you know you wouldn't be walking right back into a trap?"

Shaking her head, she dropped her hands. "I don't. I don't have an answer to any of those questions. But I do know that my life isn't worth war."

"It is to me."

"Zander, this is ridiculous." Tears burned her eyes, but she blinked them back. She was the Alpha wolf's niece. He was the leopard leader's brother. Just because he made her feel in a way no other man ever had was irrelevant. The messenger's arrival made it clear just how solid the lines were in their world, no matter how they'd begun to blur for Lyra and Zander. "I'm going back. Please take me to the resort so I can book a flight to Tennessee."

"No! Damn it." This time she didn't even get the warning growl as he shoved his fingers into her hair, jerking her up against his chest and crushing her mouth under his.

His tongue thrust between her lips, and heat exploded through her. Backing her up against his seat, he lifted her so that she was half in the Jeep and half out. Her ribs slammed against the steering wheel, but she ignored the pain and clung to his shoulders as he shoved their clothes out of the way and slammed his cock deep inside her pussy. Crying out at the tight fit, she arched her hips and reveled in the excitement that twisted within her.

Fire and ice raced over her skin, tears blurring her vision as her movements became desperate, needing to be as close to him as possible. One last time. Her heart squeezed as pain and pleasure warred for dominance within her. He set a harsh, punishing rhythm, his fangs bared as the feral side of him, the leopard, came forward. His fingers tightened in her hair, pulling her head back. He pressed his lips to her exposed throat, his tongue flicking out to lick her. He rolled his hips against hers, changing the angle, but not the rough speed, of his thrusts. "Zander."

"Mine." He sank his fangs deep into her flesh. She screamed and came so hard starbursts of light exploded behind her lids. He licked and sucked at the bite mark until she sobbed for breath, her pussy flexing again and again around his cock. "You're mine, Lyra. All mine, only mine. Forever. Mine."

"Y-yours." Tears streaked down her cheeks, and she buried her face in his neck. His hard cock continued to move within her, demanding her response. Heat built again, called to the most primitive part of herself, and she lifted her hips to meet his.

He angled his chin up, baring his throat for her. Her lips closed over his collarbone, sucking lightly at the salty flesh. His taste and scent filled her senses, drugging her with the unquenchable need he ripped from her. Zander. What would she do without him now? His bite burned on her skin, branding her as his. Undeniably his. Yes. She wanted that unbreakable bond.

"Bite me, Lyra. Mark me."

She obeyed without question, without thinking. God, yes. That was exactly what she craved. The wolf inside her howled as her fangs pierced his flesh. He jerked beneath her touch, coming in long, hot spurts within her. The coppery tang of his blood flooded her tongue as she licked the healing wound. It was carnal, possessive. He was hers, all hers. Forever, just as he'd said. Her Zander.

When it was over, he carried her around to her side of the car and tucked her into her seat. She heard him punching the buttons on his cell phone and the quiet conversation with one of his brothers as he related what had just happened with the messenger. And that they were now mated. She closed her eyes, fighting a low moan. What had she done? She'd mated on the side of a road in the middle of the desert. Contentment she'd never experienced before twisted with the practical understanding that this meant her life as a wolf was over. Done. She'd no longer have a family. Even if the Alpha forgave her, her father never would. Pain and loss rippled through her followed by sweetness and joy. She was so jumbled up inside, broken and scared.

Her eyes flared wide when his door squeaked open. He picked his shirt up off the floorboard, shook the wrinkles out, and put it back on before he got into the Jeep. A minute later, they'd pulled back out onto the road headed for Tucson. She blinked. "We're still going?"

"I have a meeting." He lifted his shoulder in a shrug. "It's business."

She snarled at him, not bothering to check the raging wolf inside her. How could he be so calm when her life was crumbling around her? "I'd heard your family were all ruthless assholes."

"Sugar, I'm the nice one of the Leonidas brothers."

"That's comforting," she muttered, snatching up her discarded shirt and shoving herself into it.

Curling into a ball against her door, she vacillated wildly between self-loathing and giddy delight the whole way to town. Zander was thankfully silent. Smart man. She wasn't sure if she'd have ripped his head off or thrown herself at him again, but neither reaction would have been rational. His meeting passed in a blur, and she was grateful that she got to sit outside the glassed-in office where she wasn't expected to make polite conversation.

The last thing she wanted was to shop, but she needed clothes, so she had to suck it up and do what she had to. But as Zander dragged her in and out of big department stores and small specialty boutiques in the mall, something nagged at her the whole way, made her skin prickle with unease. She couldn't put her finger on what was wrong so she said nothing. This day had been so insane, she wouldn't be surprised if she was losing her grip on reality. She stepped out of a shop to buy a drink from a concession stand, making sure to stay within Zander's line of sight. His insistence, but she didn't have the energy left to argue.

The hairs lifted on the back of her neck, rippling in chills down her arms. Her stomach flipped as her instincts lit up, shrieking danger. She tried to remain calm and casual, not make any sudden moves that might give her away, but the wolf in her had gone on alert and every sense intensified. Scents assaulted her, her eyes absorbed every detail around her, looking for the source. She saw nothing, but she didn't need to. Now she knew what was wrong.

She was being followed.

Ramon watched Benny tail the she-wolf through the mall. If Lyra managed to identify anyone, it would be Benny, because he was providing close cover while Ramon remained farther behind and across the wide walkway. No one would ever connect his face or scent to this operation. If Benny didn't understand that score—well, it wasn't Ramon's job to educate the hyena-shifter.

Surveillance like this was best conducted in pairs, so if she stopped, Benny didn't have to do something stupid that would only draw attention to himself, like bend over and tie his shoe, or pretend sudden interest in a perfume display. The hyena could walk right past and wait up ahead while Ramon watched her from a distance. All they needed was a few moments of her away from Zander and the crowd—a bathroom break, a trip down into a mostly empty store—and it was over. A simple snatch job, then lights out for the Marcus woman.

Ramon could collect his hefty fee, give Benny a small cut, and be on to the next assignment.

Until then, they had to be patient and watchful. Ramon had no problem with either, but Benny was a bit of a wildcard. The hyena wouldn't have been Ramon's first choice as a partner in this job, but he was the only one available on such short notice.

"*Mierda.*" He hissed the word in a voice too low to attract the notice of the humans around him when the leopard stepped out of a store to rejoin the woman.

He pulled back, slipping into the crowd and out of sight. Another delay. He didn't like it, but it wouldn't stop him from finishing the job.

Patience would reward him. The woman had to be alone some time. When she was, he'd be waiting.

CHAPTER FIVE

Killing rage pumped through Zander's system. He paced the length of Nico's office, rattling off questions, demands, observations from what he'd found at the mall. Lyra had come to him, claiming she was being followed. He'd pulled her into his arms and let his gaze scan the surrounding area as he'd hustled her and her shopping bags out to the Jeep. An odd scent had caught his attention. Not canine, exactly. But not feline, either. And there wasn't a real dog or cat anywhere in sight. No, this was a shifter. He just wasn't sure what kind. The scent had faded fast, but he hadn't wanted to leave Lyra alone to trace it. Frustration still curled in his gut. Fuck.

Every imaginable electronic gadget and three different computers were neatly arranged on desks that ringed Nico's large office. The big man dwarfed the space as he kicked back to read a sheaf of paper, occasionally glancing up to scan a wall of video monitors.

He ran a hand over his military-short hair, slanting a glance at Zander. "I think it's a professional."

Stopping, he rounded on his older brother. "What?"

"The tailing, the way they worked her over bad enough to leave her near dead, but not. It was too calculated, too good. We're assuming this is meant to start something between the wolves and leopards. I'm going one step beyond that and saying it isn't some disposable lackey doing it. Whoever wants to start this shit has hired an assassin to get the job done. Smart of them, bad for us."

"I agree. My contacts in the shifter community have pulled up dick. No one leaves a trail this clean without bringing in professional help." Adrian entered the room as Nico finished speaking, and leaned back against the door after he closed it, folding his arms. He leveled a cool stare at Zander. "To make matters even more complicated, you mated with the Alpha's niece. I could toss your ass out of Refuge so fast it would make your head spin for this, little brother."

"Are you really going to disown me for mating to a woman I love?" Love. The word came out of his mouth, and it felt right. He'd never used it in reference to a woman before, but this wasn't just any woman, this was Lyra. This was his woman. He wanted to tell her—she deserved to know. Emotions banded tight around his chest, too many to control. Love, need, and intense protective instincts for Lyra—rage, hate and the need to kill the person who wanted to hurt her.

"Love? You've known her about five seconds. Spare me. And a wolf? Jesus, Zander." Adrian rolled his eyes, glancing back at Nico. Both men wore looks of utter repugnance on their faces. "How the hell did we end up with such an open-minded brother?"

"Apparently, we didn't beat him enough when he was growing up." Nico snorted, letting his feet drop to the floor. "If the kidnapping wasn't enough, then this mating is definitely going to start a shit storm in wolf-leopard politics. Celeste was a human, and she died before anything really got started because of Jason mating to her, but this? They're already threatening war. What happens when they find out you want to tie the bloodlines with a mating?"

"Maybe then we can work out this centuries-old bullshit. Do we even know why we hate them anymore? When have they ever done anything to us or us to them?" Zander crossed his arms and met their steely gazes head on. "From where my mate and I stand, that's the best news I've heard all day."

"Not from a security standpoint." Nico sucked his teeth in disgust, his emerald eyes narrowed.

Zander sniffed. "Killjoy."

"Well, while you've been getting your rocks off, I've been dealing with a thoroughly pissed off werewolf Alpha. I may not be kicking you out of the family, but your mate's not going to be so lucky. With Celeste, Michael Lykaios has already had one woman in his family die after she mated to a Leonidas, so he's not going to be happy with this. And Felix Marcus? Talking to him was as fruitful as talking to a brick wall. Mating with her was stupid, Zander. It's going to cause nothing but problems. You'd have done better to just keep her as a lover and end it at that." As usual, Adrian was uptight, relentless, and unforgiving. All of that combined with a smooth, unflappable control made Zander want to punch him.

Especially now when he spoke of Lyra as though she were a disposable plaything.

Zander drew in a deep breath. Beating his brother to death wouldn't help anything. "I don't know, Adrian. You seem a little tense—maybe you should give this whole getting-laid thing a try."

Adrian's nostrils flared. "If I want your opinion on the matter, I'll give it to you, little brother."

Rounding the end of his desk, Nico swept both of them with a dismissive glance. "Regardless of the politics going on here, it's a security issue. That makes it my concern. I want to question her further. Alone."

"No. Not without me there." The flat denial surprised Zander, but the dangerous looks on his brothers' faces said they were even less pleased by this new turn of events. Zander opened his mouth to take it back, but that wasn't what emerged. "Absolutely not."

Adrian's icy pale green gaze sharpened, and he moved away from the door, his voice going deadly soft—a ruler displeased that his subject had turned traitor. "What do you mean, no? She can answer Nico's questions…unless she has something to hide."

When Nico tried to step around him, Zander blocked his path. Nico's face hardened. "I can kill you, little brother."

"Keep telling yourself that, little brother." Zander made his voice light, but he didn't budge. Distract, deflect, diffuse. He forced a smile that was half-charming, half-mocking. Even though he was the youngest, he was easily the tallest of his brothers. A fact he rubbed their noses in as often as possible. He would take every advantage he could claim. It was the way of brothers.

All of the Leonidas men stood over six feet tall, but the reminder that he'd always be shorter than Zander made Nico glower. Adrian just looked disdainful. "We have to question her, Zander, and we're hardly going to hurt her. This chivalrous streak of yours is getting a bit too wide to be reasonable. Jason lost his grip on reality over a woman too. Remember how well that turned out for him."

Reason. Harsh reality. Control. That was all Adrian was about now that Celeste and Hector were dead and Jason had gone to Florida to lick his wounds. Their whole family had been ripped apart with that crash. Zander still staggered under the loss. His other brothers hadn't fared any better, though they'd never admit it, even to themselves. Nico was obsessed with the idea that the airplane accident was no accident, but sabotage of some kind. Zander sighed. There was no reasoning with Nico, and there never had been. It was always best to give him room to run and let him work things out his own way. Including accepting the loss of their father.

Adrian, though. He'd become even more uptight than usual—focusing all his anger and grief at Jason for leaving his younger brother in charge of their businesses, family, and all the shifters who looked to the Leonidases for leadership and protection.

As second oldest, Adrian wasn't raised to rule, and he resented having it foisted on him when Jason abandoned the throne. On the one hand, Zander could understand Adrian's bitterness. On the other, meeting Lyra had given him a new perspective on what Jason must have gone through when his mate died a sudden and violent death. And Zander was going to make damn sure that didn't happen to him.

He offered both his brothers a cold, hard glare. "If you have something to ask my mate, then you can do it in front of me. I know you won't hurt her, but you're also not going to interrogate her. May I remind you that she's the one who was beaten and left for dead? I'm not letting you loose on her—either of you—without my supervision."

The cell phone clipped to Nico's belt chirped and vibrated. He pulled it free, punched a button with more force than necessary, pressed it to his ear and barked into the receiver. "Yes?"

Zander took that as his cue to get while the getting was good. He slid past Adrian on his way out the door; the older man gave Zander a narrow-eyed stare, but didn't try to stop him. He needed to track down Lyra. He had a few new revelations to share with her, preferably while burning off some of his frustration between the sheets. There was nothing wrong with a little multi-tasking.

And they'd both be in a mellow frame of mind when his brothers got to asking their questions.

If they thought they'd try to force her to take their side in wolf-leopard politics, they were out of their minds. Bad enough that her family wouldn't take this well. He'd never ask her to betray her kind for him. He loved her just as she was. Strong, passionate, a little wild. He already knew she was a fighter, a survivor. He had a feeling those traits would be put to the test before this was all over.

A dry, desert breeze ruffled Zander's hair as he rounded the back corner of his house. He could see Lyra through the window puttering around the kitchen, and it stopped him in his tracks. He pulled in a deep breath, the emotion he'd experienced since the moment he laid eyes on her hammering through him. It was...good to have her here. It was right. He couldn't get over how perfect it was with her when he'd always shied away from commitment with women. They'd been a convenience to warm his bed for a night or two. That was all. Lyra was anything but convenient. He'd never expected to have anyone like her in his life, but she'd swept in and changed everything before he could run. He hadn't stood a chance.

She glanced up and gave him the kind of smile that sent fire shooting through his veins. Stepping out the back door, she reached for him, that intense, animalistic need he felt for her shining in those molten silver eyes. God, he loved her. She was made for him.

Then he smelled it. The same scent that had fouled the air at the mall. Lyra's stalker.

His heart seized as absolute terror gripped him, but he didn't stop to think, just launched himself forward and tackled her, wrapping his arms around her and bringing her to the ground as a low whistle pierced the air. The stucco on the side of his house exploded to shower down on them. His breathing and pulse raced, and he reacted on pure instinct to protect his woman. Tucking his forearm over her head, he covered her body with his and wedged her up against the rough wall.

"Someone's shooting at us." Lyra's voice was a harsh rasp. Rage vibrated through her slim form, but he could also smell her fear.

He tightened his grip when she tried to move. "Stay down."

Another bullet slapped into the wall over his head, and bits of stucco rained over them. Lyra coughed and sputtered, spitting out what had gotten in her mouth. "Are you okay?"

"Yeah." Darting a glance over his shoulder, he zeroed in on their attacker. There. On a hill overlooking the resort, one of the foothills that led up to the mountains. Too far to get a good look at a face, even with a cat's advanced vision, but Zander knew the man's scent and that was all it would take to track him down. And then kill him.

Sand and gravel sprayed against the side of the house as an electric blue classic car squealed around the corner and rocked to a stop between them and the shooter. Tori barked through the open passenger window, "Get in."

Zander jackknifed to his feet, keeping low to the ground to use the car as the best cover possible, and wrenched open the passenger door. "Get out. I'm borrowing your car."

"Fuck that. I'm driving." Hunching over the steering wheel to stay down, she snorted. "This is a '56 Chevy Bel Air. No one touches my baby but me."

"Shit." He didn't have time to argue, so he slid in.

The sound of two doors slamming had him turning in his seat to see Lyra climbing in behind him. The car jolted as Tori hit the gas and peeled out across the desert, sand and loose rocks shooting up behind them as they went. Lyra arched a brow at him. "That asshole is after me, and I'm not sitting around waiting to see what happens."

He snarled but didn't trust himself to speak. Had he ever thought he liked stubborn women? He'd been out of his mind. The noise of the engine rumbled through the car, far more powerful than anything that should be in this model. They were already cresting the hill the shooter had been on, and he turned to Tori to offer a grudging smile. "You souped it up."

"Well, yeah. How else was I going to beat my brothers in a drag race?" The blonde woman gave a matter-of-fact shrug. "Look, I'm not a predator, so I can't track for shit. You'll have to tell me where we're going."

He dragged in a deep breath as the hot wind whipped through the vehicle, the scent of his prey filling his nostrils. "Take a left."

Tori obeyed, then flicked a glance in the rearview mirror at Lyra. "So, you want to tell me why someone's trying to kill you?"

CHAPTER SIX

Fury boiled in Ramon's veins, but he controlled it with ruthless force. He and Benny had been scouting the resort when the hyena had opened fire with his sniper rifle. Attacking downwind of an enemy? Shooting at a Leonidas on the leopard's home ground? Reckless. Idiotic. Careless. Hiring Benny on had been a mistake, one Ramon would rectify the second the hyena showed his face. Another fucking loose end to tie up.

Ramon could have walked away from this job a long time ago, probably should have, but it rankled to leave it undone. He was the best at what he did. He balled his fingers into tight fists at his sides, fangs erupting from his gums. The wild cat inside him growled, and he had to rein in the ocelot.

At this point, he was so pissed about the woman getting away again that he'd kill her for free. His client didn't need to know that, but he'd be lucky if the client didn't hire another operative to take out Lyra *and* Ramon. A hiss slid from his throat.

He froze in place when he saw a dust-covered classic Chevy parked outside the deep, narrow cave he and Benny had been camping out in. They'd found him. Lifting his face to the wind, he caught both of their scents, Lyra and Zander. He let a feral grin peel back his lips. Nice of them to make it so easy for him by coming out into remote territory, where no one would hear the bullets. Or the screams.

There'd be questions about the Leonidas man's death, but that couldn't be helped. Collateral damage sometimes happened. Considering who his client was, it might be an added bonus for Zander to die. Anticipation hummed through Ramon as he set aside his rifle and drew the pistol out of the holster at the small of his back.

Finally, the break he needed to finish this.

Zander bared his fangs at Lyra and hissed. She folded her arms and stood her ground against the big leopard. He'd never hurt her, and they both knew it. Her belly trembled at the idea of how much trouble she'd caused him so far. Eventually, he'd decide she was more than he wanted to handle, just like her family had.

This mating thing was insane, and there was no way it could last. She wasn't worth the kind of trouble she'd already caused him and his family, let alone what would happen when her family found out they'd mated. It was only a matter of time. She wasn't sure which scared her the most. The thought that he could still get hurt because of her, or the thought of him leaving her when it was over. She swallowed and lifted her chin when Zander hissed again. "We'll stay here while you check out the rest of the cave, but we are not sitting in the car."

Tori scooted closer to Lyra's side and mimicked her pose, jutting her jaw for good measure. "Yeah. What she said."

A growl vibrated his big body. "Don't move so much as an inch from this spot." Lyra opened her mouth to respond, but he cut her off. "Is. That. Clear?"

Nodding, Lyra said nothing as he spun on a heel to stalk away, rage broadcasting in his every movement. Oh, yeah. He was definitely going to get tired of the kind of headaches she would give him. She sighed.

A soft scrape of rocks rubbing together made her cock her head. Someone was outside the cave, walking with cat's feet on the gravel. She could sense it. The hairs lifted on the back of her neck, gooseflesh rippling down her arms. Shooting a glance at Tori, she pushed the younger woman back into the deep shadows as a dark-haired man with cold, world-weary eyes entered.

He leveled a pistol on her, and she lifted her hands. Terror and rage made her fingers shake. She drew in a deep breath to calm herself, but recognition spun through her. Fury beat out the fear. "I know your scent. From that night. You assaulted me, and I don't even know you."

"You should be dead already." His expression didn't change for even a moment and the gun didn't waver. Finally, he shook his head, his voice rough. "Stupid wolf. Estranging yourself from the clan is dangerous, made you an easy target. It took them days to even notice you were missing."

Well, that answered the question of why she was chosen out of all the people in her extended family. She bared her teeth in a smile colder than his eyes. "I wasn't as easy to kill as you were hoping though, was I?"

"Maybe. Doesn't mean you won't die now." His finger tightened on the trigger, and she snarled, her fangs sliding forward. If she was going to die now, she was taking him with her. The vengeance she'd bottled up since he'd jumped her outside her clinic burst inside her. She exploded forward, tearing from her clothes as she shifted to wolf form midair. The deep roar of a leopard echoed as Zander shot from the recesses of the cave at a dead run, and the assassin's gaze snapped to him. A bullet rang out, and she heard Tori scream, but she didn't stop. Leaping forward, Lyra snapped her jaws around the assassin's wrist, shaking it viciously until the gun went flying. The taste of his blood flooded her tongue as she sank her fangs deep into his flesh.

The wolf's animal instincts were all that mattered now, kill or be killed. Zander plowed into the gunman, ripping him away from her, and the two men tumbled away until they slammed against the cave wall. She watched Zander rear back and slam his fist into the other man's nose.

It was then she realized what happened to the one bullet their assailant had managed to squeeze off. Blood streaked down Zander's ribs, staining his shirt a dark crimson. The assassin's hand sliced through the air to strike the wound, and all the color rushed out of Zander's face, a harsh noise bursting from his lips—the sound of a wounded animal.

Horror slammed into Lyra. Years spent in a werekind clinic meant she knew exactly what a bullet wound like that could do to a man. Zander would die, and soon, if she didn't do something. Spinning on her haunches, she changed back to human form and ran for the gun. She was only a step ahead of Tori as they dropped to their knees and searched the dirt. Rocks dug into bare skin, but she ignored the pain. The light kept shifting as the struggling men moved in front of the cave entrance.

Her breath sobbed out as fear made cold tingles race over her flesh. Grunts and the sounds of fists connecting with bone and sinew echoed through the cave. She glanced back to see her mate get dragged to the ground. Oh, God. Not Zander. Please not Zander.

"Got it!" Tori held up the matte black handgun, and Lyra snatched it out of her hand. She leapt to her feet and strode over to where Zander had the gunman in a chokehold on the dirt floor. Both men wheezed for breath and her mate was ghostly pale, but his jaw was locked and fury burned in his eyes. She looked down at the man who had attacked her and left her for dead.

"Zander, back up." Her mate opened his mouth to say something. He spared her only a momentary glance until his gaze locked on the gun in her hands. He dropped the other man and leaned back only far enough to give her a clear shot. Not an ounce of remorse flowed through her as she aimed the pistol at his heart and fired twice.

Surprise flickered in the assassin's gaze as he lowered his head to look at his chest. "It wasn't…supposed to end like this."

"Who are you? Who hired you?" Zander pressed a hand to his ribs and got right down in the other man's face.

A breathless laugh ended in a cough as crimson oozed from the corners of his mouth and out his nose. "I'm…a ghost."

Zander balled his free hand in the assassin's shirt and shook him hard, determined rage stamped on his face. "Who hired you?"

Zander's voice was nothing more than a gasping rasp, and from the sucking noise coming from his chest, Lyra knew the bullet had struck his lung. Oh, Jesus. They were in the middle of nowhere, and she had no good way of treating a pneumothorax.

The dying man hacked up blood, the dark liquid gushing out of his mouth. His lips moved, forming words, but no sound came forth for a moment. "W—wolf."

"Wolf? Which wolf?" But there was no answer. The assassin was dead. Zander let him go and rolled away to collapse onto his back, coughing. His green eyes were glazed with pain and fatigue.

Lyra dropped the gun, raced forward, and ripped open his shirt, confirming her diagnosis. The bullet had penetrated his chest and punctured his lung, but there was no exit wound, so the bullet was still inside him. Her own breath strangled out, matching his as she struggled not to panic. "I should have left. This never would have happened if I had."

"I would have...followed you."

She shook her head, checking the rest of him for any other serious wounds. "No. I'm s-so much trouble. Look what being near me did to you."

"Worth it. My mate." A wan smile crossed his handsome face. "You couldn't cause enough trouble for me...not to keep you."

Biting her lip, she forced her attention back to treating him. At least the chest wound was on the right side, so it was less likely the bullet had hit his heart or any other major blood vessels. Her hands shook. The doctor and woman inside her warred for dominance. She loved him. Oh, God. She couldn't lose him. Please, God. She needed him so much. "Don't leave me, don't leave me, don'tleaveme."

"I...won't." His big hand brushed lightly over her cheek, wiping away her tears before it dropped back to the floor.

She hadn't even realized she'd been chanting it out loud until he said something. Or that she was crying. He hacked like a chain smoker, and hope exploded through Lyra. She looked up at the swan-shifter who stood staring down at the dead man. "Tori! Do you have your cigarettes?"

Shaking herself, Tori looked at Zander. She fumbled in her pockets. "Are you seriously going to start smoking right now? Ohmygod, he has a hole in his chest."

"Just give me the fucking cigarettes."

Tori thrust a crumpled pack into Lyra's hand, and Lyra carefully pulled off the cellophane wrapper to slap it over the wound. Zander's breath wheezed in a bit easier. Relief so powerful it left her weak slid through Lyra, and another tear leaked from the corner of her eye. She positioned the wrapper to form a makeshift flutter valve. Thank God. He just might make it. If they got him back to the clinic so she could dig the bullet out. She met his beautiful green eyes, and he tried to give her a reassuring smile. "Zander, I lo—"

A maniacal, whooping cackle sounded from the entrance of the cave. It made a shiver run down her spine, and her instincts screamed danger. She searched for where she'd dropped the gun as a hyena loped into the cave. He paused, his eyes reflecting eerie yellow points of light in the darkened cave as he took in the scene before him. He licked his lips, that chilling laughter bursting from him as he looked over Lyra's nude body. Hunching protectively over her mate, she bared her fangs and gave a warning growl, the wolf inside her howling for freedom to attack, but the woman stayed in control and held down the cellophane on Zander's wound.

"He's from…the mall." Zander struggled to rise, and Lyra planted a hand on his chest to keep him down, putting as much of her werewolf strength behind it as she dared.

The hyena shifted in the blink of an eye, snatching up the gun from the dirt and pointing it at her. She could see he sported an erection now that he was in his naked human form, and her stomach turned as her growls grew fiercer. Tori planted herself between the combatants. "Look, asshole—"

The report of gunfire cut across her words, but the bullet sliced through her clothes to embed itself in the cave wall behind Lyra. She watched in stunned silence as Tori's clothing fell in a heap to the floor while the woman was nowhere to be seen. Then a large lump moved, and a swan emerged from the hem of the shirt to run hissing and flapping its wings at the hyena-shifter. His eyes popped wide in shock as he scrambled back for a moment before he seemed to realize he still held the pistol and raised it to fire.

A man who looked so much like Zander he had to be a Leonidas ghosted into the cave holding a huge, deadly looking handgun. He was the scariest man Lyra had ever seen, including her would-be assassins. He didn't pause as he aimed it at the hyena. She shouted, "Don't shoot, damn it. You might hit Tori!"

"Nico," Zander gasped.

The hyena jerked his gaze away from Tori, and both he and Nico froze for a fraction of a second. Tori struck, stretching her long neck out to snap her hard beak around the hyena's exposed balls. While he yowled with pain, dropping the gun to grab his injured privates, she shifted to human form, picked up a rock, and slammed it against his temple. The force of the blow caved in the side of the man's skull, and his eyes rolled back before he sank to the floor. Dead.

Nico's eyebrows rose as he looked at Tori. A grudging respect filled his gaze.

She grinned. "What? Just because I'm not a predator doesn't mean I can't kick a little ass."

She said it so perkily it almost made Lyra laugh, but she had more important things to focus on. Her gaze locked on Nico, and she snapped out orders in her best emergency room physician's voice. "We need to get Zander back to the infirmary. I need to get this bullet out of him and get him on a saline drip so he can start healing himself."

"Painkillers would be…nice too." Zander drew in a shuddering breath.

Nico's gaze swept his brother, and he issued a sharp nod. "I called for back-up. They'll be here soon."

Lyra watched Tori stuff herself back into her tattered clothing before she addressed Nico again. "How did you find us?"

He prowled the confines of the cave restlessly, a predator thwarted from his kill. After a long moment, he grunted a terse response. "Saw you on the surveillance monitors at the resort and followed you."

"Oh." Lyra swallowed when he leveled those cold emerald eyes on her.

Everything about this man said predator, and barely leashed at that. Working in clinics as long as she had, she'd met shifters who were more animal than human, but he was something else. Just pure predator.

Well, she was a predator, too, and she forced herself to meet his gaze. A man like him wouldn't respect anyone who showed even an ounce of cowardice in front of him, no matter how terrifying he was. She had a feeling he knew exactly how terrifying he was and used it to his advantage. Lifting her chin, she held his gaze long enough for him to arch a brow…and smile. Almost.

She fought a shudder and inched just a bit closer to Zander. There was brave, and there was stupid. No need to go nearer the scary leopard than necessary. Zander hadn't been lying when he said he was the nicest Leonidas. "I believe you now," she whispered in his ear.

Startled, he glanced up at her and gave a breathless chuckle. He knew exactly what she was talking about. Weariness pulled at the skin around his eyes, bracketing them with pain. She checked the flutter valve again, but there was little she could do now until

Nico's back-up arrived. She slid her fingers in Zander's hand and squeezed. "Hang in there, my mate. Don't leave me."

"Never." His lips formed the words, but no words emerged. He swallowed and closed his eyes, his thumb brushing over the back of her hand.

Reaction finally set in, and she began to shake in long racking shudders. She turned her head to wipe her cheek on her shoulder so the tears she couldn't stop didn't drip on him as she watched him rest. She wouldn't draw an easy breath again until he was healed, but with Nico here to guard them, she wasn't as worried about another attacker showing up.

No, she just had to figure out how to survive now that Zander had taken over the focus of her world in a matter of days. She, who had always stood on her own two feet, couldn't even imagine a life without him. She closed her eyes and sent a prayer of thanks up to every benevolent deity she knew of that he was still with her. Anything else. She could handle anything else but losing him.

CHAPTER SEVEN

Zander lay back against the pillows, his hands folded behind his head. He stared at the ceiling of his bedroom, listening to Lyra's approaching footsteps. It had been entertaining to watch Lyra duke it out with his brothers for her position in the family pecking order. Damn, but Zander loved the woman. Neither of his brothers was used to any woman speaking to them as though she was an equal. Considering her position in the wolf clan, Lyra was entitled. And it was nice to see a woman go toe to toe with a Leonidas. Celeste had always been softer than Zander expected Jason to want, so she'd never stood up to any of them. She'd been downright terrified of Nico. It would be interesting to see how Lyra fared.

Sighing, he shifted restlessly, the sheet slipping down to ride low on his hips. It had been two weeks since he'd been shot, and as a shifter, he was fully healed. Yet, things were still up in the air. Lyra had been emotionally withdrawn, treating him as she would any recovering patient. He clenched his jaw to bite back a growl.

Except for her tearful pleas for him not to leave her, he'd never have known she had any feelings for him at all. And that meant he didn't know if she would disappear from his life as suddenly as she had appeared. It was intolerable. He'd already lost half his family in the last year. He couldn't lose someone else he loved. He just…couldn't let that happen. And the very idea of hunting down his mate pissed him off. He wanted things settled, and it looked as if they were going to have to have it out in order for that to happen. Uncertainty wasn't an emotion he cared for, especially where it concerned his mate.

"I...spoke to my family." She stood in the doorway, her arms crossed defensively over her breasts. She blinked rapidly, but he caught a shimmer of tears in her eyes, and his anger died a swift death.

"And?"

"It's pretty much what I thought would happen. My father disowned me, and my uncle is seriously pissed off, but he's not kicking me out of the clan. So, my dad and uncle are on the outs. Again. Because of me." She sighed and tried for an ironic smile, but it wavered and broke before it had a chance to fully form.

"Come here." He patted the mattress beside his hip, and she hurried forward to curl up next to him. He hugged her close, her back to his front. It soothed him to have her near. He could so easily have lost her. He almost had while he'd lain in that cave, helpless to stop the hyena. If it hadn't been for Tori's quick thinking— He cut the thought off, brushed back the silky black hair at Lyra's temple, and kissed her cheek. "I'm sorry about your family, sugar. I know it hurts."

"Yeah." A waterlogged chuckle broke from her lips.

His chest tightened at her pain. He'd like to strangle her father, but it wouldn't help her now, so he focused on the most important thing in his life. Lyra. "I'd make it better if I could."

"I know you would." Sniffling, she twined her fingers with his and held on tight. "I'm glad I'm here with you."

"Lyra, I—"

She jerked her face to the side, and she used her free hand to swipe at her cheeks. "Let's talk about something else."

Resting his chin on the back of her head, he smiled at her prickly refusal to show weakness. Always the wolf. "Okay. What's on your mind?"

"Interspecies genetics."

He chuckled and decided to humor her. He didn't know much about the topic, but then, he wasn't a doctor. "When different were species breed, one of them is always dominant."

"In theory, it's possible for a child with a throw-back recessive gene to be born and produce siblings of different species." Her long hair brushed over his chest as she settled deeper into his embrace. He bit back a groan and tried to pretend that even so simple a touch didn't have the power to make him hard. Interspecies genetics. Right. "While it's genetically impossible to have a hybrid child who can shift into both the mother's and father's animal species, that doesn't mean all children produced by one couple have to be all the father's species or all the mother's species, but a mix."

He swallowed and dug leopard's claws into his control. "I've never even heard of that happening."

"Like I said, this is all theory; it's never happened before that doctors know of." She stroked her fingers up and down his arm, her brow furrowed in thought. "For werekind, it's a strange mixture of animal and human genetic anomalies, so it's best not to assume it will always stay this way—we're constantly evolving. Because of the unknown factors that makes us neither human nor animal, but a combination of both, with a mixed species coupling, it might even be possible for identical twin offspring to each shift into a different animal."

"Un-identical identical twins?" That caught his attention, but only for a moment as the soft globes of her ass brushed against his now-erect cock. Jesus, she was killing him.

"Theoretically, yes." Her nails drew lazy circles on his arm, and goose bumps followed in the wake of her touch.

Sweat broke out on his forehead, and he reminded himself that he was holding her to comfort her, not to roll her over and fuck her senseless. "Why the sudden fascination with genetics?"

She sighed and looked over her shoulder at him. Secrets glimmered in her gray eyes. "I'll probably be obsessing over it for the next nine months or so."

It took a moment for what she was implying to register; then his eyes went wide and he slipped his palm down to curve over her lower belly. Shock and joy rocked through him, and a grin burst across his face. "Holy shit."

Her hand covered his, and a quiet smile curled her lips. "Yeah."

When she leaned into him, he saw her eyes widen as she came into full contact with his rigid cock. If anything, the news that he'd gotten her pregnant only made him harder. He slid his tongue down a tooth, letting his grin turn feral. "We should celebrate."

The same wrenching fear he'd seen in her eyes two weeks ago shone there again before she masked it behind the calm, collected physician. "Zander, I don't think—"

He cut her off. He had a feeling if he let her fears close her off now, he might never draw her out again, and he needed the wildness in her as much as he thought she needed it, too. "It's been weeks, sugar. That might not be long enough for a human to heal, but we both know I'm fine. Why are you stalling?"

She pressed her lips together, a troubled look flashed through her gaze, and a stubborn angle tilted her jaw. "I'm not stalling."

Arching a brow, he said nothing. She was going to have to work this out herself, but he wasn't going to let her slide by and not deal with it.

"All right, so maybe I am." She looked away and closed her eyes. "I just—everything changed so fast, and we mated, and my family, and…then you got hurt." Her voice caught. "Oh, God. I don't think I could lose you, Zander."

"Scary as hell, isn't it?" He lifted the hands they had over her belly and kissed her fingers. He knew exactly what she meant. The idea of her being hurt was enough to kill him. He could only hope that she was never in that kind of danger again, but since they'd been unable to discover who had hired the assassin, he'd had Nico beef up security around the resort. Zander wasn't taking any chances. She was too important to him.

Tears welled in her gray eyes when she opened them again. She swallowed audibly. "Yeah. Scary's a good word for it."

"I love you." He spoke the words baldly, his gaze locked with hers. Cupping a hand around her chin, he tilted her face toward him. "Come here, sugar. I need you."

Her gaze softened, and a sweet smile curved her lips. Twisting at the waist, she offered him her mouth. He took it, sliding his tongue along the seam of her lips before he pushed inside. He shoved away the sheet around his hips so that the only thing separating him from her was her clothing.

Sliding one arm under her torso, he reached up to flick his fingers over her nipples through her thin cotton shirt. He wanted her so badly his hands shook with it, and his cock ached. He had a feeling the need would never be quenched, and he didn't want it to be. Her tongue twined with his, and she nipped at his lower lip. The sweet sting made him growl low in his throat.

Her breath hissed out as she broke her mouth from his, her fangs emerging. Sliding his hand down her midriff, he popped the button on her shorts and eased them along with her panties down her legs. She lifted her hips to help him and kicked them away. He bunched her shirt in his fist and ripped it to the waist. Her breasts spilled out, and he cupped his hands around them, her hard nipples stabbing into his palms.

He lifted his leg over hers, trapping her. He coasted one hand down to caress her taut buttocks. She whimpered and wriggled against him. "I can't…I can't move. I need to move."

"Not just yet." Pushing her forward slightly at the waist, he stroked her wet pussy from behind. God, he couldn't wait. He needed her. Grasping his rigid cock, he rubbed the head against her sex before he pushed in. Thrusting his hips, he worked himself into her one slow inch at a time until he was seated to the hilt. He rolled his hips and couldn't hold back a harsh groan. The way his thigh held her legs together made the fit incredibly tight.

"Oh, God, Zander," she breathed. Her claws slid out to rip into the sheets. "You're so deep."

"Yesss," he hissed, the leopard within him clawing for supremacy, demanding he take his mate hard and fast. His fangs elongated as he struggled to stay in control. "That's so fucking perfect. I love the feel of you. You're so tight around me, Lyra." He slipped his hand over the soft swell of her belly, dipping to stroke the dampness between her legs. He flicked her clit, making her thighs jerk. He grinned, loving her responsiveness. Pulling his hand free, he licked her wetness from his fingertips. "Mmm. Still sweet as sugar."

She choked, whimpering as she watched him over her shoulder. Her pupils dilated, and she panted, her eyes burning to molten silver.

"You're so beautiful." He smiled down at her, and let the endless desire he had for her show on his face. There was nothing he'd keep back from her, she could have it all. And he wanted everything she had to give. "I'm going to make you scream before I'm done with you, sugar."

She shivered. She fisted her fingers in his hair, her body writhing against him. "Stop talking and fuck me already."

"Oh, I will." He chuckled, thrusting his hips to drive himself inside her in slow, deep strokes, knowing it wouldn't push her as hard or as fast as she wanted.

She tried to twist, but he held her down, flexing his thigh over hers. He kept the rhythm at the measured pace he wanted, didn't allow her to speed him up. He wanted to draw this out as long as possible, to savor the feel of her in his arms. He wanted her to know to her bones that she could never be apart from him.

"Zander." She moaned his name, and he loved the sound of it on her lips. "Please. More. I need you."

A purr soughed from his throat, and he closed his mouth over the mate mark on her neck. His. She was all his. Her breath caught when he licked the bite. He could feel her pulse pounding under her soft, soft skin. He arched his hips, matching his thrusts to the rhythm of his tongue. Faster and faster, giving her exactly what she asked for. More. He rolled her nipples between his fingers, plucking at the hard tips. Wetness soaked his cock as she cried out, and the scent of her drove him wild.

"Mine." He sank his fangs into her again, needing that connection. She would never leave him—he couldn't live without her. Mates.

"Yes! Zander, Zander, Zander." She screamed when he sucked on the bite. The slickness of her sheath, so tight around his cock, made his skull feel like it was going to explode.

"Tell me. I want to hear it." Yes, he needed the same words he'd given her. That final, unbreakable bond.

A sob erupted from her as she bowed in his arms, her pussy flexing around his cock. She raked her nails up his arm, and she twisted helplessly in his embrace. "I love you. I love you so much, Zander."

Some tightness he hadn't even known was banding his chest snapped free. His orgasm slammed into him like a riptide, dragging him under. His body locked in hard shudders as he came. He didn't know how it had happened so fast, but he was so grateful that he'd found her. She filled up a void inside him that he'd grown so used to he almost didn't notice it anymore.

With her, he had hope for the future again, and a quiet joy that life could once more be as bright as it was before his family had shattered. He'd survived losing them, but he didn't think he could ever survive losing her. He would make sure she knew it, too.

Every day. He would never push her away as her family had done. She was…everything to him now. All the pretty words he'd ever used couldn't capture how precious she was, but he did his best.

"I love you, Lyra."

Passions Recalled

Loribelle Hunt

CHAPTER ONE

Celeste pinched her nipples, squeezing her eyes against the image that insisted on popping into her mind to superimpose the nice, safe one she tried to cling to. With a repressed growl of frustration, she slapped the mattress with the flat of one palm. She just wanted to get off, needed to release weeks of built-up sexual tension. Was it too much to ask to get to do that and not be overwhelmed with memories? She opened her mind and stared at the ceiling. Would it matter if she came seeing his face? No one else would ever know about it, after all.

Sighing, she gave over to the need, to the desire she'd never admit to feeling to anyone but herself, and sensation shot straight to her core. Both hands returned to her breasts, cupping them, squeezing and plumping before reaching for the hard tips. She imagined Jason's face, tense with lust and longing, as she remembered his fingers. At once strong and gentle, coaxing and demanding.

Groaning, she released one nipple and reached for the vibrator. It was always like this. No matter who she met, no matter how much she willed it otherwise, her body only came alive for one man. A man who didn't want her, who'd rejected her. She gulped back a sob, but didn't stop. Couldn't stop the want roaring in her mind. To come. To feel something. To live again. It was a false little fantasy she'd created here in her lonely bed, but right now with the desire raging through her she didn't care. She'd save that for later. The self-recriminations, the fear that she'd never love or respond to any other man.

Enough, Celeste. Enough.

She flipped the switch to the on position, sighed as the toy slid easily into her pussy. It almost felt like he was there with her, stroking her, thrusting into her. Her sex grew impossibly slick and her fingers closed convulsively around her nipple. She swiveled her hips upward, as if meeting him move for move, and then releasing her breast, reached for her clit.

Her first touch was soft, hesitant. She wanted to draw out the pleasure as long as possible, but even that gentle touch made her pant, the lust building. Jason would not be reluctant if he were there touching her. His fingers on her clit would be strong, insistent. Pressing harder, she slid her finger back and forth over the hard nub. She imagined him, *felt* him, leaning over her, his fingers guiding her to orgasm, his cock thrusting home.

She could have wept from all the emotions consuming her, but the orgasm tightening her body prevented it and took her over. She exploded, splintered apart. When her mind came back together, she curled into a fetal position and cried herself to sleep only to be awakened by a shrilly ringing phone and the demands of her family.

Celeste drove as fast as she safely could in the pelting rain. Hurricane Iris may have been sweeping up the Gulf, but this, the remnants of Hurricane Helga held fast in the Tennessee mountains, unwilling or unable to release the fury of the warm Gulf waters. Irritable and leery of the harsh weather, she rubbed a wadded-up T-shirt against the fogging window. What was so important her stepfather insisted she drive from Atlanta to Chattanooga in what looked like Noah's flood revisited? She sighed. It didn't matter. Her fear of storms was irrelevant in the face of family obligation and need. When the werewolf clan Alpha called, everyone ran. Including their human sister, Celeste.

Thank God, she was close. She shuddered as small hail began to hit her window and wind rocked the car. How bad must it be down on the Gulf when these storms rolled onto shore? How did anyone stand to hang around and ride that out? She knew a lot of people did—they didn't call them hurricane parties for nothing. If a person could watch from a safe place she could see the appeal in it, had even had a taste of it herself. After all there were few forces on earth more massive, more electrifying, than a hurricane.

The streetlight illuminating the turn off to her parents' appeared in the gloom, and she sighed in relief, the knots in her stomach beginning to loosen. Almost there. Almost safe back in the arms of her family. If she felt some small twinge for something else, some wistful longing of things past, it was only normal with this storm raging around her, right? Her palms grew slick with remembered fear, her stomach once again heaving, betraying her terror of bad weather. Only a year ago a sudden summer storm just like this one took down the small jet she'd been a passenger on, and she'd barely survived the trip to the ground. All her naïve youthful hopes had crashed and burned with that plane. Life hadn't been the same since.

Right. Get over it already. If wishes were fishes her mother would say, and she'd be right. All the wishes in the world hadn't done her any good then. They were a waste of time now. She forced Jason from her mind, ignoring the tiny voice saying to give up the effort. No matter how she tried, he was never far from her thoughts, lingering like an unhappy poltergeist.

She turned down her street and watched for the house lights in the distance. When they appeared she released a pent up exhalation of tension, but it was quickly followed by anxiety. What was so important she had to come out now? Had to drive two hours in this nightmare?

Her gaze swept the driveway when she pulled in, mentally noting which car belonged to whom. Her half-brothers, her stepbrothers. The trucks, the SUVs, the odd little compact hybrid that would always stand out. No clan members. Whatever the big-ass hurry was, it really was family business.

CHAPTER TWO

She grumbled as she parked. They could have at least left her a spot near the door. Squinting through the rain, she considered trying to haul her purse and overnight bag out with her, but it didn't seem worth the effort. Then she'd be soaked along with all her things, and she probably wouldn't sleep here anyway. The house was too crowded, the people in it overprotective to the point of coddling.

Derek, her friend and date if an occasion demanded one, didn't know she was in town, but she was sure he'd welcome her. She scowled at the rain that battered her windshield. She'd called to tell him she was coming up, but he hadn't answered the phone or returned her calls. With a mental shrug, she pulled the door handle. She'd catch up with him later.

The rain drenched her as soon as the door was open a crack. She lunged out, flinging it shut behind her and sprinting for the front door. Inside the foyer she slipped off her jacket, shook off the rain, and hurriedly used the towels her mom had left on the bench to clean the mess. She heard low, angry voices in the living room, her mother's and stepfather's, with the soft timbre of one of her brothers thrown in here and there. Straightening her spine and adopting the neutral mask she'd perfected after years of dealing with werekind, she marched into the room.

As soon as she crossed the threshold, silence reigned. Not a good sign. She hoped she was wearing her objective journalist face as she approached and embraced her mother. They'd always been a united front, the two female humans in a house full of male werewolves. It took feminine solidarity to confront this much testosterone. Miranda hugged her to her side, not releasing her when Celeste would have stepped back, and gave her a tight smile. Something whooshed out of Celeste when she saw it. Some foreboding that she was really going to hate hearing whatever was coming.

The males in the room were tall, hulking. Brooding, which was so out of character she felt a real tinge of fear rise in her throat. Had someone died? Had the Wolf Council passed judgment and someone she knew was going to die? Derek immediately came to mind, and she shoved the thought away—down deep where it didn't worry. Surely not. Not her Derek, the friend who'd gotten her through Jason's betrayal, the only person who'd been brutally frank with her about the condition of her body, her face, in the hospital.

"What's going on?" she asked when, after several minutes of silence, it became clear no one was going to start. She turned to Michael, her stepfather, and met his gaze. A definite no-no when dealing with the clan Alpha. But he was also Dad, and she was human. No mating, no marriage that put her under anyone's control. She was an adult and technically no longer under the rule of clan law. Besides, she could feel her mother's agitation, and it made her less inclined to deal with the werewolf's archaic attitudes. Usually so much aggression on the part of a female would have raised his hackles. He was the acknowledged leader of clan and family. When he lowered his eyes and turned his head, she knew she was in real trouble. Her famous intuition was screaming. This night would change her life in ways she'd never imagined. Forever.

Tomas, one of her younger half-brothers and the family business heir apparent, stepped forward.

"Remember a few months ago when we were discussing the new timber mill?"

Arching an eyebrow, she crossed her arms over her chest. Of course she did. Her financial instinct was legendary in the clan. So much so she was always consulted on all business matters, and it had led her to endorse the new venture. She was sure the new mill would be a success and, if it went according to plan, it would also be environmentally responsible. Was her intuition wrong? It had only been wrong once, and majorly so then, but she pushed that thought away. She was positive the mill was a good investment—she'd helped research it herself.

"What about it?"

She had an urge to push her palms against her ears, certain the news was bad. Michael stepped into her line of sight. He took a deep breath, visibly steeling himself against his own words.

"We needed a loan for the project." He paused. "I took out a mortgage on the land."

Closing her eyes, she sucked in a deep breath. Held it until she saw spots behind her eyelids. Clan land. Family land. Her land. The only thing she had left of her human father bartered in a business deal?

"And?" she asked, knowing there was more. Knowing there was worse.

"There was a balloon payment due last week. We didn't make it."

"Can't you negotiate an extension?"

He grimaced, blushed a little, and she arched her eyebrows again wondering what the hell was going on and if it was going to take her all night to drag it out of them.

"Normally we could," Tomas said. "But Jason won't listen to reason."

"Jason?"

All of the blood rushed from her head, and she swayed, throwing up a warning hand when her brothers rushed to her side. Her Jason?

No. Not my Jason. He didn't want me.

For him, for better or worse was only an issue when it was better. She bent over and gripped her knees, sucking in big gulps of air. How long had she lain in that hospital bed and waited for him to come? And he never had. It had been hell. While her family hovered and fretted, her body broken and bleeding, the man who was the center of her universe had suddenly become a figment of her imagination.

She looked at her mother, studied her face. She'd paled to an unnatural whiteness, her eyes pinched with anxiety, and something else occurred to Celeste, something worse. Jason was a wereleopard and her father hated leopards. The animosity between the leopards and wolves, the hatred went back so far no one even remembered how it had started. Nor did they care. It just was. Leopards and wolves, enemies forever. She couldn't believe they had taken money from Jason. Had gambled and lost her father's land. Anger poured through her as she slowly straightened.

"Why?" she ground out through clenched teeth. What would make Michael desperate enough to go to Jason for cash? "Why would you accept his money? Why would he refuse to negotiate?"

Fighting the tears that threatened to flow freely, she added in a harsh whisper, "My father's land…"

The spot on her shoulder where Jason had marked her a year ago burned, as if protesting her anguish. She rubbed it absently while she waited for an answer. Michael noticed the movement and moistened his lips.

"We lied," he said baldly into the tomblike quiet of the room. "I lied."

She frowned and waited for him to go on. When he didn't, she asked, "About what?"

"I insisted you leave Refuge Resort because I thought you were getting too close to…that leopard." His distaste was palpable. "I didn't know he'd bonded with you until much later."

So what? What did that have to do with Jason's obvious dislike of her human frailties? She fisted her hands, trying not to remember how naïve she'd been. For years she'd been a freelance journalist, mostly for werekind publications, but occasionally she sold a piece to a human magazine. Last year her focus had been on the ancient rivalry between the wolves and leopards. They'd been created in opposition. To reward Leonidas of Sparta's courage against the Persians, Artemis had granted all his descendants the ability to change into a leopard. Not to be outdone, Zeus had granted the same abilities but in a different form, wolf, to the descendants of King Lycoan.

It was her extensive writing credits which had convinced Hector Leonidas to let her go to the Refuge to research. Who could have predicted she'd meet his oldest son and lose her mind? Oh, but the things the man could do with his hands. And his mouth. Wow, was that mouth talented. Her fingernails dug into her palms. Focus, damn it. She wasn't stupid. She may be human, but she'd grown up in the werewolf clan. She knew he'd mated her, and knew he didn't give a damn about that. He'd found it so easy to walk away, she'd often wondered if he'd only done it to escalate the feud between the two species, if he'd done it purely to piss Michael off. Maybe that was why her father had taken Jason's money. It didn't have anything to do with her after all, she thought bitterly. She was just a pawn in the ongoing war between the wolves and leopards and so was her land.

"So?"

"When the plane crashed, we didn't think you were going to live. We were afraid to hope and afraid to give up hope, baby doll." There was a pleading quality in his voice, something that begged her forgiveness, and she clutched her stomach in response. How awful was this going to be? No one ever brought up the accident. "We told him you died."

The shock of that audacious statement almost brought her to her knees. For the last year she'd lived with the belief that he'd forsaken her. And for the last year he'd believed she was dead? But no, wait. That couldn't be possible. She wrote for the werekind newspaper.

"And you think this is why he won't negotiate? Why?"

Michael threw his hands up in the air, a sign of his exasperation. "Revenge, girl. He blames us for taking you away from him, for putting you on that plane. He thinks we killed you."

She shook her head. "But everyone knows I didn't die."

"No," Tomas said. "Everyone doesn't. You're writing under a different pen name. You've never been back to the resort. You avoid everyone but our clan. And I've kept up with Jason. He left his family's resort and took a park ranger job in Florida, down on the Gulf Coast. A place called St. Andrews. By all accounts, he's completely cut himself off. I know for a fact he doesn't get the paper, and if his brothers even know your new pen name, you can bet they wouldn't tell him you're still alive. You know how clan politics are. Leopards don't like wolves any more than we like them."

The room started to spin, and she grabbed the back of the couch to keep herself upright. Could this be true? He hadn't come because he thought she was dead? She didn't believe it, didn't believe he wouldn't have moved heaven and earth to get to her, to see for himself. If that was true, she had no choice but to face reality. He wasn't here. He hadn't come. She'd been nothing more than a means to an end, a game piece in the ongoing war between the two most powerful clans in North American. But why wait so long to go after them, after her land? Why now?

And why on earth was he in Florida? Everything west of the Mississippi belonged to the leopards. East of it was wolf land. Most of the Gulf Coast was dolphin land, however. Jason would have had to get their permission to move into their territory. She was pretty sure his park belonged to the dolphins. Panama City was far from the mighty river's borderlands, those wild and untamed places most shifters chose not to live in, but where anyone strong enough could.

Lyra's pretty face rose in her mind, accompanied with the usual worry. Her cousin had disappeared from her medical clinic in the borderlands a few months ago. Celeste had heard through the family grapevine the cats had had something to do with it, but no one could tell her what exactly and her oldest brother, Bastien, had warned her to stay out of it when she'd mentioned asking Lyra's parents if they knew anything. Lyra's father was reported to be in a state beyond rage, so Celeste had taken her brother's advice without batting an eye. She wasn't in a hurry to face her uncle's infamous temper.

"You have to go to him," Michael ordered, the bit of pleading in his eyes jerking her out of her thoughts. "Explain our position."

She barked out a laugh. She didn't understand their position; how could she explain it? Fury rose, swelling her chest to what felt like impossible proportions, making her head ache, her fingers itch with the urge to hit something.

"How would I do that exactly?" she asked sarcastically.

"We were taking care of you. We were protecting you."

CHAPTER THREE

A glance around the room told her her brothers clearly hadn't agreed with this approach, but they'd followed their Alpha. No wolf would have dared to defy him. Even her mother wouldn't have stood up to Michael, her mate. Celeste's heart hammered, a whispered voice buried deep in her mind railing against the betrayal. It was a bitter pill to swallow. Her brothers, her mother all had given into Michael's demands, despite knowing how much it would tear her apart. Ever the loyal family and pack, willing to forgive whatever stupid decisions he might make. Celeste, on the other hand, was not a werewolf or mated to one, and she was not so forgiving.

Her whole life had changed in that instant, and the person she'd needed there the most wasn't. Now it was happening again. It was too much to take, too much information at one time. She was angry, shocked and hurt. Confused. She couldn't stay another minute and quickly walked from the room. Digging her keys out of her pocket she ignored questions about where she was going. At the door, she didn't even pause, just gulped a deep breath, and sprinted into the rain to her car. She was inside and driving before she could string a coherent thought together.

What was she going to do? She didn't believe for one minute Jason didn't know she was alive. If he'd loaned Michael money, wouldn't he have checked the family out? The Jason she remembered was fun and light-hearted, but serious minded and thorough. She'd go to Derek. She'd known him for years, but he was much older than her, ran in a totally different crowd when they were young. They hadn't become friends until she returned from college…and not good friends until the accident. He'd got her through those first awful lonely months when she'd still had to fight her body's and mind's cravings for Jason every day.

She frowned. If Jason didn't know she was alive, she had to let him know. It wouldn't be fair not to, and she didn't think she could resist the urge to find him, to go to him. But how would her relationship with Derek change?

He'd been her only friend the last year, the only one who had tried to understand how empty she felt. How abandoned. And he wanted a lot more than friendship. She knew that. He'd asked her to marry him so many times she'd lost count, but he'd never pushed her, never made demands. Just smiled and said he could wait. For a man so insistent on marrying her, and a werewolf to boot, he was very physically distant. Not that she was complaining. She wasn't sure how she felt about sleeping with someone else, even Derek.

He didn't live far from her parents, but she was forced to drive slowly in the heavy rain. She tried calling again, but she'd lost her cell signal. Probably the weather, she groused to herself. She turned off into his driveway and eyed the muddy slope. She doubted the car would make it up, and backed into the turnaround that was halfway up to park. She'd have to run for it in the rain and mud, but it couldn't be helped. Stuffing her keys in her pocket and leaving everything else, she once again stepped out into the weather and sprinted.

The driveway was slick and slippery, hard to navigate in the dark. The rain picked up as she approached the house and when she reached the yard, she took a minute under the arbor to catch her breath. Unfortunately, she chose that moment to look at Derek's front picture window.

Well, no wonder he hasn't tried to insist on anything with me.

He stood in the middle of his living room, his pants hanging around his thighs with an enormous erection jutting out. On the floor in front of him was a buxom blonde—Celeste knew, because she was getting a profile view—busily sucking on said erection. Celeste was so surprised she froze in place, thankful they couldn't see her out in the gloom. When Derek threw back his head and gripped the woman's face in his palms, she knew he was coming. His face twisted with the orgasm, as if it hurt, and he looked down at blondie with an evil grin. Celeste only had a moment to wonder why she'd thought it was evil before Derek, whose hands had not left blondie's face, gave a vicious jerk, snapped her neck, and dropped the woman to the ground.

Celeste jumped back, completely unbelieving of what she'd seen but unable to deny it. She was grateful for the heavy rain and wind—it hid the noise she made as she ran back to her car. With a human she wouldn't have had to worry. But a werewolf with superior hearing and reflexes? That could have been a major problem. As it was, she made it safely to her car and, with shaking fingers, twisted the key in the ignition. It was at that moment the wind and rain lulled to a low murmur, and she knew Derek must have heard the car from the house. She jerked it out of park and sped into the night. The question was where was she going?

She got onto the highway and turned south. She didn't dare go back to her family. Derek was powerful in his own right, and she didn't want to put them in danger. She needed time to process what she'd heard and seen tonight. But could she trust Jason? Jason who'd abandoned her when her human frailty came to the forefront? Her analytic journalist's mind said she was nothing more than a chess piece, than a pawn being used between Michael and Jason. Her gut said to go to Jason, that he would keep her safe, but, wow, had it been wrong about Jason before. Did he really believe she was dead? The idea seemed crazy. But what her family had done, what she'd seen at Derek's was just as crazy.

She couldn't see any other choice. So she drove south.

Through rain and wind that ebbed and flowed, the remnants of Hurricane Helga raging across the state, she drove. By the time she reached Columbus, Georgia the sky cleared, and she fiddled with the radio, searching for news. She knew another hurricane was coming up the Gulf and was relieved to hear it was forecasted to hit far down the coast near Tampa. One model had it veering north into the Panhandle, but the experts were discounting it.

Iris was a category one storm, so they weren't even forcing evacuations, just recommending them for low-lying beach areas. She snorted. Wasn't all of the Tampa Bay area low lying? She hadn't made it down in a couple of years, but usually she spent time with friends there every summer, even sticking around for a tropical storm one year. She knew her Tampa friends wouldn't heed those warnings. They'd ridden out many storms over the years, and perhaps their blasé attitude was contagious because eight hours later, she paid her five dollars to enter St. Andrews State Park.

It was bright and sunny and clear, no sign of the turmoil brewing on the Gulf or the storm that had just blown through. It certainly didn't mirror the turmoil inside her. Unwilling to confront Jason quite yet, she drove to the public beach, parked and wandered into the gift shop. Her time would probably have been better spent driving into Panama City and finding a hotel room, but she could never resist the Gulf. The rolling emerald water, the pristine white sand. She sighed. This was her idea of heaven.

She hadn't brought anything with her, obviously, and on a whim bought a bathing suit, sunscreen and a giant towel. After changing, she dropped her clothes in her car and headed to the sand. She had to think, had to decide what she was going to do about Jason and Derek and her family. If she had any sense she'd walk away from all of them. She was human and couldn't help but feel both sides were using her. What better place to make a decision than the perfect, pearly beaches of the Gulf of Mexico?

All right, healthy dose of avoidance and fear there too, Celeste, but way to rationalize.

She pushed the worry away, spread her towel on the ground and lay down, digging her toes into the warm gritty sand. She'd driven all night. It was still early morning. There were a couple of guys playing volleyball and a few sunbathers, but mostly she had the beach to herself. She wondered whether the hurricane's predicted landfall site had changed. Was that why the beach was so empty? Even if it had, it was only a category one, and she had plenty of time to drive inland. Safe enough she reasoned. Especially once she found Jason. He might be angry with her, might be indifferent to her, hell he might even hate her, but he'd never let harm come to her. When she'd settled on that conclusion she wasn't sure—sometime on the long drive down. Exhausted, she sighed as her mind swirled with all of the recent happenings. She drifted to sleep, warmed by the sun and sand, lulled by the pounding surf.

When she opened her eyes, the sky was dark and ugly, clouds churning as if stirred in a witch's caldron. The wind whipped her hair, and she felt a moment's unease. She hadn't meant to fall asleep or to sleep so long. Standing and dusting the sand off, she looked around. The beach was abandoned. She grabbed the towel and her car keys and sprinted for the parking lot. When she veered around the beach shop, she noticed it was closed up, shutters latched into place. Around the front in the parking lot, a few cars were pulling out onto the road and only two vehicles remained parked and empty. The second one froze her in place a minute. The F150 truck looked exactly like Derek's.

Ignoring the fear that bubbled to her throat, she hurried to her car. It was a common truck, and he couldn't know where she was. Why would she come to Florida in a hurricane after all? It had to be a coincidence.

She reached her door as thunder boomed over the ocean. The noise startled her so much she dropped the keys. The fine hairs on her arms rose and fear with it, as she bent to retrieve them. Where the hell was Jason when she needed him? She choked back an angry sob. If he hadn't been around when she needed him before, why did she suddenly expect him now?

Get a grip, Celeste, and get the hell out of here.

She'd kicked the keys under the car and had to crouch to her knees to grope the ground under the driver's side to retrieve them. She almost cheered when her fingers closed over the cold metal. She rocked back on her heels to stand. She never made it to her feet.

"Bitch. You aren't going to ruin all my plans."

She barely registered the menacing voice as Derek's before something hard came down on her head, and the world went black.

CHAPTER FOUR

Anger pulsed through him. This was not the way he wanted things to go down, not part of the plan. Celeste's death should be just one more thorn to twist in Michael's side, but it should have been on his terms, not anyone else's. And not before he'd had the taste of her for which he'd waited so long. Ignoring the tire iron in his hand, Derek stood over her and glared at her prone body, then noticed the steady rise and fall of her chest.

No fucking way.

She should be dead, but it had always been as if the woman were protected from the weaknesses of mere mortals, as if she'd been touched by one of the Gods who'd created the world's shifters. A werewolf—a were of any kind—wouldn't have walked away from the plane crash last year and yet, she'd lived. And she survived a killing blow now. Pure ass luck or something else? He wasn't willing to seriously consider the implications.

Celeste had been the perfect opportunity for him. Abandoned by Jason and smothered by her family, Celeste had been ripe for the picking. He'd earned her trust and wormed his way into the Alpha's circle. The hardest part had been concealing his true nature. Not from Celeste—she thought he could do no wrong—but from her father. Michael was a suspicious son of a bitch. He'd wondered right from the start why a strong werewolf in his clan was willing to wait so long for his daughter to come around, but as the months stretched on, he relaxed, became complacent. He didn't consider Derek a threat.

Resting on the balls of his feet, he hunkered down next to Celeste, brushed a long tendril of blonde hair from her face, and tried to decide how to use these new developments to his advantage. No one knew he was here, and he bet no one knew she was either. He'd been lucky to find her, and it was due more to instinct than knowledge.

He'd been riding the high from Marie, that special feeling he got every time he brought another slut low. And they had to be sluts. Killing more circumspect women had never been a thrill for him. He'd given it a shot once or twice, but the excitement just couldn't compare. That's why Celeste had always been safe. She lived like a nun.

Lately the women he picked were with purpose, a means to an end as well as the special kick he craved. It was too soon for Marie, too soon after the last one. He'd known that but was so excited about the progression of his plan to bring Michael down, he'd seized the chance to celebrate a little. Who knew Celeste would happen by? It was pure luck the storm had slowed at just the right time for him to hear the distinctive whine as her car's engine started.

By the time he'd rushed out she was gone and though he trembled with the need to rush after her, to protect himself, he'd made himself stop and think. First the body had to be dealt with then he'd figure out what to do. He'd known he had to act with haste. If she went to Michael, the Alpha would come after him fast and furious. Walking back into his house, he'd noticed the cell phone on a side table. It had rung a few times while he was playing, but he'd ignored it. He'd picked it up and scrolled through the missed calls—all Celeste—then listened to his voice mail. He'd grinned as he hung up, strolling over to gaze down at the corpse sprawled across his living room floor.

Michael had called Celeste for a late family meeting, about what she had no idea, but Derek was pretty sure she'd received the shocking news that Jason thought she was dead. Like the good little girl she was, she'd come straight to her good friend. Enraged, he'd broken out in a cold sweat. He'd had to find her before she fucked up everything.

He'd bet his fortune she wouldn't go to Michael. She'd already be in shock and the addition of witnessing a murder would have put her on overload. No. She'd go home. Or maybe even to Jason. Derek's money was on her Atlanta apartment. So he'd disposed of the body—making sure to dump it on Alpha land where it would surely be discovered soon—and driven to Atlanta. He'd been surprised to find she wasn't there, and he hated surprises.

He knew she hadn't gone to Michael's. His people were watching the Alpha's house. So, with only one other option, he'd driven south, despite the latest radio weather warnings that had Hurricane Iris turning toward his destination. He went straight to Jason's park, where he caught a lucky break. He found her car in the beach parking lot and, from a sand dune, he spotted her stretched out on the beach. Although not as crowded as it might've normally been, there were too many people around to approach her, so he checked out the park, looking for unused roads and paths, and found a place nearby to hide and observe. He'd narrowly avoided running into Jason who'd driven by in a work vehicle.

As the morning passed, the weather had grown progressively worse. When she'd finally stirred and hurried to her car, he'd seized his opportunity and made his move.

Now he had to decide what to do with her. Finish her off or keep her alive? The better to torment Michael with obviously.

The roar of an engine stopped him. The sound increased, and he cocked his head to the side. Definitely coming his way. It sounded like the vehicle he'd seen Jason in earlier. He made a split second decision and sprinted for his truck. Jason would probably have to be dealt with later too. The delay infuriated Derek, but he knew he'd need an advantage. The leopard was a fierce fighter, and he wasn't positive his wolf could take the cat down. Better to fight safe than stupid, a lesson he'd learned the hard way from his father's murder.

He made it to the truck and gave Celeste a last fulminating glare. Should have finished her off or taken her with him, but with Jason added to the equation, there were too many variables outside of his control. The other vehicle approached the parking lot, and he knew he was out of time. He started the truck, threw it in gear and peeled out of the parking lot, barely missing sideswiping the oncoming vehicle.

He'd wait and watch. And strike when they were at their weakest.

CHAPTER FIVE

Jason Leonidas steered the park service vehicle into the beach parking lot and growled when an exiting truck almost ran him off the hardtop. The other driver's tires squealed as he took the turn. "Reckless," Jason muttered. He would have gone after the idiot and given him a ticket and a lecture, but he saw one car left in the lot. The storm was coming in bigger and faster than the weather center's models had predicted, and its course had completely changed, leaving Tampa safe but barreling straight for Panama City. His first priority was to make sure the park was empty. Then he'd go hole up somewhere safe.

He guided his vehicle into a space next to the Honda. Grabbing his binoculars, he stepped out. He'd just run up the dune and scan the beach for stragglers. He made it to the front bumper of the truck before he froze, assaulted by familiar smells.

Fear. Blood. Celeste.

Not fucking possible.

Celeste was gone, taken from him in the cruelest way—forever. He must have finally lost what was left of his mind.

Over the wail of the wind, he heard a low mewling sound, like a kitten in pain, and he lurched into movement, quickly circling the compact car. A small figure lay on the ground, a woman with long blonde hair matted red with blood.

Celeste's hair. Celeste's scent.

Celeste is dead you idiot. Get it together.

Fur ruffled under his skin as he approached her. The logical thinking man knew Celeste was gone. The wereleopard who lived on instinct insisted this was its mate, and someone had hurt her.

He growled, low and threatening, man and leopard beginning to merge in growing fury when he knelt and carefully rolled her over.

Celeste…alive.

His chest tightened when he brushed the hair off her face, but he pushed all conflicting emotions away. No time for that now—he had to get her to safety. What the hell was she doing here anyway?

He easily lifted her and carried her to his truck. The driver's side door was still open, and he maneuvered his way in while holding her against his chest. Squeezing his eyes shut, he took a deep breath, dragging her scent deep into his lungs. A feeling he could only describe as joy overwhelmed him, and he choked on a sob. In any other circumstances he would have laughed. Big, bad, Jason Leonidas crying like a baby? But she was alive. How many times had he wished he could change the past? How many times had he wished he could go back and insist she not get on that damned plane?

Fury replaced the joy. Where the fuck had she been? She'd abandoned her mate. She'd let him think she was dead. The only thing that kept him from shaking her awake and demanding answers was her sudden moan of pain. He held her too tightly, knew she'd probably bear bruises later from his rough embrace. Gently, he laid her across the bench seat, resting her head on his lap.

He cranked the engine, put the truck in drive and headed for the ranger cabin where they would ride out the storm. He glanced down at her, ran a finger over his mark on her shoulder. Together again. Together at last.

She stirred, agitated, but remained unconscious, and he frowned. How long had she been out? Smoothing his hand over her hair, he murmured, "Shh, baby. Almost there."

His voice seemed to soothe her, and she settled. Within minutes, he'd stopped the truck and carried her into the small building he called home. He paused in the living room, wondering if he should lay her on the couch. Hell no. She was his mate—she belonged in his bed. A few steps down the hall and he was striding into his room. He pulled the blanket back, laid her down and stepped away.

He struggled to get his mind past the shock of her presence. He needed to have a look at the wound on her head, clean it up and see if he could wake her. Forcing himself to focus, he gritted his teeth and stared down at her. How had he missed the impossibly small bikini? Even that was too much concealment though, and he wanted it gone, wanted her uncovered and exposed to his hungry gaze. He remembered too well what the scraps of material covered. The small perfect breasts. The generously rounded hips and hot pussy that always welcomed him, no matter how he'd previously loved her. His cock sprang to hard, throbbing attention. She groaned again, rolling her head against the pillow and spurring him to action. First things first.

He got his emergency kit, a clean cloth and a bowl of cool water. Placing the items on the nightstand, he shifted her over enough that he could sit next to her and dipped the cloth in the water. The wound was on her right temple, and he cleaned it as gently as possible while still being thorough. She'd been hit with something, and the gash was long but not deep. The butterfly bandages in the kit would be fine to close it, but first he had to make sure there was no sand in the wound. His biggest concern was concussion, but that worry was alleviated as he worked. Her breathing was even and steady, and once her eyes fluttered open to focus on him for a few seconds. He was pleased to see no dilation in her pupils. She closed them with a sigh. It was her scent, however, that really eased his mind. He didn't catch one whiff of anything that would indicate an injury in her brain. It had been a glancing blow. It was probably a combination of the heat, surprise and the hit that had her sleeping so soundly. She'd be fine in a couple hours.

When he was sure the cut was cleaned, he disinfected the area, pressed the edges together, and sealed it shut. He exchanged the bloodied cloth for an unsoiled one and refilled the bowl with clean water. Sitting next to her on the bed, his hip against hers, he hesitated. Cleaning the wound was one thing, cleaning the rest of her might be out of line. But fuck, it had been a long time, and he couldn't not touch her.

After dipping the washcloth, he bathed her face, the fine high cheekbones, the perky nose, the stubborn chin he'd loved beyond reason. He frowned when he saw the long scar up the side of her cheek. It hadn't been there before. His gaze raked her body, lingering over the flat smooth belly and the faded scars that crisscrossed the top of her bathing suit bottoms. There were more scars on her legs, and he gently wiped away crusted sand from her knees while he thought it over. She hadn't had any of these scars the last time he'd seen her, but it had been awhile since the plane crash. Her injuries had time to fade like these.

He searched his memory of that time and knew he paled under his deep tan. His father's death in the same crash hadn't registered for months. He'd been mad with grief and consumed by fury at Celeste's family when they told him she'd died in that crash, for refusing to let him see her body. He'd blamed them for her death, still did, despite the proof she was alive. As soon as they'd realized her infatuation with the wereleopard was a great deal more than just that, they'd been quick to pack her up and send her home. A leopard in the ruling wereleopard clan wasn't good enough apparently. But she'd never made it, the small plane left the private airstrip at the Refuge Resort in Arizona only to be taken down by a sudden storm in the Appalachian Mountains.

He hadn't believed them, had been sure he would feel it if she was dead. Since he was told to stay away from the funeral and threatened with execution if he entered wolf land without permission, he refused to believe it. Until his brothers forced him to view video of the crash site, forced him to see the wreckage. There was no way anyone could have survived that mangled wreck, so he'd begun to accept it.

Now he didn't know what to believe. If she'd been on the plane, how had she survived? And why the fuck had her family told him she was dead? He'd been living with a gaping hole in his heart for a year and for what? Werewolf snobbery? His cat side hissed in response, demanding release. It wanted to run off the rage, the hurt, the shock, the fear. The new questions. If Celeste had survived, what about his father? He needed to let his brothers know ASAP, but it was all too much to take at once and with no target at which to vent.

Jason finished bathing her and cleaned up the mess. He walked back to the living room and opened the front door. It was raining hard now. The wind blew it sideways, and it fell in sheets rather than drops, but the deep porch kept most of it outside. A few drops hit the floor at the open entryway, and he went to the hall closet for a towel, dropping it down to soak up the moisture. He knew from experience that the storm would go on for a couple of days, in fits and starts until Iris passed over the area. This round of rain and wind would probably stop soon, for a short time at least before picking up stronger when the next band reached them.

Glancing in the direction of his bedroom, he stripped. There was no help for it. Worry ate at him. Every emotion under the sun consumed him. A quick run would help sort out the jumble. Then hopefully he'd be able to deal with Celeste, his need for her, and her betrayal. Because under the fury, was a bone deep hurt that twisted his insides into painful knots. He could have forgiven her for dying on him, but she hadn't. She'd left. She'd never given them the chance they deserved. It was the ultimate betrayal. He wasn't sure if he could ever forgive her for it. One thing was certain though, forgiveness or not, he wasn't letting her go again. They were mated. Whether she liked it or not.

Shifting to leopard form, he padded outside, leaving the door open behind him. He considered closing it, but dismissed the idea as quickly as it came. With the electricity out, the air conditioner didn't work. Right now that wasn't a problem, but the house would get unbearably hot and muggy very quickly once the rain died down. Plus he planned on staying near the house. Should she awaken or cry out while he was gone, he'd have a better chance of hearing her if the door was open. Decision made, he ran off into the surrounding brush.

CHAPTER SIX

There were jackhammers in her head. Even moaning hurt. Funny, she didn't remember partying last night. She frowned, and it made the pain worse. Actually she didn't remember last night at all. Rolling over, she pressed her forehead into the pillow and was immediately swamped by Jason's smell. Oh, God. Where was she?

She couldn't think past the pounding behind her eyes, but when the room shook with a crack of thunder she jerked her head up, wincing for her trouble. She hated storms. There was one window, and outside it a palm tree whipped back and forth.

Definitely not in Kansas anymore. Or Atlanta. Whatever.

Rolling back over, she took stock. Her head hurt like hell, but everything else seemed fine. Only one way to know for sure. Gingerly, she pushed up on her elbows, cursing the pounding headache that spread over her face with the strain. She sat up, gasping, and looked around the room. To call it bare was generous. It contained the bed and a dresser. The walls were empty. There was nothing to identify its owner but the scent of the sheets on which she lay.

But that didn't make sense. She looked out the window again as another gust of wind buffeted the house. Rain tapped the roof, and she cocked her head, pressing her hand to the side that throbbed the most. The sound echoed loudly in the room, and her headache seemed to pick up the rhythm, pulsing in time to the rain. It was familiar. Tin would be her guess, and that at least helped her narrow down her location to probably somewhere in the South where in recent years tin roofs had become all the rage. She wasn't sure if she was relieved or disappointed. Not the Southwest, so not Jason's home. She swung her legs over the side of the bed and set her feet firmly on the floor.

And why the hell was she wearing a bikini?

Only one way to find out, Celeste.

She had to venture out of the room, find out where she was and who else was here, if anyone. Her mind refused to accept it might be Jason, even if her body thrummed at the thought. She didn't dare wish it was so. She squeezed her eyes shut. Jason was over. Jason was the past.

She stood and took a step toward the door, but froze when a black leopard appeared and blocked the space. Her eyes filled with tears.

The first time she'd seen Jason in leopard form, she'd been very confused. His brothers looked like typical leopards in their were forms, tawny and gold with black spots. Jason was dark, his coat black, his spots brown to cream colored. He'd explained that sometimes nature threw a genetic anomaly out there, in the leopard and wereleopard worlds. Melanistic leopards were often born in litters with regularly colored siblings, probably an evolutionary advantage for jungle ranging leopards. All of the big cat species had melanistic or black versions. The same held true for werecats. Black was not a common color to see, but not rare either.

Looking at him now, she remembered the pain of that conversation. His pain. She'd felt his loneliness and had wanted to soothe it. He'd identified himself as the outsider in his family, but she'd seen how much they loved him, how much they needed and respected him. Although, none of that had really mattered to her. She'd thought he was beautiful. She'd loved him beyond reason. She should have known better, she thought bitterly with the benefit of hindsight, but the observation didn't make one damn bit of difference in her reaction.

He padded closer, stalking, and she clenched her fists. She would not reach out and bury her hands in that fur, would not give in to the tears threatening to fall. The big body pushed against her, his head butting and rubbing against her thigh in a show of affection, and she couldn't help the sigh that escaped. He pushed her until the backs of her knees hit the bed and she sat, giving in to the temptation and sinking her hands in his pelt.

Soft. Silky. So, so dark and lit with light at the same time, like the mysteries of the midnight sky. And definitely Jason.

She was afraid to speak, afraid to shatter the spell. It was the best damned dream she'd had in over a year.

He moved closer, sat on his haunches and rested his front legs along her thighs. Then he licked her, a long swipe of his tongue up the side of her face, over her old scars. The raspy stroke woke memories. This tongue, this man. Months alone and lonely and heartbroken in a hospital bed. Yet she shuddered as her body responded to him, recalled the out of control feeling of being in his arms.

Memory shattered the dream.

Except it wasn't a dream, was it? She pushed against the cat and scrambled back on the bed. Shifting, the man followed, crawling up her body and pinning her under his weight. A growl rumbled deep in his chest.

"No," he ordered, refusing to allow her to retreat.

She tried to push him away, but he grabbed her wrists and held them next to her head, while forcing her thighs apart with his knees and settling between them. His erection pushed hard and throbbing against the juncture between her thighs. She grew slick, felt the swelling in her clit and saw by the way his nostrils flared he knew it too.

"So long," he muttered, before his lips descended on hers.

God help her, she couldn't resist. She opened her mouth to him, accepted the stroke of his tongue. His pelvis ground against hers in a matching rhythm, and she was positive the only thing keeping him from plunging into her was the thin fabric of the bikini. It wasn't much of a barrier, and she wished he'd throw it away. She'd toss it herself if he ever let her wrists go.

The kiss was all too short as he broke the contact and trailed his lips along her jaw, down her neck, and finally closed over the old mark on her shoulder. He nipped it lightly and her back arched, her pussy flooding with cream as an intense orgasm froze her. God, she couldn't respond to him like this, so quickly, after so many months absence. It was mortifying, and she strained against him. She needed a minute to collect herself, to attempt to build some kind of barrier around her heart. She feared she was too late. Maybe she'd never managed to do it in the first place.

He released her wrists, rolled onto his back and moved up the bed, pulling her across his chest with one arm around her waist. Somehow during the move he removed the bikini bottom. His cock insistently pressed against her center and with his eyes he begged for admittance, but he was leaving the choice to her. How could she resist? Her body had been dead for a year and now it screamed for the fulfillment only he could give her.

Refusing to acknowledge the niggling worry over where he'd been or where she was or even if it was real, she sat up on her knees and moved over his hips. She held her breath, closed her eyes and allowed the fantasy to take over as she took him inside her. Slow. So slowly. If this was a dream she didn't want to ever wake up.

She felt his hands behind her neck, over her back. Shivered at the sensation of fabric sliding free of her skin. He was finally seated all the way inside her, when his hands closed over her breasts. Her entire system threatened to melt down.

"Look at me," he demanded.

His thumbs flicked over her nipples. She opened her eyes in time to see his nostrils flare, to see him lean forward and flick his tongue over one hard point. He sucked it into his mouth, bit down. It was just this side of painful, and she grew wetter, felt her body rushing to accept him. She shuddered, then groaned. Didn't even fight the orgasm she felt rising from the very center of her, the heart and soul. Nothing had ever equaled being possessed by Jason. Nothing ever would, she realized with sadness. As if he sensed her slipping away he moved his hands around her ribcage, let her nipple fall free of his mouth, and squeezed a little.

"Slow and easy is not going to cut it right now."

She nodded. She knew. Maybe later he'd let her pet him, stroke him. When the leopard was appeased. He rolled her over, reached to wrap her legs around his hips, and plunged into her. She grabbed his shoulders and hung on. He wasn't slow or smooth or even gentle. He was wild. Out of control. His fingers bit into her hips, holding her still and she tried to shift a little, tried to at least meet his thrusts.

He growled a low warning, and she waited for the spike of fear. She'd always been a little afraid of his primitive side and he'd been careful not to scare her, not to push her too far too fast. The old alarm didn't come. She'd learned to be strong after the crash, found that she liked that about her new self. She ran her hands down his shoulders, over his pecs. Paused a minute to flick her fingers over his nipples. He growled again, and she almost smiled. She wasn't scared at all. She was really, really turned on.

"When did you get so brave?" he asked, voice guttural with lust.

About a year ago. The answer froze in her throat. His eyes had turned from their natural green to the narrow amber slits of his cat and she knew he was losing what little control he had. She liked it. Liked that she could push him to it. She didn't answer, just shook her head, arrested by his expression, by the need and desire stamped across his face.

Not that he gave her a chance to frame a suitable reply. He reached between them and pressed his thumb against her clitoris. Every thought fled. Every worry. Everything but sensation. And sound. She heard herself screaming as she came, heard skin slapping against skin, heard him grunting as he came seconds later.

She didn't know how much time passed, thought she'd probably dozed off. When she came back to her senses she was sprawled over Jason's body, one arm around his neck, one leg thrown over his hips. She smiled at the familiar feeling, almost forgot a year had gone by since she'd seen him, but slowly came back to herself, became embarrassingly aware of the leopard beneath her.

She shifted a little, intending to move away, to gather herself but he held her still. One hand convulsed on her ass, the other caressed the nape of her neck. He was gentle, quiet, but his breath sawed from his lungs as if he'd just run a marathon. She struggled to remember how she'd ended up here, but the effort just brought the headache back.

"What am I doing here, Jason?" she whispered.

She had to figure this out.

He lifted his head to meet her gaze, eyebrow arched.

"You don't know?"

CHAPTER SEVEN

She caught her bottom lip between her teeth, biting back the exasperated retort that hovered. She tried to pull away, but he wouldn't release her. He moved her further over so she stretched from head to toe across his body. His erection pressed against her belly and with a sigh, she spread her thighs to straddle him, felt him nudging the lips of her pussy seeking entrance. She tried hard to ignore the spark flaring to life inside her.

"Not a clue," she grumbled. The wind howled outside. "Maybe we could start with where am I? And why does my head feel like someone beat on it?"

He scowled.

"Because someone did. I was hoping you would tell me who."

She thought about it, and her temples throbbed. Shaking her head, she answered, trying to ignore the rising panic.

"Nothing. I don't remember anything. Where are we?"

"Florida," he said, then grunted.

She wasn't sure if he was angry or as confused as she was, but a disturbing thought niggled. Florida seemed…familiar. She needed to remember something important. One thing clicked at least, and she looked at the window with alarm.

"Hurricane Iris?"

"So you remember something of the last few days at least."

"Days?" she asked, alarmed. "Have I been here that long?"

He shrugged. "I don't know. I found you a couple of hours ago in the beach parking lot. Laying on the ground and bleeding." His voice turned menacing. "I need to know who hit you, Celeste."

She was surprised at the quiet vehemence, as if he actually cared. She snorted.

"Why?"

He'd always moved fast, but she was still shocked when he reversed their positions and she found herself flat on her back and pressed under his weight again. His cock nestled against her pussy and unable to resist, she tilted her hips just enough to take the head inside her.

"Because no one attacks my mate and lives. No one." He thrust deep.

She blinked. Surprised and seriously pissed. She found the strength to push him off of her, to push away the tears. His mate. Yeah, right.

"Your mate," she whispered and then ground her molars against the angry words threatening to spill out.

One learned to be careful with words when one grew up in an Alpha werewolf's household. She wanted to scream and pace, but tried to resist the urge. Well, to hell with that. He wasn't a werewolf, and she owed him nothing.

"My mate," she said, putting as much scorn as possible into the word. "My mate would not have left me alone for months in the hospital. My mate would not have left me alone when the doctors told me I'll never have children. My mate would have been there for the months of physical therapy and half a dozen surgeries to fix my face."

She wrenched free and jumped off the bed, putting as much distance between herself and his seductive body as she could, pointing a shaky finger at him.

"Don't talk to me about mates, Jason."

He rose slowly, rounded the bed and paced toward her. He looked a little green under his tan. Probably didn't like to be reminded of his failures in the mate department, or hers in the human. His cock jutted out before him, stiff and proud and damned near impossible to resist.

"Well, that explains that," he whispered.

He kept advancing, and she retreated until her back hit the wall. She went to duck around him, but his hands slammed against the wall, his hips pushing into hers and pinning her, caging her between his body and the hard place at her back.

"What did they tell you, Celeste? That I didn't want you? You want to know what they told me?" He waited until she met his eyes before continuing. "They told me you were dead."

She gasped. At this range she could feel the heat, the fury, rolling off of him. She wanted to protest, but for some reason she was certain it was true. He slid his palms down the wall, gripped her hips and lifted her. He entered her roughly. No finesse. She didn't need it, already impossibly wet, immediately convulsing around his cock.

"It won't happen again, Celeste. They took you from me once and now that you're back from the dead, I'll never let you go again."

Tears stung her eyes. It was so, so good, but as much as she wanted this fantasy, it wasn't right. Not that that thought stopped her body from responding as he thrust into her, worked her into a frenzy of want and desire and another orgasm. When he slowed, when his movements inside her became as lazy as the tongue lapping at her breast, her brain reengaged. She started to worry again.

"There's something I'm not remembering," she whispered, more to herself than him. "What day is it?"

He looked surprised at the change of subject.

"Thursday." His cock was still hard inside her. She closed her eyes and concentrated.

"Thursday...I remember Dad calling me Wednesday night and insisting I come home." She blushed, remembering how she'd masturbated to Jason's memory before that phone call. "So between yesterday afternoon and now I drove from Atlanta to Chattanooga to here. Where is here exactly?"

"St. Andrews Park. Outside Panama City Beach. Florida."

She looked around the room. She couldn't imagine him in Florida. Dolphin land.

"Why?" The question seemed to confuse him more, and he stepped back, giving her room to breathe. "Why are you in Florida? Why aren't you living at the resort and helping your brothers run all the Leonidas businesses?"

"I left a long time ago. Everywhere I turned...I saw you. I couldn't live with it."

His voice was emotional, raw. She couldn't say why but she believed him. She wanted to hate him, had half hated and loved him for the past year. Now he was back, screwing with her resolve to get on with her life, with her plans to meet someone else and get on with her life. Oh, shit. Derek! She was almost dating him and had just fucked the wrong man. Twice. How had she managed to forget that? She clapped a hand over her mouth, afraid she'd blurt it out and pretty sure Jason would go ballistic. He couldn't miss her panic, damn the man. He released her slowly, let her slide down the wall until her feet hit the wooden plank floors, but kept his hands on her hips.

"What is it? You remembered something."

She shook her head and tried to get free, to walk past him, but he wouldn't let her.

"There've been too many secrets, baby," he whispered. "What is it?"

His voice was soft, cajoling. But how long would that last? And why was she so relieved? Something about Derek... It just wasn't there anymore. But he was her friend, the one who'd got her through Jason's abandonment. Surely this awareness, this fear, was unfounded.

Jason moved his hands on her shoulders and held her still. "What is it, Celeste?"

"Didn't you try to get on with your life? Find someone else?"

He grew very still, and she knew she was in trouble. She hated to hurt him and hated herself for caring, but what could she do? What should she have done differently? He'd disappeared from her life. Was it wrong for her to long for companionship? Just a little of what she'd lost?

And Derek... Well if that was a little too comfortable a relationship, so what? She'd had wild and passionate and look what it got her. But now she had to deal with Jason, and he grew more livid by the moment.

Grabbing her by the waist, he pulled her close and sniffed her. It was possessive and proprietary, and it pissed her off all over again. It was entirely too up close and personal for a casual werekind acquaintance. Despite just having had sex with him, could she call him anything more than that?

He didn't smell anything but himself—couldn't have—and relaxed marginally.

"Explain yourself, Celeste. Tell me what you're holding back. Now. Or so help me, God, I'll bend you over my knee, and it won't be like old times. You won't like it," he threatened.

She met his gaze, hard and glittering green. He'd changed. She thought he probably meant just what he said. But she'd changed too. Was harder, tougher than he remembered. How to diffuse the situation? She shrugged.

"It's been a year. It's been a long time since I knew you wanted me."

"So what? You're fucking someone?" His voice got very, very cold. "Living with someone?"

"No," she whispered, knowing with the possessive urges of a mate that he was going to explode even though the situation was innocent, trying like hell not to care. "Dating. A little."

He released her as if she burned him, sudden and abrupt.

"Don't leave this house," he ordered, then shifted and ran from the room.

CHAPTER EIGHT

As he ran, he decided to kill her father and spread pieces of him across the southern states. It was just possible—maybe—that Celeste didn't understand the full nature of a mate bond, but Michael sure as hell did. Michael knew it was very unlikely Jason would ever commit to another woman. To allow Celeste to become involved with someone else when he knew Jason was unaware she lived—it was infuriating. Jason had never experienced such rage, so he had to escape the house. He didn't want to take it out on Celeste.

But Michael. Michael had a lot to answer for.

And who was she dating? She hadn't mentioned his name. Was he human? A werewolf? Was she fucking him? Jason stopped and dug his claws into the ground. He cut off the thought and started running again…getting overwhelmed with rage wouldn't help him or her. He couldn't afford that; he had to deal with the mystery of why she had shown up now. But maybe it wasn't such a mystery.

Several months ago a werewolf approached him. He had a plan to take over Michael's clan and a small role for Jason to play in it. To Jason the role wasn't so insignificant though.

When Celeste died Jason had been in the process of branching out. He'd dreamed of having werekind-safe resorts like Refuge around the world and so began his career in real estate speculation. None of his plans had come to fruition—she'd died, and he'd taken off. But he found the risk of land development too addictive to give up. He'd just switched gears away from hotels.

So when the werewolf—Derek—came to him with a plan to ruin Michael, part of which was to take his prime piece of land, Jason had jumped on it. He couldn't care less about the rest of Derek's scheme and hadn't asked. That land was Celeste's, the only thing left of her, and he wanted it. He hadn't believed Derek when he insisted Michael would contact him to mortgage the land, but he'd jumped on it when it happened, skipping the in-depth background checks he usually went through. If he'd done them, he might have discovered Celeste was alive. Then she sure as hell would've been here already instead of showing up now injured and unable to remember most of the last twenty-four hours.

The rain let up, and he slowed to a loose-limbed lope while he worked it through. Michael had accepted insane terms for the mortgage, terms no rational person would take. He either had the money in reserve for the first balloon payment, was certain he would or just didn't care about losing the land. Since he was using it for his new business venture, that couldn't be it. If he had the cash, he wouldn't have needed the loan, which left being certain he'd have the money. So, why didn't he? Normally before Jason decided to hand out so much money, he demanded business plans, financial records and made personal background checks. Normally he made people jump through hoops. In his haste to get the last piece of Celeste, he'd skipped all of that. But he bet Derek hadn't, and that made Jason nervous. What was Derek's motivation for going after Michael? Simple greed for power or something else?

A familiar scent came to him on a sudden gust of wind, and he lifted his head to search it out. Wolf and, since there were no wolves indigenous to this park, it had to be werekind. Stopping still in his tracks, he looked around but didn't see anything other than storm debris and rain. Taking a deep breath, he didn't smell anything other than salt water either. It was either his imagination or the werewolf was gone.

When the unfamiliar feeling of dread inched its way up his spine, he turned, running full out for home. He wasn't sure how he knew, but Celeste was in danger.

Celeste stood frozen in place when Jason made his hasty exit. She felt rejected, confused and angry. The confusion she understood, but the other two? She'd accepted his rejection a long time ago and the new rejection, the new anger over something she should expect, fucked with her mind as well as the peace she'd carved out for herself.

To hell with this.

Curling her fingers into fists, she redressed quickly, took a final look around the room and walked out. He was off running in his other form, so it was the perfect time to get out of here. Listening to the howling wind and driving rain, she walked down the hall—he'd left the front door open—and onto the porch where she winced, her stomach clutching in dread. Wind blew the trees flat, and the relentless rain collected in pools around the yard. There was no way she was driving in that, and she couldn't believe he'd gone out in it.

Fear for him was bad enough, but this new emotion was more like terror—at the realization she wasn't going anywhere. She'd have to stay until this storm blew over and if she couldn't avoid him, she was afraid she'd fall in love with him all over again. Snorting, she walked back inside.

Like I ever really stopped?

She had to figure out why she was here. She squeezed her eyes shut, willing the memory to come. Nothing did.

Pushing the door mostly closed, but not catching the latch in case Jason returned in wereleopard form, she walked back into the small living room. The wind blew the door open behind her, and it banged into the wall. She flinched and whirled around. Why was she so jumpy—because of the storm or something else? She walked over and slammed the door shut. He could just shift and use the knob like normal people when he returned.

Standing in the small living room, she sighed. Now what? She needed a phone, needed to call her mom and see what she knew. Frowning, she looked around. Where was her purse? Her phone? Where was Jason's phone for that matter? She hadn't seen one yet. She peered through the doorway on her left and saw a refrigerator, but when she entered and found a phone it was dead. She slammed it down in frustration and went to search the house. There had to be a cell phone. Maybe it would work.

She started with the nightstand in his bedroom and got the shock of her life when she pulled the drawer open. It couldn't be the same box, but she knew as she reached for it with trembling hands that it was. Lifting it out, she set it on one open palm and frowned. Her chest expanded, shrank and swelled again. It took a moment for the sobs to register, and she gulped them down. He hadn't kept the ring, had he? The ring she'd left with him when she'd flown home to explain things to her family. It was like watching a train wreck, her train wreck, as she flipped the lid open, saw the blazing red ruby circled by diamonds. She bit her lip and pulled the ring from the box. She held it a moment before sliding it on and holding it up to the light. He'd kept her ring. What did that mean? What else had he kept?

She set the box on the bed and stood. Hands on her hips, she looked around, wondering where to start. Afraid she'd find something else as disturbing in the dresser, she headed for the closet and opened the doors. She quickly flipped through everything in front and pushed them out of the way when she came to the items hidden in the back—the clothes she'd left in his quarters at the resort. Had he kept everything? She shrugged off the curiosity. Did it matter?

At least she could get out of this bikini now. She tugged a tank top and then a pair of jeans off hangars and carried them into the bathroom. Setting them on top of the closed toilet, she pulled the shower curtain back wondering if her shampoo and conditioner would be there, too. Thankfully, they weren't. That just would be too creepy.

Turning the water as hot as it would go, she got in and soaped up, careful to avoid the bandage on her temple. With the electricity out she figured she didn't have a long time before the water turned cold and hurried through the process. She squeezed some shampoo in the palm of her hand and fingered it through her hair. After she rinsed it, she stepped out of the shower, wrapped a towel around her hair and one around her body. She eyed her clothes and tried to remember if she'd left underwear in his bungalow a year ago. If she had, did he still have them? Not sure if she wanted the answer to that she decided to go commando and pulled on the jeans and shirt.

The material rasped over her sensitized skin. Her pussy grew wet against the hard crotch of the jeans and her nipples pebbled when the shirt brushed over them. She groaned. Would even her clothes conspire against her to keep her ready and willing for Jason?

She wanted him again already, with that deep craving she'd hoped to defeat. Turned out she'd only partially managed to numb herself to her body's demands. Now that it was fully reawakened she didn't think she could turn it off. Wasn't sure if she even wanted to. It was a problem she wasn't ready to deal with quite yet. She was stuck with him until the storm passed, might as well enjoy him while she could. She just had to keep her heart out of it so that when the inevitable happened, when he left her, it wouldn't hurt as bad as before. He may have thought she was dead, but she didn't have that excuse. She hadn't insisted on speaking to him herself. She'd withdrawn in hurt and anger. Eventually he'd probably see her failure to contact him as a betrayal, or worse, cowardice. She couldn't really argue he was wrong, either.

Sighing, she pulled the towel off her head and let the length of her hair fall down her back. A quick search of the bathroom drawers gave up a single comb but no brush. She decided to let her hair air dry while she searched the rest of the house.

She came up empty except for the romance novel she'd left in Jason's bungalow at the resort. No phones. No computer. No outside communication. Grumbling, she went to the kitchen. Her stomach rumbled as she entered, and she wondered how long it had been since she'd eaten. Not that it mattered, since she was hungry now.

The electricity was out. The stove was electric, but there was a camp stove pushed to one corner of the kitchen counter next to a case of water. Jason had obviously prepared for the storm. She cleared a space for the camp stove and fiddled with the knobs, trying to remember how they worked. One of the burners lit. Satisfied she could get something warmed, she turned it off to search the pantry. It was almost bare, and she wondered what Jason lived on. He was leaner, but by no means small. He had to be feeding his bulk, but damned if she could tell how. She found more cases of water, a box of MREs and the odd can of veggies and soup.

She pulled out a couple of cans of beef stew and bread and then retrieved cheese and mustard from the refrigerator before she rummaged for a saucepan. She dug a handheld can opener from a drawer and used it on the can before she poured the stew into the pot. Then she placed it on the burner and relit the camp stove. She was making cheese sandwiches when the front door banged open.

She winced at the sound and heard Jason walk into the small room but, instead of acknowledging him at first, she finished covering the bread with slices of cheese and started squirting circles of mustard on the opposite slices.

She felt his gaze on her. Desire rushed through her, heating her skin and accelerating her heartbeat into a wild staccato rhythm. Knowing he could hear it, she turned to face him.

"Found some clothes, I see," Jason said when she finally lifted her face to meet his gaze.

He stood in the doorway, rain dripping off his body. He seemed tense, twitchy and he looked around the room before his gaze finally settled on her. He was naked, all rippling muscle, not an ounce of fat, and his cock was hard. He made no effort to hide it, and she couldn't avert her eyes. Moistening her lips, afraid of the crushing urge to approach, drop to her knees and take him in her mouth, she crossed her arms over her chest and tucked her hands under them, leaning back against the counter.

He stalked to her and tugged her arms loose, lifting up her left hand. She'd forgotten about the ring—it had felt so natural to leave it on—and jerked free. Pulling it off, she held it out to him.

"Sorry. I found it when I was looking for a phone."

CHAPTER NINE

She wondered if he'd fly off the handle at her snooping, but he just smiled and caught her hand again. He slipped the ring back on her finger and pulled her close, one hand flat on her ass to hold her still.

"It's your ring. I don't expect to see it off your finger again."

The stew started to bubble and pop. He reached over and turned off the burner, moving the pot to the cold side. Then he pulled her back into his embrace and kissed her. Hungry, raw, demanding. His tongue stroked hers while his thumb rubbed over the small scar on her shoulder. His hips pushed against hers, and he maneuvered her until her back was to the counter. His erection pressed against her belly and pussy grew slick with need. His grin was wicked.

"I know what you want, baby." He took several steps back, took his cock in his hand and slowly stroked up and down. She nibbled at her bottom lip, watching, wanting to take him up on the invitation, but unsteady, unsure.

"Celeste." There was command and temptation in the growl that she couldn't resist. Moving forward, she knelt. She placed her hands on the back of his knees and slowly drew them up, over his thighs, to his ass. His skin was smooth, his muscles hard and flexing under her touch. She breathed deep, taking in the masculine, outdoorsy scent that was only Jason's—that drove her crazy. Leaning forward, she traced the contours of his cock with her tongue, ran it down the top of his length, then the bottom, before taking him between her lips. They groaned together when he slid past her teeth, into the warmth of her mouth to bump the back of her throat.

She pulled back, sucking as she withdrew, until only the head was left. She suckled it, running her tongue over the weeping slit. He hissed out a breath and his fingers gripped her head, urging her forward, urging her to take him deep again. She did, but only repeated her earlier actions. She was too caught up in his taste, in teasing him to give into his subtle demands and after too brief an exploration he took over, holding her still so he could thrust in her mouth, until she was certain he was going to come and she moaned her anticipation. Then he stopped, pulled free and yanked her to her feet, crushing her lips with his.

When he broke the kiss she almost protested, but before she could form the words, his mouth closed over her nipple. She gasped, pushing against him, grabbing the counter at her back for support. He sucked at the swollen tip of her breast, suction then gentle bites, alternating until she thought she would go mad with desire. He broke the contact abruptly and jerked the tank top over her head.

"What was wrong with the bikini," he mumbled before his lips closed over the opposite nipple.

Her eyelids slid shut, and her body started to shake. She knew the orgasm would overtake her soon, would leave her weak and still needy, because she hadn't felt him thrusting inside her, yet. Suddenly she needed that more than her next breath. Releasing her grip on the counter, she reached for his cock. Warm and wet from her mouth, it jumped in her hand, and she tried to see around Jason's head, to see her hand gripping him. He released her nipple with a pop, and she groaned in protest.

"You're playing with fire, baby." His voice was gruff, and she knew he was on the edge too.

"I like fire," she whispered, walking her fingers to the head of his cock.

Collecting the pre-cum there, she rubbed it in, then down the length and resumed her grip, beginning a slow up and down stroke. He released a long hissing breath and stripped off her jeans. Unwrapping her fingers from his length, he stepped away and grinned. He looked her over, a lascivious, possessive gleam in his eyes.

"Two can play that game," he replied, then lifted her to the counter.

He set his hands on the inside of her knees and slowly caressed upwards. As he did, he spread her thighs wide and sank to his knees. When he reached the apex, he draped her legs over his shoulders and tugged her forward until her butt rested right on the edge. The first swipe of his tongue over her pussy made her grit her teeth to hold in the scream. If she started screaming now she'd be hoarse by the time she came, and she knew from experience he'd keep her on the edge forever if he was enjoying her cries too much. She didn't think she could take that after a year of celibacy.

He lifted his head. "Stay with me, baby." His smile was slow and knowing. "No holding back."

He bent back down, and his lips found her clit. He sucked it, applying just the right amount of teeth, and she moaned. It sounded impossibly loud to her, and she wondered what insanity had made her think she could control her reaction to him. As if to reward her vocalizing, he suckled harder, adding an extra bite of teeth and a finger thrusting into her pussy. She clamped around him, felt the shudders of an orgasm begin, and he moved his head, biting the inside of her thigh, the sharp pain reminding her who was in charge.

"Too soon," he said.

She wanted to sob. How could it be too soon? That first time, a little while ago in his room, had been the first time in months and it wasn't nearly enough to take the edge off.

He worked another finger inside her, then another, stretching her cunt to accommodate his girth. His fingers hooked to rub against her G-spot, and she arched against him, again biting back a scream. He laughed softly.

"What is it, baby? If you're ready to come, all you have to do is ask."

He stopped stroking with his fingers, keeping them still and in place. She tried to move her hips, get the action going again, but he held her still. It was maddening—she was right on the edge.

"Oh God," she moaned.

She rolled her head against the cabinet behind her. He wanted her to beg, and she was going to end up doing it eventually. Might as well stop fighting it. Her body was so tight with need it wouldn't take much.

"What's it going to be, Celeste?"

There was a little bite in his tone and a lot of enjoyment. He was enjoying taunting her, enjoying the control he had over her body and, unless she missed her guess, he thought of it as a small punishment for thinking she was dead. His tongue trailed lazily up her inner thigh, explored the outside of her pussy with the same lazy disregard while avoiding her clit. She wanted him to make better use of it.

"Jason. Please. Let me come."

"Hmm, maybe in a minute, baby."

His fingers straightened away from her G-spot and began a slow gentle glide in and out of her. The fire that burned in her veins increased and when his teeth nibbled on her clit, she didn't hold back the scream. She panted with the need to come.

"Jason, quit teasing and fuck me already," she yelled.

He lurched to his feet, murmured, "I thought you'd never ask," and claimed her mouth and pussy at the same time. A thrust of his tongue in her mouth and the stroke of his cock in her cunt were all it took, and she came apart. Her body shook with the force while her mind shattered. She was aware of him moving inside her, faster and harder, until he too cried out.

They stayed still for several minutes, spent and breathing hard. When he lifted his head and pushed her hair from her face, his finger lightly rubbed over the old scar.

"Dinner?" he asked.

She shrugged. "Sandwiches and stew. I was hungry."

He stepped back and grinned, helping to set her on her feet and steady her. He bent and handed her her clothes.

"Almost like old times." He kissed her on the forehead. "I'm going to grab some pants. Then we'll eat."

He strode from the room, leaving her breathless. She turned and stared at the stove. Yes, it was like old times. Jason leaving in the morning, and her having dinner ready when he returned. A little sex to heat things up first. Shaking her head, she searched the cabinets for plates and set two out, doling out the sandwiches before turning the search to bowls, which she set next to the plates on the small kitchen table. Then she hurried from the room to get cleaned up. She used the small half-bath off the living room and returned just before Jason reentered the kitchen.

She leaned her hip against the counter and studied him when he entered. She didn't know what to make of his mood. He seemed calm, unaffected, as if she didn't just have a mind blowing orgasm and had every right to do so in his kitchen. As if he expected her to be there, or she'd never left. If only she could remember how she'd ended up here.

"Are we eating?" he asked and arched an eyebrow when she shrugged instead of answering.

He reached for the handle of the pot and carried it to the table, while she skipped out of his path, watching. Silently, he ladled stew into two bowls and set the empty pan back on the stove before pulling out a chair.

She just stood and watched, wondering where the angry man from earlier was. Were they pretending the last year hadn't happened?

"Sit down and eat, baby. We'll talk about it after dinner."

No longer hungry, she sat and reluctantly picked up a spoon, swirled it around without lifting a bite. She refused to meet his gaze. The situation was too surreal to be believed. She was afraid if she blinked she'd wake up back home in her bed. Alone.

"So we're just going to pretend like we've been doing this every day for the last year? No big deal?"

He smiled and took a bite of the stew. "Yep."

"Why?"

Jason set the spoon down. She noticed he was almost finished anyway, as he leaned back in his chair and crossed his arms across his chest. In anyone else, it might have looked like a defensive posture. She only saw the bulk of his arms, the expanse of his shoulders. Jerking her gaze up, she met his and caught his smile before he hid it. She frowned. Being so transparent in her appreciation was only going to hurt in the end. He let her watch him for several seconds before he answered.

"It's a fantasy." He shrugged. "Do you have any idea how many times I dreamed you were with me? That you didn't die in that crash? It never occurred to me after I saw pictures of the wreckage that you could be alive. One of our kind wouldn't have survived. Hell, my father didn't. Why should you have?"

"I must have a stronger will to live than you imagined then," she whispered. She wanted him to understand where that will had come from. She lifted her chin and added in a louder voice that wobbled at the end, "I kept expecting you to come. Even weeks later."

He concealed the hurt that flared in his eyes so quickly she almost missed it, and she regretted her words. Nothing could change the past. There was no point in dwelling on it, hammering it home over and over again. Even if he were human, he would be dominant and protective. His nature, his character wouldn't allow someone he cared for to suffer without aid or friendship at the least.

The question was, was there a future for them? And if so, what would it be? After Jason filled his family in on her family's deceit they would never accept her, and hers had never accepted him. She wanted to curl into a ball and cry, wanted to shove the returning memories into a dark hole where they couldn't hurt her. She'd loved Jason, been happy and excited at the possibility of a future with him. Then there'd been nothing but pain, physical and emotional. She couldn't go back to that, but she couldn't see a way around it. After the year of lies, she didn't believe he could want her for anything other than sex anyway and that wasn't enough. Not for her.

He stood and circled the table, pulling her out of the chair.

"You're overthinking things."

"No. I don't think I am." Lifting her hand, she caressed his face, ran her thumb lightly up and down his cheekbone. "I'm sorry. I should have realized."

His hands on her shoulders, he shook her a little.

"You will not blame yourself for something Michael did, Celeste," he ordered.

She nodded her head in agreement but felt tears fill her eyes. She couldn't believe she was so emotional. She seemed to be zinging all over the place. Maybe it was the way he'd come in and taken her in the kitchen. So familiar, so like old times.

He lifted her and carried her down the hall, had her stripped in one minute and screaming with desire in the next. Her last thought before she succumbed to the lure of sleep was she could never go back.

CHAPTER TEN

Derek hunkered down in his truck. He was on a road that looked unused as near as he dared to get to the cabin where Jason had taken Celeste. It was time for a little recon. He'd have to be cautious to avoid Jason's detection. When a lull came in the storm, he jumped out, stripped and shifted. Euphoria rushed through him—the game was on.

The wolf wanted to run, to hunt down its prey. Its instincts were primitive and bloody, and Derek had to fight with his other half for control. As much as the idea of ripping out the throats of his victims appealed, he knew the cat would never give in easily. Derek grinned. No, the cat would make one hell of an opponent. He'd make Derek work for victory. The wolf growled its willingness and lifted its muzzle. Derek barely restrained the howl of challenge welling in its throat and set off at an easy lope through the underbrush.

He studied the ground while keeping his nose alert for Jason. The last thing he wanted was to get caught before he had a chance to plan. The terrain had promise. It was marshy, the ground vegetation not as thick as it had been before the last hurricane blew through but more than enough to hide a couple of bodies. There was a sudden splash to his left, and he jerked his head around in time to see an alligator swimming away in the pond he skirted. If the wolf could have arched its eyebrows, it would have. Could this set-up get more perfect? Ready-made body disposal. He could use a gator back home.

He started to catch scents of the wereleopard the closer he got to Jason's cabin, so he slowed his approach. It didn't smell fresh, as if he had been here, but was now gone...out prowling the grounds. Derek's relief was immediate. He'd come too close to getting caught on one of his earlier forays.

Derek could see a clearing up ahead through the trees and crouched low to the ground, taking his time to inch forward, careful to stay upwind and as quiet as he could manage. The wind aided him. While there was currently a break in the rain, the wind never seemed to slow. In fact, it seemed to be picking up.

He reached the line of trees at the front of the house and looked around for a hiding place. He found a small depression under the exposed roots of a cypress tree and worked his way under it, twisting and contorting his body until he found a comfortable position. He had a good view of the house but they wouldn't be able to see him, or smell him as long as the wind direction didn't change. It was foolish to get this close, but he'd always liked living on the edge. Making an enemy of the wereleopard was definitely one way to do that.

Jason's scent was strong here, and he took a good look at his surroundings, noting the long scratch marks on the trees next to him. Did the cat mark its territory or was it simply to sharpen its claws? Derek couldn't ignore the unease that thought invoked. His plan to ruin Michael had come too far to blow it all to hell by getting himself killed here. But he couldn't let Celeste live after what she'd seen and now that Jason was involved, he had to die too. That was a cryin' shame. Jason had been useful and rash, not asking the questions he should have, not behaving in the calculated manner he did with his other business ventures. When Derek approached him, the wereleopard had only been concerned with revenge.

The wolf snarled with contempt and disdain. While it understood the need for vengeance, the lengths males would go to over women were a mystery to it. Women were for sex, for breeding. Too many of them didn't know their place in the natural order. They had been allowed too much freedom under Michael's rule. No doubt due to Michael's infatuation with his human mate. Things were going to change when Derek took over.

His rage rose again over the disruption of his plans. He'd wanted Jason to take the land from Michael. Losing such prime real estate would put the Alpha in a position to be challenged. Throw in the recent spurt of murders of women connected to the clan, and he was practically begging to be challenged. Derek had waited years for this time to come. His claws dug into the mud, a low growl welling up from his throat. Everything would have gone perfectly if Celeste hadn't found out Jason didn't know she was alive. Hadn't seen him kill the blonde woman.

He'd been able to piece together some of what happened. Rumors flew quickly in the clan. Celeste had been called home and hadn't been told her mate thought she was dead. Derek had stumbled on that knowledge accidentally a year ago and kept it to himself, saved for some time in the future when he might be able to use it. And it had worked, making it possible to maneuver both Jason and Michael into the land deal. No one seemed to know why Celeste was given that information after so long, and he'd kept his speculations to himself. He still couldn't believe Michael told her. Derek had badly miscalculated, certain the werewolf would stand by and watch the land go before he confessed his deceit to his only daughter.

A new scent came to him on the wind, and he lifted his muzzle to take it in. Celeste, mixed with Jason and the heady, musky smell of sex. He growled. She'd have to pay for that. It hadn't taken her long to forget him, had it? Derek had never bedded her. He wanted to. Wanted to possess her, own her, but he'd held back waiting for the right time. Forcing Michael to watch his rough treatment of her after he was removed as Alpha and unable to come to his daughter's aid would only add to the other wolf's humiliation. Derek had been looking forward to that humiliation, dreaming of it for years. All those plans were now shot to hell. He had to salvage whatever he could.

Jason and Celeste had to die. Here. Tonight. No one would be able to pin the murders on him, and his little side hobby would return to be a more secret, safer pastime. In a few days he'd approach one of Jason's brothers about buying the land from them. He would at least still be able to challenge Michael, demoralize and ruin him. Then maybe he could finally put his father's spirit to rest. But for now, he had to figure out how to take out Jason.

He'd seen the wereleopard fight once, and he was formidable. In a fair contest, Derek knew he couldn't take him. Good thing he didn't care about fighting fair. He kept a hunting rifle in his truck, the better to fit in with his human yokel neighbors. Maybe he'd use it to kill Jason, quick and easy, then he could take his time with Celeste. He couldn't let her faithlessness slide with no punishment. He wished he could keep her alive a little while, take her home and use her the way he used other women, but he doubted even the trauma of seeing her mate murdered would keep her in line for long. No, eventually she'd rebel, and he'd have to kill her anyway. Too risky. It would be much easier to dispose of the bodies here.

The rain started up again, and he wiggled his way up from under the shelter of the tree. He stared at the house a minute, allowing his excitement to rise. It would all be over soon. Turning, he let the wolf loose and ran back to the truck. It was time to put his plan into action.

CHAPTER ELEVEN

When he was sure she was asleep, Jason rolled out of bed. He stood and watched her a few minutes, grinning like a fool. A woman so well pleasured she passed out was a beautiful thing.

My woman.

Leaning over, he pushed a strand of hair out of her face and brushed a kiss over her lips. Then he walked out to his truck.

The only way to keep her safe was to get information. Celeste was so upset over dealing with her family's betrayal that he was afraid to push her for the reason for her sudden appearance. But the storm was roaring closer to land, and he needed answers quick. The phone in the house was dead. He hoped to God the satellite phone would still work.

He retrieved it from the glove box of his truck, ran back inside through the pouring rain and turned the phone on. It had a dial tone. He exhaled a gusty sigh of relief he hadn't been aware he was holding and punched in Michael's number. Tomas, the brother he remembered as Celeste's favorite, answered and quickly handed the phone off to his father.

"Is Celeste with you?" he demanded gruffly. Did he actually think Jason was going to let him control the conversation? He snorted. Not in this lifetime.

"Now that was a stupid question," he drawled. "The smart question is why you sent her to me after all this time and in a fucking hurricane."

"She didn't tell you? It's about the land, of course—getting an extension on the balloon payment. Why else would I send her?" Michael's tone was all arrogant bravado and all Alpha. It made Jason's teeth itch. The werewolf needed Jason's help but still couldn't bring himself to tone down the attitude. Like most of the old school werekind leaders, Michael was autocratic. Abrasive. Was certain he knew what was best for everyone. Look what he'd done to Celeste.

Fury rolled through Jason at Michael for sending her into danger during a hurricane, and at Celeste for agreeing to it—for coming to him over her precious land. Jason's thoughts bounced back and forth, and he stood poised on the balls of his feet, ready to pounce at an enemy he couldn't see before reason started to return. Celeste could not have changed so much. Whatever had sent her running to Florida—to him—it wasn't the land. Michael's explanation didn't fit with the evidence of her attack, her amnesia, but he was certain Michael knew a hell of a lot more than he was saying.

"Why else would you send her? That's a very good question, isn't it?" He let the silence drag a moment. "Because she didn't get to me before someone attacked her, and now she doesn't remember anything that's happened over the past twenty-four hours or so."

He heard a muffled gasp in the background on Michael's end and knew her mother was listening in. He felt a brief pang of sympathy for her and wondered what the fuck Michael was up to.

"She's fine by the way," he said sarcastically when the other man didn't respond. "I take care of my own. And let's get that clear right from the start, Michael. She's mine. You won't take her from me again."

Michael huffed, and Jason could imagine his grip on the phone turning white knuckled. He grinned. He could really learn to love one-upping Michael.

"So why don't you tell me what's really going on? You sent her here. Why? To protect her or because you need help? And don't give me some bull about the land."

Michael's growl turned into a groan, and Jason muttered, "Shit."

"We could have easily made that payment." Michael sighed. "Except things kept going wrong. Broken equipment, late deliveries, personnel problems."

"Sabotage?"

Michael's laugh was short and harsh. "We didn't think so at first, but then Celeste got close to someone who helped her recover. Emotionally started to rebound, I mean, and he—Derek—started offering to help us out of the mess. With a hefty percentage of the business going to him, of course. Even that didn't make me really suspicious. Not at first."

Jason gripped the phone so hard the plastic casing cracked in his hand. Derek was the mysterious boyfriend? Like hell that was just a coincidence.

"It was the women," Michael said.

What the fuck was he going on about now?

"Come again?"

"A suspicious number of women have gone missing recently. There wasn't any kind of pattern, no connections between them—except they were all humans from this area."

"Until?"

"The last three have all been connected to my family in some way."

Fuck, and Celeste had almost been the fourth. How close had it been? How had she escaped? He remembered the truck that had almost run him off the road at the beach.

"Do you know anyone who drives a white F150?"

He heard movement in the hallway and turned to meet Celeste's gaze. She was pale and shaking, and he immediately stepped toward her. She and Michael answered his question at the same time, Michael by swearing and Celeste with a shiver.

"Derek," she whispered. "It's Derek's truck. I saw him kill someone."

Jason set the phone on an end table and pulled her into his arms.

"It's okay, baby. You're safe here."

She pressed her head against his chest and shook it.

"I'm not. He'll keep coming. He's relentless in everything else he does, and what choice does he have now?"

Jason's chest rumbled in response. "Let him come. I protect my own. You have to trust me to take care of you, Celeste."

114

She leaned back, tilting her head to smile up at him.

"For some crazy reason I do."

They heard yelling through the phone receiver, Michael trying to get his attention. Releasing her, he stretched an arm out and picked the phone up. My dad? she mouthed. He smiled in response.

"What else, Michael? I can see him wanting to cover up what he's doing, but why target women important to your family? Why the business arrangement?"

Wind gusted against the house, banging debris against an outside wall, and Michael's answer was garbled. The phone lost its signal before Jason could ask him to repeat himself. Frustrated, he turned it off and tossed it to the couch where it fell between the back and a cushion.

"Fuck," Jason muttered.

Celeste had backed away and huddled in the entry to the hallway, instinctively going for the interior walls when the wind picked up. She bit her lower lip and tried to hurry her mind through the last few minutes' revelations. First, there was the dream recounting her family's deceit and Derek killing the blonde woman, and now what little she'd overheard of the phone conversation.

"What women?" she finally asked.

She felt a sense of urgency, knew they needed to work it all out quickly. Celeste felt watched, stalked. Goose bumps broke out across her arms, and the back of her neck tingled. They couldn't hear much over the wind and rain, but she knew Derek was out there somewhere. Watching. Waiting.

Jason didn't answer right away. With one hand on his hip, he bent his head forward and massaged the back of his neck with the other hand. He retrieved the phone and put it in the hall closet. When he returned his gaze to her, there was a feral gleam in his eyes.

"You were involved with Derek?"

She almost smiled at his emphasis on the past tense and nodded. His expression hardened, and he approached her slowly with the stealth of a big cat. A predatory, pissed-off cat. Her heart skipped a beat. She glanced down the hall behind her and considered making a run for the bedroom.

"I wouldn't if I were you."

"Wouldn't what?" she whispered.

"Run."

"Wouldn't dream of it."

Like hell she wouldn't. He was within arm's reach when she took a nervous step back. It was reflex more than desire to get away, but if he realized that he didn't care.

Jason pounced before she could retreat any farther, taking them both to the floor with a thud. His hand swept under her head, protecting her from the fall as well as pinning her under him. He ground his hips against her belly, and she opened her legs to accommodate him, groaning when he readjusted himself and his erection pressed against her pussy.

He shoved her shirt up above her breasts and took one nipple into his mouth while his hand fisted in her hair and tugged so she arched her back, pushing her chest up to him. Both stung a little more than was good, coming down more on the pain side of her pain/pleasure comfort zone than pleasure. She yelped a protest, Jason released the pressure on her hair, his teeth abandoned her breast to be replaced by soft kisses, gentle licks. When he lifted his head and met her gaze, she trailed her fingers down the side of his face.

"It was always you. Only you."

"Damn right," he growled. "And it'll always be me."

The door banged open, and Celeste's alarm spiked. She craned her head, trying to see around Jason's body, to see what was coming. Storm or monster?

Derek strolled in, a rifle propped on his shoulder and an insane look in his eye that made her shudder in terror.

"Well, isn't this sweet. Lovers reunited. Too bad for you, it'll be so short lived."

Jason jerked the shirt down over her chest and leapt to his feet, dragging her with him and shoving her behind him.

"Derek," he greeted him coldly. "What brings you to the neighborhood?"

"Just a quick visit." Derek looked at her and sneered. "I'm so disappointed in your lack of fidelity, sweetheart." He returned his gaze to Jason. "My girl here is a liability. I was delayed in coming after her. Small matter of disposing of another body, you understand. Come to think of it, you're a liability too."

Jason growled low in his throat, and she clutched his wrist, afraid he'd attack and get himself shot.

"She's not yours. Never was and never will be."

Derek chuckled. "No, I'll give you that—she really wasn't. But she made good bait, didn't she?"

She tried to peer around Jason, to see Derek, this man she'd thought she knew and was obviously clueless about, but Jason held her immobile behind him, his strength easily overpowering hers.

"Let's see her, Jason. I want to watch her face when I kill you. Then she and I have some unfinished business to tend to."

CHAPTER TWELVE

She gritted her teeth against the scream welling inside her, the anger building in her. He was crazy. Insane. Certifiable. She wasn't ready to die, yet, especially now that she'd found Jason again.

"She's just fine where she is," Jason answered.

"No, I don't think so. Come out, come out, Celeste. Or I'll just shoot your mate while he tries to guard you. Fair trade don't you think?"

His voice had a singsong, loony quality to it and, knowing he meant what he said, she wrenched free from Jason's grip and stepped into the living room where she could at least see what was going on.

"Ah, there you are, love."

She sensed more than saw Jason bristle at the endearment. Arching an eyebrow she addressed Derek, hanging on to her cool by a thread.

"I never was your love though, was I?"

His laugh was more a cackle, and it grated on her nerves, making them raw and alert. How could they get out of here alive? She was determined to live. Watching Jason in her peripheral vision, she was certain he felt the same way.

An eerie quiet descended outside. She was so used to wind screaming and rain pelting that it threw her for a loop. What the hell? The sudden calm was unnerving. She looked at Jason, and he was looking up.

"We're in the eye," he said.

In the eye of the storm? That couldn't be good, even if it was a small hurricane. The highest winds were on the back side of a hurricane. If it passed directly over them, they'd get the worst of it, regardless of the psychopath in the living room with a gun. And here she'd thought her luck might be changing. Not.

Jason met her gaze, then reached out and took her hand, squeezing it gently. There was a hard look on his face when he turned back to Derek, and she hoped it meant he had a plan to get them out of this in one piece. Releasing her hand, he shrugged, somehow combining it with a smooth step closer to Derek that the other man didn't seem to notice.

"If you're going to kill us, we might as well know why."

"Why not? Celeste may not even know the story. Michael's always spent too much energy protecting his human daughter." Derek's grin was pure malice and the way he sneered human made her skin crawl.

"Once upon a time, there was an Alpha who was challenged by his Beta, and the Beta killed him." He frowned theatrically. "Sound familiar yet, Celeste?"

"My father. Your father." She shrugged and tried to look nonchalant. She hadn't had a clue he held a grudge about that. No one had. "That was what? Fifteen years ago? Isn't that old news?"

"Old news." He sneered. "For y'all maybe. Michael killed my father and stole my clan. I've watched and worked and waited for years to get it back. Destroying his family in the process is just an added bonus."

"Well, I don't have a problem with that on general principal you understand," Jason drawled, and she glared at him. This was helping? "But Celeste is my family, not Michael's, so she's hardly a target for your revenge."

Derek shook his head in mock sorrow. "I might have let her go, but she saw something she shouldn't have. It's better if she dies here really. It'll be quick, Jason. And it'll destroy Michael. One more woman he's responsible for that he couldn't protect."

"About the women." Jason stood calmly with his arms crossed over his chest as if it was perfectly normal to stand in his living room in the middle of a hurricane and hold a conversation with a madman, as if it was simply curiosity that made him inquire. "I get going after his business. I was ready to take the land. But how do the women fit into the plan?"

"Ah, you spoke to Michael. He told you about the women." Derek's eyes were wild and he gave her a smile she could only describe as creepy. She wished Jason would hurry the hell up and get them out of this. She tried not to watch as he took another step toward Derek, tried not to give the movement away. Derek waved a dismissive hand in the air. "They were only human. Well, except the first one."

She sucked in a deep breath as realization hit her. She remembered the whispered conversations.

"Michael challenged your father because he thought Darren killed his youngest sister. But it was you, wasn't it?"

Derek grinned at her. It made her skin crawl, and she tried to edge closer to Jason, but he'd managed to put too much distance between them.

"So you do remember. Irresponsible of me to kill one of our kind though. I didn't make that mistake again."

"So you target human women," Jason said, admiration in his voice, part of sidle-up-to-the-crazed-killer-to-take-him-out act. She hoped like hell he knew what he was doing.

"I knew you would understand, Jason."

"Oh, I get it all right."

The wind and rain picked up again outside, and Jason lunged at Derek. Before he could take aim, the rifle flew from Derek's hands and skittered across the floor. She grabbed it as they fell in a tangle. Both men lurched apart and shifted as the eye passed over the house and the wind built to a roar. It was as loud as the tornado that ripped through her neighborhood a few months ago, and she tried to get a look out the window. She couldn't see anything but knew tornado or not that much wind was very dangerous. They needed to find shelter fast.

A growl made the hair on the back of her neck stand on end, and she spun her attention back to Jason and Derek, both now in their animal forms. They circled each other, the gray wolf huge and growling, the black leopard quiet and stealthy. His complete focus on Derek was chilling. She got the impression the wolf was trying to induce fear and found it laughable—he wasn't nearly as scary as Jason.

She lifted the rifle to her shoulder and found Derek in the sights, but jerked her finger away from the trigger when he leapt at Jason. Jason twisted out of the way with feline grace, a smooth efficient movement. But he wasn't quick enough, and she held her breath when she saw blood dripping down his side as they separated.

The blood agitated the wolf. He snarled, the sides of his lips peeling back to reveal rows of sharp teeth. Jason stayed between them, and she was afraid to take a shot, afraid with the way her hands were shaking she'd miss her target. Before she could steady herself again a burst of wind hit the roof, pulling back one corner that flew away into the storm. She eyed what was left warily. It didn't look like it would take much to bring the rest down on top of them.

"Hurry, Jason," she muttered, knowing she shouldn't distract him but afraid they were out of time.

The wolf and leopard circled each other again, each taking swipes at the other and missing. She got the impression they were testing each other, their respective reach, speed and strength, and she grew more frustrated. Neither ever stopped moving, and her hands didn't stop shaking. Another huge gust of wind swept through and, amid the constant roar of the rain, there was a loud boom somewhere outside. Everyone's reaction to the sound was different. She jumped. Derek froze. And Jason attacked.

He leapt across the space between them and clamped down on the wolf's neck, hitting his jugular. Flesh tore, blood spurted and the leopard straightened, giving Derek a vicious shake before dropping him. Jason didn't waste any time over the body but returned to Celeste's side. She dropped the rifle, and he lifted his muzzle, gripping her wrist and dragging her down the hall to the bathroom where he pushed her into the tub. He shifted and climbed in with her, wrapping his arms around her and protecting her with his body.

She didn't have a chance to wonder what had happened to Derek. The wind hit the roof, peeling the rest of it and the hall wall off. She watched from under Jason's shoulder as the side of the house where Derek's body lay was blown away, Derek along with it. Even if by some miracle he'd survived the damage to his neck, not even a werewolf could survive getting swept away in hurricane force winds. That part of the nightmare was over at least.

CHAPTER THIRTEEN

The storm raged for several more hours. After the worst passed, Jason had gone out to his truck and found a blue tarp for them to huddle under. They moved into the bedroom. The ceiling was gone but at least they weren't cramped in a tub. The tarp helped keep most of the wind and rain off, but they were still soaked through by the time morning dawned. The sun came out by late morning, and they left the ruin of the house to stand in the ruin of the yard.

She was amazed to see the truck still in place and all in one piece. Even more shocking was the calm, pretty day in the midst of so much destruction. She stood in her bare feet on what was left of the front porch and tried to take it in. It was overwhelming. How could he live in such a place? How would she? Assuming of course, he was serious about them being together. She didn't have the guts to bring that up yet.

"I thought category ones weren't that bad," she said instead, sticking to a safe topic.

"They aren't," he answered. "When it changed course yesterday it stayed on open water longer, warmer water. It made it a stronger storm. It hit land as a cat three."

She arched an eyebrow. How did he know that?

"I got the radio to work for a few minutes this morning while you were asleep."

"I see. Now what?" she asked.

Standing next to her, he took her hand and lifted it to his lips, pressing a soft kiss against her palm. "Now you go home while I clean up the mess."

She jerked free. So much for working things out.

"Tomas is on his way now. I spoke to him this morning. He was already on his way down."

He'd been on the phone for hours before the sun came up, when the storm had begun to abate. She hadn't had any idea he was making arrangements to send her away, though, and tried to hide how deeply it cut. It had been a nice fantasy, but it was over now, and she wasn't going to make it worse by crying or screaming or begging. She bit her lip against the urge to do just that and turned her back on him.

"Hey." His footfalls were heavy as he followed her, and she tensed when his hands landed on her shoulders, pulling her back against him. "It's just for a couple of weeks, sweetheart."

"Right," she whispered, fighting the moisture gathering in her eyes. Her fingers twisted together, and she looked down as a tear escaped and landed on the ruby glittering on her hand. Her voice broke. "Just a couple of weeks."

"Celeste." He growled and spun her around. "You can't stay here right now. There's no power or water or, hell, even a house."

"Of course."

No there were none of those things. But there was Jason, and she'd been under the foolish assumption he wasn't letting her go again. She clenched her jaw and ignored the ache in her chest. She'd survive—she always had. Inside the satellite phone rang, and he left her to answer it. She heard him return, but didn't turn to face him.

"Tomas is here. He's waiting for us at the gate."

"Fine," she said, moving toward the truck, but before she reached the door an eagle flew into the clearing, huge and majestic. It shifted into a tall, gorgeous woman with short, spiky white hair. She inclined her head slightly at Celeste and Jason stepped in front of her, blocking her view of the woman.

She had to be a Messenger. Celeste knew a few of them—she grew up in werewolf land and the birds territory was right smack in the middle—but she didn't know this one.

"I'm Ajax Petros," the woman said. Frowning, Celeste poked Jason in the back until he let her step out. Why was the Messenger

Commander coming to Jason? He didn't respond to her, just waited her out in silence. The woman smiled just a little and Celeste caught a flash of amusement cross her face. Celeste got the impression, and she'd heard enough over the years, to know Ajax Petros was not a woman who could be intimidated. The birds she knew spoke of the eagle with a reverence reserved only for God.

"Do you have a message?" Celeste asked, curiosity getting the better of her.

Ajax turned that measuring glance on her. Celeste had to force herself to be still, to be calm. To stare the other woman down. If she'd learned one thing after the crash it was that she was a hell of a lot stronger than she'd ever given herself credit for. Or anyone else for that matter. She lifted her chin and met the wereeagle's gaze. Ajax grinned.

"Spine. Good." Then she turned to Jason. "I have a message for the Leonidas brothers from Tonina Guerra."

She didn't know the name, but Jason did. His reaction was subtle but immediate. He gently nudged her behind him, his muscles tensing as if to leap forward and grab the Messenger by throat. It alarmed her and she stroked his back, murmured soft encouragement and the tension eased a little from his body. Messengers were neutral. Messengers were off limits.

"What's the message?" he asked.

"She apologizes for the assassination attempt on your brother's mate and hopes you understand she knew nothing of it."

Jason nodded.

"She also thought you'd like to know who paid her mate for it," Ajax continued, pausing for effect.

Jason shrugged, but the bond between them pulsed. She knew he was desperate to know who had paid for the attack on his sister-in-law, who she'd discovered through the long night was her cousin, Lyra, mated to his younger brother, Zander. "Of course."

Her gaze shifted to Celeste, softened. It was clear the woman knew more about Celeste than she knew about her.

"A werewolf named Derek. She doesn't know his last name."

Celeste was numb with shock. She couldn't imagine why Derek would want to kill her cousin, but she was no longer surprised. Not by anything. The bird was waiting expectantly and Jason finally nodded.

"We won't hold her mate's actions against her."

Ajax nodded. "I'll let her know." And with those words she shifted back to her bird form and took flight. Celeste held her breath until the bald eagle was gone from sight.

Jason didn't move, didn't look at her. She knew he was struggling with his leopard side for dominance and waited him out.

"How many Dereks are there?" he asked.

She shook her head. "I have no idea. But…it has to be him. Why, Jason? Me, I can understand, but why would he go after Lyra? She ran away from the clan years ago."

"I don't know, baby, but we'll find out." He finally hugged her, pulled her close.

"How?" she whispered.

"Nico. I'll call Nico. This is the kind of thing he does."

But he was estranged from his brothers. They hadn't spoken of it, but she knew. He squeezed her shoulders.

"Don't worry, this is family. And speaking of family. Tomas is waiting for us."

That's right, he was pushing her out of his life. Everything else seemed to pale in comparison. There was no point in delaying, so she got in the truck, quietly latching the seatbelt. The quick drive was made in an uncomfortable silence. She shuddered when they passed the empty beach lot and wondered where her car was, but the dismay was wiped away when they reached the entrance of the park a few minutes later and she saw Tomas waiting, leaning against the hood of his car. She reached for the door handle before they'd even come to a complete stop and launched herself from the cab. She didn't make the gate before Jason stopped her, dragging her into his arms with a crushing kiss.

Sighing into him, she gripped his shirt in her fists and tried to take it over, tried to soften it. She'd miss him. She'd recover, but it would be hard and as goodbye kisses went, this was not what she had in mind. He didn't let her have control though. His lips were bruising, his tongue demanding. If his intent was possession it was a rousing success. He let her go abruptly, and she staggered back, one hand coming up to cover her mouth as if she could hold the feel of him there.

"Two weeks, Celeste," he said, breathing hard.

"I understand." She said it softly, sadly. She understood she wouldn't see him again. Why couldn't he just say goodbye? He pulled her back into his arms, and this time the kiss was easy and slow. Lifting his head, he picked her up and put her down on the other side of the gate.

"You don't understand shit. This is not an end."

He met Tomas's gaze.

"Take care of my mate, wolf."

Then he spun around and strode back to the truck. She watched until he was out of sight and jumped when Tomas spoke.

"You look like hell, babe. What happened here? All Jason said was Derek is dead and y'all made it through the storm."

Sighing, she walked to the car and got in. He joined her and cranked the engine before she answered.

"It's a long story."

He grinned. "We have a long drive."

"Atlanta's not that far."

Would the drive fly by or drag? And how long would it take to slip back into her calm, ordered life?

Tomas snorted. "I don't think so. I'm taking you home."

She glared at him. She wasn't ready to face Michael yet, didn't trust herself not to lose it when she saw him.

"Hey, Jason insisted. Said something about it being the last time we'd get to see you in a good long time. He's seriously pissed at us."

"I don't blame him. I'm seriously pissed at y'all." She sighed. "But you don't have to worry about it. I doubt any of us will be seeing him again."

He frowned at her. "You're crazy if you believe that."

She just shrugged and stared out the window. Maybe he would come but so much had happened. Too many lies, too much hurt. She wouldn't blame him for disappearing. The ring was heavy on her finger, and she considered taking it off but couldn't quite make herself do it. She'd cling to the fantasy for just a while longer.

It was a long drive, and the last couple of days had taken their toll, finally catching up to her. She slept most of the way, jerking awake when the hum of the car was silenced. She blinked at the front of her parents' house, not sure she wanted to enter. It was the lure of a hot shower that got her moving in that direction.

The whole family was waiting when she walked in, but she just shook her head when one of her brothers opened his mouth to speak.

"Not now," she said and went to her old room.

CHAPTER FOURTEEN

Jason watched her leave, watched until the car disappeared around a curve in the road, and still stood rooted in place. She thought he was letting her go and nothing other than his coming for her would convince her otherwise. Fine. He'd just work double-time. But first…

First he had to deal with family issues. The fact that the ocelot who'd tried to kill his sister-in-law, his baby brother's mate and his mate's cousin, was hired by Derek complicated the shit out of things. Maybe it was nothing more than Derek trying to weaken Michael's position in the clan. Or maybe his brother Nico was right. Maybe something was seriously off in the shifter world and it started with the crash that was supposed to have taken the life not only of his mate, but also his father. The leopard clan leader.

He pulled out his cell phone as he turned to the truck, cranked it as he scrolled to the recorded address book. Pushed send as he put it in drive. Nico answered on the first ring.

"Jason. Make it through the storm okay?"

"Fine. Celeste is alive."

There was a brief pause. "If Celeste is…"

Nico didn't have to say anything more. If Celeste was alive, Hector's, their father, chances had just improved. Jason filled Nico in on the bird visit and message, then hung up and got to work. He had a mate to claim.

The next week passed slowly. Eventually she spoke to everyone, listened to their apologies and justifications. Told her father about the message from the werebird. But Celeste wasn't sure if she'd ever be able to really forgive them, and an uneasy kind of peace fell over the household. She prowled the house in silence, going stir crazy and ready to bolt at any minute. Jason didn't call—a fact she was positive of since she jumped every time the phone rang and refused to let anyone else answer it.

The more time passed, the angrier she became. He really was willing to let her go a second time. Fine. But she'd be damned if he got away unscathed. He'd made her love him again, had reawakened her body and made her hope. Damned if he was going to do that and just walk away.

She began to plot her escape. She couldn't get beyond the porches without someone following her, and no one was willing to hand over their car keys even if she could. Of course they had to sleep sometime, and she decided she wasn't above liberating a car from one of them in the middle of the night. She considered it small repayment for the lies they'd fed her. The best part by far though was planning what she would say to Jason. She was torn up with hurt and anger, and she wanted, needed, him to feel as badly as she did.

It was a warm breezy summer day, and she'd put on what she often joked was her flower child outfit, a long flowing skirt and tank top. She was lying in her favorite place, in the hammock on the back porch, in the middle of planning her tirade when she heard a vehicle pull into the drive. Pushing her foot against the porch rail, she set the hammock lightly swaying and idly wondered who the new arrival was. Another clan member coming to gawk under the guise of worry for her no doubt. She closed her eyes and pretended to sleep as footsteps came down the back hall. She just wasn't up to being the center of attention today.

The door creaked. She ignored it but jerked when a light stroke glided down her jaw to her neck. Of all the presumptuous nerve. Her eyes flew wide open, and she opened her mouth to give whoever it was a piece of her mind, but the words froze in her throat.

Jason loomed over her in tight jeans and a tighter shirt. Her mouth watered at the sight, and her brain finally reengaged. She was beyond mad at him. She swung out of the hammock and shoved past him. When she felt as if she had enough distance, she spun around.

"What are you doing here?"

He arched an eyebrow. "Not quite the reception I had in mind."

She narrowed her eyes. "You sent me away, remember?"

"And I told you it would only be for a couple of weeks. I didn't have anywhere for you to stay."

She huffed. "Oh, please. I made it through a hurricane and a madman. I don't think the lack of four walls and roof was that big a deal in retrospect."

His eyes gleamed at the sarcasm, and he took a step toward her. She retreated with one of her own, but not out of fear. She felt gloriously alive for the first time in days.

"Well, I did. Next time you can stay and sleep in the bed of the truck with me. I'm sure we can find a better use for your smart mouth there."

She gasped, glaring at him and ignoring the tingle of lust that strummed through her at the crude suggestion. He rubbed a hand over his face and sighed.

"I'm sorry. That was rude and uncalled for."

The apology surprised her, and she nodded agreement.

"Yeah, it was."

He grinned. "Not that the idea doesn't have appeal, you understand."

Her body was keyed up, ready. Desperate. But she wanted to vent her anger and frustration before giving into the craving for him. She smiled sweetly. "Not in this lifetime."

Laughing, he shook his head. "I can see that. Why are you so pissed? I told you I'd come, and I'm here. A week early."

"I…"

She let the answer trail off into nothing. Why was she pissed? She hadn't believed he still wanted her and had spent a week getting good and angry over that, but he was here now. He knew when he sent her off she believed that, too, and didn't try to contact her during the last week to convince her otherwise.

"You could have called," she grumbled.

He grunted. "I would have if I hadn't been working twenty hours a day. So I could bring you home sooner."

When he put it that way, she felt a little bitchy. Not too much though. Surely he could have managed a phone call somewhere.

"I don't think this is really anger here," he said gesturing between the two of them. "I think it's fear."

"Fear? No way."

He smiled and sauntered closer to her, smoothly, easily as if he knew she'd run at any minute. He cupped her face in his palms and looked into her eyes. She felt as if he could see into her soul, see all of her deepest secrets, and she realized why he thought her anger was born of fear. He may even be right. She saw it all reflected in his gaze.

"I'm scared, too, baby. I lost you a year ago, and I'm terrified of going through that again." He kissed her, a quick featherlike brush against her lips. "But I love you, and we're going to make this work. Hell, I'll even learn to live with your family."

Cheers erupted from the open doorway behind them. They turned to look, and Celeste wished she could sink into the floor. The whole family crowded in the small space.

Michael grinned at Jason and offered him a jaunty salute. "We heard that, and we'll be holding you to it."

Jason groaned and dropped his forehead to rest on top of hers. "Great. What have I done?" he complained.

Laughter bubbled from her throat, and she shook her head in mock sadness.

"You invited a wolf—no a family of wolves—into your home. So much for that old leopard-wolf rivalry, eh?"

He straightened, turning serious. "They won't visit unless you're there."

"Guess you'll have to get used to them then, huh?"

He released a gusty sigh. "You didn't have to make me sweat so long."

She shrugged. "You made me sweat for a week."

"And she made us suffer for it."

The family was still gathered in the doorway, Tomas leaning on the frame and grinning at her. She made a shooing motion with her hands.

"Go. Away."

Reluctantly, everyone backed away but Michael.

"You'll take care of her," he said, more demand than question.

"Of course I will."

Michael nodded curtly. "See that you do." Then he disappeared into the house with the others, pulling the door shut behind him.

Jason tugged her back to the hammock and lay down, pulling her with him. She shoved a foot against the ground to get them swinging and stared out into the yard. This was one of her favorite pastimes for lazy summer days, though usually she had a book.

"Nice skirt."

He reached down to her ankle and slowly slid his hand up her leg under the skirt. Her breath quickened then stopped altogether when he reached her pussy.

"No underwear?" he whispered in her ear, his breath tickling her, arousing her. He pushed his cock against her ass. She avoided the question as his fingers began to stroke her.

"I need a hammock in Florida."

He nuzzled her neck and murmured. "I'll get you a dozen."

He rubbed her clit and pushed one finger slowly inside her. She clutched around it, moving her hips back, grinding against the hard body behind her.

"Good."

He chuckled. "Which part? This part?" He moved a second finger inside her, set up a steady in and out rhythm, and gave her clit the lightest pinch. She trembled and bit her lip, afraid she'd cry out. Right on the edge of coming.

"My whole family is inside, Jason."

"Hmm. I don't care." He nibbled on her neck. "I always was the bad boy in my family, you know."

She grew slicker, hotter when she felt his teeth scrape over her pulse. She was so close, but she didn't want to come like this. She needed him inside her, filling her. Unable to turn around, she reached one hand behind her and rubbed it over the hard bulge in his jeans. He groaned.

"Playing with fire again," he said.

She grinned, fought down a giggle. Suddenly, sex in broad daylight on her parents' back porch sounded pretty damned good. She wondered if they dared get naked? As if he could read her mind, he moved her hand and unsnapped his jeans. The zipper sounded impossibly loud in the quiet afternoon, and he lowered it so slowly she'd thought she'd go mad. Then she felt him free, pressed up against her ass. He bit down on her neck, a little hard, an attention getter.

"Last time to say no."

"Not on your life. Now, Jason."

He pulled the skirt up to her waist, lifted her thigh over his and thrust into her in one smooth movement. Then he rearranged the length of the skirt so it covered their actions and started moving in short shallow strokes that left her unfulfilled and drove her mad. He wrapped his arms around her, one hand lightly plumping her tight nipples while the other pressed flat against her abdomen holding her still and in place for his thrusts. He kept his face buried in her neck, kissing, biting or sucking the tender skin there. All his movements were slow and measured, designed to keep her on the edge and wanting. She knew exactly what he was doing, felt his resolve, and she smiled. It was a claiming, body and soul. But as much as he owned hers, she knew she also owned his, and she relaxed against him, releasing that last bit of her resistance.

He sighed when she went pliant and deepened his thrusts, quickened his pace. The bites came harder, the fingers closed on her nipples tighter. She panted, wrapped her fingers through the mesh of the hammock and held on. They swayed, rocking in an increasingly fast rhythm until she had to clamp down on her bottom lip or scream out and alert those inside the house. They came together, and he bit down hard on the sensitive skin between her shoulder and neck. She knew she'd bear two marks from him now. She grinned. Doubly claimed.

After he withdrew from her and put their clothes to rights, they fell silent, just enjoying the aftermath and being in each other's arms, when she thought about the destroyed house and the odd visit from the Messenger.

"What was Derek up to? Trying to cause a further rift between the leopards and wolves or what?"

Jason's arms tightened around her body. "I don't know. Nico's looking into it."

She couldn't repress a shudder. Nico was scary under the best of circumstances. She decided to change the subject.

"Where are we living by the way? Not the back of your truck," she said with alarm. She was just a little too girly for that.

He laughed and teased her. "But, honey, I thought you said, implied at least, you'd live with me anywhere?"

She craned her neck back to look at him over her shoulder. "Don't joke, Jason."

He grinned. "A borrowed RV. A very small borrowed RV, but it's in that little tourist park right outside the gate so it's close to work. And it has electricity and running water."

She smiled. "Ah well, it's perfect then, isn't it?"

"Long as you're in it with me."

"Oh you had your chance to get rid of me. Now you're stuck."

She laid her head back against his chest and kicked the floor again.

"I am waiting to hear one thing from you, you know."

She smiled and closed her eyes, breathing his scent deep into her lungs. She knew exactly what he wanted.

"I love you, too, Jason."

Fleeting Passions

Crystal Jordan

CHAPTER ONE

Strong male hands slid up Cleo's back to curl over her shoulders and pull her down, seating her fully on a long, thick cock. He was so big the stretch of it almost hurt, but she craved more, wanted him deeper, harder, faster. *More*. She closed her eyes and threw her head back, reveling in the sheer carnal bliss of a man's hands on her skin, his cock filling her. The muscles in her thighs flexed as she lifted and lowered herself on his pulsing dick.

God, it was so good. So perfect. So sweet. Nothing had ever been this good before in her entire life.

She knew it was a dream, so she let herself enjoy it. The fantasy called to the primitive lioness within her, and her fangs slid out as his hot scent flooded her nostrils, sank into her blood. Her nipples peaked tight, and she wanted his mouth there.

A smile curled her lips as her dream answered her unvoiced desires. His mouth closed over the taut crest of her breast and sucked strongly. Pinpricks erupted down her arms, and she shuddered at the sensation. Her fingers lifted to slide into the short silk of his dark hair. His wide palms cupped her hips, working her on his cock. She was so hot, so damp. Her wetness slipped down the insides of her thighs, and their flesh slapped together in the silent room.

"More," she pleaded.

He growled low in his throat, the sound of a dangerous feline caged. *"Yes. I'll give it to you, angel."*

Something about the voice tugged at her memory, but he rolled his hips beneath her, changing the angle of his deep penetration. She was swept away on the sensations rocketing through her body.

Her breath sobbed out, and they moved together towards orgasm, thrusting, grinding. Skin slipping against naked, sweaty skin.

"Yes, yes, yes." Something in this man called to her very soul. Mate. Her other half. Perfectly matched to her. A phantom possessing her dreams.

Desperation whipped through her. She was close, very close. She licked the salty sweat from his shoulder, sucking his essence into her mouth, tasting his flesh. His lips opened over her collarbone. She felt his fangs prick her skin. It was the only warning she had before he growled, buried the sharp points into her and sucked at the bite. Her pussy contracted hard as she rocketed over into sudden orgasm. Her own fangs sank deep into his shoulder, mimicking the carnal possession of her dream lover.

They'd marked each other. *Mate* marked.

"Mine." His deep rumble was the last thing she heard before she collapsed, orgasm still rippling through her system.

So perfect. Too perfect to be real.

A small groan pulled her from deep sleep. Was that her voice? Her head pounded with fierce purpose, and her mouth felt as if she'd stuffed it with cotton before she went to bed.

The groan sounded again. And it wasn't coming from her throat. She sucked in a breath and caught a whiff of familiar scent. *His* scent.

Oh. Shit.

She sat up fast. Mistake. Her mind spun from the alcohol she'd consumed the night before. Those last four Jack Daniels shots must have done it. Or was it six? She'd meant to toast to making good on her escape from her ex-fiancé, and she'd gone a little overboard.

Obviously.

Pulling in a deep breath, she assured herself it couldn't get much worse than it already was, and if she hurried she might get out of here without him catching her. The coward's way out perhaps, but she'd never met a man who relished a hung over woman in the morning. This was her first one night stand—and her last—but she couldn't imagine it being much different from her other interactions with men.

Including Trevor.

She shuddered in disgust at the mere thought of her ex. Rubbing her hands up and down her arms, she was grateful that for once they were free of bruises, free of the marks of his abuse. The incredible healing abilities of a werelioness made them fade quickly, but Trevor had always made certain she was never without. Yes, he *always* provided for her. A bitter smile twisted her lips.

Every werekind species could trace its existence back to a benevolent deity. For lions, it was the Egyptian god Aker. For the leopards who ruled the western half of the United States—and that all lions pledged fealty to—it was the Greek goddess Artemis who blessed the sons of King Leonidas of Sparta. For werebears like Trevor, it went back to the Native American legend of Rhpisunt, a chief's daughter who married a bear and birthed halfling twin sons. The thought reminded Cleo too much of how close she'd come to marrying Trevor, and she shivered.

Her fingers clenched on her biceps. Thank God, she'd gotten the job at Refuge. The resort was more than a thousand miles from Trevor and his hard fists. She'd never have to deal with that again. Not from any man. Her spine straightened. She'd had the strength to leave him, and she wasn't looking back. Her only regret was staying with him so long, but they'd gotten engaged when she was nineteen. Too young to know any better—to know that the cruel things he said to her weren't what she deserved. Too naïve to realize that the hateful words would escalate to physical abuse.

Using slow, deliberate motions that wouldn't set off the pounding in her head, she slid her legs over the side of the bed. The smoothness of the Egyptian cotton sheets on her skin made her shiver as a flood of memories flashed back from the night before. Her imagination must have been filling in some details because no man was *that* good in bed. She sighed, her mind dragging her away from the mystery man of the night before and back to one particular man—Trevor. She'd kept putting the date off for their marriage—not until she finished college, until they had some money saved up, until, until, until.

She might have stayed, might have married him, *mated* with him, but she'd found out she was pregnant. The thought of allowing Trevor near a child was revolting. No way in hell would she raise her baby in that environment. So she'd put out quiet feelers for jobs. With a degree in public relations, she could go anywhere in the werekind community or vanish into the normal human population.

Dragging in a breath, she caught the familiar scent of Refuge. So, wherever *here* was, it was on the exclusive werekind resort. She wasn't sure which was worse—if she'd slept with a fellow employee or if she'd slept with a guest. Standing, she tiptoed to the bathroom to splash water on her face. She hoped his hearing wasn't as sharp as hers. Every drop of water that hit the basin boomed like an atomic bomb in her ears, but she couldn't walk around where anyone could see her with smudged make-up and wild sex hair. She refused to let herself look in the mirror as she shut off the faucet and went to gather her clothes from where they were scattered on the floor.

It was the extensive security of Refuge that convinced her to take the job, and that the Leonidas family who owned the resort had a fierce reputation for protecting their own. That they were also the rulers of all cat-shifter species didn't hurt. A small Southwestern-style bungalow came with the position, so she could live on the grounds. She'd only been here a week, and already she loved it. Something about the place had put her at ease from the moment she stepped on the arid desert property with stark mountains rising in the distance. She felt safe here, and it was a feeling that she hadn't experienced in so long it caught her off guard. She couldn't resist. The Leonidases needn't know why she came to Arizona so long as she did her job as the new public relations officer well. And she would.

Her eyes slid closed, and she fought a moan while the last horrible memories of Trevor paraded through her mind. She often woke up in the dead of night with nightmares of it.

She'd flown out to Refuge six weeks ago for her interview with the Leonidases: Nico, Adrian, Zander and his very pregnant wife, Lyra. There was another brother, Jason, but he lived in the south somewhere… She forgot where. She'd have to look it up in case anyone ever asked. It was her job to always have the answers and deliver them with a smile. Even if the last thing she wanted to do was smile.

Swallowing hard, she laid a hand over her flat belly.

When she'd returned from her interview, it was to the hard blows of Trevor's fists. He'd found out somehow. He knew. Cold washed through her body in tingling waves. Nausea clenched her throat. The memories wouldn't stop. Trevor backing her into a corner, his fists coming down on her again and again. His werebear strength overpowering her as it always did.

No escape. She couldn't get away. Not then.

Not even from the memories now.

Collapsing to the floor and hunching over, trying to protect the child growing within her womb. His boot drawing back to kick her. Blood pouring down her thighs to coat the floor in a dark, sticky pool. The blackness of unconsciousness taking her away. The feeling of gratefulness… so grateful to escape for even a brief moment the knowledge that she had failed to save her child. Failed.

She'd spent a week in a werekind clinic, telling the same lies that she had always told before to protect Trevor. He was sorry. He was always sorry after he hurt her, but this time she just felt numb, dead like the baby she'd lost. Hollow. A call had come in on her cell phone from Zander Leonidas asking her to come to the Refuge. Most of the conversation she couldn't remember. Most of the hospital stay had been a blissful, blank nothingness.

Trevor would have been wild with rage when he found she'd slipped from her hospital bed and disappeared. She didn't envy the nurses, but she didn't regret it. They had hospital security to protect them from him, and she had no one but herself. She had nothing left. Nothing but the job offer in Arizona, so she'd clung to that to get her through.

Her gaze landed on the man in the bed, jerking her back to the present. She stooped to gather her clothes in her hands, holding them to her breasts. Who was he? She wanted to get out of there, but she needed to know what his face looked like in case he remembered more than she did and they ran into each other later. God, how humiliating.

Padding on silent cat's feet, she clutched her clothes close to cover her nudity, and bent to look at him.

Horror exploded in her veins. She knew him. Adrian Leonidas. The leader of the Leonidas family, ruler of all leopards, all cats. Her new boss. No that wasn't quite right, Zander ran the resort, and she answered to him. *He* answered to Adrian. What had she *done?* She needed to get out of here. He'd smell her on his sheets and have a damn good idea of what happened last night, but a good idea was a whole lot different than being confronted with your naked employee. She backed away slowly. She'd dress in the living room and hope like hell no one saw her leaving.

Then Wagner's *Ride of the Valkyries* pierced the silence of the room, and Adrian bolted upright in bed.

Shit.

CHAPTER TWO

Adrian's eyes cracked open in the harsh morning sunlight. A naked woman stood frozen at the end of his bed, her eyes held a hint of panic as her gaze darted between him, his ringing cell phone and the door. She was obviously trying to sneak out, her clothes in her arms. He dragged in a breath, trying to catch her scent, trying to remember what she might be doing in his bedroom. His nostrils flooded with the smell of her and him and sex. Memories flooded his mind from the night before.

Jesus, he hadn't—

He wouldn't have—

His gaze dropped to her collarbone as his hand lifted to his shoulder. An electric shock passed straight from the mark on his skin to his cock.

"Shit."

Her amber eyes widened as she followed his movement. Her hands fumbled her clothes, and she stroked her fingers over her collarbone. He groaned low, possession gripping his gut at the sight of his mark on her creamy flesh. His *mate* mark.

"Shit," she breathed.

This woman, this stranger, was now his mate. The thought rocketed through him, hitting him with the subtle force of a sledgehammer. How had he let this happen? He was a man who controlled everyone and everything, especially himself and his women. His fingers pinched the bridge of his nose as he tried to make what his instincts told him fit with what his mind knew.

"Who the hell are you?" His anger was more directed at himself than her, but her flinch told him she'd taken his tone as a direct hit. He bit back another curse.

He'd let a situation slip from his control. And he'd seen in his older brother, Jason, what that kind of weakness, what letting a woman get under his skin, could do to a man. How *the hell* had this happened? And with a stranger.

Her face looked familiar, but he couldn't place her. She wasn't a guest. Of that he was certain, so how did he know her?

She swallowed and straightened. Her clothes shifted as she did, and he got a peek at one rosy nipple before she covered herself once more. A damn shame. He wanted to see more. And his body clamored an immediate agreement, his cock rising.

He had the distinct memory of what her skin tasted like on his tongue, and he craved more. A bone deep addiction.

"Cleo Nemean," she whispered.

He knew that name. He wracked his fogging brain, waiting for the synapses to connect in coherent thought.

Damn, but he needed coffee. And about ten aspirin. It had been a long time since he'd had so much to drink. He'd already had one too many by the time he'd seen her across the bar and approached her. He'd offered to buy her a drink and one had turned into…a lot. The rest was an alcohol soaked blur.

He narrowed his eyes on her face. Wide amber eyes dominated a face framed in a smooth mane of golden waves. She wasn't stunning or even beautiful, but something about her drew him to her. Her look was quiet, coolly enchanting. But it was her eyes that caught him. Haunted, pained, secretive. The whole package made him want to explore what was hidden from first glance.

She wouldn't be here unless she was werekind or mated to werekind. He winced. Well, now she was mated to werekind, and the prick of her fangs in his shoulder made her a shifter of some kind. "You're a…"

Blinking, she tilted her head to the side. Confusion filtered through her gaze for a moment before she grinned. "Lion."

The smile kicked him in the gut, hard. God, she was lovely. And *his*.

He swallowed. What should a man say to his mate?

Hell if he knew.

He jerked a thumb at his chest. "Leopard."

The grin bloomed into a charming smile. "I know, Mr. Leonidas."

That was it. He knew her now. He groaned, and the sound made hammers pound in his head.

What the hell had he done? He'd gone and mated with an employee. As the CEO of all Leonidas business interests and ruler of the leopard species—among others—he kept strict non-fraternization standards for himself with the staff and guests. Dalliances with either type of woman was a bad idea. He blew out a long breath. "The new head of PR."

"Yes, sir." Her spine snapped straight.

He'd been away on business for the week she'd been here. Zander had called to let him know she arrived, but that's all he knew. Damn it. How had he let it go so far last night? It wasn't like him.

"I'll just…" Her voice trailed off, and she tilted her head toward the bedroom door. She turned as though to make good her escape, and rage flowed through his veins. Possession unlike he'd ever known fisted in his belly.

His mate.

He wanted her back in bed with him, wanted to memorize every detail of her lush body, wanted it with a fierceness he'd never known before.

Mate.

Everything in him screamed for her, this woman he knew nothing of. Lust, possession, and…something sweeter twisted tight in his chest. He tried to cut it off, to distance himself, to regain control. And failed.

"Wait!" he snapped. His anger was unreasonable. He knew it, but it didn't seem to make a bit of difference in how he reacted.

She wavered in front of him, flinching at his harsh tone. Some emotion he couldn't identify flowed through her amber gaze before a professional mask slipped over her features. "Yes, sir?"

Another wave of anger rolled over him that she could keep her calm when he could not. Damn it. *"Adrian.* You'll call me Adrian."

Her chin bobbed down in a quick nod, and a small dart of fear flashed through her eyes. If he hadn't been staring at her so intently, he would have missed it. What was she afraid of? Him? He hadn't made a move toward her.

Was she afraid he'd have Zander fire her? He held back a snort. As if he'd let her go so easily. No matter how little he knew of her, she belonged to him now. *His.* She'd simply have to get used to it.

Dragging a hand down his face, he rubbed the back of his neck. *What a mess.*

He hauled himself out of bed, and her gaze slid to his cock, which twitched and stiffened in response to her attention. He let a slow, hot smile curve his lips. She wasn't as immune as she was pretending. *Excellent.* He barely contained a purr.

"See something you like, Cleo?"

Her gaze jerked up to meet his, and a wild blush tinted her cheeks. "I, um, have to get to work. Right now."

"Have dinner with me. Six o'clock in the lounge." It wasn't a question, and he didn't expect an argument. No one but his siblings ever argued with him.

Her brows rose in response, she swallowed, and her gaze dipped to his erect cock again before glancing away. "I—yes, sir—Adrian."

Turning, she bolted from the room. Within moments, his front door slammed shut behind her.

He forced himself not to go after her. He would see her later. It would do, for the moment. He needed to regroup, to regain some control. He wasn't the kind of man to let it slip through his fingers. Losing it would make him weak, make him vulnerable, and he couldn't allow that. Not ever.

When his father and his brother's mate had died in a freak airplane crash, Jason had walked away from everything. The family, his responsibilities, his duties as ruler to the leopards. Everything. As second oldest, Adrian had had to step up and take over the reins. He hadn't asked for the position of heir, but he'd be damned if he messed it up over a woman. And he'd resented the hell out of his brother for the better part of the last year for dumping everything on him and running. Weak, that's what it was. Not being able to cope, to handle himself, to maintain control.

He sighed. Things were complicated as hell with his brother. He'd heard Jason's mate had been found alive, hidden by her family because they thought a wereleopard an unacceptable mate for a werewolf's *human* step-daughter—especially since the werewolf in question was the Alpha wolf, and their two species had been at odds for centuries. As if a Leonidas was some throw away bastard. He growled. They hadn't really spoken in months, but his brother hadn't deserved that.

Then again, Nico was obsessed with the idea that the airplane accident had been no accident at all, but an assassination attempt against their father, Hector. Adrian had thought his younger brother unreasonable and unwilling to deal with his grief, but since Celeste was alive, the wild idea seemed to have a hell of a lot more credence.

It was just one more bad coincidence for the Leonidas family. Or was it? Zander's mate, Lyra, was the werewolf Alpha's niece, an enemy clan to the leopards. Usually, wolves stayed in their own territory, east of the Mississippi River. The only reason Zander met the woman was an assassin had been hired to kill her and dump her on leopard land. Adrian had always assumed it was an attempt to start something between the two warring species. But was it really? Nico sensed something deeper, and Adrian knew his brother's instincts were rarely wrong. Too many coincidences. Too many unsolved riddles. One more thing he wasn't certain how to deal with—which didn't help his foul mood this morning.

He scrubbed a hand through his hair and wandered into the shower. A cold shower. His dick still stood erect, aching with want for the woman who'd just fled his home.

He should have the maids wash the sheets—they reeked of sex. On second thought, he'd leave them. For now.

The cold tiles on the bathroom floor stung his feet. He twisted the dial to start the shower, his mind wandering back to his brother. Jason hadn't come home when Celeste had been found. He still worked as some menial park ranger in Florida. Zander and Nico, his younger brothers, still had contact with him, but Adrian preferred otherwise. They hadn't seen each other at all since Jason ran away. Adrian had never understood why his brother ran, and he doubted he ever would.

He was distracting himself with thoughts of his family problems. None of this would help him figure out what to do with the lovely slip of a woman he'd mated himself to in an alcohol-induced stupor last night.

He stepped into the shower and adjusted the water as hot as he could stand it. To hell with a cold shower. The water sluiced down his body, washing away Cleo's scent. But it couldn't erase the mark on his shoulder, couldn't take back what their drunken recklessness had done.

He winced, a small part of him glad that Jason wasn't here to harass him for having a one night stand and ending up mated like some regular human in Vegas with an Elvis impersonator.

A mate. What a nightmare.

A mate. What a nightmare.

Oh, God. Oh, God. What had she done? Cleo hadn't bothered to dress, she'd just dumped her clothes on Adrian's living room floor, shifted into her lion form, and made a beeline for the door. Her golden forelegs stretched before her, claws digging deep into the sandy earth as she raced toward her bungalow in the early dawn light. The chill of the desert morning swirled around her body as she moved, and the crisp air cleared the last dregs of alcohol from her mind.

And then she panicked.

Oh, holy Jesus. She'd never intended to mate with anyone after she left Trevor. How could she have bound herself to a stranger for the rest of her life?

No matter how safe she felt at Refuge, it was superficial. Trevor would come for her. It wasn't a matter of *if*—it was a matter of *when*. How long would she get to pretend normalcy before he ripped her life apart once more and she had to run, to hide, to start over again? Fear skittered down her spine.

And now she was mated to Adrian Leonidas. Her stomach clenched at the thought, but the rest of her body loosened, heated. She shuddered, and a slow ripple of sweet desire filled her. Her cream-colored stucco house came into view, haloed by the morning sunlight, and she fled toward it as though her life depended on it. She'd just run from Trevor. Was she insane to want Adrian so much, so quickly? Nothing like this had ever happened to her before.

Matings among the werekind couldn't be undone. Not ever.

She slammed the door shut to her bungalow and slumped to the floor in the entryway. The doors had been specially designed for the resort to let shifters in their animal form get in.

Her heart raced, and her chest bellowed as if she'd sprinted a marathon instead of across the resort grounds.

She didn't think anyone had seen her. She hoped no one had. What was she going to do? She didn't know.

Shifting back into her human form—the hair retracting, her bones molding into human formations—she walked into the bathroom for a hasty shower. She had about thirty minutes until she needed to be in her office. She and her assistant both started work at seven. Stepping under the heated spray, she shivered as the water hit the mark on her collarbone. Her nipples crested as though fingers brushed over them in the lightest of caresses. Her breath caught. She'd never guessed a mated mark could be so sensitive. Heat flooded her sex, and she grew wet with want.

Adrian's face flashed through her mind, his jaw clenched, his features flushed, passion in his pale green eyes. Her pussy spasmed. She wanted him. Right now. Would he try to touch her at dinner? Could she resist something that pulled at her very soul? Should she try to get out of it?

Somehow she doubted he would tolerate it. And, unlike with Trevor, the possession in his gaze didn't scare her. It comforted her, wrapped her in a feeling of belonging. How was that even possible? The total acceptance that filled her scared her to death. She'd been with Trevor for almost a decade and had never felt this way.

What was she going to do? The question nagged at her again.

Act as if nothing was wrong, as if nothing had changed. She was desperate to keep a low profile, to regain her balance. Last night was not going to help her with that. Refuge was a world-renowned resort. The Leonidases were public figures in the were community. Mating into that family was not a way to fly under the radar.

She was doomed.

CHAPTER THREE

Adrian leaned back in his leather desk chair and pulled the file toward him. Cleo's file. Nico, as head of security, did a background check on all of their prospective employees. Most of them never knew how thorough that check was, and they didn't need to know. If they were offered a job here, they passed the check. End of story.

His intercom beeped. "Mr. Leonidas, I'm headed home for the day. Is there anything else you need?"

"No. Thank you." There was nothing anyone could do for him. This he had to do for himself.

Cleo. Her name rolled through his mind, more powerful than the most pungent alcohol. Addicting, enticing. *Mate.*

"Not a problem, sir. Have another *wonderful* night with Ms. Nemean." His secretary, Tori, chirped. As a bird-shifter, she couldn't help it, though it had taken some time for him to get used to her chipper voice and irreverent personality. Zander's mate, Lyra, thought it was good for him, and he'd long since learned when to let the woman have her way.

Adrian rolled his eyes and bit back a retort for his secretary relishing every piece of gossip about the Leonidas family. How she got her hands on the details of their affairs, he wasn't sure he wanted to know. He cleared his throat. "Have a good evening, Tori."

He had bigger issues to deal with than a nosy little bird, so he dismissed her from his mind. Cleo would meet him at the lounge in half an hour. It was where they'd been last night before they'd gone to his place. He ran the tip of his finger around the rim of his scotch. Last night. He sighed and sipped the drink.

In between conference calls about problems with a new investment he was considering and dealing with squabbling factions that fell under leopard clan leadership—his leadership—he'd managed to read her file four times today, trying to wrap his mind around the woman. He needed the facts to be prepared. When he was with her his body reacted, and his mind shut down. He wanted to know the woman's past, know everything about her. He supposed he should feel guilty for the advantage his position gave him, but he couldn't. The thought of facing her unarmed, stripped of all control, was more than he could handle. He needed to know.

The pieces were a jumble. Her parents' death dates were there, the length of her relationships, her school transcripts. He saw a dedicated student, a woman who excelled in every job she'd ever had. It had been what had made them hire her. The rest of the file, the personal details, was what disturbed him.

The number of trips to the hospital, the moving to different cities when too many emergency room visits raised questions, the fear that filled those amber eyes when he'd gotten angry this morning, lead to one simple conclusion—Cleo had been abused.

Only the fact that she'd lived in borderland cities along the Mississippi River that divided leopard and wolf lands had concealed it for so long—places where violence was more likely to erupt and one injured woman could easily fall through the cracks.

Rage made his fingers tighten on the tumbler in his grip until the glass cracked. He eased his hold before it shattered. Her ex had beaten her, hurt her. Bile rose in his throat, and his stomach heaved at the thought of her in pain and helpless. The connection he felt with her was bone deep, inescapable. It scared the shit out of him.

So, here he was, desperate to learn more, to regain his perspective. Spending the day apart from her, deliberately not seeking her out, hadn't lessened the grip of this unknown feeling in his chest.

"Trevor," he growled. The file gave the werebear's name and address. Cleo's former address. He'd already had Nico begin tracking the man down. He'd never threaten Cleo again. Whatever else happened between them, as mad as it all seemed, she was his responsibility. His mate. He swallowed.

How had she wound up with a man like that? Why hadn't her family protected her? If anyone had lifted a hand to his very pregnant sister-in-law, he would have ended the man. And if he hadn't, Nico or Zander would have.

Who had protected Cleo? No one. What kind of strength would it take to survive? To leave?

The woman was a puzzle. All he had were dry facts. He needed more. He was going to have to get the rest from her.

Anticipation punched his stomach. More. Would the need ever ease? Would it get stronger as they spent time with each other? God help him if it got stronger. He knew next to nothing of the woman, but it felt right. All of it did. He forked a hand through his hair. He felt as if he was being jerked in forty different directions. It was crazy, and he couldn't draw himself back from it. So, he had to move forward. But he wasn't giving up control for any woman.

Cleo would just have to get used to that.

Decision made, he stood, flicked the file closed, straightened his tie, left his office, walked out the front doors of the sprawling building that housed the corporate offices for Leonidas Industries and headed toward the lounge. The building had the Southwestern feel as the rest of the resort, designed to blend in and not appear to be the headquarters of an international operation. The lounge had the same Spanish-inspired architecture of the larger buildings, but none of the formality. Small, round tables filled the space between the long, gleaming wooden bar and the stage for live music.

He caught sight of Cleo already sitting at one of the tables, her body strung in a tense line. He knew the moment she smelled him, because her shoulders flexed and her chin jerked in his direction, but she didn't look at him.

Right. So that was the way she wanted to play this. Fine.

He approached the bar. "Hi, Katie."

The buxom redhead behind the curve of polished wood smiled a welcome. "Wow, two nights in a row. This is a first. To what do I owe the privilege?" Her eyes cut to Cleo, and a knowing grin kicked up the side of her mouth. "Or should I say *who?*"

He cocked a brow. "You shouldn't."

"Noted." She nodded, sobering. Katie had been with his family since her mother came to work for them as a maid. She'd never left, just moved around in their staff until she landed in the lounge. According to Zander, business had never been better than when she ran the place, and she was fiercely loyal to his family. "What can I get for you?"

"What's she drinking?" He didn't specify further. Katie knew exactly who he was talking about.

"Just seltzer water." Her smile turned wry. "Couldn't tempt her with anything else."

Cleo needed to relax, but not as relaxed as she'd been last night. No hard alcohol for either of them tonight. "Wine, then. Red."

Katie dipped behind the bar and came up with two glasses and a bottle. He hooked a finger around the neck of it and tugged it from her hand. She arched a brow, but said nothing and handed over the glasses. "I'll send someone out to take your dinner order."

"You do that." He grinned and saluted her with the wine bottle.

"Yes, sir."

Cleo's head tilted to the side as he approached. "Does everyone always obey you?"

"Yes." He hooked the chair opposite her with his foot and sat down. Setting the glasses on the table, he poured them each a generous serving. "Have you had a chance to look at the menu?"

"I have it memorized."

He glanced up to meet her eyes. "Oh?"

"I'm in public relations. I make it my business to know everything about Refuge that the public might ask. I don't like to be caught off guard." One slim shoulder lifted in a shrug.

"Nor I." He sipped his wine and just let himself look at her. A tailored blue pinstriped pantsuit did nothing to hide her lush body. He wanted to strip her and bury himself in her sweet, hot pussy until she screamed out her release. As she had last night, her desires calling to his. "I wonder what else we have in common, my mate."

She hissed out a breath. "Do you have to say that quite so loudly?"

"It's a fact, Cleo. This isn't open to interpretation." And he wouldn't let her hide from it. They needed to deal with this head on. There was no pretending it hadn't happened. And he sure as hell wouldn't let her deny the connection between them. He forced himself to grin. "Mate in haste, repent at leisure."

Taking a gulp of her wine, she waited a moment before speaking. "We don't even know each other."

"I imagine time will take care of that for us."

A waiter approached and took their order. Adrian topped off their wine glasses before he sat back. Perhaps if he appeared at ease, she would follow suit.

She pulled in a deep breath and picked up the conversation where they'd left off. "We could hate each other."

"I doubt that. And we can get to know each other tonight and tomorrow night. Neither of us is going anywhere." He leaned forward, bracing his forearm on the table. "Tell me, do you want children?"

She blanched, all the blood draining from her face. "I—I always thought so."

"What happened?" Something was there. A sore spot for her. Could she have children? He'd never contemplated having them, but it seemed a good place to start the personal questions. Wasn't that something mates should know about each other?

Her eyes went blank. "I miscarried a baby. Not long ago."

"I'm sorry." His gaze met hers. "Are you all right?"

"Fine." She moved as though to rise.

He snapped a hand out to close around her wrist. She sucked in a breath at the contact, and an electric shock went running through him. Her amber eyes softened, heated. Her breasts lifted with each slow breath, and her gaze stayed locked with his. She licked her lips, and his gaze dropped to watch the sensuous movement. The moment stretched, heavy with meaning. "Stay," he said softly.

The waiter set their plates in front of them, and Adrian nodded to dismiss him. He faded away and left them to their meal.

"Eat." She settled in her chair and obeyed. They ate in silence, and her tension seemed to ease by degrees when he asked no more questions. Watching her was a visceral pleasure. His teeth ground every time her full lips closed over her fork. He could picture those lips wrapped around his stroking cock. He'd like to fist his fingers in her silky hair. Her tongue flicked out to catch a stray drop of wine, and he barely contained a groan. His dick rose hard and full in his slacks, rubbing against his fly. He shifted in the seat, trying to ease the strain. Jesus, the woman was going to kill him.

When her gaze flicked up to meet his, she flushed and glanced away. She swallowed, her hands shaking as she reached for her wine glass. "You're staring."

Her scent filled his nose, intoxicating. She was turned on. He could smell her desire. He wanted to taste it too, feel her come against his mouth. "And you like it."

"Yes," she whispered. Her scent intensified, and he growled low in his throat.

"Are you finished with dinner?" Standing, he stepped away from the table.

She rose, but glanced at his plate. "You haven't eaten much."

He let his desire show in his eyes as he swept his gaze down her body, zeroing in on her hard nipples outlined by her blouse. "I wasn't hungry…for food."

She closed her eyes and pulled in a ragged breath. "Adrian, I—"

His hand closed over her elbow, savoring the delicate feel of her bones beneath his fingers. "Let's go."

"Where?" She followed along beside him, taking two steps for every one of his. He checked his stride to allow her to keep up.

"I'm going to walk you to your bungalow."

"Oh. Okay." Her voice sounded dazed, and need pumped in his veins as her scent surrounded him, aroused him. The darkness of night had settled over the resort while they'd eaten, but he could see just as well in the dark as the light. Better, usually. When they mounted the steps to her porch, he spun her to press her back to the door and lifted her chin until she met his gaze.

"I'm not going to fuck you, angel. You said we should get to know each other better. Let's start here." She needed to know he could maintain control. After what he suspected Trevor had done to her, she needed to know she could trust him never to hurt her. He had to keep himself in check. Last night's slip was caused by too much alcohol, nothing more.

He lifted his hand and sifted it through her golden hair. So soft and silky. His thumb stroked along her jaw. She swallowed and closed her eyes. He dipped forward to kiss her, his mouth settling over hers. His movements were a gentle caress, his tongue moving along her bottom lip before slipping inside to taste her. So good. She tasted as sweet as he remembered. She moaned, the sound filling his mouth. Heat flooded his veins, drove him wild. He cursed softly and started to step back when her fingers clenched on his lapels, pulling him back to her.

"More, Adrian." He watched the rise and fall of her breasts as she panted for breath. She arched, pressed herself firmly to him, and rubbed her stiff nipples over his chest. "Please."

Groaning, he complied. He swooped down to capture her mouth once more, his palm lifting to cup the weight of her breast. His cock ground against the soft juncture of her thighs.

She whimpered and tried to climb him. A wildfire blazed in his blood, her hot, wet scent spurring him on. He gripped her rounded hips in his hands, pulled her up to brace her against the door. Her legs wrapped around his waist, and she moved on him through their pants.

Their mouths mated with each other in rough abandon, nipping, sucking. It felt so amazing. A few more minutes and he would come in his trousers. A few more minutes and he'd take her right here on the porch, breaking his promise to her.

Damn it.

"Stop, Cleo." He tugged her legs down, and let her slide down his body. They both groaned. He made himself let go, but had to grip both sides of the doorframe to stop from reaching for her. "Go inside."

Confusion and lust spun together in her hooded amber eyes. She swayed toward him. "But—"

"*Go.* I'm hanging on by a thread here, angel. I said I wasn't going to fuck you, and I meant it." She turned, fumbling with the latch until the door opened. He winced when it shut in his face. Still he didn't move for long moments as the blood rushed through his veins. His hands fisted, and he ran his tongue down one of his protruding fangs. Lust tangled in a tight knot inside him, and he forced his feet to turn for his house. He stopped on the wide patio outside, not wanting to go in alone. Her scent would be there, on his bed, in his bathroom. Her clothes would still be dumped on his living room floor where she'd left them this morning.

No. He stripped down, shifting into his leopard form as he did. He needed to go for a run before he could face a night in his bed without Cleo. One night he'd had with her, and already he didn't want to sleep without her. Racing for the underbrush of the desert that surrounded the resort, he let his tan and black spotted paws stretch in front of him and ran without aim or purpose, just with the burning need to leave his troubles behind for a moment, clear his head so he could *think*.

How the hell was he going to deal with this? It was unacceptable. How was she doing this to him? He barely knew her, and she laid him out. She was under his skin, and he needed to figure out what to do about that before he touched her again.

Too much was up in the air. Too much uncertainty. He didn't like it. As much as he wanted to possess her, this *thing* between them possessed him just as fiercely. He was skating dangerously close to losing control of himself.

He forced himself to picture the ragged agony on Jason's face when he'd been told his mate had died. Adrian didn't want that. He never wanted to give so much of himself to a woman that he couldn't function without her. Not even Cleo. *Never*.

So close. Leaning her forehead against the closed door, Cleo gripped the doorknob so hard it shook. She'd almost had sex with him, and her body wept juices that showed how very ready it was for more of Adrian's possession. If he hadn't stopped them, they *would* have had sex.

Damn him.

But she knew sleeping with him would only make it worse for both of them when she had to run. Dread skittered over her nerves, stretched them tight. What would Adrian do when he found out exactly what kind of mess he'd mated himself to? She shuddered at the thought of his anger. She couldn't blame him. She would be angry in his position.

And what if Trevor tried to hurt Adrian? She knew from experience just how dangerous the werebear was when he was provoked. And even when he wasn't. The thought of Adrian hurt sent horror spinning through her. No. She couldn't let that happen. He was too important, too vital. She didn't want to examine why, but she knew it was true.

She had to leave before this went any further. She ignored the fact that they were already mated. That wouldn't stop Trevor. It would probably make it worse for everyone.

Oh, God. *Calm down*.

She forced herself to pull in a deep breath and think clearly. What she smelled sent her panic spiraling into terror.

Trevor. Here. In her house.

But, no. Even he couldn't have found her so fast, could he?

She took another deep breath. There was no denying the sour, musky stench of werebear. One specific werebear. She'd know his stink anywhere.

The last of the sweetness of being with Adrian tonight drained away.

Trevor had found her. It didn't matter how little time it had taken him. She had to run. There were no other options.

She froze, waiting for the slightest noise to tell her if he was still here. His scent was fading as though he'd come and gone. But he could be outside waiting for her. It would be just like him to lay in wait and savor her panic.

He was toying with her. Anger and fear flashed through her, but she shoved them back. This wasn't the time. She had to think, had to get out of here before he caught her. Before Adrian got caught in the crossfire.

Walking forward on shaking legs, she stepped on broken glass. It crunched under her shoes. Her eyes swept over the room. Even in the weak light coming from her kitchen she could see the place had been violated, ransacked. The furniture was shredded by bear claws, the mirrors and knickknacks that had come with the place crushed beyond recognition. She stepped into her bedroom. More destruction, this time including her clothes, make-up. Everything she owned.

She fished her cell phone out of her purse and punched in a number she'd programmed into speed dial the day she'd arrived. "Hello. I'd like to order a cab, please." She forced her voice into calm as she gave them her address. Forty minutes. More than enough time to do what she needed to do.

The floorboard of the hall closet lifted. Inside was her stash of cash, a small backpack with clothes and toiletries, and a wig she'd put on after she left. Her heart pounded, and sweat slicked her palms, but she made herself sit and wait for the cab. Made herself *not* call Adrian.

She would walk away clean, no excuses or explanations. There was nothing she could say that would make him understand. She didn't see him as the kind of man who would let his woman leave him, no matter how short their acquaintance. And she didn't see him as the kind of man to forgive. Once she left here, it was done.

Finished. If she had any regrets on that score, she'd just have to tell herself that sacrificing Adrian meant he'd be safe.

She'd already failed her child—she wouldn't survive failing her mate too.

Gravel crunched under wheels as headlights flashed in front of her windows. She peeked out the window to see if it was, indeed, the cab she'd called. She took a deep breath and heaved a small sigh of relief when she didn't smell Trevor anywhere nearby. Jerking the door open, she sprinted for the cab, slid in, and locked her door behind her. "The airport. Now."

A wizened old man glanced in the rearview at her as he sped away from her bungalow. "Yes, ma'am. You late for a flight?"

"Something like that. Please hurry." She twisted in her seat, watching as Refuge faded into the night. The darkness began to obscure her view, but she stayed that way, gazing out the back window until they turned onto the highway.

Her heart stumbled in a painful, broken beat. *Adrian.* God, she hoped this kept him safe. Pinching her eyes closed, she prayed harder than she ever had in her life. She swallowed back tears. Please let him be safe.

CHAPTER FOUR

Two weeks had passed since she'd run from Trevor. From Refuge. From Adrian. Her soul cried out for him, twisting her on the sheets of cheap motels night after night. She couldn't sleep, couldn't rest. When she did, she dreamed of him, wanted him. She'd bounced all over the southwest on buses and planes, wherever her cash could take her. Santa Fe, Phoenix, and now Las Vegas.

And Trevor had found her. Again. She knew he would. She'd made herself easy to track this time, hoping to lure him away from Refuge. It worked. And now that she knew he'd followed, she needed to shake him loose. She just hoped she could. No more hiding among the werekind. She'd have to make her way with humans. Only then might she have a chance.

He was waiting for her outside her hotel. She could smell him. Her heart hammered in her chest, and sweat dampened the back of her shirt. She pulled her pack over her back and tightened the straps. Creeping down the back stairs, she slipped into the kitchen. Smiling at the staff, she walked fast enough that no one bothered to question her. After she opened the backdoor, she peeked out to look both ways to see if Trevor was out there. With the constant traffic on The Strip, she'd go farther, faster on foot.

Darting out of the door, she jogged down to the end of the alley. Rain—so unusual for Las Vegas—fell in a steady downpour and had for hours. She was soaked within a few minutes. She peered around the corner…and she saw Trevor. He stood at the back entrance of the hotel, waiting for her. And he'd seen her. Spinning around, she sprinted down the alley to the front of the hotel and out onto the sidewalk.

The deep roar of an angry bear split the loud sounds of city. It spurred her to new speed. She desperately wished she could shift into lion form, go faster. *Faster.* She needed to run faster. Her heartbeat jack-hammered. Sweat slid down her face with raindrops to sting her eyes. She didn't bother to wipe it away, just ran. Glancing back, she caught a glimpse of Trevor's face, mottled red with fury. Her feet slapped down harder on the wet pavement as she sprinted.

She turned a corner and slammed into a broad chest. A familiar broad chest. Adrian. Tears welled in her eyes—she was so relieved to see him. But, oh holy Jesus, Trevor was right behind her. "We have to get out of—"

Her words trailed off when she actually looked at him. Oh, shit. Out of the frying pan, into the fire. His jaw flexed as he gazed down at her, silent rage darkening his face. He glanced over her shoulder, then back down at her. A hard hand closed over her upper arm. She jerked back, and his grip tightened. "Get in the car, Cleo."

"You don't understand."

"Get. In. The. Car. Cleo."

She swallowed, turned, and climbed into the passenger seat of a sleek black BMW. Her door locked, and she had a feeling if she tried, she wouldn't be able to get out. He wasn't letting her escape.

Bastard. But her panic had receded. As angry as he was, she didn't think he was angry enough to hurt her. Not like Trevor would if he caught her. Of the two, she'd rather deal with Adrian.

He loped around the car, popped his door open, and slid behind the wheel. The car purred to life, spinning away from the curb. She craned her neck to see behind them, searching for Trevor through the rain-blurred windows. "Where are we going?"

He ignored the question. "You're not very good at running, Cleo."

"Well, I went to college, not spy school." *Asshole.* Her fists clenched in her lap, but she kept that sentiment to herself. "Where are we going?"

"Somewhere safe. Don't worry."

"The hell you say. I'm worried. That man—" She jerked her thumb over her shoulder. "That man will kill me without blinking. He's spent weeks hunting me down, and he's not going to give up. And since he got past the world-renowned security of your resort, you'll forgive me if I have to question your definition of *safe.*" Her chest heaved as the words rushed out.

He snorted. "Are you done?"

"Fuck. *You.*" Rage exploded in her veins, and she felt her fangs slide out before she hissed at him.

His fingers stroked down the wheel, and he didn't even bother to look at her. "I believe that's what got me into this mess."

Hurt slammed into her, hitting her like a hard slap across the face. She gasped at the harshness of his words. They were true—she knew they were. But coming from her mate, they clawed at her soul. Her mouth snapped shut, and all the fight drained out of her. She looked out the passenger side window as the Las Vegas Strip sped past in a blur of neon lights.

"I'm sorry. I would never have dragged anyone into this on purpose. I hope you believe that, if nothing else."

He cleared his throat. She could feel his gaze on her, but she refused to look. What more could she say? She had no excuses. Alcohol soaked bad judgment wasn't good enough for putting someone's life in danger. She closed her eyes and rested her forehead against the glass. All the weeks—years, if she were honest with herself—of fear and tension caught up with her, rolling over her in a wave of exhaustion. It was hopeless. She'd never escape Trevor. She was a failure at hiding.

A warm, strong hand wrapped around hers, tugging it from her lap. She twisted in her seat to look at Adrian. He lifted her hand to his lips and pressed a soft kiss to her fingers. "Forgive me, angel. I shouldn't have snapped at you."

She blinked at him, surprise darting through her. He didn't seem the kind of man who even knew what an apology was, let alone how to offer one gracefully.

"I'll keep you safe, Cleo. No matter what, we're in this together." He slanted her a quick glance out of those icy green eyes before focusing on the road.

"You shouldn't have to be stuck with me. No one should. You can still walk away."

He arched a brow that clearly meant to question her sanity. "We're mated. I can't walk away from you."

She closed her eyes, her shoulders sagging in defeat. "I'm so sorry."

"I'm not."

"What?"

He heaved a sigh and ignored her question again. "We're going to a house out by Lake Mead my family owns. It's where we used to go during summers when I was growing up to escape and have some down time."

"A retreat from everyone else's retreat?" She lifted her eyebrows.

"Yeah. The resort is our business—one of many—but not our vacation."

"I understand." She let herself smile. "I love it there, though. Refuge."

"Good, because you'll be spending the rest of your life there. Except when we're on vacation."

"Adrian . . ." Wariness slid over her. She wasn't even sure enough to plan for the next day, let alone the rest of her life. She just wanted to survive long enough to die of old age. That wasn't too much to ask, was it? "I don't—"

"I do. We're mated, we're going to get through this, and then we'll figure the rest out." He slid his thumb in soothing circles over her palm, and she relaxed into the soft leather seat, while the car's heater wrapped her in warmth.

She blinked slowly. When was the last time she'd slept? She shook her head, trying to force herself back to wakefulness.

"I'll keep you safe, Cleo. I swear it."

She shouldn't believe him. She barely knew him. Maybe it was the mating that made her want to trust implicitly, no questions or doubts. But she *felt* safe for the first time in forever, her fingers cradled in his strong hand, his big body radiating assurance. She was desperate for that, for some small chance at hope. She couldn't do this alone anymore. She was always alone. A wave of self-pity washed over her, and she couldn't seem to push it back as she usually did. She pressed her lips together to keep from crying.

He continued to rub his thumb across her hand. "Just relax now. Nothing will happen to you while I'm here. Try to sleep."

It didn't seem she had a choice. She obeyed the soft command. She wanted to believe him. She wanted to matter to someone besides the obsessed Trevor. She wanted to be safe. Just for a little while, she assured herself. For a little while she'd take advantage of what he offered before she ran once more. It was selfish and stupid, but she needed him. Adrian.

"Sleep," he said again. Her body relaxed bonelessly into the heated seats and within moments the world had faded to nothing but the soothing swish of windshield wipers and the rocking of the car. Safe, protected, cherished.

Fury pumped through Adrian's veins as he watched Cleo curl up in obvious exhaustion. Dark shadows smudged her eyes. What had she been through these past weeks? His jaw clenched as he fought the urge to shake her for running from Refuge. It was done now, and he had her back. His younger brothers were meeting them at the lake house, and he suspected Trevor wouldn't be far behind. A nasty smile curved his lips. Nico took his job as the family's security expert seriously, and he was damn good at his work. And severely pissed at the slip that had allowed Trevor to get in—Nico angry was enough to chill the blood.

Adrian took a circuitous route to the lake, just complicated enough that it should take Trevor a day or more to track them, but not too difficult that he wouldn't be able to find them. And then he could face whatever Nico had planned for him. Adrian didn't trust himself to deal with the man, and he had enough to handle with his runaway mate.

Still holding her hand in his, he sucked in a deep breath and caught Cleo's sweet smell. Some small pressure let loose in his chest. More than the blind rage he'd felt when he found out she ran was the terror he couldn't stop. Zander was the one who'd told him, and he'd seen her trashed bungalow. A cold chill ran over his skin at the memory. Trevor could have killed her, kidnapped her, and Adrian couldn't have stopped it. He would never allow that to happen again. Never.

Whether he liked it or not, wanted it or not, she was vital to him. And he'd damn sure keep her safe. No more running. He pulled in another breath, waiting for the reality of her safety to sink in. Nico had tracked down the cab company she'd used, and they'd been following her ever since. And following Trevor while he tracked her.

He turned the car down the long gravel drive that led to the lake house, the bumpy ride waking Cleo up. She jolted up right, startled to wake in an unfamiliar place. Panic flashed over her face. He squeezed her hand tight. "We're almost there, angel. Everything is fine."

She pushed the soft fall of her hair out of her eyes and glanced around just as they broke into the clearing in front of the lake. "It's beautiful."

"It is at that." He peered up at the house through the windshield and pulled the car up to the front to park. The big place had been built just before he was born and looked like a classic hacienda surrounded by palm trees.

He'd had the house stocked with enough dry goods that they'd be comfortable, but not so much that it was obvious to Cleo that he'd planned this. He was positive she would never agree to him using them as bait or waiting for Trevor to come to them. She'd gone to a lot of trouble to get away from the werebear and, if Adrian had his way, she'd never have to see the man again. If Nico and Zander's plan worked out, Cleo might not ever know that they were bait. And that would be just fine for Adrian.

"Stay here and let me check things out."

"You don't think—"

"No. But I won't take a risk with you." He took her chin in his hand and pressed a fast, hard kiss to her lips. Damn, but he wanted more. That little taste wasn't nearly enough. Later, he promised himself. Later he would have her. Over and over until he burned off the fear that had sat like an anvil on his chest for the past two weeks.

Grabbing an umbrella from the backseat, he handed it to Cleo. Flipping his collar up, he tugged his own overnight bag from behind the passenger seat, popped open the door, and jogged to the house. His key slid into the lock, and the knob turned in his hand. He took a breath and found only the musty scent of age, and the newer smell of himself. He hoped Cleo couldn't tell the difference between the scent of him here yesterday to drop off supplies and the scent of him here now. He made a quick tour of the house to spread his smell everywhere.

Then he stepped out onto the porch and waved her in. She hopped out of the car, opened the umbrella, and hurried up the steps. He wrapped her in his arms, wanting the feel of her soft curves against him. She laid her cheek on his chest. "How far are we from other people? I smell others."

"Not too far. There are cabins nearby, people who live here year round." And a team of security experts who were patrolling behind the scrub brush and rocky hills to try and catch Trevor, but he kept that information to himself.

He pushed her into the house and shut the door firmly behind him. She dropped her bag beside the door and went exploring. He watched the slow sway of her hips as he followed her into his old bedroom. His cock hardened, straining the fly of his jeans. That bed needed to be put to good use. He'd have to check in with their security detail after nightfall, which was soon, thank God. And then she was his. All night.

Anticipation clenched his gut. He'd missed her so much. It was insane, and he didn't give a good damn at this point. He'd had two weeks of hell to know that he wouldn't let her leave his side for the rest of her life. And he intended to see that it was a long, long life.

She looked back over her shoulder at him, the heat building in his body reflecting in her eyes. That was all it took. He reached for her. To hell with it, he wasn't willing to wait. He had to have her now. She made a small noise and spun into his arms. Then her tongue was in his mouth and his hands were buried in her soft, soft hair. He backed her up against the nearest wall, and they both groaned when their bodies made full contact, her sweet curves fitting to his harder angles. Need made his dick ache. It had been so long since he'd fucked her. *Weeks.*

Shoving his leg between hers, his forced her to spread for him. Her hips rocked, grinding herself against his thigh. He flexed the muscles, and she whimpered into his mouth. He thrust his tongue between her lips to a rhythm that matched the movements of their bodies. She twisted to get closer. Her fingers balled in his shirt as she worked her pelvis faster and faster.

She broke her lips from his and her head fell back against the wall. "Hurry. I want you inside me, Adrian."

The words made every coherent thought slip from his mind. "Yes. Right now. Yes."

Fire licked over his skin as he wrestled with her zipper. He popped the button and jerked her pants open, shoving them to the floor so she could step out of them and her shoes. He laid his palm against her belly, sliding his fingers down into the soaking curls between her legs, stroking over her hard little clit. He dipped into her heated pussy, filling her with one, two, three digits.

She cried out, her movements becoming frantic as she reached for his belt. In moments his throbbing cock was in her stroking fingers. He hissed. That felt *too* good. If she didn't stop he was going to come before he ever got inside her. Damn, he needed to regain control of this situation. He pulled her hand away, freeing himself from her grip.

"Adrian, please." She panted for breath, her pupils dilating with desire. The musky scent of her need was heady.

He bracketed her waist with his hands, lifting her against the smooth wall. Cupping his palms under her thighs, he held her in place. She snapped her legs around his waist and arched her body in offering. The head of his cock rubbed against her hot, damp lips. Sinking into her until he could go no further, he had to clench his jaw to keep from groaning at the exquisite agony of finally joining with her again. Her wet channel gripped him in little spasms.

He heard a sob catch in her chest, and a single tear slid down her cheek. "So long. It's been so long."

"My mate." He kissed the tear away, but he couldn't find it in him to be gentle. Not this time. Later…much later, he could savor her slowly. Later he would make her swear never to be parted from him again. Now, he needed this carnal connection with her. He jerked her thighs wide so he could thrust deeper and began a hard, punishing rhythm that drove them both to the edge in moments. God, it was so good with her.

Whimpering little cries poured from her mouth each time he filled her. He pushed himself to go harder, faster. More…he always craved more with her. Sweat formed on his forehead and back, sealing his shirt to his body. His muscles tightened as he hammered his cock into her slick pussy. The fire inside him reached a flashpoint, and he held on to his control by a thread. He buried his face in her neck and bit deep into the soft flesh there.

"*Adrian.*" She screamed, convulsing in his arms. Her pussy fisted tight around his cock, and it was more than enough to send orgasm running through him. He closed his eyes tight and jetted into her damp sex, emptying all the fear and pain of the last few weeks into her.

"Cleo," he breathed her name. Everything else he thought or felt or needed to say tangled inside him. "Cleo."

They stayed where they were for a long time, his cock filling her, his mouth sucking lightly at the bite he'd left on her neck. She shivered and pushed at his shoulders until he released her. He watched her gather up her jeans and slide them back on. It was a damn shame to watch her cover all that pretty skin, but it just meant he could strip her again later. The thought almost made him purr.

She finished fastening her jeans, and her stomach gurgled loud enough for him to hear it. He chuckled.

"Built up an appetite, huh?" A satiated smile tugged at his lips.

She blushed and slapped a hand over her flat belly. She'd lost weight in the last two weeks, he noted. Just like that, the sweet afterglow of orgasm vanished. It made him angry all over again, knowing that she'd suffered even that small amount. He bit back a snarl as harsh reality returned with a sharp snap.

"Follow me." He spun on a heel and led the way into the kitchen. He pulled soup out of the pantry, opened the cans, and dumped it into a pot on the stove. "Should be done in a few minutes."

She sat on one of the stools at the kitchen island and eyed him warily. "So…are we going to talk about it?"

Neither of them needed to specify which *it* she was talking about. Her leaving him. The rage lingering like a bitter taste on his tongue. He clenched his fists tight. He opened his mouth and then snapped it closed. "No. No, we're not. I'm pissed as hell at you, and anything I say will only make it worse. So let's get you fed and then go twelve rounds about how *stupid* it was for you to run."

"You don't understand what he's like."

He arched an eyebrow. "You think that makes this all right?"

"No."

"Good." He turned and grabbed some bowls from a cupboard, rinsing them out in the sink before dishing them up a generous helping of soup. They ate in silence, and she constantly glanced up at him.

He swung wildly between wanting to shake her for running and wanting to bend her over the island and claim her until she knew she was *his* and could never leave him again. He was already uncomfortably hard…taking her once hadn't been enough, would never *be* enough.

She pushed back her empty bowl and met his gaze. "Okay, I'm fed. Let me have it."

He chuckled. She was the perfect woman for him. He was never letting her go. Ever.

"I know about Trevor. I know he used to beat you. I'm guessing he had something to do with the baby you lost, and I cannot believe that you'd be foolish enough to throw yourself in his path *alone* by running. You should have come to me, damn it. I would have taken care of you."

"I can take care of myself. But, you know, it's funny. Trevor used to say the exact same thing to me." Her amber eyes narrowed to dangerous slits.

A low snarl ripped from his throat, and his hand slapped down on the countertop. "Do not ever compare me to him. I would never hurt you."

"I know." She didn't flinch away from him, even though he was bigger than her, stronger than her and obviously angry.

Good. She was learning to trust him. As she should.

Still, he tilted his head and asked, "Do you?"

She sucked in a breath, but never looked away from him. "Yes. I know not every man is like my ex. My father wasn't."

He let the comment about her ex go for the moment and latched on to the information about her family. "Tell me about him."

"Who?" Confusion shone in her eyes, and she looked at him for a few moments, obviously trying to determine what his angle was.

He smiled to throw her off even further. "Your father. Your family. Tell me about them. How the hell did they let you end up with Trevor?"

"They didn't." She shrugged and looked down at her folded hands on the counter.

"No?"

She shook her head. "My parents were both only children, and we were never close to the rest of their families. So…it was just the three of us. They died my freshman year of college in a horrible car accident. A ten-car pileup with a semi hauling gasoline. It exploded. No one survived."

"And Trevor?" How had someone like her, beautiful, smart, and sweet, ended up with an asshole who abused her? His hands fisted at the thought.

She sighed. "He was a mistake. I thought he was like my father. But Trevor was a selfish bastard. My dad was just a dominant man—he would never have done the things to my mom or me that Trevor did. That I knew he would do to my child. My dad would have died to protect his family, would have done anything to make us happy. And we knew it. We *always* knew he loved us." Tears welled up in her eyes when she looked up at him, and it ripped his heart out. "It's just…when they died I was so lost, so *lonely*. I would have sold my soul to have someone care." She choked on a sob. "Isn't that pathetic?"

"Not pathetic." His voice came out as a gritty rasp. His hand actually shook when he reached to push her hair back from her face. "I'm sorry, my mate. Sorry for what you went through. Sorry I didn't know you then, and sorry I couldn't save you. But I can promise you this—I am nothing like Trevor, and you'll never be alone again."

He opened his arms, and she dove for him, wrapping her arms tight around his waist. He breathed in her scent, savored the softness of her hair under his chin. He closed his eyes and just held her.

She snuffled against his T-shirt. "Don't let go. Just—just for a little while."

"For as long as you need." For the rest of her life.

His. All his.

He sat back on his stool and pulled her into his lap. She curled against him and cried. It killed him a little, every one of her sobs stabbing into his chest. He hugged her tighter, helpless to do anything to erase the horror she had known.

Her sobs quieted to low hiccups. He stroked her hair, ran his fingers through the silken locks, and massaged the back of her neck.

She sighed and purred softly in pleasure. "Thank you."

"Any time." But night had fallen while they sat in the kitchen. *Damn it.* He hated to leave her alone even for a few minutes, but he needed to check in with Nico, make sure everything was going smoothly, and that Trevor hadn't shown yet. It should be at least another day before he did, but Adrian wasn't willing to take that chance. Not that Cleo would really be alone. There was a security team surrounding the house, camping out in the brush.

"I need to make a run around the property. Just to make sure everything is safe for the night. Will you be all right by yourself?"

She tensed, and the fear came back into her face. He cursed himself for putting it there, but he didn't have a choice. Nico and Zander wouldn't hesitate to come in, guns blazing, if he didn't keep to their schedule. They'd assume something was wrong. She gave a tight nod.

"Hurry. The storm is getting worse."

He stroked his thumb over her cheekbone. "A little rain never hurt anybody, angel. I'm locking the door behind me. *Do not* open it for any reason. I'll be back in a few minutes. Don't worry."

CHAPTER FIVE

Lightning streaked across the night sky and rain poured down in pounding torrents. This was freakish weather for Nevada. Cleo paced in front of the window. Where was he? Adrian had been gone for fifteen minutes already. Anxiety knotted her belly. Where was he?

Fifteen minutes wasn't that long, was it? Her hands trembled as she shoved them through her hair and gripped the long strands. Another jolt of terror shot through her. God, he mattered too much to her. Already. She wanted to blame it on the automatic connection of mating, but she couldn't. It was everything. The sex, the way he came after her and refused to let her disappear into oblivion, the way he protected her, the gruff way he cared. She was brutally honest with herself, didn't allow her to cop out of what her heart knew.

She was in love with him. Her chest tightened, and tears pricked at her eyes. It was the worst possible timing, but she couldn't deny it. Not what he meant to her and not her own feelings. The wonder of it wrapped her in sweet warmth.

What she wouldn't give to survive this and have fifty years with him—her mate. Her body had known him the moment they'd met in the bar. He was meant to be hers, and she was his.

Yes.

But being with her was going to get him killed. Her stomach turned, and a tear slid down her cheek.

Hopeless. It was all so hopeless.

She wanted to stay with him forever, but it could be a death sentence for him. And she didn't think she could survive losing him that way. But what could she do? He'd already found her once. And the hours since had only drawn them closer, made the connection deeper. He'd find her, no matter where she ran. And Trevor would be right on his heels. She pressed shaking fingers to her eyes.

She loved Adrian so much. The sweet pain of it flooded her. Sucking in a deep breath, his scent filled her nose. Adrian. She ran the few steps to the door and threw it open.

The tawny and black spotted leopard materialized from the dark. He shook his coat off on the porch and walked in. Predatory grace reflected in his every movement, and his eyes tracked her like succulent prey. His body stretched and flowed as he shifted back into his human form. His naked human form. His cock curved up in a long, thick erection.

"I told you not to open the door."

Eyes locked on his cock, she shut the door and felt coherent thought spinning out of her grasp. "I knew it was you. I could smell you."

"Look at me." Her gaze snapped up to his face, and a flush heated her cheeks. A slow, hot smile curved his lips and lit his pale green eyes as he leaned back on the dining room table. His arms folded across his wide, muscular chest. "I told you not to open the door."

She swallowed, excitement exploding in her veins. Her body ached with a need so deep it made her shake. Fucking him earlier hadn't even begun to take the edge off of the weeks without him. "I—"

"Come here." His voice purred in a guttural order.

Her heart hammered so loud she could hear it. Wetness slicked the lips of her pussy, and she squeezed her thighs together to ease the burn between them. "I don't—"

"Now, Cleo. Come here."

Her legs shook as she stepped toward him.

He didn't move from his relaxed stance against the table. "Strip."

What would he do to her? She wasn't afraid of him. She knew deep in her bones that he would never harm her. Anticipation of whatever he had planned to pleasure her with hummed through her. She shimmied out of her jeans. Her fingers shook as she slipped the buttons from her shirt. Shrugging, she let it drop to the floor. She wasn't wearing a bra, and Adrian's eyes flared at the sight of her naked breasts. Her nipples hardened almost painfully.

She grinned and repeated his words back to him from their first time together. "See something you like?" Had it only been two weeks ago? So much had happened since then.

He straightened, his arms dropping to his sides. He nodded to where he'd been leaning. "Bend over the table."

Shock stopped her breath, and her eyes widened. Excitement twisted inside her like a wild thing. "W-what?"

"Trust me." A wicked grin pulled at his lips. "Bend over the table."

Her breath heaved out in torturous pants, and eagerness hummed in her blood. Oh, God. Her knees felt liquefied, as if they couldn't hold her weight. She set her palms on the table to brace herself so she wouldn't fall. She squeezed her eyes closed when she felt his heat wrap around her. He was right behind her, but not touching her. Her pussy clenched on nothingness, aching to be filled by his thick cock.

One of his fingertips grazed her ass cheek, and she jerked in response. More. She needed *more*. Still he only touched her with the one finger, letting her know that he was in control of her pleasure. And his. He dipped between her legs, stroking over her swollen sex, her hard clit. "I love the feel of you, Cleo. Hot and wet for me."

"Yes," she said on a soft breath. God, she needed him. That one finger was driving her mad. "Please, Adrian. I want more."

"No." He withdrew his finger from her pussy and teased the insides of her spread thighs. She choked on the want clawing within her. "You'll never run from me again, Cleo. You're my mate. Mine. Do you understand me?"

Her heart clenched at the quiet possession in his voice. Her breath shuddered out in quick gasps, and she fought to focus, to think. "I did what I thought was right."

"What's right is us staying together. We're *mates*. I can't protect you if you run off." A leopard's hiss filled the room. He stepped close to her, the head of his cock brushing the lips of her sex.

His hand settled on the small of her back, arching her as he slid all the way into her soaking pussy. Her eyes closed as the love she'd so recently acknowledged and the burning need for him these past weeks coalesced into something sharp and painful. "Adrian."

"Say that you're mine, Cleo. My mate. Always. Mine." He pulled out of her until the bulbous ridge of his dick caught on the edge of her pussy. Then he slammed back in. Hard and fast.

"Oh, God. Adrian." A moan tore from her. He set a deep, pounding rhythm that took her right up to the edge of orgasm, but didn't push her over. She twisted in his arms, but the way his hips shoved her against the table caged her movements. He worked inside her, pushing her closer and closer. Taunting her with the glimmer of release.

He covered her hands with his, pinning her down, surrounding her, dominating her. She couldn't escape him. *Oh, yes.*

He growled in her ear as he bent close. "Never leave me again, Cleo."

"I won't." She bowed her back and tried to push her hips back, tried to take him deeper, faster. *Something.* Anything to push her over the edge. She needed it, needed him, needed the surcease that only he could grant her. Her mate.

"Swear it." He shoved all the way into her. And stopped.

A cry ripped from her throat. He couldn't deny her now. Desperation slammed into her. She was so close. So very close. One more thrust of his hard dick and she would come. Her claws slid out to rake the table, the lioness within fighting for supremacy. She opened her mouth and hissed before she gave him what he wanted. *Anything* to make him move. "I swear. I'll never leave you. I'm yours. Yours, yours, *yours.*"

Turning her head, she bit his arm. Hard. He roared, his hands clenching around hers as he pounded forth inside her. She orgasmed, her pussy tightening in rippling waves. She threw her head back, and an animalistic scream erupted from her. Still he thrust deep, and deeper still. She was so full, and he was so big, that she came once more. Starbursts exploded behind her lids as he went wild on her, in her. Yes. She loved this—him working in her almost to the point of pain, where she skated the very edge of agony and ecstasy. "Yes. Adrian. *Yes.*"

"*Cleo.*"

She collapsed on the smooth wood of the tabletop, tears leaking from the corners of her eyes. Aftershocks of orgasm still ripped through her system. A soft sob escaped from her throat.

Adrian's hands went around her, his fingers pushing her hair back, running over her body. "I—I'm sorry. Don't cry. Please. Did I hurt you, angel? I just…lost it and—"

A watery chuckle slipped free. She turned in his arms to cup his handsome face. He looked so panic-stricken. She shouldn't enjoy it, but it was nice to see him not so in control for once. It made her feel better, as if they were on the same level in this crazy situation that fate and a bottle of Jack Daniels had thrown them into together. "I liked it. I like that you're not always in control. That I can push you into losing it. In fact, I love it. Let's do it again."

She tugged him down for a kiss, standing on tiptoes to get closer. After a long moment of his mouth playing over hers in a dance of lips and teeth and tongues, he stepped away and blinked down at her. "Whatever makes you happy, angel."

"It does." *You do.* She didn't say it out loud, but it was there in every stroke of her fingers, every caress as she pulled him back to her. *I love you. Don't leave me. Be safe. I need you forever. I love you.*

Hours later they lay curled together on the couch. She was sprawled across his chest, panting from another round of sex. The man was insatiable. And that was just fine with her. Yawning, she closed her eyes. She shivered as the sweat on her skin chilled. He tugged a blanket off the back of the sofa and threw it over them.

He chuckled. "Was it good for you too, angel?"

She snorted and bit his nipple lightly. He jerked and snapped his arms around her, rolling her under him. She giggled until she saw the mask of rage that slid over his features.

"It was great for me…angel. Thanks for asking." Trevor's voice sounded from across the living room. Horror streaked through her. No. God, no. Not him. Not here. Not with Adrian so close. How had she missed smelling or hearing Trevor's approach? She was usually so alert, and the one time she'd let her guard down, let herself get distracted by love and sex, it might get Adrian killed.

Tears welled in her eyes as she looked at his beloved face. "Adrian, I—"

"Shh," he whispered. "Later."

Only there might not be a later for either of them, but she said nothing more as he hauled them both to their feet to face the man who'd done so much to hurt her. She fumbled with the blanket, pulling it tight around her body.

Trevor's hair hung in dark, greasy strands down his back. He ran his tongue over his teeth. "My little lioness. It was so good to hear you purr, darling. Too bad it's with him. You'll be punished for that. Later. For now, let's deal with this little…*pussy.*"

"Touch her and die." Adrian stepped in front of her, but she moved to stand beside him.

"That's a pretty bold statement for a stark-ass naked man with no weapon." Trevor's shaking hand clenched on a handgun, his finger poised on the trigger, and Cleo fought not to flinch. Please, *please* don't let him shoot Adrian. It was her worst nightmare come to life. Her mate, the one man she was destined for, could die right here and now in a wash of blood and rage from the one man she'd thought she could escape.

"We're mated, Trevor. I know you can smell it on us. And you know I'm not talking sex. Mated. You can't undo that." Her heart raced. Cold sweat formed sticky and clammy on her scalp. Her stomach churned with a dread unlike any she had ever known.

How could she stop this? What would make Trevor stop? She knew the answer to that question. Nothing. Nothing she had ever done, including run like hell, had ever stopped him.

"Oh, that's all right, Cleo." His hand steadied the gun, aiming it at Adrian's chest. Even werekind couldn't survive a bullet to the heart. "I know just what to do to make your mate disappear. A widow isn't mated, is she, Cleo? A widow can be claimed again. Because we both know you're mine. I was patient for years, Cleo. I was good to you."

"*Good* to me? How many times did you put me in the hospital, Trevor? How many times did you beat me until I couldn't stand?"

She balled her hands into fists. Fury exploded through her that he would even suggest touching Adrian. She would never let that happen. She needed to get him away from her mate. Stepping forward draw his attention, she made sure to stay just out of his arm's reach. His eyes followed her as she made herself an open target. He swung the gun to aim it at her, but she didn't think he'd shoot her. Not yet. Not when he took such pleasure in the sound of his fists hitting her flesh. He liked her fear and helplessness best, and beating her was how he savored it.

"There's a problem with your little plan. I'd have to claim you as mate too, Trevor. And I'd rather die."

"That can be arranged." A rusty chuckle slid from him. "You still don't understand, do you? If I can't have you, no one will. Not him, and not some guy somewhere down the road. It's me or no one."

Hate twisted with the terror inside her. The bastard had murdered her unborn child, and now he wanted to strip her mate from her. No. Hell, no. She was through running. She'd run and cowered before, and it hadn't saved her, hadn't saved her baby.

Her heart tripped at the thought of her lost child. *Don't think about it,* she ordered herself. *Focus.* She'd never have another chance for more children if she and Adrian didn't make it out of this. And she'd be damned if she let Trevor win again.

A low snarl exploded from her throat. "What are you waiting for, then?"

She flicked a glance back at Adrian, but he wasn't there. When had he moved? Her gaze scanned the room for him. Trevor seemed to notice the big wereleopard's absence at the same time she did.

Adrian dove for Trevor in his leopard form, his jaw snapping around the other man's wrist. She hit the floor as the gunshot rang out. A sub-bass bear's roar chilled her blood, and when she looked up she saw the two huge predators now circling each other. Trevor's shaggy brown coat stood on end as he roared. Adrian snarled and swiped a paw out to claw Trevor's nose. Blood gushed from the wound, and he charged the leopard. They went crashing through the front door and tumbled out onto the porch.

Cleo grabbed the gun off the floor and ran after them. She danced around the fighting animals, trying to see a clear shot to Trevor, but they kept moving in a blur of dark fur. Damn, damn, *damn.*

No way would she risk hurting Adrian.

Adrian leaped on top of Trevor, digging his claws deep into the bear's back. Trevor reared back, slamming Adrian into the porch roof. They both toppled sideways, and she couldn't get out of the way fast enough to avoid them. She hit the porch railing hard and slumped to the floor, dropping the gun. Spots swam in her vision for a second.

"Cleo!" Adrian appeared beside her, human once more, and his arms wrapped around her. "Angel—"

She saw Trevor scoop up the handgun and point it at Adrian's back. *"No."*

Lunging forward, she shoved Adrian out of the way as the gun went off. She couldn't lose him. She tensed and waited for the hot pain of a bullet in her back. But Trevor missed. Adrian's arms enfolded her, rolling them away from the spray of splinters as the bullet slapped into the wood. Trevor ran forward, the gun rising to aim again.

"Adrian, behind you!"

Adrian kicked out, catching Trevor in the knees. The gun rattled away and both men scrambled to get to it first. They wrestled for it, grunting as fists hit bone and sinew. They tumbled across the porch until they hit the railing.

A single shot rang out, and then there was nothing but silence. No birds called. Not even the rain fell. Dead silence. She'd never understood the meaning of the phrase until just now.

A scream of absolute agony ripped from her throat. *"Adrian."*

Her heart stopped for the longest moment in history as both men collapsed in a heap. She swayed on her feet, her whole world focusing on her mate.

A sob of relief clawed its way free when he moved. Slowly, but he moved. He groaned and rolled to his feet as Nico sprang up the steps and on to the porch, a deadly looking weapon drawn.

And the only thing she could think was Nico shouldn't be here. He should be in Arizona. "H-how did you get here so fast?"

CHAPTER SIX

"Nico." Adrian nodded. His chest heaved as he stood beside the fallen Trevor. He looked to Cleo, assuring himself that she was all right. She scrambled for the discarded blanket and wrapped it around herself while he ignored his own nudity under the rush of intense relief. He closed his eyes for a moment. *She was all right.* Thank God. Thank *God.*

"Adrian." Nico jerked his chin at a massively tall man who walked up the steps behind him. His youngest brother. "You got him, Zander?"

"Yeah. I always get stuck with garbage duty. Explaining this to the authorities is going to be a barrel of laughs. I could be home with my mate right now, but *nooo*, Nico's got me running around in the rain." Zander hauled Trevor's body upright and flipped him over his shoulder before walking out into the night. "Hasn't anyone ever told you people cats don't like to get wet?"

"Weakling." Nico snorted, ignored him, and cocked a brow at them. "You two all right?"

"You could have gotten here a few minutes earlier." Adrian grunted, thrusting a hand through his hair.

"You did just fine on your own." Nico sighed and rubbed his hand over the back of his neck. "We were distracted when one of our men didn't check in on schedule. By the time we found what was left of him, the gunfire had already started going off. We got here as fast as we could."

"There's more of you?" Cleo's gaze flashed to Adrian, her mouth hanging open. "You knew Trevor was coming. You set us up as bait."

He slanted a glance at his brother. "Give us a minute."

"This is going to be all over the werekind papers tomorrow. Adrian Leonidas disappearing after a secret mating stirred up a shit-storm already." Nico bared his teeth in a feral grin. "That bear got here awful quick—maybe now you'll listen when I tell you something's going on. Dad, Celeste and now this. I'm not—"

Lifting his hand, Adrian sighed. His brother was right—something deeper was going on here. Too many coincidences that ended with ugly consequences for his family. Too many questions left unanswered. But there were only so many fires he could put out in one night. "We'll talk about this when I get back to Refuge." He slanted a look at Cleo. "For now—*give us a minute.*"

Nico shook his head as he looked from Adrian to his mate. "Weakling. Soft over a woman. All of you. Jesus," he muttered under his breath as he stepped out the door, pulling it closed behind him.

A few minutes of tense silence passed before the roar of an engine started and faded into the distance. They stared at each other, neither moving.

The flap of giant wings reached him a second before the newcomer's scent carried in on the wind. He snapped his head around to look. "Fuck. What now?"

Cleo went rigid when an enormous bald eagle swooped down to land on the porch railing, and Adrian hauled her into his arms, his eyes pinned on the bird of prey. It shifted into a tall, regal woman with spiky blonde hair. She nodded to him as she stepped down onto the porch. "Leopard king."

He narrowed his gaze, a warning to come no further. "Leopards don't have kings. Only the birds have royalty."

"It doesn't matter what you call it, the truth is the same, cat." She lifted a cool brow, her expression impassive. "I've come to speak to you about the problems that your family's been having. Especially with the wolves."

He tilted his head, looking for tricks. Cleo stirred against him and addressed the bird directly. "Who are you?"

"Ajax Petros. Commander of the Messenger Corps." The words had no inflection. A statement of fact to a question she'd been expecting.

It raised his suspicions to new heights. Messengers lived a warrior's existence and clung more fiercely to bird neutrality than anyone else. "Why are you here? Birds don't involve themselves in the conflicts between shifter species."

"Except when they start the conflict." A flicker of rage entered her eyes, the first sign of life he'd seen in her.

He let go of Cleo, pushing her safely behind him as he stepped forward. "What are you saying?"

Ajax swallowed, and he watched her wrestle with some emotion before she answered him. "Your father, the crash, the assassination attempt on your sister-in-law, even your mate's werebear fiancé. I've been investigating all of these *problems* on my own. Quietly. I've only been able to come up with one answer. None of it was an accident. Worse, I think one of my own is behind it all."

"Who?" His fists clenched. Here it was, the answer to all the mysteries, all the dangers.

"I don't know who or why, but I intend to find out." The look on her face left no doubt in his mind what would happen to the traitor in the bird clan when she rooted him out. Good. "I refuse to let my people become embroiled in a war, or to start one between other shifter clans. It occurs to me that you have as much or more interest vested in ending the danger to you and yours. If necessary, can I count on you for support in this?"

"Yes." He wanted to see the threats against his family ended once and for all. He wanted to know the truth. If this woman could give him that, he'd do everything in his considerable power to help her.

"Expect to hear from me in the future." An ironic smile twisted her lips. "Congratulations on your mating, leopard king."

With that, the woman stepped off the porch and shifted midair, winging away as quietly as she had come. Nico would want to know about this as soon as possible, and he'd never let Adrian live it down that he was right about everything. But that could wait. Adrian had to finish dealing with his mate. He turned to Cleo standing in the shadows of the porch. She pulled in a deep breath, and he couldn't help but stare for a moment at the way it lifted her lush breasts. His cock hardened. Would his reaction to her ever ease? He hoped not.

"Well, then. I'll put together a press release about Trevor and...our m-mating...when we get back, try to minimize the damage."

He blinked, and blinked once more. Anger bubbled up inside of him, rolling to a slow boil. After everything that had happened tonight, after what they'd been through since they'd mated, *that* was all she had to say? Even without the new puzzle of the wereeagle's visit, his hands were still shaking from seeing her ex hold a gun on her. Shoot at her. A centimeter to the left and he would've lost her. It hit him again like a fist to the gut. He hissed. "You think I care about the damn media? Are you all right?"

"I—yes, I'm fine." Confusion spun in her amber eyes. A strange blankness settled over her face. Shock, he realized. "Are you?" she asked. "You look...fine."

Two strides took him to her side, and he cupped her shoulders in his palms. She trembled in his grasp, her pupils huge as she stared up at him. He shook her lightly. "Talk to me, Cleo."

Tension ran through her muscles, and she jerked away.

"I was so terrified, and you set him up. You used us as *bait*. And you didn't tell me." She drew back her hand and slapped his chest. A sob heaved her chest, and she hit him again. And again. He pulled her to his chest. She tried to hit him once more, but he caught her wrists, pinning her to him. She broke, collapsing against him, tears streaking down her face to dampen his chest. "I was so scared, Adrian. I thought he was going to kill you. I can't—I c-can't—"

He buried his face in her hair. "Shh. I have you. It's all right."

She sniffled and pulled back, smacking his chest again. Fire blazed in her amber gaze. "You used us as bait, damn you."

"I did." He couldn't deny it. Once he'd found her, he knew Trevor would keep coming for her. And he wasn't a man to run and hide. "You couldn't run forever, Cleo."

"You could have been killed."

"You damn near were," he growled. Remembered terror speared him. He'd forever have the image burned into his memory. His mate in danger, helpless to save her. His jaw flexed.

"You think I care about the danger to me? You could have—I was almost responsible for—" A low whimper of pain pulled from her throat, and she closed her eyes.

He knew that pain. He felt it himself. For her. Lifting his fingers, he tangled them in the strands of her hair. He needed to touch her, to make her understand what she meant to him. Remorse bit deep as he thought about losing her without her ever knowing what she'd come to mean to him in the past few weeks. No matter how fast their mating had been, he'd never regret it. Never. "I care. *I* care about the danger to you. I'm sorry, angel. I'm sorry you almost got hurt. Jesus, I'm so damn sorry."

She threw herself into his embrace, wrapping her arms around him.

Yes. Oh, yes. He needed to touch her, feel it to his bones that she was unharmed.

"Adrian."

"Cleo." He picked her up, cradling her slim form to his chest. Walking into the house, he mounted the steps, carried her to their room and laid her on the bed. He dragged in a slow breath, pulling her scent to him. Soft, feminine woman. Feline. His mate. Aroused for him.

She arched her body under his gaze, letting her blanket fall away. She reached for him, her fingers brushing over his chest. Her nails raking his nipples lightly.

His breath tangled in his chest.

"Please, Adrian. I need you now. I need you so much."

He groaned, lowering himself over her. He wanted to be gentle, to cherish her. To show her what words could not. She'd had enough words from Trevor. For years. Nothing he said could prove what he felt. He wasn't even certain he could put the depth of it into words. He'd never felt something like this for any woman. Only Cleo. Bracing himself on his elbows above her, he leaned to the left to raise his right hand and run his fingertips over her hip. Her breath caught, and her thighs parted as she arched herself in offering. A hot smile curved her face, and she bit her bottom lip. His chest banded tight in emotion just looking at her.

Only Cleo.

She twisted under him, groaning when he slipped his hand up to cup her breast. His lips brushed over hers, and she opened for him. Their tongues stroked together. She moaned into his mouth, and a punch of lust hit his gut. She bit him, her fangs sliding out to scrape his lip. The tang of blood in his mouth drove him wild, her taste shoving him over into feral need. His cock had been hard the moment he touched her, but her excitement fed his. His cock was rigid, full to bursting. He wanted her. Craved her.

Trailing his hand down her torso, he pressed his fingers between her legs. He stroked over her hard clit. She cried out and clamped her hand over his wrist. He pulled back to look down at her. "Something wrong, angel?"

"Not a thing." One side of her mouth kicked up, and she shoved his fingers deeper into her pussy, into the hot channel. He groaned, his cock jerking.

"Damn, angel." Heat slammed into him, tightening his gut as he moved his hand on her. Her wetness coated his fingers. The musky scent of her arousal sent him skating to the ragged edge of his control.

Her hips squirmed, working his digits inside her. He thrust in, angling his fingertips until he—*ah, yes*. That was the spot that made her scream. An animalistic shriek ripped from her throat. Her pussy flexed on his fingers, and she closed her knees over his forearm. He stroked inside her over and over, loving the clench of her inner muscles on him.

"Adrian." Her voice caught on a soft sob. "I love your hands on me. I love the feel of you. Make love to me. Please."

He needed no more encouragement than that. Yes. Oh, yes. He growled low, all the pent up need inside him ripping free. Moving over her, he settled between her thighs. The silk of her flesh slid against his hips as she wrapped her legs around his flanks and made him groan. Guiding his cock to the wetness of her core, he sank to the hilt within her. Her sweet warmth clenched on his dick. He swallowed and closed his eyes to savor this moment. The band around his chest tightened further.

Her claws slipped out to curl into his back, raking down his skin. Oh, *God*. His hips bucked hard, slamming home. She screeched and arched to rub her nipples over his chest.

"You feel so good, Cleo. So good . . ."

"Yes. More. Please." She lifted her head, offering her lips to him.

He took her mouth hard, thrusting his tongue into the moist cavern. Desperation rode him hard as he ground into her. Her scent, her hot skin was too good. Too much. Her soft, excited moans into his mouth drove him on. He felt as if his head were going to explode.

Her hand moved to cup his jaw, a smile on her lips. "So perfect."

Oh, yes. Perfect. Sweet relief wrapped around his soul that she was safe, and she was here, and she was his. Something inside him loosened and broke free at the knowledge. He *needed* her. He couldn't live without her. He opened his mouth and finally found the right words for it, this emotion that slammed into him like a tidal wave when she was near. "I love you, Cleo. I'll always love you."

A tear streaked down her cheek as she bowed in his arms. Her sex fisted on his cock rhythmically. "I love you too. My mate. My Adrian."

"*Yes.*" He clenched his jaw to fight the orgasm, to draw it out for her, for them. Slipping his hand between them, he worked his fingers over her clit. His fangs slid out as control spun from him. Only Cleo. Only Cleo could strip him bare. He threw back his head and roared, jetting his come within her soft body.

Her pussy flexed on his cock so tight that he could feel the deep contractions. The lioness within her shrieked as orgasm took her, calling to his leopard. He loved watching her come, the hot flush of satisfaction on her face. He shuddered, held her close when he collapsed on top of her him, and rolled so she lay on his chest. Her arms curled around his shoulders, and she buried her face against his neck. They panted together, just holding each other as they came down from the rush.

"I love you, Adrian." Her body relaxed, and her eyelashes brushed over his skin when she closed her eyes.

Within a few moments, her breasts moved against his chest, lifting in the deep rhythm of sleep. Good, she needed to rest. His hand cupped the back of her head, and he turned to lower her to the mattress.

He stroked her golden locks away from her face. She was so lovely.

His chest tightened with that almost familiar band of emotion. Now he knew what it was.

Love. Deep and lasting. Mated love. *Yes.* It was so right. It shook him to the very core.

He had no control with her, and it scared the hell out of him. But he wouldn't walk away from her for anything. Ever. He'd learn to cope with the fact that she made him crazy. She'd thrown herself in front of a damn bullet for him. Fitting his body to hers, he lay beside her, steeping himself in her scent, in the feel of her silky skin.

She curled on her side away from him, her back pressed to his chest. He sighed, contentment winding through him. He closed his eyes, letting relief wash through at the knowledge that she was all right, that she was safe.

He'd set them up as bait, but Trevor wasn't meant to get past Nico. The werebear was never supposed to be near Cleo. Adrian swallowed hard. Losing her would be more than he could handle. He'd never survive it. Needing her so much terrified him, but there was no denying it now.

How had his brother survived? Jason had lost his mate, and he'd watched the soul leech from his brother. Now he knew why. And he knew there was one more thing he needed to do tonight. Rising silently from the bed, he scooped up his cell phone and punched in the speed-dial for his brother in Florida.

"Hello?" Jason's deep voice boomed through the phone.

"Hey, Jason."

"Adrian?" His brother's tone sharpened. "Is everyone all right? Lyra and the baby?"

"Yes. They're all fine. Lyra's not due for another couple of months." He swallowed, uncertain how to put into words what he was feeling. Things had never been easy between him and his older brother. A natural rivalry had turned into an inability to connect, to communicate somewhere along the way. "I—I'm getting married. I mated to a werelioness. Her name is Cleo."

There was a long pause on the phone, and Adrian thought his brother might have hung up. Then he heard a sigh crackle the phone line. "Congratulations."

"I didn't call to tell you that."

Jason grunted. "No? Well, get it said, brother."

A chuckle pulled from Adrian's throat. That was Jason. No patience, just the facts. "I wanted to say...that I'm sorry." He blew out a breath. "I thought that you were weak for leaving after Celeste died. Or we thought she died. I didn't understand why you left, why you walked away from everything."

His gaze landed on the smooth curves of his mate lying naked in his bed. Her soft breasts rose and fell in the slow rhythm of deep slumber. He sighed. Was there anything sweeter than watching your woman sleep? The thought of losing her, of how close he had come to the grief his brother had known for so long, almost drove him to his knees.

His voice came out a harsh rasp. "I'm sorry, brother. I didn't know what it could do to a man—loving a woman."

Jason snorted. "It'll rip your heart out. And that's if you found the right one."

"I did." A small smile curved his lips. "I want you and Celeste to come to the wedding."

Another long pause greeted that invitation, and Adrian swallowed. Regret pierced him. Too much time had passed, too much had come between them for his brother to ever come back home. He reached out and curved a hand over Cleo's silky hip. Just touching her was a comfort.

"We'll be there." He started at the sound of Jason's voice. A soft feminine murmur sounded in the background. Celeste. His brother's mate. Jason chuckled in response to whatever she had said. "I have to go. Celeste…needs me."

Sure she did. Adrian grinned. "Tell her I said hello. And have fun filling all of her…needs."

"A man's work is never done." Jason's voice took on a long-suffering tone. Celeste sounded an obvious protest at that, but it dissolved into a giggle. "Bye, brother."

"Bye." He clicked the button to turn off his phone, and Cleo sat up in bed.

A small smile curved her lips, and she reached for him. "Come back to bed."

He slid in next to her, pulling her into his arms. She cuddled up to him, dropping back into sleep. Contentment wound through his chest. Perfect. He let himself go, let himself enjoy this one quiet moment with her.

His life stretched out before him, open to incredible possibilities that weren't even there two weeks ago. Thanks to Cleo. He never would have imagined anyone like her as his mate, never would have allowed himself to touch her if he hadn't gotten drunk that night.

He shook his head and smiled. Life was one hell of an amazing thing that way.

He closed his eyes and drank in the scent of her.

His mate, his heart, his soul.

Renegade Passions

Loribelle Hunt

CHAPTER ONE

Nicodemus Leonidas stopped the rental car, turning off the engine while he studied the house's long front porch. He hadn't warned Jason he was coming. His brother lifted his head but didn't move from his position wrapped around the human woman in a slightly swaying hammock. He couldn't make out his brother's expression, and it was a good thing Jason couldn't see his in return.

His lip curled in derision. His scorn wasn't even at taking up with a human associated with the werewolves. That was bad enough. Hell, his youngest brother had gone further and mated a werewolf. No, it was because Jason was completely whipped. It was one thing to shack up with a woman. His practiced eye looked her over, and she was one hell of a woman, but mating? Mating made you weak. Mating made you stupid. He'd seen it over and over again the last few months as each of his brothers fell. Definitely not for him.

Calling on his experience as the family's security expert, he schooled his expression into one of disinterest and got out of the car. The north Florida humidity hit him like a blow. Dolphin territory. Even in early winter it was warm and balmy. How could anyone live here? The leopard clan claimed everything west of the Mississippi, and he'd be glad to get back to his own land and more specifically home, to the family's resort, Refuge, in the Arizona desert. At least they had seasons.

Scanning the area as he walked, he strode through the yard. Scrub and small trees. There was nothing appealing in it and its proximity to the wolves just made it worse. The Gulf Coast may belong to the dolphins, but almost everything east of the Mississippi was wolf land. Jason had escaped here after Celeste's alleged death and other than finding her alive hadn't had much luck with the place. This was the area where Jason had a fought a werewolf and a hurricane. The need to take action also ruffled his fur.

As he approached, the couple moved. Jason came to meet him at the porch's edge while Celeste remained seated on the hammock. She watched him warily, suspicion and unease clear on her face. Nico tried to force some of the predator that lived in him farther below the surface. He needed answers from the woman. Scaring her silly was unlikely to get them.

"Brother." Jason stood with his feet braced apart and his arms crossed over his chest. "What brings you here?"

It was like that, was it? Could be he had the cool reception coming. He hadn't been very diplomatic the last time they spoke, but his focus was single-minded. He cocked an eyebrow.

"You know why I'm here."

He and his brother both looked at Celeste. She shifted under the double scrutiny, and Nico was shocked to see her expression and body language change. Gone was the timid mouse, replaced by someone harder, someone bolder. A she-wolf readying to protect her own. He wondered why that image popped into his mind. Her family may be wolves, descendants of King Lycoan and his one hundred sons granted the ability to shift into wolves by Zeus, but she was human. That must be it.

She stood, and he approached, forcing his features to relax, hoping his smile wasn't a grimace. When he'd first met her over a year ago, she would have shrunk back from his advance regardless. Now she stood her ground, eyes stony. Jason joined her, and she took his hand. Nico noticed it was shaking a little. Not as brave as she pretended to be, but there was no smell of fear from her, no sign of retreat. He had to admire her backbone.

"Celeste. It's good to see you well."

She nodded. Curtly. Once. "Thank you."

He sighed. This was going to be more difficult that he'd anticipated. He turned to his brother, forcing his voice to be free of censure. "I had to come. Dad wouldn't have given up on any of us."

Instantly, he knew it was the wrong thing to say. Jason stiffened, his eyes growing glacial and a low growl welling in his throat. Nico's statement hadn't only accused his brother of giving their father up for dead but also his mate. He was relieved when Celeste slid her hand up the inside of Jason's arm and calmed the beast lurking inside him. She turned cold, angry eyes on him.

"I do have one thing that may help you." She held up a hand to hold off the questions rushing through his mind. "Inside."

He followed them to a small kitchen and sat at the table she pointed out. Jason sat across from him and glowered. Nico was on thin ice here in the warm southern winter. Celeste poured three cups of coffee and placed a bowl of sugar on the center of the table. When she would have taken her own seat, Jason pulled her into his lap. She sat there easily, and Nico ignored the twist in his gut. He didn't want that. The easy companionship. The warm willing woman who would always be his responsibility.

He stirred sugar into his cup and waited for her to speak. The silence stretched, and when he looked up again she had a faraway look on her face. He cleared his throat, and she jerked. Jason's arms tightened around her waist, and he glared at Nico. Celeste rubbed circles on his arm and whispered in his ear. He relaxed, but only marginally. Nico almost sighed again. He didn't like this armed truce that had developed between him and his brothers. Celeste twisted and looked him in the eye.

"I don't remember anything. That hasn't changed. No amount of badgering me is going to change that either."

It was irritation not awkwardness that made him want to fidget. There was no way being dressed down by this human slip of a woman embarrassed him. He forced himself to sit still. He needed her information too badly to go cat on her right now. She was the sole—and surprise—survivor of the plane crash that had taken his father's life. But if the human had lived in secrecy, why not the wereleopard leader?

"I don't remember," she emphasized again. Did he imagine the apology in her voice? "But my dad finally told me that it was the birds who found me. The plane…went down in their territory. It was a Messenger—Ajax Petros—who found me and notified my family."

He shut his eyes and took a deep breath. The birds who made up the Messenger Corps were reputed to all be trained fighters and they zealously protected the neutrality of the group. This Messenger though, this Ajax Petros, kept popping up, kept feeding his family pieces of information. Now it appeared she had another connection to them, a more tangible connection. He was the only Leonidas brother not to meet her yet, and he was damned curious. He'd been on his way to see her when he'd decided to visit Jason first. Now he was glad he did—it provided the perfect excuse to enter bird territory.

It was a start. It was something to go on. He knew the crash was on bird land, of course, but other than a video they'd sent only after he badgered them into it, he knew almost nothing about it. Now he had a name to go by at least.

"Thank you, Celeste," he said gently. Looking at the tense lines around her eyes, he had an idea how much it cost her to try to remember that time. He stayed only long enough to be polite. Determined to find answers. Determined to find the truth.

CHAPTER TWO

Nico stomped through the woods wanting to howl his frustration. After two futile days of searching for Ajax Petros he was beginning to think the woman didn't exist. Not only that, but everyone refused to speak of the crash. Someone had finally taken him to the site but after a year there was nothing left to be found.

Two days on the werebirds' land wasn't going to be nearly enough time. They owned several hundred acres in the middle of wolf land in the Tennessee Smoky Mountains, but there was no central town or city in which to track people. Instead there were small enclaves dotting the mountainsides, and they were difficult to spot. Mostly high up in trees, always concealed as part of the landscape. If he weren't in the middle of a mission he'd find it fascinating. The leopard in him was naturally curious about the aeries.

There were no roads. He'd had to hike in, which turned out to be a problem. It had gradually grown cold over the days. A biting, bitter wind blew in from the west and brought black, ugly cloud cover with it. If the temperature continued to drop he knew those clouds could mean snow, and he didn't want to get caught out in the open in an early season blizzard, so he was making his way down.

It pissed him off.

He wasn't getting anywhere with his search and now he was being forced to put it on hold until the weather improved. In a normal situation, he'd just find local lodging. But to his extreme annoyance there was none to be had. Not that it was full, just that there *wasn't* any. No hotels. No inns. No rooms for hire. He'd been sleeping outside, but that wouldn't be possible tonight.

He came around a bend in the path, cursing when in his distraction his foot caught on a concealed stone. Pausing, he shook out the twist in his ankle, reaching for the water bottle clipped to his belt. Before he could take a swig, he heard a flutter of wings and looked up. A huge bald eagle was flying straight for him. He forced himself to remain still, not to flinch, as the deadly talons grew closer.

He watched the flight with an awe he'd never admit to. The bird circled his head, then landed a few feet before him and shifted in an explosion of color. A woman stood before him, tall, proud, and gloriously naked. Athletic. Incredible boobs. Each shifter species could trace their beginnings to one deity. Marathon, the greatest of message bearers may have inspired Hermes to give the gift of flight to his descendents, but he wouldn't be surprised if her fierce beauty was from Aphrodite herself.

She cocked her head to one side and twisted to look down the trail behind her. Exceptional ass. Her hair was short, white-blonde and spiky. His leopard lifted its nose to take in her sweet, womanly scent. She turned back to gaze at him. Her glowing blue eyes froze his tongue.

"Like what you see?" she asked.

Hell, yeah. If he didn't have other pressing obligations, he'd be happy to spend a week showing her just how much. Before he could frame a response that wouldn't get him decked another bird flew into the small clearing. It landed and shifted into a tall, heavily muscled man. Ignoring Nico, he turned to the woman.

He had to fight a low growl welling up from his throat. He'd never been possessive of women and shifters weren't prudish about nudity, but the idea of any man looking at her naked body awoke jealous instincts in his leopard. If they were aware of it, the two strangers ignored his struggle.

"Storm's coming in fast," the man said. The woman nodded. It was a regal, dismissive motion. He finally seemed to notice Nico and hesitated. "I'll see you later?"

Nico took an antagonistic step forward, but her expression never changed. "Perhaps." A cold wind gusted through the clearing. "You better go."

The man bowed slightly at the waist before stepping away, shifting and taking flight. She turned to Nico, and he noticed she was shivering. He shrugged out of his jacket and circled her, letting his hands linger just a moment on her shoulders. He wanted to touch, to stroke, to pet. She turned around, breaking the contact to face him.

"Thank you." Cool. Contained. He wanted to break her reserve, snap her control. He shook his head. This wasn't like him. The sooner he got away from her, the better. His cat growled at the thought of leaving her.

"I understand you've been looking for me," she said. She'd pushed her arms into the coat's sleeves and held a hand out. "Ajax Petros."

He didn't like surprises. Someone should have warned him. Shifter women came in all shapes and sizes and looks, from ugly to plain to drop dead gorgeous. Ajax Petros was on the heart attack inducing end of the spectrum. He'd never seen a more beautiful woman, shifter *or* human. She wasn't at all what he'd expected. Not from a Messenger and not with a name like Ajax.

"Isn't Ajax a man's name?"

Her hand fell to her side. "Do I look like a man?"

Hell no. His gaze swept down her body, head to toe and back up again, pausing to linger over the white thatch of hair between her legs before lifting to look into her eyes.

"Is Ajax short for something?"

"Alexandra." Now that fit. A beautiful name for this exquisite woman. What was the story behind the nickname? Never mind. He'd get to that later.

Edging closer, he reached out for the aborted handshake. She set her palm in his and the skin-to-skin contact was electrifying. He didn't release her until she pulled free. Pissed at being kept from touching the woman, the cat within him started to pace. He gritted his teeth and resisted to urge to pounce. "Nico Leonidas."

The wind blew again, and goose bumps rose on her exposed skin. He edged closer, not bothering to fight the need raging in him to keep her warm. "Is there someplace we can talk? You need to get out the weather."

Her eyes narrowed. "I've been taking care of myself a long time."

"Badly if this is typical behavior."

Her eyes seemed to flash blue fire. She clenched her jaw. Her body language screamed aggression and command. He was reminded that bald eagles were predators, but even those masters of the sky were no match for a full-grown male leopard. He wondered if the rumors were true. Were Messenger birds all trained to be elite soldiers? If he showed her some of the cat would she run? Or would she submit?

He moved forward until his chest brushed against hers. He could feel her breasts through his thin jacket, felt the shudders in her body she fought to control. Probably from cold, but in that moment he determined they would be for him. Every hard, edgy line of her body broadcasted her role in the bird pecking order—right at the top. Too bad. He wanted her—he was going to have her. Awareness lit her eyes, as if she could read his intentions, but she didn't back down. He smiled. He looked forward to tangling with her. She shrugged off the jacket and handed it back to him.

Pointing into the woods and underbrush on his right, she spoke, "There's a path on the other side of those bushes. Go one hundred yards up. I'll meet you there."

Then she shifted and flew in the direction she'd pointed out. He set off into the underbrush. After a few feet he came to several intersecting paths and went down the one that led the right way, the one where her scent was strongest. He'd lost sight of Ajax and ran to catch up.

The trail climbed up the side of the mountain. He began to think he was going in the wrong direction when it ended in a small clearing. There was no sign of the woman.

"Up here."

He looked up and saw the house. He'd seen many of these houses in the last two days. Werebirds seemed to prefer being high even in their human forms. But this one was different. This one was huge. Ajax leaned against a porch railing wrapped in a long robe and grinned down at him. It was the first non-neutral expression he'd seen on her face, and it damned near stopped his heart. He searched for a way up and found switchback stairs around the trunk of a huge tree.

At the top he looked around. It wasn't all one building after all. A rope bridge in front of him led to a separate space, and he could see others leading in other directions like the spokes of a one-sided wheel.

He turned away from them, his senses opening up, tracking her by scent and sound. He found the railing she'd leaned on and trailed his fingers over it, imagined he could feel her warmth lingering in the wood. Her scent was stronger here. Jasmine, vanilla and something unique he couldn't name. He followed it around the curving deck and through a set of double glass doors.

She had her back to him, pouring water into a coffee maker. He watched silently. Studied her. She removed the filter cup, rinsed it in the sink and measured grounds into it. Her movements were smooth and efficient. Her head tilted to one side a little as she worked. He found himself fascinated by the line of her neck. It was elegant. Graceful. Kissable. He could see her pulse hammering there and wanted to nibble. He didn't resist the impulse. Using his cat's stealth, he padded forward on silent feet. She jumped when he set his hands on her hips, held her breath when his tongue swiped the alluring spot on her nape.

"What are you doing?" she asked breathlessly.

"Tasting," he murmured before setting his teeth to the tantalizing skin. She let her head fall back against his chest, giving him better access and groaning. God, he loved that sound. It almost undid him. And it snapped him back to reality. What the hell was going on here? He dropped his hands like they'd been burned.

CHAPTER THREE

When the leopard set his hands on her hips, she had to grip the counter for support and bite her lower lip to keep from begging for more. His lips brushed her skin, and her blood rushed. Then his teeth scraped over her pulse. She groaned, and he released her abruptly as if he was burned by the heat rising in her body. She felt the same way.

Slowly, she turned to face him, study him. She'd just arrived home a few hours ago and everywhere she went had been told a leopard was in their mountains asking for her. Nico Leonidas. One of the leopard king's brothers and the only one she hadn't met until today. Considering everything that had been going on with the leopards recently, she'd decided it would be better if she found him first.

She'd expected him to seek her out sooner, had been informed by her source inside Refuge Resort that he was investigating the plane accident his father had died in. She had her own suspicions about that crash, suspected one of her own was behind it. She would be forced to move against him soon. The man's arrogance, his greed threatened the balance of power in the shifter world and the bird's place in it. She wouldn't allow that, but she couldn't strike without some kind of proof. Such rashness would shake the foundations of her clan.

So she'd done the unthinkable, broken the bonds of neutrality by sharing her suspicions with Adrian Leonidas. She couldn't explain that compulsion to share the information with the leopard family, but it wouldn't happen again. Her duty was to *her* people. She'd been waiting for the Leonidas' arrival, had been sure she could deal with him and send him off quickly.

Now that he was here, she knew that belief for the mistake it was. As the leader of the Messenger Corps, she came into contact with many different werekind species. She'd often dealt with wereleopards. This one's domestication was a thin veneer. Not a problem in and of itself. She'd known a few predator weres over the years that were barely human. But this one. This one was *hers*. And not at all happy about it if his expression was anything to judge by. To tell the truth, she wasn't either, but his rejection still stung.

"Don't like what you see that much after all, huh? Don't worry. I don't either."

His eyes narrowed to angry slits as she brushed by him. It took every ounce of control she had not to reach up, soothe his brow and apologize for her angry response. She didn't have time for a mate. If she had any sense at all, she'd shift and get out. Fly far away and wait to return until he'd left. Her body refused her mind's orders to do so immediately. The sense of self-preservation apparently didn't trump the lust. She was in real trouble.

She avoided looking at him as she opened the freezer and rummaged around. Her mother usually stocked it with casseroles while she was gone, and she pulled something out that might be lasagna. It was in a glass pan with a foil lid, and she put it in the oven. Turning the knob to three hundred and fifty degrees, she looked over her shoulder.

"Hungry?"

Another mistake. Nostrils flared, he stood very still and stared at her. His hands clenched and unclenched at his sides. For the first time she wondered if she might be in danger and felt a spike of fear. He reacted like she'd thrown cold water on him, jerking and prowling around the room. He stopped by the doors, didn't turn around when he spoke.

"There's no need to fear me. I won't harm you."

Was that hurt she heard in his voice? With his back turned she allowed herself the opportunity to really look at him. She could see his reflection in the glass and caught her breath.

He was a magnificent specimen of masculinity. Not much taller than average height, maybe a little over six feet tall, with defined muscles she itched to touch. His hair was very short, dark, almost black, as if to match the darkness she sensed in him. But his eyes were bright, grassy green. He met her gaze in the glass and held her snared. She suddenly wished she'd taken time to put more on than just a robe. As if he heard her thoughts, he let his gaze trail over the reflection of her body in the doors.

"I think I preferred you without the robe."

His voice was low, husky with arousal. She held her breath, wondering if he'd tell her to remove it, wondering if she'd comply. The problem with being raised as the heir to a throne was you never met a man who could really take charge, who you wanted to give over control to. It could only be in bed, but it was a kind of freedom she secretly yearned for. Except his earlier rejection still rankled. It was clear from the bulge in his jeans he wanted her, so what was that about? She didn't know what to think and fell back on cool disdain.

"I can find some clothes. No point in walking around without them. I try not to fly around inside."

His smile was slow, a little cruel and all dominant male. "I'd just have to remove them."

Her heart hammered, and her sex clenched in response. Her mouth was too dry to respond. He approached her, stopped close enough she could feel his chest rise and fall against hers. She stood frozen in place as he lifted his knuckles to stroke her cheek, down her neck and over her collarbone.

"How long before dinner?" he whispered.

"Um." She gulped. Impossible to think while he stood so near. While he petted her. "An hour maybe."

"Good." The heat in his eyes faded a little. "Ground rules. You agree or you don't agree. If you don't, nothing happens between us. Understood?"

She nodded, still aroused but bemused by the sudden change in tone and conversation.

"Just two things really," he said going back to stroking her neck. She tilted her head to give him better access and waited to hear his rules. "One, I'm in charge."

His lips touched her skin and she gasped as he suckled it. "Whatever I say, whenever I say it."

She didn't know if she could go for that, but she was intrigued enough to let him go on. "And two, while I'm here, you're mine. I don't share." The last ended on a growl. That was fine with her. She knew she wasn't ever going to be able to look at another man. What gave her pause was the implication he'd go on to other women, but she forced the savage jealousy away. She didn't want a mate after all. She had enough problems.

"Oh…" His teeth nipped at the vein pulsing in her neck. "Okay."

Hands moving to grip her hips, he straightened to his full height, looked down into her upturned face. He nodded, but he didn't smile as he reached for the tie on her robe, face hard and possessive. Her heart skittered. Maybe this was a mistake, but it was too late to change her mind. She didn't deny the need in her. Couldn't even if she wanted to. Her nipples were hard, her pussy wet.

He spread the lapels of the robe open, let it slide slowly off her shoulders. It dropped to the floor, and his hands circled her wrists like manacles and pulled them behind her back where he held them in one hand. He backed her up till her butt hit the counter, and then he just stared down at her. The gaze was so hot, so carnal and full of need her legs shook. He leaned forward slowly, and she closed her eyes when his mouth was just an inch from her nipple. Anticipation rushed through her. She wanted his mouth, his teeth, his cock. The need consumed her. Overwhelmed the protesting voice in her head. She waited and nothing happened. Opening her eyes, she saw him standing tall again, frowning down at her. He released her and reached for her robe on the floor, pulling the belt free of the loops. He jerked his head towards the table.

"Lay down."

She almost protested, but remembered his rules. She chafed under them, but wanted him too much to refuse. Walking over, she sat down and lay back watching as he prowled the kitchen and found a knife. He held the belt so the ends were equal then sliced it with the knife. She gasped and went to sit up. *Damn it.* That was her favorite robe. One look at his face held her in place though. He wasn't going to brook any kind of defiance.

It was a small table, round and made only for two. Her torso barely fit on it and her ass was dangerously close to the edge. He stalked closer, the ends of the robe tie held in one hand as he trailed his fingertips from one hipbone to her shoulder. He traced them over her face, lightly, the touch sensuous and promising, before taking one wrist gently in his and pulling it down towards the floor. He tied it to the table leg then repeated the action with the other arm. She was breathing hard by the time he finished. She'd never been tied down. She felt her wings struggling for freedom while she fought for calm. He stood back and watched her a moment before ripping his shirt over his head.

"You're unaccustomed to being restrained."

She nodded, more a jerk, and focused on the muscles rippling across his torso. He spoke softly, but there was no denying the menace under his tone.

"Answer me, Ajax."

She lifted her gaze to his face, felt a measure of relief at the stark control stamped across his features. "Yes. I am."

He unsnapped and unzipped his jeans. Pushed them down over his hips. He wasn't wearing underwear and his cock sprang free, erect and long and hard. She took a long deep breath, licked dry lips. He stepped closer and ran a hand through her hair.

"I won't hurt you," he whispered. "I'd never hurt you."

He wrapped his hand around his erection, stroked it slowly up and down while she watched. She wanted to taste him, wanted to know if he tasted as good as he smelled. All masculine and woodsy. Primitive and tempting. He was the ultimate bad boy. Hers if she was willing to take him.

He stepped closer to her, a bare inch from her mouth and she darted her tongue out. Caressed the tip before he groaned and moved closer, letting her take some of him into her mouth. She suckled, moaning at the salty tang of him, at the width and steel in him. He rotated his hips, lodged himself deeper and deeper, faster and faster until he hit the back of her throat. She felt his control slipping and reveled in it. Then he pulled back, popping free of her mouth. He glared at her, and she glared back. The look said she'd done something wrong. What the hell could that be? She was tied to the damn table. She pulled at the bonds, suddenly sick of the game and wanting to be free. He moved to the other end of the table, gripped her hips and held her still as he knelt down.

"Oh no, baby. You agreed."

The table was so small her ass was right at the edge. He slid his hands down and in, traced the creases between her thighs and sex as he did. His touch was gentle, undemanding as he moved inwards, spreading the lips of her pussy to his gaze. She groaned, embarrassed and turned on at the wanton sight she knew she made.

When he leaned forward and licked her, the groan became something else. He took his time, avoiding her clit as he explored her, tasted her. He pushed his tongue into her pussy, and she bucked against him. Her temperature spiked impossibly high, her heart pounded as if she'd run a marathon. Frustration and lust raged through her. She was so wound up it would take nothing to make her come, yet he held her back.

Nico had no idea where his control was coming from. Her taste was perfect. Ambrosia. She drugged his senses. He felt the lust and need coming off of her in waves, wanted to fuck her until she forgot her name, until it didn't occur to her to do anything but to submit to his every whim. But the leopard in him wanted something else. It wanted to possess, to own her heart and mind, body and soul. Wanted to cherish. Wanted to protect. It wasn't like him at all, but he couldn't fight the dual urges.

Knowing he couldn't wait much longer, he found her clit with his tongue. Flicked it and enjoyed her loud moans, enjoyed her pleasure before inserting one finger into her cunt. Then two. His reward was immediate. She cried out as she came, thrusting hard against his hand, her cream sweet and wet and warm on his tongue. He stood on unsteady feet and moved between her legs, gripping her knees and holding them high as he thrust into her.

Dear God, she was going to kill him. She was tight and almost blistering hot, convulsing around him in orgasm as she came again. It felt too damned good not to make it last. He slowed and gentled his thrusts, leaned forward to suck one pert nipple between his lips. As soon as he tasted her, his incisors lengthened and he had to fight the leopard from biting, from claiming and marking her. He forced the sharp points to retract, forced instinct under control. Recognizing the danger they were both in, he lifted his lips, increased the depth and speed of his thrusts and let the orgasm rush through him.

As it broke over him, he couldn't fight the animal in him. His fangs broke free, found the gentle slope of her breast and pierced her tender skin. The taste of her blood exploded over his tongue and something shifted inside him. Something primitive, primal. She was *his*. Irrevocably and forever. He'd known it and hadn't wanted to admit it when he'd seen her on the trail, but now it was a fact neither of them could escape.

He collapsed over her, sucking in deep breaths. Taking in her scent, their combined scents and sex. Trying to reconcile what he'd just done with what he'd always promised himself he wouldn't do. Reminding himself he'd come here to find out what happened to his father not get wrapped up with a woman.

When he regained some semblance of control he rose on his elbows and studied her. She was still breathing fast and deeply, her eyes closed with a small smile on her face. He lifted his fingers to the side of her face, tracing the high cheekbones. She opened her eyes and met his gaze. Calm and reserved again. It pissed him off. What right did she have to control when he was in so much turmoil? Her expression changed under his glare. Softened, soothed.

"Will you let me up now?"

It was a softly spoken request, but he didn't miss the command underlying her tone. She was used to being obeyed. He cocked an eyebrow as he stood. She wasn't going to get a pliable mate in him. He moved around the table. Leaned over to flick his tongue over one nipple. It pebbled with the contact.

"I think I prefer you like this. At my mercy."

He sucked the nipple into his mouth, biting a little. She moaned and arched up into the caress of his mouth. His eyes closed. So responsive. So perfect. So his. He let the hard nub pop free from his lips and studied her straining body. He hadn't put her in the most comfortable position, but she hadn't complained. He knew her arms had to be sore by now. Reluctantly he released her, rubbing each shoulder as he did. He'd make it up to her later. She lifted her arms and sat up slowly, watching him as her hand rose to his bite on her breast. She sighed.

"The last thing I need right now is a mate."

CHAPTER FOUR

It was like a slap in the face, never mind he'd been thinking something similar. It had never occurred to him he'd be rejected by his mate. The two sides of his nature warred over a response. The human half agreed wholeheartedly, but the animal half, the leopard, was furious in a way only cats seemed capable of. It paced just under his skin while Nico struggled for control. It wasn't until he smelled the slight tang of blood in the air that he realized his claws had burst from his fingertips and cut his palms. Ajax took a step away from him, her fear suddenly a cloying, heavy smell between them, finally causing the leopard to settle down.

Nico knew it was only temporary, but he heaved a sigh of relief at the reprieve. His leopard side was always close to the surface and damned near impossible to fight. He usually saw no reason to, usually didn't bother, but her fear was like claws raking across his chest. It hurt like nothing he'd ever experienced. And it was an insult. He may be barely tame, but he'd never hurt his mate. His growl was low, just this side of audible but she heard it.

"Your fear is fucking offensive."

She took a deep breath and the scent receded. "You'll have to forgive me. I'm new to this."

Reaching down, she picked up the robe and pulled it on then leaned back against the counter with her arms crossed over her chest. The posture was defensive, but her expression was that same earlier mask he'd seen. Calm. Remote. He might prefer her being afraid to hiding behind this composed woman. He had to move before he did something drastic to effect that change. She cocked an eyebrow and watched him as he paced around the open kitchen and living room.

After a moment she straightened and disappeared down a hall. He heard water running shortly after and ground his teeth against the sudden need that surged through his body as he imagined her standing under it, imagined it caressing all her lush curves and secret places. Lucky water. He wanted to go to her, but held himself back. Held the leopard back with the promise of a run, with the reminder they should make sure the area was secure. Still nude, he opened the doors he'd come in through and pulled them tightly shut behind him. Then he shifted, letting his cat side take over, and took to the trees.

Deep inside the cat, the man looked around in wonder, knew this was his natural habitat. Leopards were meant to live high above the ground, to live in jungle and forest, not desert despite how long his family had been in Arizona or how much he liked it. The land didn't sing to him the way this place did.

It didn't hurt that her scent was everywhere. When it started to fade, he turned and hunted until it was strong again. Naturally, he stayed near her home until he discovered the paths. Her scent was strong on two of them, leading in opposite directions. He followed one to its destination, another house a few hundred yards away. She obviously spent a lot of time in the house, and the leopard growled its disapproval. No one had the right to compete with it for her attention. But then another smell came to him, and he lifted his nostrils, edged closer down the length of the branch it rested on, tested the scent, the familiarity. Family. Whoever lived in the house was a relative, and female, judging by the sweet benign flavor that coated his tongue. He turned away, knowing the woman in there probably wasn't a threat to his mate.

He continued his perimeter circuit and came to another path, another place where her scent didn't lessen but just kept moving on. He followed the trail for a while from above until it became clear he wouldn't soon come to her destination. Many other scents joined hers on the trail and there was a noticeable drop in temperature from just an hour ago. Eventually he turned back, loath to leave her alone and unprotected. The man knew she'd been alone a long time—there was no scent but hers in her home—and had probably taken care of herself for some while. She'd told him as much, hadn't she? But neither the man nor the beast was willing to risk her now that she belonged to them.

She was dressed when he stepped back into the house, once again facing away from him and towards the counter. He growled his displeasure when he stepped up behind her, but this time she didn't flinch and no fear wafted through the air. Good. She was learning. Still the clothes had to go. He was already hard and heavy. He hadn't put on his clothes upon his return, and he pushed his hips into her buttocks, nuzzled her neck. He was rewarded with a rush of sensation. His own body's response. Hers. Her pulse kicked under his lips, and her arousal was a heady scent in the air.

"Dinner," she whispered as she rocked back into him, grinding her ass against his erection. His teeth closed over the soft shell of her ear and bit. She yelped, and he stepped back, allowing her to turn around with two plates in her hands. She stepped around him, walked the short distance to the table and set them down. He sighed. She was all the nourishment his body craved, but for once the cat lifting his nose to air disagreed. She grabbed two forks from a utensil drawer, and he followed her to the table. The cat might be right. The lasagna did smell incredible, but she'd forgotten something.

"Drinks?"

She started to stand. "I forgot."

He waved her back down. "Sit. Eat."

He opened the refrigerator and found a bottle of wine. After a brief search of the cabinets he returned to the table with it and two glasses. He poured for them both and waited till she raised her glass.

"To newfound mates," he said softly.

She gulped, but her eyes didn't say anything about not wanting him. She nodded. "Mates."

She sipped and set the glass aside, concentrating instead on her dinner. He watched her silently from the corners of his eyes, careful not to put her on her guard, to let her relax. They had to discuss the situation, had to make plans for her to move to the resort with him. He suspected she would balk at that order. Mentally, he shrugged. *Oh, well. She'd get over it.*

Finishing her meal, she pushed the plate forward and picked up her wine glass. She leaned back in the chair. The refrigerator hummed in the background, the only thing breaking the silence and piquing his curiosity.

"No power lines."

"Underground." She took a sip of the wine. Her expression was bitter and he wondered why. It wasn't from the sweet white wine. "Cost the royal treasury a pretty penny."

For some reason, he was certain her bitterness was not about the money, but he'd save that question for later. The lights flickered and her lips twisted in a rueful grin. "Not that it helps much. Everything down slope from us is above ground."

"And the sewer systems?"

"Septic. Pipes run through the concrete supports."

Ah, he'd noticed them but hadn't given them any thought.

"You never said why you were looking for me," she asked, changing the subject.

A piercing shaft of guilt. *Fuck*. He'd actually forgotten his search for his father while he was distracted by her. It made him angry. He didn't even know the woman and already she was intruding on his well-ordered, disciplined life. It wouldn't do at all. He focused.

"The plane crash last year. I understand you found Celeste Leonidas and brought her out."

All expression left her face, and his every instinct screamed at him.

"Yeah. So?"

"Were there any other survivors?"

She blinked. Not the question she'd expected. What the hell was going on here?

"No, there weren't."

Something wasn't right. There was a ring of uncertainty in her reply.

"You're sure?"

Her chin went up stubbornly. "Of course. I would have been informed if there had been."

She stood and carried their plates to the sink. He couldn't see her expression with her back turned to him, but he could smell her response to the questions. Fear again. And deceit. The leopard clawed for release.

"Why?"

"I'm the Messenger Corps Commander. I'm privy to all bird business, to everything that affects the clans."

An incomplete answer. The bitter smell of her dishonesty lay heavy between them. He rose and moved so quietly she couldn't have heard his approach, yet she didn't flinch when he placed his palms flat on the counter caging her in.

"I can smell a lie, Ajax." She stiffened. "Don't lie to me."

Her spine went straight as a rod, and she shoved against him. He stepped back, allowing her the illusion she was in control, but his cat paced the confines of its cage in his mind. It was enraged. So was the man. A mate didn't have the right to keep secrets, to lie and deceive. The animal in him wanted to spring. To lick and taste and demand answers. Nico had never had to fight his leopard so much in the span of one evening before. It was infuriating, but also invigorating. He loved women. What male didn't? But he'd always preferred them submissive and biddable. This one was anything but.

CHAPTER FIVE

It was only years of court training that allowed Ajax to regain control. She used old breathing techniques to get her pulse and lungs functioning normally. Old lessons learned at her father's knee to school her expression into one of casual interest. Nothing more. Could he really smell a lie? Her panic threatened to return and with lessons taught by brutal experience she forced it down, forced it into a small corner of her mind to observe while she watched the predator stalking her home. Stalking her heart and body and threatening to take over. Already she craved him with a fierceness that terrified her. This was a strong man. A dominant man. A leopard at the top of the food chain. What would he say? How would he react when he realized his mate was meant to be Queen? An involuntary shudder shook her. He'd never submit to anyone, much less a bird. Even less a mate.

Her sight was keener than any other predator in the world. She was quick and agile. Her talons would, and had, rend the flesh from the most dangerous of enemies. But none of those things protected her heart from the leopard who'd already managed to worm his way in. It would destroy her if he turned away from her, if he left her. So she buried her secret, her deceit, deep in her mind. It wasn't like she was in a big rush to rule anyway. She'd been avoiding the duty for years, letting her cousin rule as Regent in her stead.

She ground her molars against the frown gathering in her thoughts and on her face. That was a problem. Mathew was consolidating. Reaching. Soon his power would eclipse hers. It wasn't because of arrogance that that rankled. Already he was doing things, making decisions that she disagreed with. They'd fought over and over again, loudly and bitterly, over his actions. He only responded if it was such an issue for her she was welcome to take over. He knew she didn't want to rule so it was an easy thing for him to suggest. As long as she didn't take the power for herself, it was his to do with as he wished.

She sighed. The time for holding back was fading fast. Her cousin's actions left her no choice. She would have to take the Eagle Throne, like it or not. She cast a longing look under her lashes, watching her newfound mate prowl the large room. Would she lose him when she did so? Likely. She'd never wanted to be in this position. Never wanted to lead or be queen. Certainly never wanted to be mated. She'd seen how much being queen had isolated her mother and watched her steady decline since the death of her mate until the point that she'd stepped down and made Ajax make decisions about the throne. Mattering that much to one person, depending that much on one person, petrified her. Yet here she was mated and contemplating her next move in the werebird world. Consolidating and calling on her power. Taking her throne. Taking responsibility for every werebird in North America. She just hoped like hell she didn't end up like her father.

She knew Nico's questions were about his father, had watched the entire were world tremble with the news of Hector Leonidas's death. Her heart ached for him. For a very personal loss she knew all too well. If her suspicions were right, that plane crash had been no accident. Would he react to the murder of a father the same way she had? She peeked at him from under lowered lashes. Of course he would. The memory rose sharp and sudden. It caught her in its teeth and wouldn't let go. She felt Nico stalk closer as her eyes slid shut, as her heart thudded at the recall of what had been done and what she'd done in retaliation.

Knuckles gently traced the curve of her cheek. The touch soothed her as nothing else could. "What is it, Ajax?"

She shook her head. "Remembering."

"The crash?"

She smiled a little. He was completely focused. "No. My father."

He moved his body closer to her, sharing his heat, and she realized she'd started to shiver. "Tell me," he ordered.

She scowled. She didn't take orders from anyone, but against her better judgment she started to speak. She told herself it was because he needed to know where she'd come from. That her independence and strength had been forged in blood.

"I was thirteen when he died. We went for a morning flying lesson." She didn't mention he'd been teaching her battle tactics, didn't mention part of the household Guard had been with them. "We were attacked by a group of rebel vultures."

She turned her face into his chest and rubbed her nose over his breastbone as he stroked her back. Nico ached for the girl she'd been. No child should have to see her father murdered. How had she survived? And who had punished the vultures? He got control of his protective rage, reasoned with the cat. If someone hadn't already done it, he would. Later. Now he needed to take her to bed and spend hours loving her body. He started to nudge her in that direction but she backed away.

"I'm not done." She sighed. "All of my kind knows this story, but no one speaks of it. I'm not sure why I'm telling you now."

He did. He'd accused her of keeping secrets. For some reason, she didn't want to speak about the crash so she was giving him this instead. The box around his heart cracked.

"I was too young to do anything about it at the time. Too weak." She shrugged one shoulder. A nervous gesture he hadn't seen yet. Afraid of how he'd react to whatever she was about to tell him? She fisted her hands.

"I waited five years. Then I gathered…some friends." Why that hesitation? His cat sniffed the air and raged. More deceit. "We tracked the vultures down."

She stared at her hands. Spread her fingers wide. Her voice when she continued was fierce, unapologetic. "I killed four of them myself."

Man and cat went still. This was more than a secret in exchange for one she wasn't willing to give over. This was the story of how a girl had become the woman standing before him.

His emotions were mixed. Rage that no one had kept her safe. Terror for what one wrong move during that operation could have cost them both. And pride. Sharp, bright satisfaction that she'd made those who'd hurt her pay. Both man and leopard agreed. An eye for an eye. Life for life. It was fitting that she'd killed the vultures. He would have done the same in her situation. It was the natural order in their worlds.

Twisting her fingers together, she turned her back to him and stared out the doors. The snow had begun and wind howled, battering the glass and shaking the house.

"You're stuck here for a few days," she whispered.

She was afraid again, but this time the fear didn't seem to be of him. Her body was stiff and even though she saw him coming in the reflection on the door she winced a little when he rested his hands on her shoulders.

"Why the fear, little bird?"

She tensed, pulled free of his embrace, and turned to face him. Eyes narrow and cold, she set her hands on her hips. Her voice was glacial. "I know you didn't just call me little bird."

"Don't like that huh?"

There was no scent of fear from her now, only extreme irritation. As endearments went, little bird was definitely out. Fighting a grin, he held his hands up in mock surrender.

"How would you like me to call you kitten?"

"I wouldn't try it if I were you," he managed to say through clenched teeth, the very idea of it appalling. He sucked in a deep breath. She'd made her point—time to change the subject.

"Why Ajax for Alexandra?"

The tension left her shoulders, and he knew he was on safer ground with the question.

"My father started it. He always joked Alexandra was too much of a mouthful and besides Ajax sounded tougher."

She smiled a little as she answered, obviously caught in memory. Returning to the doors, she resumed watching the snow, growing quiet and thoughtful. He was drawn to her again, unable to resist moving closer and leaning down to nuzzle her neck. Would it always be like this? Would he always feel like he had to be touching her to breathe?

"The crash was pretty spread out." The subject change surprised him enough he bit harder than he'd intended, hard enough to sting. Instead of a protest, she softened against him the scent of arousal on her skin growing. He licked, soothed the ache and waited for her to go on. "There are two enclaves near the area. One on each end. I was visiting one. We checked out our end. Celeste *was* the only survivor there. If the storm passes, I'll take you to the other one tomorrow. Maybe you'll find the answers you need there."

He murmured agreement, ignoring a twinge of guilt. The crash and his father's fate were not the center of his attention at the moment. His brothers would probably cheer this new development. And rub it in his face. Ignoring that for now, but well aware he owed several apologies, he picked her up and carried her down the hallway he knew led to her bedroom. She felt fragile in his arms and didn't protest the move.

Her fingers curled around the nape of his neck, brushing over the shorn hair there. She didn't let go when he lowered her to the bed, tugging him down on top of her. Her eyes glowed in the dark room, but not with the confidence he expected to see. They were questioning, a little shy, sad. Lifting her head from the pillow, she kissed him. He didn't like his women aggressive in bed, but her actions spoke less of trying to gain control and more of a need to be held. In that he was willing and able to oblige her, desperate to eradicate the wounded feeling he glimpsed in her eyes.

He took her mouth in a slow kiss not bothering to reign in his possessive instincts. He wanted her body and soul. *Needed* her body and soul. More than that, he needed her to recognize it, to see it and submit to him, let him take care of her. It was selfish, but he didn't care. He couldn't change his nature.

He withdrew from the seduction of her mouth and sat up on the side of the bed. She lay back and watched. Silent but not withdrawn. No longer the closed-in, reserved woman he'd met only hours ago. That shell was broken, at least for now. He undressed her. Taking his time, watching her carefully as he went, he removed first her shirt and bra, then her pants and underwear.

Her skin was creamy white. He set his palm flat on her stomach and enjoyed the contrast of his dark hand against her paleness, purred with satisfaction at the way her belly spasmed under his touch. He slid his hand up, slow, wanting to map every inch of her body. He felt the ridges of old scars and eyed the faded areas.

"What happened here?" he asked, lingering over a long obviously old scratch that stretched across her ribcage.

She met his gaze with a small smile on her face. "Some birds are just as dangerous as wolves and leopards, you know. That one was from training. My own fault. Wasn't fast enough."

His growl was low and menacing. It took a lot to scar a wereleopard. He knew the same was likely true for a wereeagle. That someone had permanently marred her flesh infuriated him. He knew she felt his anger, but she didn't flinch when he bent to trail kisses over the old hurt. Breathing deep, she lifted a hand to his head. His hair was almost military short, but she ran her fingers through it, massaging his scalp with her long nails. The growl became a purr. The cat liked being petted, stroked. So did the man.

He continued kissing his way up her body. She tensed, her anticipation a thrilling taste on his tongue, when he reached the underside of her breast. He flicked his tongue over her nipple, used the leopard's superior night vision to watch it harden into a tight nub of sensation as he repeated the action. Her breathing became a pant, and her hands clutched at his head as she thrust the breast up. He took her nipple between his teeth. Bit. Suckled.

Rolling off her, he propped himself on one elbow at her side and switched to the neglected breast. With his free hand, he skimmed her body from shoulder to hip. Learning her curves and skin, claiming what was his. He explored the downy white curls at the apex between her thighs, reveled in her low moans when his thumb flicked over her clitoris. Slowly he pressed his index finger into her waiting pussy. She mewled like a kitten. He added a second finger to her warm heat, thrust them slowly in and out. The orgasm came over her so quickly he hadn't anticipated it, hadn't been able to hold her back. She convulsed around him, her entire body stiff yet shaking.

His cat side was done waiting, done playing, and Nico let it take over. Still stroking his thumb over her clit, he rolled over, covering her body with his. She reached between them, took his cock in her tight little grip and guided him to her entrance. He froze for moment, resisting the urge to shackle her wrists over her head and show her who was in charge. She leaned forward, found his nipple with her tongue and a satisfied purr of her own.

"Nico. Now. Please," she whispered, breath feathering over his skin in carnal invitation.

"Greedy, Alexandra?" He used her full name, liked the feel of it rolling of his tongue.

A brief frown marred her forehead. "Only for you."

The cat preened its pleasure. Only for him. And she'd only ever be for him from now on. On that thought he could no longer resist and entered her in an unhurried, measured glide. He wanted to keep it slow, wanted to draw out the pleasure for both of them, but she wrapped her legs around his waist, dug her heels into the small of his back and gave him a look of such yearning he couldn't refuse her. It was impossible.

Still inside her, he sat up and grabbed a pillow. Placing it under her ass, sitting back on his heels, he was unbelievably deep. He gripped her hips and set a steady, even pace. He had to be careful. It would be so easy to lose control in this position, so easy to hurt her accidentally. The leopard was already desperate, wanting to rut. To fuck. To claim. Would that feeling, that urge, ever go away? Would his animal half ever be appeased? Ever accept there was no alternative for either of them—she was theirs. He'd had a hard time accepting it. Maybe when she accepted it, the leopard would calm. But right now it growled, hating being shackled, held back. It would prove to the woman some things were irrevocable. She must have seen or felt his struggle. Lifting her hands, she stroked his face. Petted his shoulders and back.

"What's wrong?" she whispered.

"Nothing," he grunted, increasing the speed of his strokes. She shouldn't be able to think with his cock buried in her. He met her gaze. Saw her confusion. "There's no going back, Ajax."

She actually grinned and tightened her grip on his shoulders. "No. I don't suppose there is. So are you going to fuck me like you want to? Like I want you to?"

The cat caged in his mind snarled for release. "Careful what you wish for, baby. I'm no tame house cat."

"And I'm not a sweet, fragile swan that needs coddling."

He wondered if she'd ever met his brother's secretary. The swan's cheerfulness irritated the shit out of him, but she sure wasn't weak. That bird had a backbone of steel.

And, he realized, so did his mate. He should let her see him now. At his most dominant, his most possessive. There was no way to temper those traits. No way to ease her into his life. Not that he'd been doing that. So he fucked her. Hard and fast. Until her cunt clenched tightly around him and she screamed her release like an eagle's battle cry. Seconds later he roared his own release.

He sensed her withdrawal almost immediately. Rolling over, he pulled her across his chest, anchoring her to him the best way he knew how. She wasn't hiding. She wasn't running. He refused to allow it. She was his.

CHAPTER SIX

Ajax woke to weak daylight reflecting off the window, the cloud cover hadn't abated during the night, and languid sensual heat. The big cat who'd invaded her life and home was pushed close, his chest against her back, one thigh between hers and an insistent erection against her ass. Her head was pillowed on one thick biceps. His other arm was wrapped tightly around her waist.

His breathing was deep and even with sleep, but she didn't dare move, didn't try to exit the bed. She told herself it was because she knew any movement on her part would rouse him, but a secret needy part of her mind recognized the lie. She liked being held in his embrace. She hadn't felt so safe, so protected, in years.

An unfamiliar ring tone jarred her from the disturbing direction of her thoughts. His cell phone was on her nightstand and she reached for it, hoping to answer before the shrill tone woke him. He got to it first.

"Yes?" he barked.

She bit her bottom lip against a smile while rolling to her back. Clearly, her big cat didn't like having his sleep disturbed. He leaned over her, and she traced the stubble on his chin. The man on the other end of the line said his name and Nico jumped up, pacing to the other side of the room. He kept his back to her, one hand on his hip and stared out the window. Part of her mind registered that the snow had stopped, but she was so distracted by his scrumptious ass she missed the first part of the conversation.

Wereeagle ears were sharp and even standing several feet away and murmuring she heard the relevant parts. No wonder he thought his father was still alive. The conversation ended quickly, and he turned to face her, body rigid and eyes flinty.

"You heard?"

"Some of it."

"If he's alive, there's a reason he's not contacting us."

She knew anger made her eyes the angry slits of her bird. "Surely you're not suggesting my people are keeping him captive."

She barely restrained herself from emphasizing *my people*, reminding herself just in time he didn't know he was accusing the royal heir of holding his father hostage, but even she heard the edge of doubt in her voice. She only knew one person gutsy enough to make that kind of move without her approval. Her cousin was already on her shit list. She was almost positive he'd hired the ocelot assassin Ramon Guerra to kill Lyra Leonidas, formerly Lyra Marcus and incidentally the niece of Michael Lycaon, the werewolf Alpha, and pretty certain he bankrolled a werewolf named Derek's attempt to oust Michael and install himself as Alpha. But if he were behind the disappearance of the wereleopard leader even being family wouldn't save him. She'd rip his throat out herself. She took a deep breath and forced herself to calm down, to think. She had her own concerns about that crash. Concerns she'd have to share soon.

Rising from the bed, she reached for the robe tossed across a chair and pulled it on. When he opened his mouth to speak, no doubt to protest the covering, she held a hand up for silence. She was amazed when he complied. Out of shock more than anything else probably.

"I'm not rushing to any judgments. After breakfast we'll go to the other enclave and see what they know."

She exited the room and walked down the long hall, sensing him following close on her heels. In the kitchen she got out bacon and eggs.

"You could fill me in," she suggested while cracking and beating eggs in a large bowl. Silent and broody, he started the bacon sizzling in a cast iron pan and glared at her.

"You heard."

Exasperation finally won. She threw her hands up in the air and paced. "That's my fault? You were in the same room. You know my hearing's as sharp as yours. I don't have the background knowledge to go with what I heard."

While she moved, the robe's makeshift tie loosened. She scowled at him, remembering what he'd done to the other one, but wasn't quick enough to prevent the lapels from falling open. She knew she should pull them closed, but was arrested by Nico's sharp inhalation and the heat that flared in his eyes. So much better than cold anger.

"Hector, my father, had a private bank account no one knew about. I only discovered it a couple of months ago."

He approached her with feline grace. Smooth. Silent. His hands settled on her hips and, leaning over, he nipped at the sensitive skin under her ear. Gasping, she let her head fall back. He took full advantage of the increased access and bit his way down her neck to her collarbone then licked his way back up. His rasping tongue set her blood on fire.

"Someone's been transferring money out of that account," he murmured between nips of his sharp teeth. "We finally traced it to a local bank. A bank owned by a bird conglomerate."

"Oh," she moaned, not sure if it was a response to his words or the fingers that teased her nipple into hardness.

His lips continued their southward track, and he sank to his knees to suck her other nipple between his teeth. She grabbed onto his shoulders, holding on for dear life as sensation flooded her. He paused a moment and looked up into her face.

"Aren't you going to share now?"

"I thought I was," she teased. He bit her in response, but she doubted it had the effect he wanted. She groaned and hung onto him harder. He growled when her fingernails dug into his skin, but it was a sound of pleasure not protest.

"We carry messages in bird form as you know and also own the werekind airline."

"Mmm hmm," he murmured while his tongue swirled around her navel. He licked a straight line down her belly to the curls hiding her pussy. Spreading the lips, he found the hard nub pulsing there. Licked. Bit. She groaned. God, he was going to kill her. His voice, mouth pressed so close, hummed straight to her core. "You were saying?"

"The crash was ruled an accident, but one of my mechanics doesn't believe it."

The change was so abrupt it was like flicking a light switch. He stood, all sensual play gone, gripping her hips so hard she knew he'd leave bruises. His normally green eyes became narrowed amber slits. Totally cat. She realized the leopard had taken over too late to get out of the way.

"Why weren't we informed?" The demand was harsh, guttural.

She made her body go soft, non-aggressive, and her voice coaxing. "I don't know who to trust, Nico. Until I know something for sure, my people will continue to investigate quietly."

His eyes still glittered severely, angrily at her. Lifting her hand, she stroked the side of his face. Tried to soothe, tried to placate. Instinct told her she wasn't out of danger yet.

"The last year…it almost looks like someone's instigating a war between the leopards and wolves. My Messengers have been dragged into the middle of that. It threatens our neutrality."

She continued petting him and breathed a sigh of relief when his eyes returned to normal. He was still furious, but he was in control. He let go of her hips, but before she could move away grabbed her shoulders with a small shake.

"You should have told me," he growled.

"I can't trust anyone with this. Not until I have answers."

The whisper was a harsh reminder that they may be mated, but they didn't know each other. He let go of her like he'd been scalded and stalked off, paced around the connecting areas of the living quarters.

"Is there anything else you've neglected to tell me?"

His voice was coldly furious, and he kept his back to her. She ached to go to him, to rub against him, offer what meager comfort she could. Viciously, she forced the urge down. Too many secrets left to go, and surely he'd turn against her when he learned them all.

She was beginning to get a sense of him, of how black and white his world was. Of how fierce his pride was. When he learned who she truly was he'd reject her. Maybe not because of her position, but because she'd kept it from him. She opened her mouth, but then snapped it shut. She wasn't ready to lose him yet.

Turning away, she walked to the counter and finished breakfast. He joined her when it was ready. Silent. His mood dark. She didn't break the silence, quietly cleaned up when they were done, steeling herself against what was still to come.

"The enclave we're going to is like a...military outpost."

He cocked an eyebrow and waited for her to go on.

"Our clans are broken down by species, but we're all ruled by one queen. There's a lot of inter-clan bickering and the queen is always an eagle. The eagles are the only ones who can really keep everyone else in line and cooperating." She shook her head. Some of the other breeds were ridiculously childish, their issues with each other stupid and petty. The others were...dangerous, covetous. And she was supposed to be the referee. It could really suck being at the top of the food chain. "Right now, we have a Regent. One of her cousins." She should have said one of *my* cousins, but still shied away from the inevitable.

"I knew this already."

"Right." Of course he did. "Anyway, this particular enclave belongs to several members of the Royal Guard. They live there. Train there. I haven't been there in years. I'm not sure what we'll find." Hopefully they wouldn't give her away but she wasn't holding her breath. "You have to be careful there. Let me do the talking." She frowned. "And we'll have to go in were form. It's too difficult to get to in human form. You'll need clothes."

He scowled. "What about you? You won't need clothes?"

"They'll have something for me," she replied. She could see the question in his eyes, but he didn't ask why. After a few seconds he nodded.

"I can handle the clothes."

He disappeared down the hall and came back a moment later with the backpack he'd been carrying when they met. He pulled jeans, a sweatshirt and a small bag out. Rolling the garments up, he stuffed them inside and zipped it shut. He held the bag up. It was half the size of his backpack and had two straps.

"You'll have to put it on after I shift."

He showed her how the straps would wrap under his shoulders to snap into place, then he stepped back and changed. She held her breath as she watched. She'd seen leopards before. They were big, powerful cats. Beautiful. She'd never felt such awe at seeing one. But this was different. He was hers. He butted his head against her thigh until she knelt and dug her fingers through his fur. He purred, let her explore a few minutes before stepping back and picking the pack up between his teeth. He dropped it at her feet and, sighing, she strapped it on him.

She wished she could delay this meeting and enjoy her cat for a while, but she could read the impatience in his gaze. She removed her own clothes and stepped out onto to the deck, shutting the door behind them once he followed. He jumped onto a tree branch, then a lower one and another until he waited on the ground below her. He grunted, and she realized she'd been staring. It was hard to rip her gaze away and concentrate on her shift. He was stunning.

Once she'd embraced the change, became the bald eagle her other half was, she quit thinking of Nico. Quit worrying about his leaving or clan business. Since he didn't know where they were going she stayed under the canopy, following the trail as far as it would take them. She let the exhilaration take her over, wind rushing under her wings as she flew dangerously fast just feet above the ground. He was forced to run to keep up but it was no hardship. His lope was strong, ground eating fast, and she felt an inexplicable pride in him. Her mate.

Too soon she had to slow her crazy flight to turn off the trail. There was only a narrow path going up the steep incline on the side of the mountain to the Guard's enclave. Normally she'd go above the treetops, but she wouldn't be able to lead Nico if she did.

The higher they went, the more she had to pull in her wings and slow her flight. He scrambled up the rocky mountainside easily, and in moments, they were standing on the huge ledge that led into the enclave. As soon as they came into sight, a sentry whistled, and she shifted, knowing news of her presence would spread quickly.

She bent to unbuckle the snaps holding Nico's pack on. He was standing and dressed when someone rushed out to meet her with clothes. She hurried to get into them before a crowd gathered. Patrick was first on the scene, and she inwardly groaned.

CHAPTER SEVEN

Nico recognized the man as the one who'd spoken to Ajax the previous afternoon. His every step was aggressive, territorial. He glowered at Nico. Nico wasn't sure if that was because of his presence in a place few were allowed or because of the woman at his side. Maybe the stranger thought he had rights to her. When he reached for Ajax, Nico growled and shifted his position to stand in front of her. He didn't know what the hell was going on here but no one was laying a hand on his mate. She shoved at his back and tried to step around him. He simply moved with her.

"Oh, good God. Nico. You're making me look bad," she hissed. Sharp talons scratched his back. He got the feeling if anyone else had dared block her she would've attacked. It pleased the cat that she held back with him. "Move."

Reluctantly, he stepped aside, closing his hand around her forearm. He didn't know what was going here, felt unexplained undercurrents, high tension, and growing anger. It seemed directed more at him than her, but he wasn't taking any chances.

She stood straight and tall next to him, glaring at the gathering crowd. Proud. And very, very angry. The scent rolled off her in waves. But other than that she showed no outward sign of any emotion. He almost growled. He was sick of seeing this façade of remote control. Then the other man moved and her control broke. She wrenched free of Nico's grasp and stepped forward. His heart literally stopped beating. Toe to toe. Nose to nose. With a man much bigger than her. Probably faster. No doubt stronger. He was planning a counterattack when her voice rang through the clearing.

"Back off, Patrick. *Now.*"

The other man cocked an eyebrow. "You don't have the right to order me around, Ajax."

There seemed to be a collective gasp from the crowd and then it waited, breath baited for her response. Nico frowned. What was he missing?

Ajax crossed her arms over her chest and smiled. It was the coldest, most chilling thing Nico had ever seen, and he had a damned hard time reconciling this woman with his mate.

"Is that right?" Her gaze swept the crowd. "Need I remind you, all of you, that oaths were sworn? Blood oaths."

Patrick tilted his head to one side. "Conceded. But you haven't lived up to your side of those oaths either."

She took a deep breath, and he had to force himself to focus on her face and not the way the action lifted her breasts. "That time has passed."

A ripple rushed through the crowd. He smelled their exhilaration. Their approval.

"We need to speak. Privately."

The man, Patrick, inclined his head. "Of course, Majesty. This way."

He turned and walked towards a building carved out of the mountain. Three others peeled out of the crowd and followed before Ajax took a step forward. Nico stopped her with a tight grip on her elbow, but forced himself to release her and follow. He wanted to throttle her. To yell and rail at her. She'd had plenty of time to tell him that she was the queen. Right on the heels of anger was confusion. Why was a Regent ruling in her place? Why had she led him into this blind? What else was she keeping from him? His cat prowled the confines of his mind. It wanted answers *now*, and following four strange men into a building to talk was not likely to get them.

He was the last inside and pushed the door closed behind him with a little too much force. The sound echoed. Ajax wasn't able to repress a wince. Good. She should understand how pissed off he was, how dangerous it was to anger a predator cat—and her mate—so much. He watched her move through slitted eyes and though her back was ramrod straight, her attitude screaming for a fight, he knew this wasn't the time. He took a calming breath and looked around.

It was a large room with a long meeting table in the center. He'd expected it to be dim as closed in as it appeared to be, but huge skylights carved into the ceiling filled the place with light.

The four men sat at one end of the table and Ajax joined them. Nico prowled, too restless, too furious, to sit still.

"Nico," she said softly, the slightest edge of command under the tone. He turned to glare at her.

"Don't push your luck, Alexandra."

She raised both eyebrows and sat back, again crossing her arms over her chest. This time he recognized it as a calculated move, something meant to convey ease, but he smelled the exact opposite. She was nervous. Anxious. Why? He concentrated. No fear so why the worry? Unless she thought this news would make him reject her. He snorted. That was impossible. Even if his father's fate didn't hang in the balance, she was his mate. Leaving would be like cutting off his right arm.

"Careful, Ajax," one of the other men said softly.

She turned to look at him, waited for him to go on.

"Cat. Bird." He shrugged. "Might want to watch how far you push him."

"I thought you had more spine, Jack."

They exchanged a long look, a look filled with history. "I have plenty of spine," he said quietly.

"Point taken. I apologize."

Nico had his suspicions. He caught Ajax's gaze, jerked his head to man. "He was with you?"

A look could communicate a lot. She knew he wanted to know if this man had been with her when she'd gone after the vultures who murdered her father. She nodded. Once. Slowly. Precisely. As if that time was too much for her to remember, and the pieces started to fall into place.

He stopped pacing, pulled the seat out beside hers and took her hand, lacing his fingers through hers. Some of the tension went out of her body.

"We'll talk about it later," he said. "For now..." He let the rest trail off. She knew what needed to be dealt with now. He watched the change come over her features and squeezed her hand.

"Don't do that."

Startled, she met his gaze. "What?"

"That change you do. That woman you become."

Across from him Patrick arched an eyebrow and grinned. "That's the queen."

"I don't like it," Nico snapped back.

She laughed softly, turned her head into his shoulder and bit. Her free hand moved to his waist. Stroking. Petting. Her touch soothed the cat, soothed the still present anger. Lifting her head, she nipped at his lower lip before turning to face the room, but it was Ajax that did so, not the remote shell.

"Start with the crash," she prompted. Steel in her voice, eyes clashing with Patrick's. Nico felt a pride he acknowledged he probably hadn't earned. He may not have the control over her he'd like, but *no one* was pushing his mate around. She would never allow it.

Patrick reached for the laptop at his elbow and spun it around. "Definitely sabotage."

He and Ajax both leaned in to study the screen. One half was filled with schematics, the other with a photograph.

"What am I looking at, Patrick?" she asked.

Patrick stood and leaned over. "This line?"

"Yeah."

"Here it is on the schematic. It's part of the hydraulics."

"And?"

"We combed that site. Picked up everything. That's why it took so long and I can't be sure, Ajax. Some of the pieces were too damaged to be of any use. You understand?"

"I do. Go on."

"Okay." He clicked one of the pictures, a long hose. "See this hole?" He waited until she nodded before continuing. "It's too precise."

"Tool made," Nico said, and Patrick nodded.

"Yeah."

"Okay," she said, leaning back and absently rubbing his thigh like she felt his turmoil. "Then the questions are, who did it and who was the target?"

Nico scowled. "First question is the target. That'll point us to the other questions. But there's another question to be addressed even before that. Where is my father?"

"Told you he was smart, Patrick. That he'd figure it out."

The voice came out of his dreams, and he turned slowly, drawing the anticipation out, to see the face that went with it.
"Dad."

CHAPTER EIGHT

"Well that answers that question."

Ajax repressed a wince of sympathy at the cold fury in Nico's voice even as her own rose to match it and turned, slowly rising to meet this man, this *dead* man, who was her mate's father. He moved with the feline grace she'd come to expect from the Leonidas males, but that's where the similarity began and ended.

Hector was shorter, bulkier, somehow *harder* than his sons. He let his hair flow to his shoulders, and his eyes were dark, bitter chocolate. She presumed the brothers' green eyes were a legacy of their mother. And she suddenly wondered why she'd never heard anything about the woman. She concentrated on the scene unfolding before her. That was a mystery for another time.

Nico strode forward and embraced his father with a quick squeeze. When he turned to face her, she forced herself to stand still and tall even though the accusation in his eyes cut her to the bone. She wouldn't defend herself or her lack of knowledge. This was her fault. If she'd been willing to step forward and take her place before, she would have been in this enclave often. Would have known Hector was there. She ground her teeth together. The hell with that. She wasn't taking all the blame. Patrick should have informed her. She'd make him answer for that later. First she had to deal with Nico, which meant regaining some of the emotional reserve he hated so much.

"Don't," Nico growled in warning, holding his hand out to her. He was tense, radiating rage, and it scared her a little. Was he trying to assert his dominance or responding to something else, the tension in the room, the secrets that kept getting revealed one after the other? "Don't push me right now, Ajax. Come. Here."

Hector raised an eyebrow, and she knew what he was wondering. Was the werebird queen going to bow to the demands of a leopard? Of his son? In front of her most senior advisors no less. Biting her lower lip, a nervous gesture she couldn't seem to break, she met Nico's gaze, watched as his softened a little. He kept his arm extended. Waiting for her to move.

"Ajax." A definite warning in his voice this time, one everyone in the room heard. She sensed her lieutenants tensing for a fight and knew she had to diffuse the situation fast.

She wasn't sure who would be the victor in a battle of wills between she and Nico, and if she tried he would try to make her pay for it later. She shivered in anticipation, remembering the ground rules he'd started off with. Submitting to him in private bedroom games was exhilarating, freeing, but it wasn't going to happen anywhere else. Looked like she needed to establish her own rules. How did you tame a cat? The thought of the fights to come sent a spike of adrenaline through her system.

She grinned. "I do like to live dangerously."

"If you don't move your ass, I'm going to give you dangerous."

Laughing, she shook her head. "You shouldn't assume that you're the most dangerous predator in the room. I realize that west of the Mississippi everyone probably follows your lead. Here they follow mine." She lowered her voice, "You're going to have to find a way to accept that, Nico, or this isn't going to work."

He cocked an eyebrow, incredulity stamped across his features. "You expect me to submit? Not fucking likely, baby."

Submit? Probably not. But he had to at least defer to her when there were others around, had to stop expecting her to submit to him in everything. Her stomach rolled and she took a steadying breath, knowing what had to be said, knowing it was going to hurt like hell to watch it happen.

"Then you should take your father and return to your lands."

He growled. "That's not happening either. Someone has to stick around to protect you from yourself."

God, the man was infuriating. She stepped close enough to poke him in the chest with her finger. "I don't need a protector, cat. I've been doing it myself for a long time. Why are we having this conversation again?"

"Because you aren't any good at it?"

Outrage coursed through her. Of all the gall. Hands fisted, her talons thrust through her fingertips and bloodied her palms while she struggled against the instinct to attack. If anyone else had dared speak to her like that, dared make that suggestion, she wouldn't have held back. She reminded herself, repeating it like a mantra, that he'd never seen her fight, this was the first time he was seeing her outside of her home.

Someone snickered behind her.

"Quick. Put him on the payroll. Anyone who can rein in the adrenaline junkie is worth any amount of money," Patrick drawled. He knew her well enough to know she was fighting the urge to attack, knew her body was keyed up for the excitement of a good match.

She spun around and glared at him. "How would you like to have your eyes gouged out?"

He smiled, slow and just this side of taunting. "Try it."

A hand closed around her wrist, and Nico yanked her back against his chest. "I don't think so," he said coolly, but he was speaking to Patrick not her.

Patrick shrugged, but he was smiling. "Another time, then. Better to get the business part finished first anyway."

Nico's arm was a tight band around her waist, and she stroked her hand slowly up and down its length. "Let's get this over with," she murmured before stepping forward. He let her go, and this time when she returned to the table, she sat at its head. He took the chair on one side of her and Patrick the other. Hector sat next to his son. She met his gaze levelly, forcing any sentiment she might feel towards her mate's father to the back of her mind.

"Start at the beginning," she ordered. He may be the leopard king, but she was queen here.

Nico reached for her hand absently as if he didn't realize he'd sought comfort from someone else. He laced their fingers together, held their entwined digits against his thigh and lightly traced her knuckles while he focused on his father.

"How did you end up here? Why haven't you contacted us?" Nico asked. She didn't think anyone else heard the hurt in his voice, but Hector's eyes flashed with understanding.

"It was too dangerous. I was very badly injured. I'm amazed Celeste survived. I almost didn't. We agreed—" he jerked his head to include the other birds in the room, "—to keep my survival secret until I was stronger."

She narrowed her eyes, furious over the deception, and looked him over. "That's obviously been a while." Then she turned to Patrick. "You should have told me."

Nico's fingers clenched around hers. A warning? Comfort? Patrick met her gaze steadily.

"You weren't ready to take over, and I promised your father we wouldn't force it on you. Under the circumstances it was safer for you."

She forced her jaw to unclench. "I've never picked safer."

He smiled and this time it was with warmth. Respect and remembrance. "No. You have your father's strength."

She ignored the implication that her mother *didn't* have any. Her father's death had broken her mother. Everyone knew that. It was no wonder to anyone that she'd spent the fifteen years since her father's death avoiding personal relationships and the throne. She studied Patrick. But maybe they'd resented her refusal more than she realized.

"What do we know?"

"It had to be someone with access to the plane at Refuge," Hector said. She shivered at the calculating rage in his voice. She'd hate to be the one responsible when the leopard tracked him down.

"We'd need a complete list of everyone who was at the resort at the time."

Even as she stated the obvious she had a knowing, a foreboding. She knew who was behind this, behind everything the last few months, even if she couldn't prove it. She didn't have to as it turned out.

The door slammed open, and Mathew walked in with enough arrogance in his swagger to make her gums hurt from grinding her teeth. She watched him approach, watched his gaze sweep the room and take in the presence of the two leopards and realization of the older's identity dawn. His eyes finally settled on her, and she rose to face him.

"Another survivor," he drawled. "I obviously need to come up here more often. How many others are you hiding, Ajax?"

She smiled coldly. "Just the two."

Leaning against the opposite end of the table, he seemed to consider her words, accept them before moving on to something else. "It's true then," he said.

She wondered what he meant. It was obvious she'd taken a mate and that meant Mathew's position was in jeopardy. It was almost unheard of for a mated heir not to take the throne. If a Regent was necessary it was almost always a mate. Nico would have the right to demand her cousin hand over control of the clan if she didn't take it for herself, if he were a bird. She struggled to remember their history—certain at some point in the distant past there had been a non-bird Regent. Only an eagle could sit on the throne, but there wasn't actually anything in law barring other species from holding the Regent's position. That was simply tradition. But maybe he was only reiterating Hector's obviously very alive presence to himself. If her suspicions were true and her cousin had tried to kill the cat, then his life was forfeit.

"What?" she asked.

"It doesn't matter." A slight shake of his head. "Challenge."

Her jaw dropped. A challenge could be issued by anyone in the clan. With just cause. It rarely happened if leaders were strong, and she was strong. She also had the right to have a representative fight in her stead. She'd never exercised that right before, always had chosen to fight her own battles. As queen, they probably wouldn't let her. In the past it would have gone to Patrick, but now Nico would have first choice. She wasn't about to put him in that position. She moved away from the table, out in the open of the room where she could maneuver if necessary. Nico shadowed her.

"Grounds?"

She didn't ask what she really wanted to know, didn't want him to realize how suspicious she'd been of him and his actions for months. Not until she was ready, until she had more information. But she wondered, why now? Why wait till this moment to challenge her? There was a slim possibility it might remove his only obstacle to total rule over the birds—her—but what did that have to do with all his machinations with the leopards and wolves?

"Supremacy. Purity," he said with a glare at Nico.

"Ah. That old argument." She hadn't realized Mathew was part of the small minority that believed there shouldn't be any interspecies mating. It didn't ring true as the reason for his challenge though.

She shook her head. "I don't think so. What are you really up to?"

His grin made her skin crawl. "You'll see soon enough, cousin."

Damn it, she should take him out now. Forcing herself to stand still, she pressed her lips together. A challenge had been issued. She couldn't make a move against him before morning. Honor and the rules demanded that much.

"How does this challenge thing work?" Nico asked Patrick who'd moved between them at Mathew's entry.

"He issues his challenge. She has until morning to meet him. Or her representative has until morning to meet him." The smile he turned on her cousin was feral. "You know we aren't going to let you fight her. You aren't worthy of that battle. You haven't earned it."

The protest died on her lips, hearing his words and seeing the reflection of his feelings in the other eagles' faces around the room. It was a part of their command structure she'd never liked. She could fight her own battles, was encouraged to, until she accepted the title. Then she was expected to give her defense over to someone else. She hated that. Chafed under those cultural rules. And Mathew knew it. His gaze was mocking when he met hers. He expected her to overrule her advisors, and it made her even more suspicious. Contrary. She nodded at Patrick.

"Make the arrangements."

She pivoted on her heel, but Nico caught her wrist before she could leave. "Wait."

She faced him and raised an eyebrow. She was shaking and struggling to conceal it, a combination of adrenaline and excitement and fear threatening to overrun her system.

"This representative. Who has first choice at that?"

Her heart pounded. She didn't want to drag him into this, but she'd already spent too much time not telling him important things, things he needed to know. She tried for nonchalance. Shrugged. "Mates have first dibs. Then senior advisors. Patrick most likely."

Looking over, she met his gaze and he bowed deeply. "Of course, Ajax. I'm at your service."

Nico moved to her side, the movement breaking her concentration on Patrick. They stared at each other for several long seconds.

"So it's my right, correct?" Nico asked Patrick not her. She held her breath. She didn't want this. Did she?

"It is."

"Fine." He glanced at Mathew standing near the door then back to Patrick. "Make it happen."

"No problem," Patrick murmured while ushering Mathew out the door. The other three werebirds followed them. She was left alone with two leopards, one of them really pissed off. Hector chuckled, but there was an undercurrent, a glee to it that made her suspicious.

"Think I'll leave you two alone. Ajax, dear, your rooms are always kept ready, you know."

What the hell was Hector up to? Charm seemed so out of character. Then again, she wasn't likely to be catching him at his best.

"Thanks." She nodded and chanced a look at Nico. His expression was inscrutable.

"Lead the way," was all he said.

The enclave was carved into the side of the mountain. Meeting spaces were on the bottom level where they were now and living spaces higher up. All of the enclaves had guest rooms, but this one had quarters specifically for the royal family, for her. She went through the door Hector had come in that was tucked into the back of the room and walked down a short corridor. They followed a set of wide steps up a level where it branched into a long balcony before breaking up into two new staircases. She took the one on the left, hugging the inside of the mountain. Huge window seats were carved out but she didn't take time to enjoy the view with the cat prowling at her back.

Finally they came to the end of the long climb and turned left into a corridor leading through the mountain. Every few yards they passed closed doors until stopping at the end of the hall before the last door. Twisting the knob, she paused and sucked in a deep breath. The last time she'd been here was the morning her father died.

Entering was like stepping into a time warp. She forgot Nico was with her as she wandered around the living area. She swore she could still scent her father—hear her mother's soft teasing laughter.

The place was laid out like a human apartment with a small kitchen and living area in the center flanked by two master bedrooms. She walked to the French doors and threw them open. Stepped onto the stone ledge and spread her arms to feel the wind ruffling her feathers. At this height there was always wind.

She was brought back to the present when Nico wrapped an arm around her waist and pulled her back inside, firmly shutting the doors behind them. Ready to face the music, she turned to face him. He was scowling out the glass panes.

"There's no rail on the porch. Do you have any idea how high up we are?"

She couldn't help it. She laughed. His expression just grew darker, and she moved closer, lifting a hand to caress the side of his face.

"I'm an eagle remember? We like heights and falling isn't exactly a problem."

"It's a problem for cubs," he muttered still glaring outside.

A vice squeezed around her heart. He was speaking of children. *Their* future children. In mixed were matings one parents' DNA always reigned supreme. Would it be his or hers? That could be a problem. A cat couldn't rule the werebirds obviously. She shook her head once.

"Impossible."

He broke away, and her gaze followed him as he moved around. Her leopard was a pacer.

"My genes will be dominant, of course," he said stroking the back of a leather couch. She shook her head at his confidence, biting back a laugh. Like he could just issue a command and there you go. Cub instead of eaglet. She considered arguing with him over it, but didn't think it would be worth it. Her father had taught her to pick her battles and it would be a minimum of several months before they could know the outcome of this one. Besides, neither one of them had any control over how the genetics would work out. She was confident it would be in her favor and it would be oh so fun to watch that dominant streak bite him the ass. He looked up, and his gaze was sharp, eyes steely.

"There are more important things to deal with right now though." He came around the couch on soft feet. Eerily quiet. She knew she was being hunted by one of the world's most dangerous big cats, and she retreated until her back hit the stone wall. He lifted his hand, grazed her cheek with his knuckles. "You are in so much trouble, Ajax."

The protest lodged in her throat. She wouldn't make excuses. She should have told him everything from the beginning. She knew that. But that wasn't why she held her tongue. It was the heat coming off his body, the erection pressed against her belly, the pure male scent of his skin.

Excitement gripped her with hard teeth. This was a man who would never let her rule him, who would give as good as he got and make her melt while he did. She loved him for it. A crazy thing to be thinking so soon after meeting him, but it felt right. Felt true. She wanted to mark him, bite him with teeth made beak hard and complete the mating he'd started.

CHAPTER NINE

Nico felt the change, the shift in her and knew she'd accepted him as her mate. He watched her tongue trace over little sharp teeth and held in a groan while his leopard roared for release. It wanted to lick, to bite, to assert its dominance, but he held the beast in a strong grasp. Once he started, he'd hold her at his mercy, and there was something she needed to do first. He lifted his hand to cup the back of her head and nudged her forward.

"Do it before I lose control, Ajax," he rasped.

Teeth. Hard biting teeth. He clenched his jaw hard enough to break and threw his head back with a growl. When he realized there was no getting control of his impulses, no holding back, he let his claws burst through his fingertips and shredded her T-shirt. It floated to the floor in a tattered ruin, but he ignored it, caught and held instead by round breasts, by nipples made into rigid points of arousal. He took one in his palm. Explored. Shaped. Releasing it, he grabbed her hips and slid her up the wall so her breasts were at his eye level. Then he pressed forward and sucked her nipple between his teeth. She wrapped her legs around his body and cried out.

He let go and admired the moisture he'd left, the shocking redness. He wasn't worried he'd hurt her. He could feel wetness through her jeans as she ground her pelvis into him, soaked in her moans and whispered words of encouragement. She was driving him crazy, and that need mixed with the deep fury he still felt at her deception had him riding a lethal edge.

He reached behind him and unhooked her ankles. Set her on the ground and stepped back. She met his gaze with lust filled eyes. He tore his shirt over his head and reached for the snap on his jeans.

"Get your jeans off," he ordered. Her eyes followed his movements as he carefully tugged his zipper down. She stood frozen in place. "Now," he growled shoving his jeans over his hips and down his legs. He kicked them off as she finally started to remove hers.

Too damned slow. She was struggling with her zipper when he took over. He wasn't gentle. He didn't have any gentleness left in him. The offending jeans were yanked off, gone in seconds, and she was left exposed to him. He spun her around and placed her palms flat against the wall high over her head. He growled a warning close to her ear when she tried to lower her arms. She froze, but he was pleased when he smelled no fear only excitement on her skin.

He took a steadying breath, fought with his cat's enthusiastic approval of her current position—fought its need to take over. Instead he gave into the urge to explore, to stroke and pet, assuaging the leopard's tactile need for touch. Her skin was pale and clear. Unblemished except for the few scars he'd already discovered. Soft. So soft.

He trailed his hands over her shoulders. Down her back. Stepped closer when he shaped the rounded globes of her ass. She groaned when he spread her and rubbed his thumb against the tiny puckered hole there. He nudged her thighs apart with his knee and let his cock slip between her legs, groaning at the heat and cream that escaped her pussy. She rolled her hips. The friction was exquisite. Tempted him to rush when he was determined to go slow. He slapped her ass hard enough to leave a rosy print.

"Stop that."

She whimpered but held still as he went back to his exploration. He used his thumb to press a slow steady rhythm against her asshole, but he didn't seek entrance. Instead he read her reaction. Her heart beat faster, the sweet scent of her arousal grew stronger.

She turned her head to the side, one cheek pressed against the hard wall. She was flushed, a pink tint to her skin. He slid his fingers lower, thrusting them between the folds hiding her slit. Groaning, she jerked against him, and he bit her nape in warning. When she was still again, he dipped a finger into her cunt. Just rimming the entrance, he tortured her. Tormented her. A fine tremor had taken over her body, and he knew she was struggling not to come, fighting an orgasm she knew he wasn't ready for her to have yet.

Her submission, her compliance, satisfied the cat like nothing else could. He edged his fingers a little farther into her channel while reaching around her torso, the wall scraping his knuckles as he made just enough room for his hand, palming one breast. Her breath hitched when he took her nipple between his fingers and squeezed. At the same time, he thrust his fingers all the way into her.

"Come now, Ajax," he growled against her throat, exulting at the way she clenched around him and screamed her release.

He didn't give her any time to come down. Removing his fingers from her, he repositioned himself pushing his cock slowly up. Deep. He rolled his hips, loved the way she convulsed around him. No protest. No resistance. Even though he held her pinned against the wall and, as he was learning, she was just as dominant in personality as he was, she gave him complete and total power. One day, soon probably, she'd want to try reversing that, want to take the sexually dominant role. The idea had never appealed to him before, but he was intrigued. He could give it a shot with Ajax, give her that kind of control. That kind of trust. But not now. For now he was in charge.

She trembled, and he knew she was going to come again. Knew he could hold her off or make her respond over and over all night long if he wanted to. But he didn't have that kind of control in him right now. He wrapped his arms around her waist and lifted her. He stayed lodged inside her as he carried her to the back of the couch. Gritted his teeth against the seductive friction as he positioned her leaning forward over it.

He ran a hand up and down her spine. Goose bumps rose in its wake, and he explored them a moment, fascinated by this new sign of her stimulation. They couldn't hold his interest long though, and he started to move in slow but hard strokes designed to push them both beyond reason, beyond thinking. He leaned over, covering her body with his and dropping small kisses up her back until he reached the nape of her neck.

Following instinct, allowing the leopard to rule his actions, he clamped down, holding her still with his teeth. He felt a fresh wave of her cream drench his cock and shuddered, clenched his jaw, fighting the orgasm that was coming on too soon. He couldn't hold off long so he reached between them and found her clit. One rough rub and she shook, her entire body caught as she exploded again. It was all he needed to break his bonds and he pounded into her, holding her in the submissive pose until he also screamed in release.

Dismayed, he realized he smelled blood and found he'd pierced the skin on her throat when he'd lost control. Lapping at it, he groaned and stood, but he only released her long enough to turn her around to face him. A tremor wracked her body, and she looked a little shell-shocked. A wave of remorse and tenderness threatened to undo him.

He should apologize, but he couldn't promise it wouldn't happen again. He could show her more easily than express the words anyway. Picking her up, he moved to the front of the sofa and lay down with her. She curled up against him, head pillowed on his chest, hand clenched over his belly. He petted, soothed, felt her relax enough to mold herself against him and drift off to sleep. He held her like that a long time, then reluctantly rose and carried her to one of the bedrooms, tucking her in and murmuring soothing words when even in sleep she protested being left alone.

He was in the living room pulling on his jeans as the knock came at the door. His fur rose in menace, the cat pissed at the intrusion, but it settled when he picked up his father's scent. He opened the door and stepped out of the way when Hector and Patrick walked in. He would have bristled at the other man's presence but it was clear from his scowl he could smell what had happened in the room earlier.

The wereeagle stalked in and glared at Nico. The look focused on his neck and he refused to lift a hand, to touch the mark Ajax had left. She was his. He was hers. His annoyance lifted to be replaced with a sense of rightness. Of belonging. It was an odd feeling for a loner leopard.

"Where's the queen?"

Nico raised an eyebrow at the demand in the tone. "Sleeping."

"She should hear the arrangements." Patrick was trying to exert rights over his queen. Not on Nico's watch.

He smiled, letting his expression go cold and feral. It had little effect on the bird, just a slight shift in his eyes of knowledge. Nico spread his feet into a fighting stance and crossed his arms over his chest.

"The way I figure it it's her job to rule all the birds and yours to advise her. Right?"

Patrick nodded clearly suspicious.

"And who protects her from you all? Who shields her from the petty demands of an entire race?"

Patrick's fists clenched. "This isn't exactly petty."

"No." Nico shook his head. "But we might as well start the way we're going to continue."

"With you as go between?" Patrick asked derisively.

"No. With me as protector." Everything settled inside him at the statement. The turmoil. The questions he hadn't been able to address yet. "Her safety is my responsibility."

"You're staying?" Hector asked.

"Of course I'm staying." Had there really been a question about that? "Where else would I would go?"

A gasp behind him. A sense of relief. He fought the urge to whirl around and face her, let her approach on her own. He'd been so focused on dealing with her advisor he hadn't heard her rise from bed or scented her presence as she approached.

She stopped beside him, a little behind. He could easily step in front of her if she was attacked and he realized that's why she'd positioned herself as she had. Not that she couldn't defend herself, but because she knew he wouldn't let her. Her fingers curled around his shoulder and squeezed. A sign of solidarity, of support from one mate to the other.

CHAPTER TEN

"You have news?" Ajax asked. She slid her hand down Nico's arm and linked her fingers with his as she stepped forward. He tensed but kept his protest to himself. She smiled inwardly. Her cat was learning.

Patrick inclined his head just enough to be polite. "Tomorrow at dawn." She could feel Hector watching her with interest but ignored him as Patrick paced around the room. He met her gaze and jerked his head at Nico. "You want to explain the rules or should I?"

Hell, no. She wanted to enjoy the rest of the day and not fear for what morning might bring. Nico stepped behind her and wrapped his arm around her shoulders, tugged until she leaned back into the embrace. "Tell me, Patrick."

Patrick looked him over. "I hope you're as good as you think you are."

A growl welled up in Nico's chest, and she set her palm flat on his thigh. His muscle spasmed at the touch, but he quieted. "I am."

The other wereeagle nodded. "You'll need to be. Mathew's one of us, a Guard. He's only been Regent the last few years since Ajax's mother stepped down as queen, but he's kept in fighting shape."

"Why was he Regent and Ajax not queen?"

Patrick shook his head. "That's for her to tell."

"I refused," she said softly for Nico's benefit and pleaded with her eyes for Patrick to understand. To forgive. They'd been good friends once. Comrades. "The throne killed my father and destroyed my mother. You can't blame me for…resenting that."

Patrick held her gaze a long time and finally nodded. "There's a lot to do now."

Acceptance. She couldn't fight her relief, and Nico hugged her tight in support.

"Let's deal with this first. Mathew's behind it all, isn't he?"

It was hard to concentrate with Nico pressed against her back, but at least it saved her from being overwhelmed by the *what ifs*. What if she'd taken the throne when she was eighteen? What if she'd become suspicious of Mathew sooner? How many people had died in the last year because of her inaction?

"No guilt," Nico whispered in her ear. "You can't change the past."

Tears pricked her eyes, and she hurriedly blinked them away. She'd been taught to show no emotion, had spent years pretending she didn't feel remorse, and in two days, he'd blown that control to hell. She had an urge to turn around and hide her face in his shirt. Yesterday it would have freaked her out, but it no longer worried her.

She shifted a little so she could put her arm around his waist, but he kept her close, tucked up under his shoulder. For the first time in years she felt like she belonged. She felt whole.

He'd said he was staying. Her first terror dealt with. The second wasn't so easy.

"The rules," she reminded Patrick.

He tilted his head to one side and studied her before answering. "I expected more protest from you actually."

She snorted and looked up at the wereleopard standing so close. "Wouldn't have done me any good. Seemed like a waste of words."

Patrick grinned but his gaze was assessing. "True. You were always quiet for a girl."

She smirked. "Watch it, buddy. I can still kick your ass."

"You could try."

"You're on."

"I hate to interrupt old home week," Nico drawled, "but could we get back on target?"

They sobered and Nico spoke to Patrick. "Why would she protest?"

The male wereeagle looked back in forth between the two of them and she shook her head slightly. She knew Nico would just get pissed off again. Patrick ignored her. He shrugged.

"It's not like she hasn't been challenged before. Happens all the time, and she deals with it. But traditionally, once an heir accepts her rule, she can't fight her challenges herself anymore. Queens are too valuable. Besides, it's rarely done. The heir has usually more than proven herself by this point."

"What happens if her representative loses?"

Patrick narrowed his eyes. "Would it be better if I do it?"

Nico snarled, and she turned her head pressing a kiss against his bare chest before biting down. His hand stroked the back of her head, and the snarl stopped. God, he was touchy.

"It was a logical enough question to ask," he said, voice cold with anger.

"Then the Council convenes and chooses another female from the ruling family to take the throne." He paused. "That's never happened before."

"Okay. What are the rules?"

"There's really only two. You can fight clawed, but since you're different species, not in a full shift. And it's to the death."

And *that* was the part that made her blood run cold. It didn't even give Nico pause.

"I wouldn't expect anything less."

There was a knock on the door. Patrick went to open it pausing at Nico's sharp, "*Who is it?*"

"I took the liberty of having lunch sent up. And a few other things your father thought you might find useful."

Nico nodded a go ahead and the door was opened. Two women from the large enclave staff pushed in two rolling carts. The first contained food. It was pushed into the kitchen where the top was unloaded onto the island and the hidden compartments on the side into the cabinets and refrigerator.

She arched an eyebrow at the second. Nico took the rolling desk from the woman pushing it and placed it on the wall between the front door and the bedroom then pulled one of the armchairs over. The food cart and employees disappeared while he unwound the various cords that went with two laptops and a couple of phones.

He had a happy distracted look on his face. Like a kid in a candy shop. The three of them gave him space. She ate one of the sandwiches at the counter and grabbed a bottle of water from the fridge watching while he plugged in various wires and booted up the computers.

"Bring me one of those, baby," he said while focusing on a screen and typing commands, his tone distracted.

She sighed. Of course she'd end up with a mate fascinated by modern technology. The stuff made *her* head hurt. After handing him the sandwich, she stood at his shoulder and stared at the screens trying to figure out what was so absorbing. She didn't have a clue.

"What are you doing?"

"Checking the resort records to see if your cousin was around the week or two before the flight." She knew what that was. Refuge's logo was clear on one of the screens. Frowning, she leaned in closer to look at the other one. "This one?"

He leaned back with a satisfied gleam in his eyes when the Messenger airline's database opened. She scowled. He shouldn't be able to access that.

"Hacking your airline." He grinned up at her. Patrick and Hector both crowded close at his words.

"Anything interesting?" Hector asked.

"Mathew was at Refuge. Arrived a few days before you and Celeste left and departed two days later."

"So that puts him there," Patrick said softly. "He's a pilot. Most of us are, so I'm sure he could pull it off. The question is, why?"

"Power," she said, ignoring the churning in her gut. She understood this kind of greed, but she couldn't relate to it. Nico absently took her hand and rubbed her knuckles while watching his screen scroll. The unconscious offer of support soothed her, but Patrick watched her, waited for her to go on. "We're the wealthiest clan in North America, but not really powerful. Neutrality has always been at the core of what we are. The two don't really go hand in hand."

Nico looked up at her. "That's just a different kind of power, baby."

She smiled a little. She knew. But it obviously wasn't enough for her cousin. She went to the refrigerator for another bottle of water twisting the lid off as she slowly walked back over.

"Here it is," Nico growled while reaching for the phone. "What?"

He gave her a startled look like he'd forgotten she was even in the room. She rolled her eyes. The man had to work on his communication skills.

"The list of mechanics on duty the week before the crash."

She noticed the cats tense a split second before she heard the voice, didn't realize until later that their sense of smell must be much keener than hers.

"Oh, I don't think that'll be necessary."

She whirled around to face that voice but it was too late. He must have come in through the balcony doors, an easy enough feat for an eagle. Mathew grabbed her, arm around her throat, talons sharply poking her neck. She felt a trickle of blood and knew that if he moved a fraction of an inch he'd pierce her jugular. Not even a shifter could survive that. She was amazed that Nico didn't roar his rage. It was there in the murderous gleam in his eyes, the edgy lines of his body. He wanted to act yet couldn't. His hands were effectively tied. She needed to buy some time and she *wanted* all the answers.

"Why, Mathew? Why fuck with the other clans like you did or come after me like this? You know I'll fight you. You could have challenged me months ago."

His talons dug deeper into her throat at that last reminder, and she felt the blood flow trickling down her throat increase.

"I didn't need to challenge you before. I was in charge. Then you had to go mate this cat and take the throne."

She struggled to breathe as his hand convulsed around her neck and it pissed her off. She should never have got herself into this position. She was a better warrior than this.

"The clans," he went on and she felt his chest shift against her back, knew he shrugged. "The weaker, the lesser organized they are, the stronger we are. And if I can get rid of the Leonidas and Lycoan families I can replace them with someone I control."

"Power," she whispered. "It's all about power."

She looked at the other three men in the room. "They won't let you leave here alive."

He leaned closer, his hot breath blowing over her skin. "Maybe not. But they've destroyed my plans. My dream. So now I'm going to destroy the most important thing to them. Two of them at least.

How do you think your cat and advisor will feel forced to stand there and watch you bleed out?"

Patrick moved, rolled to the balls of his feet. She could see his struggle, knew he wanted to lunge and dared not.

"Oh, I wouldn't if I were you, Patrick," Mathew drawled. "She'll just die faster."

His talons dug deeper and she knew if she survived this, she'd have a new scar to add to her list. Had Mathew always been this sadistic and she'd never noticed? It didn't matter. She had to act, someone had to act, or she would die here soon. She wanted to know what it would be like to live, to rule, with Nico at her side. To know whose DNA would turn out to be the most dominant one. Watching him closely, she hoped he knew that, hoped it saw it in her eyes.

CHAPTER ELEVEN

Rage couldn't even begin to describe the emotion that consumed Nico. He'd felt rage before. This was much more violent than any urge he'd ever experienced. If Mathew harmed her, the leopard would tear his throat out. Already it demanded retribution because the man dared lay hands on its mate, for the trail of blood flowing down her neck. His fury matched the cat's, merged and became something terrifying. The man would die. Hard and brutal, but not fast. Fast was for those deserving mercy, and this one didn't.

Appeased, the leopard crouched, prepared itself for the hunt. Nico would give it free reign once Ajax was clear of those talons. He circled them, thinking, planning.

"Ajax," he spoke softly, not wanting to spook the eagle holding her into doing more damage than he already had. "Remember the last thing we did before we left your house?"

She cocked an eyebrow. He would have thought she was entirely too blasé about the situation if not for the scared look in her eyes. He railed silently. What kind of security expert was he that he couldn't even protect his own mate? After a moment her eyes cleared and she smiled, her expression softening. Shit. He hoped she wasn't thinking about when he'd fucked her. Not yet anyway. He needed her to shift, fast, and get the hell out of the way.

Her nod was so slight he almost missed it. And then in a quick flash of movement she became her eagle, slashing her talons in a downward sweep as she dove out of the way. Blood welled across Mathew's face and chest, and he turned, screaming his outrage. Before he could lunge after her, though, the leopard crushed his throat then jerked the body until the neck snapped loudly in the silence.

Nico was lost deep in the leopard's fury. It had wanted to toy with the man, drag out his suffering. The death was too quick. Too easy. It was only the petting hands, the soothing voice of its mate that got it to unclamp its jaws, to release the carcass. She wrapped her arms around his neck and tugged him back. He gave the body one last vicious swipe before complying, stepping away and shifting.

Patrick and Hector hefted the body. "We'll dispose of the trash."

Ajax followed them to the door and turned the lock then did the same with the glass doors. He hadn't even noticed when they'd been opened, and it had almost cost him everything. The rage, the bloodlust was still riding him hard as he looked her over, examining her body from a distance for other signs of injury. It wasn't enough. He needed his hands on her, his cock in her. The desire swept over him with the force of a tornado. He knew it was a bad idea in his current state but he couldn't help himself.

"Come here," he demanded. She hesitated. "Now, Ajax."

She sauntered over, smile slow and sultry. He knew that little extra swing in her hips was for him and suddenly everything in him calmed, centered. She stopped in front of him, and he set his hands on her waist. Slowly moved them around to mold her butt and yanked her closer. He leaned his forehead against hers and breathed in her scent, convinced himself she was alive and well.

"If you ever scare me like that again, I'll spank your ass."

She laughed and leaned back, looked him straight in the eyes. "I love you too, Nico."

A vice clamped around his heart, and he exhaled a gusty sigh of relief as he crushed her to him. "'Bout damned time you admitted it. I love you, baby."

He kissed her. Inhaled her. Sucked in her essence, her soul. Then gave all of himself to her. Irrevocably.

Forever never felt so good.

EPILOGUE

Hector stood off to the side, holding the kind of glass his mate had always liked—delicate and fragile—incongruent in his big beefy hands. He flexed one fist, watching the movement, wondering what she would have thought of this gathering.

He looked around. She would have loved it.

All their sons, all their *mated* sons, were here to celebrate Adrian's wedding to Cleo, a werelioness. Interesting woman, Cleo. A fine match for Adrian.

He counted the rest of them.

Celeste and Jason, finally come home. He stood tall and relaxed, though he never let her move from the shelter of his arm.

There were Ajax and Nico. The werebird queen and his third son, more besotted than he ever expected to see *any* of his sons.

And finally Lyra and Zander. The wolf. The hugely pregnant wolf. She approached him, Zander's gaze following her closely even while holding a conversation with Adrian.

"Having a good time?" she asked, sipping a glass of water.

From the corner of his eye, he watched Ajax excuse herself and leave Nico with Adrian and Zander. She stepped forward with that regal, smooth glide he was growing accustomed to, linking her arm through Lyra's.

The women faced him together. A united front. The two predators, by more than virtue of species, mated to his sons.

Neither of these two women were ever going to be controlled, be handled. He admired their gumption if nothing else and grinned, not caring if it was just this side of feral. They could deal with the sometimes murky politics of a predator shifter's family.

Both narrowed their eyes at the look, both did that little subtle shifting of stance that warriors did when preparing for battle. Oh, yes. Worthy women. And if the future brought what he suspected it would for *all* shifter species, if that dark cloud looming on the horizon came to pass, they would need to be. But he wouldn't dwell on that today. Today he'd enjoy being in the presence of his family, ignoring the ever-present pang of grief and guilt caused by the one who refused to be with them. Another secret he'd kept from his sons, another lie he'd told. For their own good, or for his? He didn't know anymore. He shook his head. There would be time enough for that later.

He saluted Lyra with his glass. "To the next generation of Leonidas leopards."

She cocked an eyebrow and took a drink from her glass. "What makes you so sure they'll be leopards?"

He choked on his wine, and Ajax hit him just a little too hard on the back while he coughed. He knew by the look in her eyes she was aware of what she was doing and took enjoyment in it. Ignoring her, he focused on his youngest son's mate.

"Of course they'll be cats. Dominant DNA and all that."

He waved a hand through the air knowing he shouldn't have to explain it to a doctor. At least he thought not. Ajax and Lyra exchanged a long, knowing look and both burst out laughing. He glared. They'd probably both refuse to have leopards just to spite him.

The others approached. Celeste with her gentle smile, Cleo trying not to show her hyper-awareness of all the strangers in her house. His boys. Tall, strong. Good. With everyone gathered around it was time to get down to business.

He looked at his oldest, Jason. His pride and joy, the one who'd broken when he thought his mate had died. This was his chance at redemption. "Have you decided?"

Jason pulled Celeste to him, wrapped his arms around her waist. Slowly he nodded while holding Hector's gaze. "I'll come home and take my place as CEO again. And look after security since Nico's taking up with the birds."

There was an audible sigh of relief through the group, but it seemed to be most heartfelt from Adrian. The boy had taken on an unusually hard task when Jason had left. One he hadn't been trained or prepared for, but he'd done well. Hector allowed himself a small bit of pride. He'd been hard on his boys, but they'd grown up strong, smart.

There was one other matter to settle and he kept close watch on Ajax with gleeful anticipation when he delivered it. They'd been butting heads for weeks, he and his newest daughter-in-law. He knew she'd flown to Arizona expecting to leave him behind when she returned home. Little did she know.

"Adrian, I don't care how you and Jason work it out, but you two are in charge. I'm retiring officially and going back to Tennessee with Nico and Ajax."

Ajax was speechless for only a moment. "Absolutely not!"

"I'm afraid my mind is made up, dear."

She narrowed her eyes to dangerous slits. "Listen, cat, I've had enough of you. It's someone else's turn."

His other daughters-in-law were all quick to jump in to support his choice. If he didn't find the whole thing so amusing, he would have been insulted. The boys, he noticed, were all suspiciously quiet. That was fine too. He was happy just to see them together, everyone speaking to each other. Life was good again.

Smiling, he slipped away, leaving all his children to squabble amongst themselves, to find a quiet place to watch the sun set.

ABOUT THE AUTHORS

Crystal Jordan is originally from California, but has lived and worked all over the United States as a university librarian. An award winning author, Crystal has published paranormal, futuristic, and erotic romance with Kensington Books, Harlequin Books, and Entangled Publishing. Visit her at ww.crystaljordan.com.

Loribelle Hunt is a beach bunny at heart, but in a pinch she'll settle for a pool. An Atlanta native, the Army relocated her to southern Alabama more years ago than she cares to remember. Since it only snows once every two decades or so, she decided to stay. She lives with her husband of twenty years, their three kids, and way too many English Springer Spaniels. She writes science fiction and paranormal romance often with a Southern drawl. Visit her at www.loribellehunt.com.

If you enjoyed *Forbidden Passions*, you'll love *Forbidden Passions, Volume 2*.

Turn the page for a sneak peek at the first two chapters!

Forbidden Passions, Volume 2

Romance among weres is never simple.

Secret Passions by Loribelle Hunt

When the discovery of human/animal DNA makes werefox Sara Beth Reynard a tabloid's lead story, she laughs the whole thing off...until some goon attempts to kidnap her. As a result, she is sent to the wereeagles for her own protection, but she's not happy about it.

Wereeagle Patrick Aquila takes one look at Sara Beth and wants to peel away her layers. Yet one night of exploding passion pits him in a race against time. Time to convince Sara Beth they belong together, and to find the snitch who is feeding information to her stalkers.

Illicit Passions by Crystal Jordan

As a pretty swan-shifter, Tori Haida was born a stereotype, and has spent a lifetime living it down.

Wolf-shifter Bastian Lykaios is just the kind of dominant male who drives her the wrong kind of crazy. And yet, Tori can't help wanting him.

Unfortunately, there's no time to indulge an affair—not while a werekind traitor is leaking information to the human press. But when Tori is kidnapped, Bastian's is willing to go to all lengths—including betraying his own kind—to get her back.

CHAPTER ONE

Sara Beth Reynard had been on edge since leaving her house that morning. Her apprehension had eased when she reached the job site and was surrounded by the work crews, but as everyone began to leave for their lunch, the feeling intensified so much she decided she'd better finish and leave too, rather than be the last on site. She loved the house she'd designed and its country setting, but it had never felt so isolated before today.

It was that damned tabloid reporter's fault. Somehow a handful of scientists had gained access to blood and tissue samples from werekind. Sara Beth didn't believe for one second it had happened by accident—someone inside the community had to be responsible. The world's shapeshifters had kept their existence secret far too long for a small group of humans to accidentally discover them. Most of the scientific and news communities had dismissed the findings, but Jeff Nichols, the crackpot journalist, was all over the story.

Worse, he'd identified her as a werewolf. *A werewolf!* The wolves were descendants of King Lycaon, who, along with his sons had been granted the ability to shift by the Greek god Zeus. They were completely unrelated to the foxes, who'd been created by ancient Germanic gods as warriors. Their common ancestor was Reginhard. As the legends and fables were passed from generations and crossed cultures, Reginhard became the surname of the werefox alpha, Reynard.

She had no idea how Nichols had stumbled on her, but he could at least get the story straight. She was a fox, dammit, not some overgrown, bad-tempered puppy. Her clan thought it was hilarious. The whole mess appealed to them. After all, foxes were known as pranksters in most mythology and felt honor bound to live up to their history. Of course, they weren't the ones with their faces plastered all over those awful rags, were they?

She heard a truck crank up and—glancing out the window—saw it drive away. She finished washing the grout off her hands and hurried upstairs. The house was almost finished. She'd come to see how the final stages were progressing and had been roped into assisting with tiling the kitchen backsplash. Truthfully, she didn't mind. It was the kind of thing she loved and also the reason she'd got degrees in architecture and design. After school, she'd joined the family construction business. She'd only been in charge of the residential side of the company for three years, but she'd been working in it since she was a kid.

The stairs opened onto a large landing that had been designed at the client's request as a library/lounge area. The second story had natural teak floors, which contrasted nicely with the crisp white built-in bookcases that surrounded the landing. The bedrooms on either side of the library differed only in color. She went through the guest room before moving to the opposite end of the landing to the master suite. She'd given the client exactly what he wanted and had to admit the man had good taste.

The back wall was all windows and French doors that led to a balcony, which stretched the length of the house. The room had a sitting area in an alcove that managed to feel private even though it was open, and the bathroom was to die for. She took her time checking it out. It was done in warm earth tones, had a huge walk-in shower and a tub she was convinced would hold four. It was positively decadent. Sighing, she flipped off the light switch and went back downstairs.

In contrast to the traditional upstairs, the first story looked like something out of a slick urban magazine. The floors were polished concrete and the front half of the house was an open living, dining and kitchen area. A small guest bath was tucked into a short hall which led to the final room. The house featured the first studio she'd built for a working artist and so far it was the least-finished room. Only the floors and walls were complete. She had an appointment with the artist later in the week to discuss work surfaces and storage areas.

She heard the front door close as more of the guys left and hastened to follow them. As soon as she stepped outside, she felt watched. Damn, she was getting sick of this. She let her fox side rise to the surface and sharpen her vision, but she didn't see anything or anyone who didn't belong when she looked around. Was danger really lurking or was she just paranoid? It seemed ludicrous to believe someone was watching her, but she couldn't shake the feeling. She decided to swing by her parents' house. One of her brothers was bound to be there for lunch. It would be easy to rope one into having a look around.

She stepped off the porch to the sidewalk, giving the area another visual sweep. Nothing looked suspicious. There were a couple of guys getting in a truck and another couple on the far side of the yard, packing up the tools by the new retaining wall. She waved as she headed toward her own vehicle. She'd arrived late and had to park a bit down the street.

It was broad daylight, bright and growing chilly as the first storm of the season moved in. She felt like she was walking through town alone at night, though. She dug her keys out of her pocket, eyeing the tree line beside her, and activated the remote when she was in range. By then her senses were screaming. She took a deep breath to test the air. At first all she scented was woods, the last honeysuckle of the season and fresh cut grass. Then there was the faintest hint of man. When the scent's owner stepped out from behind a tree, she cried out, more from surprise than fear.

She was damned glad she had when she met his gaze and took another deep breath. His scent was putrid in a way she'd learned to associate with violence. Malevolence. His eyes glittered, his expression anticipatory. He was several inches taller than her, bulky the way bodybuilders were, balding and scary as hell. Then he lunged for her. Her heart thudded in her chest and she backpedaled, just managing to stay on her feet and pivot to run away. She had agility and a shifter's heightened speed on her side, but if the last two guys on today's crew—both werewolves—hadn't been so close she would have been caught. She felt something sting her shoulder through the thin long-sleeved shirt she wore. The two shifters, raced toward her in human form, yelling her name. She made it another couple of steps before her knees went out and her vision dimmed.

The yelling woke her, but it took several minutes before the conversation sounded like more than jumbled syllables. The words came together slowly, one here and there. Attack. Daughter. Tranquilizers. She frowned—at least she thought she did—as she struggled to make sense of the fog in her brain. She forced her eyes open and then turned to shield her face from the glare of the overhead light. The room reeked of fear and fury, and it took a minute to get her bearings. She was in her old bedroom at her parents' house, and they weren't yelling as she'd thought. They stood by the door talking with Michael, the werewolf alpha.

Shit. What had happened? She sat up, ignoring the dizziness that rushed over her, and struggled to remember. She'd been checking out a house that was almost complete. No, she'd been leaving and a man had stepped out from the trees and had tried grab her. She rubbed a sore spot on her shoulder and remembered feeling a sting before she passed out. Someone in the room had mention tranqs. Had the man attempted to drug and kidnap her? It wasn't the skeevy reporter. She'd recognize him. Maybe it was just a random incident. She knew it couldn't be, though, and dismissed the idea about the time the others noticed her sitting up. Scents assailed her. Anger, relief. Fear. She groaned. Well, hell. She was so screwed. It had taken years to wrest her independence from her father. This would make him impossible.

"How do you feel, baby?" her mom asked, rushing to her side.

"Fine," she croaked, and reached for the water bottle on the table, surprised at how parched she was. "What the—heck—happened?"

Her mother cussed almost as much as she did, and her father always griped at them about their language. Her mother hadn't missed the almost-slip and winked as Sara Beth's father and Michael, the werewolf, approached and stopped toward the bottom of her bed. Michael held up a small dart. She scooted forward to take it from him, then brought it up to her nose and sniffed. It was a common animal tranquilizer.

"Did they catch him?" she asked. She remembered the two werewolves racing to her rescue.

Michael shook his head. He didn't look particularly worried, but an expression that crossed his face made her nervous. It was almost expectant, anticipatory. What the hell was that about?

"Well, it wasn't the sleazeball reporter," she said. "This guy was a lot bigger and meaner looking."

"Which is what concerns us," her father said, his voice trembling in anger. Will Reynard glanced at the others, and Sara Beth got the feeling they'd made some decision she was really going to hate. While her father was alpha of the small local fox clan, the clan itself was under the protection of the much bigger werewolf clan. Michael's word was law, whether she liked it or not. And she really didn't.

"Michael believes until we find out who the guy was and eliminate the threat, it's best if you go into protective custody," her father said. "I agree."

Oh he did, did he? This was worse than she thought. She turned, narrowing her eyes on the werewolf, wondering how it benefitted him if she disappeared for a few days. Michael never did anything without ulterior motives.

"I don't think that will be necessary. I was surprised today. I won't be again and I'll make sure I keep my pistol with me." She was the best shot in the clan, but she rarely carried the weapon anywhere but the range. "I have too much to do to take a forced vacation. Besides, I might be able to help. I got a good look at him."

She wasn't the best artist, but she was confident she could sketch an accurate likeness.

"You do most of your work from your home office, Sara Beth. And there is no way you're getting more involved in this," her father pointed out in a tone that told her just how determined he was to protect his adult daughter. "You can take everything you need with you."

She sighed. She knew when she was facing a losing battle. "And where am I going?"

"To the eagles. They have the most secure lands," Michael said. He sounded innocent enough and maybe that was the problem. Sara Beth got the feeling from his voice he was only interested in her as an excuse to visit the eagles. But why did he need one?

She supposed it didn't matter. She hadn't seen Ajax or her girls in a couple of months so a short visit would be nice, and she knew from experience she wouldn't have any problems accessing the internet or phone lines. But that wasn't why she still resisted the idea.

"Okay," she said, giving her father a stern look. "But only for a couple of days."

"This isn't up for debate, Sara Beth," Michael said. His words were pure alpha and set her teeth on edge.

She nodded acquiescence and prayed to the gods she could avoid the one person on the eagle's mountain who posed any danger to her. Patrick Aquila. She hadn't spoken to him in a decade, though she caught the occasional distant glimpse when he came into town. But she hadn't entered his territory in years and he was one of Ajax's advisors. What were the odds he wouldn't get told about this? Hopefully, their paths wouldn't cross. Given half the chance, he'd steal her heart and soar away with it. And he probably wouldn't even realize he was doing it.

Thankfully, he was Ajax's First Consul. He'd be the last choice for bodyguard duty.

CHAPTER TWO

Patrick Aquila was looking forward to finishing this last minute meeting and getting back to Guard headquarters on top of the mountain. He'd been accused of being antsy and claustrophobic, but neither was an accurate description of his mood. Feeling confined wasn't what caused his impatience. This was more like apathy, and hell, going back probably wouldn't help. He'd come down because he'd been bored training new members of the Queen's Guard.

He needed something to shake things up. A little excitement. He was tempted to blame it on his ancestry. Wereeagles had been granted the ability of flight by Hermes, after a runner carried word to Athens of the Greek's victory over the Persians at Marathon. The urge to soar was part of his DNA.

He glanced over at Nico and Ajax, the wereeagle queen. Her head was bent over reports, but her mate was bouncing Alex, their one year old daughter, on his knee to the girl's delighted chortles. Ayla, her four year old sister, in eagle form, was wildly careening around the ceiling. Every few minutes she'd dive at Patrick so he'd pretend he was afraid of the elder royal daughter. He grinned as she made her next pass. There was never a dull moment with Ajax's daughters. He didn't want that much excitement, but he had to admit the girls kept things interesting.

"Why are we here again?" he asked Ajax. "I thought we were through catering to Hector Leonidas's whims. No offense, Nico," Patrick added, not *quite* apologetically to the former wereleopard leader's son.

Ajax laughed. "As long as he's holding Ayla or Alex, you can insult him all you want. And I don't know any more than I've already told you. Hector says Michael is bringing someone he wants us to protect."

Ajax didn't say it, but Patrick knew he'd be the one to get stuck with babysitting duty. This better not be about werewolf or wereleopard politics. Though since the four Leonidas brothers had mated—two of them to wolves—the hostilities between the two species had cooled so much he often thought nothing of it to see them together. But he still didn't want to get stuck on a protection detail. He had every intention of pawning it off to one of the squads in the Guard.

And he'd like to get on with it. What was taking so long? He stood and ducked as Ayla dived once again. He paced to the window. There were no roads up the mountain so the residents used four-wheelers for guests or transporting things from the mountain base. As he watched the dirt path Michael would use, he heard the faint hum of the vehicle approaching. Finally, Michael, Hector and the stranger came into sight and parked under the house. Patrick didn't get a good look at the occupant, who wore a coat and hood. Since his first duty was to protect the royal family, he stepped out to intercept the newcomers. He hadn't been briefed, had no idea if the mystery guest was a threat.

The balcony circled the house. He had to walk around to meet them at the stairs.

He froze when their unexpected visitor took the first step. She was a female fox. Her scent was intoxicating—sweet with a hint of fire—and she was irritated. He would be too, after who-knew-how-long with Michael and Hector.

He held his breath as she came around the curve in the stairs. She carried a backpack and small duffel bag and was wearing an unzipped cream-colored, faux fur lined coat with a tight pink shirt under it. He grinned at the glittery hammer emblazoned across her chest. Her jeans were form-fitting, and her scuffed work boots obviously saw hard use. When she looked up, still several feet below him, her big brown eyes flashed with recognition but it took him a second to figure out how he knew her. She threw back the coat's hood and rich, dark auburn waves spilled around her shoulders with streaks of white framing her face. Her scent should have been familiar, and when he took a deep breath he recognized the girl he'd known.

"Well hello, foxy," he drawled when she stepped onto the balcony.

Damn, she had pretty eyes. Her chilly gaze should have left him a pile of ice on the floor, but it started an entirely different kind of reaction. He blocked her when she tried to step around him, prompting a subtle, almost imperceptible change to her scent. Fear. Not only was it a slap in the face, it provoked protective instincts much deeper and darker than he'd known he was capable. He couldn't stand for her to be afraid of him any more than he could let her run from him.

As Michael and Hector came into view, quietly arguing with each other, Patrick took Sara Beth's hand and gently tugged her farther onto the balcony and closer to Ajax's family. He walked backward so he could keep an eye on her, though if he was honest, he'd admit he watched her so closely because he couldn't stop drinking her in. So he saw her nostrils flare, saw the way she relaxed when she realized he was taking her into a crowd. He wanted to pull her close and shelter her from whatever had scared her. The girl he'd known was fearless, and as he watched, she conquered her fright and looked more like the fox he remembered.

He smiled, hoping to put her at ease while wondering how long it would take before he convinced her to let him hold her and stroke all those lush curves she didn't bother to hide anymore.

"You've grown up," he teased.

She rolled her eyes. "You haven't."

"Oh, foxy," he said, looking her up and down. "We've *both* grown up."

He could hear her grind her teeth and hid his grin. He knew she hated being called that, which was why he'd used it when she was a young teenager trying to follow around the older kids. The nickname pissed her off, had made it easier to keep her at a distance. A three year age difference was no big deal now, but it had been in high school. He'd been drawn to her even then. But damn, the woman had grown into the name. Whether she liked it or not, it suited her now.

He realized she didn't know that though. He'd given her the perfect opportunity to flirt back, but she didn't respond to his teasing. Instead she withdrew, despite her scent taking on a subtle hint of longing, and her eyes were suspicious—like she questioned his interest, didn't believe it. She didn't have the air of a woman confident in her sensuality. It made no sense. Were the foxes and wolves in her life idiots? It didn't matter. He wanted to be the one to show her. Didn't want to share her. Emotion gripped him and twisted his insides. He was amazed at the unexpected possessiveness and forced himself to shut down and step back. He'd never been possessive of a woman and he wasn't sure what to do about it.

He led her into the house and moved into the background. Ajax and Sara Beth had been friends since they started walking, so Patrick knew his queen was perfectly safe with her. Nico, arms now free, stepped up to his side.

"Where's Alex?" Patrick asked.

"Nap," Nico answered. "One minute she's babbling away and the next she's out cold."

It might have sounded like a complaint but it was impossible to miss the fatherly pride. Patrick smiled. Alex charmed everyone who knew her.

"Not who I was expecting," Nico said, nodding toward their visitor. Patrick couldn't keep his eyes off her. He wondered if he'd ever get over the compulsion.

"Sara Beth Reynard," he answered. "She's the werefox alpha's daughter."

"Ajax's school friend. She never comes up here."

No she didn't, Patrick acknowledged, and realized Nico must have met her someplace else. He knew his queen and Sara Beth saw each other in town on rare occasions, but mostly communicated by email and phone. Patrick had never wondered why before but with each hostile look the werefox gave him, his curiosity grew.

"She's very pretty," Nico said noncommittally.

Though the two of them had worked out their distrust of each other years ago, Patrick had a damned hard time not lunging for his friend. Nico had the gall to laugh.

"Well, isn't this interesting?" Nico drawled.

"It's nothing," he snapped.

"Really?" Nico cocked his head to the side, a gesture like that of a cat. "So I should call one of the soldiers to handle this protection detail?"

"Do it and I'll break the no killing the consort rule," he growled.

Nico laughed and clapped him on the shoulder. "Yeah, that's what I thought."

"I have no idea what I'm doing," he muttered, knowing he was acting out of character.

He should let Nico call someone else in. His response to her presence was too intense and inexplicable. She was hot but he knew plenty of hot women. What was it about this one that was so different? The more he thought about it, the less he cared. They were both adults. She glanced over at him, heat flaring in her eyes. There was no way he was letting her out of his sight, and hopefully his bed, until he figured out what it was that drew him so strongly.

"Damn," he murmured.

Nico stepped in front of him, blocking his view of the women. Patrick would have snapped if not for the serious look on his friend's face. "What?"

"You can work out seduction plans later. Right now," he said with a glance over his shoulder, "we need to find out what's going on. What happened that they had to send her here?"

That question sent the closest thing to panic he'd ever known shooting through him. Sweet Hermes, how had he forgotten that? He followed Nico to the sofa where the women sat in time to overhear the end of the conversation.

"I can't stay here, Ajax. You have a family to protect."

"Our lands are the safest in the country."

Patrick watched Sara Beth press her lips together and give a small shake of her head. "Still, I won't take that risk."

"Don't worry, foxy," he said, stepping closer. "You won't put them in danger. You're coming home with me." He looked up as the door opened and Michael and Hector stepped inside. "Now would someone please tell me what I'm protecting you against?"

Instead of answering, Sara Beth opened her backpack, pulled out a sketchpad and tore out a page. She handed it to Ajax. "He tried to kidnap me this afternoon."

It took a second for her words to register and when they did Patrick wasn't sure if it was wrath or fear that filled him. He felt like a vice had clamped around his heart. He was torn between rushing out to find the monster or grabbing her and running to hide her away. When he realized his hands were shaking, he took a deep breath and regained control.

"And before anyone asks," she said, "we have no idea who he is. But it isn't the tabloid reporter who's been writing about me."

Ajax handed the sketch to Nico. Patrick stepped up next to him to look. The first thing he noticed was Sara Beth was quite good at capturing the menace in the man's eyes. They were a little crinkled, lines on the side indicating he was older, but she'd somehow put a mean glint in them. Patrick would put him in his early fifties. His features were just shy of too sharp. He looked distinguished and cold.

"I'll run it through the facial recognition program," Nico said. "Hopefully we'll get a hit."

Sara Beth told them exactly what had happened, and when she finished, Nico turned to Michael. "Did your wolves see how he got away? A vehicle?"

He shook his head. "No, but we emailed the sketch to the pack. If anyone sees him, we'll know."

A sudden gust of wind buffeted the house. "That's my cue to leave," Michael said. "I need to get home before snow closes the road up here."

Hector accompanied him and a few minutes later, when Patrick guided Sara Beth out to go to his place, the werewolf and wereleopard were still huddled together at the ATVs whispering.

"It's weird enough they're friends," Sara Beth muttered. "Now they're keeping secrets? That can't bode well."

It was a damned strange friendship, werewolves and wereleopards having been enemies for centuries. Patrick had become accustomed to them though, so he almost dismissed Sara Beth's comment as coming from someone who just hadn't seen them together much. On closer observation, however, there was definitely a furtiveness to the other men. He wondered what they were discussing. If it was anything to do with Sara Beth or the pack, he needed to know about it. Unfortunately, they noticed they were being watched and before he could butt in, they mounted the ATVs and left. He shrugged off the odd behavior—frankly, it wasn't that odd—and turned her toward the path home.

Look for these series from the authors of Forbidden Passions:

Crystal Jordan

Wereplanets
In Ice
In Heat
In Smoke
In Mist

Twilight of the Gods
Viking Fire
Viking Desire

In the Heat of the Night
Total Eclipse of the Heart
Big Girls Don't Die
It's Raining Men
Crazy Little Thing Called Love

The Night
Embrace the Night
Night Games
Edge of Night

Loribelle Hunt

The Elect
Protector
Guardian
Warrior

Delroi Connection
Invasion Earth
Leaving Earth
Stolen Earth
Claiming Earth

Delroi Prophecy
Freedom
Irresistible
Redemption
Absolution

Delroi Warrior
Shadow Warrior
Dark Warrior
Star Warrior

Genesee District Libraries
Baker Park Library
3410 S. Grand Traverse
Burton, MI 48529

F FOR
Forbidden passions